Tumbling Dice

Tumbling Dice

Nick H. Carter

bridge
books

First published Britain in 2005
by
Bridge Books
61 Park Avenue, Wrexham
LL12 7AW
on behalf of the author

© 2005 Nick H, Carter
© 2004 typesetting and design Bridge Books

This edition published in 2005

All Rights Reserved.
No part of this publication may be reproduced,
stored in a retrieval system, or transmitted
in any form or by any means, electronic,
mechanical, photocopying, recording or
otherwise, without the prior permission
of the Copyright holder.

This is a work of fiction.
All persons mentioned herein are entirely fictitious.
Any resemblance to any real persons, living or dead, is purely coincidential.

A CIP entry for this book is available from the British Library

ISBN 1-84494-021-7

Typeset and designed by
Bridge Books
61 Park Avenue, Wrexham
LL12 7AW

Printed and bound by
Cromwell Press
Trowbridge, Wiltshire

1

'Jimmy, are you up yet? It's half seven and I'm not calling you again.' This was the daily routine for Helen Challoner.

Having seen her husband off to work she then had to rouse her only offspring. James Arthur Challoner, Jimmy to his nearest and dearest, was struggling to wake but reluctant to leave the comforting warmth of his bed. It was February and his room was still dark but even so he could clearly see the thick frost patterning his window. This to Jimmy was reason enough to stay right where he was but he was bright enough to concede that this would be his last call. If he wasn't to be late for school he would have to move fast. Gingerly he stretched out his legs and felt for the bedside rug with his feet. He had once made the mistake of jumping out of bed straight onto the cold lino. It had been like plunging his feet into icy water and the shock was such that now he always made sure that the rug was in position before he emerged.

Jimmy dressed quickly in an attempt to recapture the warmth he had been forced to abandon.

'I should've been born into the landed gentry, at least we could've afforded a bit of heat around the place' Jimmy muttered as he went downstairs.

'Oh, you've decided to get up then.'

'Well it's freezing down here Mum, can't we get a gas fire?'

'Of course it's freezing, it's the middle of winter. We just can't afford luxuries like gas fires.'

Jimmy grunted and retreated into the little scullery off the kitchen to warm himself in front of the oven. At this hour the gas stove was the sole source of heating in the Challoner household.

Yesterday's ashes still lay in the grate but even if it had been laid earlier the fire would not have been lit. It was an unwritten rule that the fire was never lit before two o'clock in an effort to eke out the one bag of coal they were rationed to each week.

'If you're off to the lav it's frozen up again,' his mother's voice rang out from the kitchen. Jimmy shrugged as he opened the back door and an icy blast of freezing air enveloped him. Just why lavatories couldn't have been built inside the house instead of at the bottom of the yard was beyond Jimmy's comprehension. 'Good thing I only need a pee,' he thought to himself as he made his dash across the cobbles. Pulling the handle of the long chain that hung from the wooden cistern he heard an ominous clunk instead of the sound of water flushing. He had forgotten that the cistern was frozen over. Grimacing he raced back into the kitchen to give himself a quick, (very quick if his mother was otherwise occupied) 'lick and a promise' at the kitchen sink. The kitchen sink was all purpose in the Challoner household serving to wash clothes, dishes and Challoners alike. As the icy cold water splashed his face Jimmy wished for the umpteenth time that a hot water supply wasn't something they couldn't afford.

'Come and eat this porridge before it gets cold.'

Jimmy's eyes scoured the table for the sugar, 'Where's the sugar Mum? I can't eat porridge without sugar.'

'Well you're going to have to, there's no more to be had 'til the week end. Put a spot of syrup on it, it'll taste just as good.' Mrs Challoner hoped she sounded more convinced than she felt as she handed him the tin.

Jimmy took it, and dipping his spoon in, he extracted a generous helping of the precious syrup.

'Just put half of that back. We were lucky to get that tin and it's got to last you know.' As he drizzled the syrup back Jimmy wondered how much longer food rationing was going to last. His Dad had said that come the end of the war things would get back to normal but it was now 1946 and at twelve years of age Jimmy had yet to see any improvement. The only thing that was apparent was the increased numbers of men around now that the soldiers had come back from the war. Liverpool was as he had always known it. If change was coming it was taking its time thought Jimmy.

'Hurry up with that breakfast and stop day-dreaming. Peter will be here in a minute though goodness knows why he puts up with you. Every morning you keep that poor lad waiting,' scolded Mrs Challoner.

'He's my best mate, that's why,' Jimmy said through a mouthful of porridge as his mother went to answer the knock on the door.

'Hello Peter. Come on in. He's not quite ready yet.'

'So what's new? Hello Mrs Challoner. Hello Jimmy.' Peter grinned, glad to be stepping into the comparative warmth of the Challoner's kitchen.

'Hi Peter, coming now,' said Jimmy flashing Peter the kind of disarming grin that was to serve him well in future years.

'Done your homework?' asked Peter

'Suppose you have.'

'Certainly have, it wasn't too bad. What did you think?'

'Oh pretty easy' Jimmy replied airily as he made for the door.

'Well t'rah then and mind you come straight home tonight,' said Mrs Challoner as the two boys let themselves out of the door. She watched until they were out of sight. Peter and Jimmy had been inseparable since they were born within weeks of each other and Helen Challoner for one was grateful. The Turners were a decent family and young Peter was a steadying influence on the sometimes headstrong Jimmy. Not that they weren't proud of Jimmy. He'd really surprised them by passing that scholarship to the Liverpool Collegiate. Peter had been expected to pass but it had been a real relief to know that now they would be starting at the new school together. Helen often thought it was uncanny how similar the Turners were to her own family, with both men working on the docks and both having just the one youngster, something of a rarity in their neighbourhood.

As soon as they were out of sight of Jimmy's mother Peter handed over a blue exercise book. 'Ta mate, I should be able to get it down if I miss assembly' said Jimmy.

'I suppose you were planning that world trip.' Peter couldn't resist a grin as he teased Jimmy.

'You won't laugh when I'm on it, I'm going to be rich one day make no mistake about it.'

'I don't doubt it but right now I should get a move on with that maths if I were you.'

Walking home after school Jimmy was unusually quiet. When Peter asked him what was wrong he gave a low whistle before replying. 'To be honest I was thinking about that Easter trip the head was on about in assembly.'

'You what, you weren't even in assembly. How do you know what he said?'

'Terry told me and he's put his name down already. I'm fed up with not being able to afford any of these trips. Aren't you?' Jimmy turned to face Peter eager for his reply. His friend sounded resigned, 'Course I'm fed up but we've as much chance of finding a spare three pounds for a school trip at home as flying to the moon.'

'The thing is, what if we got the money ourselves?'

Peter raised his eyebrows.

'We could nick it' Jimmy said coolly.

'Are you daft? We'd be bound to get caught and our dads would murder us.'

'We wouldn't get caught if we had a plan.'

'Trouble with you is you've read too many comics, just forget it will you,' Peter said.

'Listen, you do what you want but I'm going on that trip. Whatever I have to do, I'm doing it.'

'Well you're on your own then,' Peter said. The rest of the walk home was marred by an uneasy silence.

As they turned into Chesham Street where they both lived Jimmy finally said, 'I've thought how to do it, it'll be dead easy with no risk at all.'

'I told you once. I don't want to know.' Peter was starting to look nervous as he began to realise Jimmy was serious.

'OK, forget it. But when I'm off to London and you're stuck here remember you had your chance.'

'I'll remember. See you in the morning and try being on time for once.'

'It's not me, it's you coming too early,' Jimmy laughed.

Peter had walked half way across the street when he turned and retraced his steps to where Jimmy was just about to open his front door.

'Out of interest, where exactly is this money coming from?'

'Oh, interested now are we? Well it's easy. The milkman collects his money in a bag every Saturday morning. He ties the bag to the handle of his milk float and I'll just wait my chance ...,'

'You're bound to get caught with that daft idea,' said Peter, shaking his head.

'We'll have to see about that, won't we?'

Jimmy realised that stealing the money would be the easy part. The tricky bit would be thinking up a plausible explanation for his mum and dad as to where his new found wealth had sprung from. He wouldn't be able to say that he'd found it because his mum would be sure to make him report it to the police and there was no way that he had time to earn that kind of money. After a few minutes deliberation, Jimmy came to the conclusion that he must put his plan for stealing the money into action and worry about explanations later.

As he entered the house he was pleased to note that the fire was lit and the freezing temperature of the morning had given way to a cosy warmth.

He went into the scullery where he knew his mother would be starting the tea and decided to broach the subject of the Easter trip. He knew a certain amount of distraction on her part could only serve in his favour.

'Guess what mum. There's a school trip to London at Easter and it's going to cost three pounds.'

'Sounds very nice love but you know we can't afford three pounds. It took us all our time to buy the uniform.'

'I know that mum. I'm not asking you to pay. I was wondering if you would let me go if I paid for it myself.'

'Well yes. But I don't think there's much chance of you coming up with three pounds, do you?'

'Might get a job or something now I know you'll let me go.' Jimmy smiled to himself, things were going well.

'Now don't you get too excited too soon, you'll only be disappointed' warned his mother.

That was one thing that Jimmy didn't intend to happen.

He knew the milkman called at nine o'clock so the plan was to follow him from that point and wait for the right moment to strike.

At five o'clock Mr Challoner came wearily through the door. His lined face belied his thirty eight years. Too long spent struggling to make ends meet, thought Jimmy. He knew that it would destroy his mum and dad if he was caught but instead of acting as a deterrent this only served to make him even more determined.

On Saturday Jimmy was up early, which came as no small surprise to his mother who was usually still trying to prise him out of bed at ten o'clock.

'What got you out of bed so early?' she asked, glancing up from the sink where she was washing up.

'I'm going to look for a Saturday job to get that three pounds.'

'Well good luck love. We're really proud of you for having a go.'

If they only knew thought Jimmy as he hurriedly slid out of the back door just as the milkman was knocking on the front.

Jimmy trailed the milk float round the near deserted streets but the milkman never seemed to leave it for more than a minute. On the one occasion that he had nearly been tempted to make his move, a man had appeared out of nowhere, forcing Jimmy to wait. One thing he didn't intend to do was to take unnecessary risks. His patience was rewarded when the milk float turned into the back yard of the local pub. Jimmy knew he might have a chance because it would take the milkman a good couple of minutes to walk up the long yard to the back door of the pub, collect the money and walk back. He knew this as he'd often done it himself when collecting his dad's Sunday jug of beer. In spite of it being a bitterly cold day, Jimmy felt himself starting to sweat as he tried to anticipate the milkman's moves. He sighed with relief as the milkman took two pints out of a crate and briskly set off for the back door of the pub. As soon as the milkman disappeared from view Jimmy raced down the street, glancing from side to side, until he reached the money bag hanging in its usual place. He plunged his hand into the bag and drew out a bundle of notes and cash. He started to run and didn't look back until he reached the corner at the end of the street. Jimmy grinned as he watched the milkman clattering on down the street, completely oblivious to the drama that had just been played out under his unsuspecting nose.

Jimmy felt exhilarated. His heart was pounding. Carefully he counted the money and smiled to himself as he relived his triumph. It was still only ten o'clock, too early to go home without arousing suspicion. He decided to go down to the docks to kill time and as he made his way through the narrow streets he came across a scrapyard. 'Rags Bought for Cash,' the hand written notice said. Jimmy grinned, this could be the solution to his problem.

On arriving home Jimmy adopted a dejected air. 'No luck with the job Mum, could you find a few old rags for me to sell to the scrapyard?' Mrs Challoner immediately searched out a few old rags and to add to the credibility of his planned story Jimmy knocked on a few doors further down the street. He managed to collect quite a bundle of rags, even impressing himself with his wide eyed tale of woe about not being able to join in the school trip. People felt driven to go to great lengths after hearing it to find him a rag or two. The man at the scrapyard paid him three shillings for his bundle and took his name and address.

Once home he announced to his delighted mother that he had made two pounds, six shillings and sixpence. 'Well Jimmy you deserve to go in that case. Your dad and I will give you the rest as you've tried so hard. I know one thing, you'll enjoy it even more because you've worked for it yourself.' Jimmy gave a sly grin.

When his dad returned Jimmy found himself on the receiving end of yet more praise. He couldn't believe his luck, he had found an easy way to get money which not only had been fun but put him in good books at home. Jimmy was so pleased with the outcome of his plans that he made a promise to himself. No more doing without, from now on if he needed anything he would take it. Things, thought Jimmy, were looking up.

At about eight o'clock that evening Jimmy was reading a comic by the fire and his mother sat beside him darning a pile of woollen socks. Mr Challoner was washing and shaving in readiness for his weekly Saturday night visit to the local pub. When a knock came to the door Mrs Challoner went to answer it. Jimmy heard muffled voices but ignored them and continued to read his comic. However he dropped his comic in shock when he heard his mother call out to his dad in the scullery, 'It's the police, they want to see you about something Jimmy did today.' Jimmy's face paled and for the second time that day he started to sweat.

2

Peter was enjoying his Sunday breakfast when his father turned to him.

'What has young Challoner been up to? They had the police there when I went past last night.'

Peter felt a wave of nausea sweep over him. It could only mean that Jimmy had been caught stealing. He had been to see his mum's sister in Southport yesterday and hadn't been able to see Jimmy.

Mr Challoner waited expectantly. 'Nothing as far as I know,' mumbled Peter.

'Can I go now mum, I've had enough.'

'Well that's what I call a waste of good food and you know how hard it is to get a fresh egg these days.'

'Sorry mum,' Peter tried to sound nonchalant as he informed them he was going round to Jimmy's but he felt sure both him mum and dad must be able to hear the frenzied beating of his heart.

Trying not to run he made his way across to Jimmy's house where he was greeted by a far from contrite Jimmy.

'Blimey, you're early. Do you want to come in and wait? I won't be long.'

Peter couldn't believe his ears. Jimmy sounded completely normal. 'Will you be coming down to the river today?' he asked tentatively.

'Course I am, why wouldn't I be?'

'Dad saw the police here last night, that's why.'

'Oh, that. They came to see dad.' Then hearing his mum approaching he put his finger to his lips.

'Hello Peter. You're out early.' Peter was mystified. She too seemed perfectly normal. He had been convinced that Jimmy's mum and dad would have been inconsolable.

'What do you think of our Jimmy then, earning himself two pounds, six and six so that he can go on that school trip?'

Jimmy flashed him a look which suggested that he shouldn't ask embarrassing questions just yet. Mrs Challoner continued, 'I forgot, you were in Southport weren't you? Well our Jimmy went out collecting old rags to sell to the scrapyard. That's how he earned his money.'

Peter looked bewildered, 'Old rags?'

'Yes but the snag was you need to be sixteen before you can sell rags at the scrapyard.'

'But Jimmy isn't sixteen.'

'Exactly. The police were keeping watch on the scrapyard when Jimmy sold the rags. They called to warn us not to let Jimmy sell anything else there.'

'Isn't Jimmy in trouble then?'

'No the policeman was very nice about it, said just to make sure that Jimmy didn't go to the scrapyard again.'

When they had left the house and were walking up the entry towards the street, Peter, who was almost bursting with curiosity turned to Jimmy and said breathlessly, 'Well, what happened about the plan, did you get the money from rags or not?'

I sold a few rags but that was only so that I'd have an excuse for the money. I got most of it from the milkman like I said I would. He never even saw me.' Jimmy allowed himself a self satisfied smile.

'Weren't you scared?'

'Only a bit. It was more like exciting than scary.'

'You wouldn't do it again though would you?'

'I wouldn't bet on it. Why shouldn't I have things that other people have?'

As far as Peter could tell Jimmy did abandon his life of crime at this point. He never gave any indication that he had any spare money, something for which Peter was grateful. He was fond of Jimmy but he knew that if he made a habit of stealing it would affect their friendship.

But Jimmy hadn't given up any thoughts of stealing. He just hadn't found it necessary. As his dad had promised things had eventually improved. Mr Challoner was able to work more overtime down at the docks and life was easier.

Jimmy was fifteen before the need arose again. He and Peter were walking back from the local cinema deep in conversation about the western they had just seen. They were taking a short cut through the entry between two streets when suddenly a light snapped on in one of the back bedrooms. Instinctively they looked, up. 'Look it's Mavis Johnson,' Jimmy said.

Peter didn't need asking twice. The two boys stood mesmerized as Mavis started to undress. They watched in silence as Mavis removed her jumper and skirt.

'She's taking off her bra,' Jimmy said softly.

Peter merely nodded, too overcome to speak as Mavis unhooked her bra and tossed it to one side, still in full view.

I've never seen bare tits before. Have you Peter?'

'No. They're massive aren't they?'

They resumed their silent vigil each praying Mavis's knickers would be the next to go. Their joint groan was clearly audible as suddenly the room went dark. Reluctantly they resumed the walk home when it became clear that Mavis had gone to bed.

I've never seen anything as good as that. I wouldn't mind a date with her.'

'You're mad. She's working and you're still at school, she wouldn't be seen dead with you.'

'She would if I spent a packet on her.'

'Oh yes? And where would you get that sort of money from?'

'Nick it of course.'

'Don't do it Jimmy. It's not worth the risk.'

'I've told you before, plan the job properly and there's no risk. I'll ask her out and if she says yes I'll get as much as I need.'

Walking to school two days later Jimmy announced to Peter that he had asked Mavis out and she had said yes.

'She really said yes?' Peter said. 'What did you say to her?'

'I just asked her if she fancied coming out with me. When she looked a bit doubtful I told her not to worry, I could afford to give her a good night out.'

'Where will you take her?'

'Well I thought a meal would be good and then the pictures.'

'But where on earth will you get the money to cover that lot?'

'I worked it out and I reckon I'll need a fiver. I know where to get it but I'll need your help.'

'Oh no. I told you before, count me out.'

'You won't have to do anything. Just keep watch at the house I'm nicking it from.'

'But that's breaking and entering.'

'It's not because I'm going to go in, not break in. That's why I need you to keep watch.'

'And just where is this house?'
'The Spencer's in our street.'
'But they've got no more than us?' Peter sounded baffled as well as shocked.
'Ah well it won't be their money will it?' It'll be the insurance man's.'
'I don't get it' said Peter.

Jimmy explained that he had overheard his mum and dad saying that on Thursday nights Mrs Spencer entertained the insurance man while Mr Spencer was at the pub. Jimmy had decided to follow this up and had gone into the Spencer's backyard the next Thursday night. Sure enough the insurance man had left his coat over a chair in the kitchen before following Mrs Spencer upstairs. 'So you see,' Jimmy went on, 'the wallet with all his takings in it will be left alone and I can just quietly go and help myself.'

'Sounds easy enough. But if I help you, I still don't want anything to do with the money.'

'Suit yourself.'

They arranged to meet at half past seven the following Thursday night, half an hour before the insurance man was due.

Peter looked edgy, 'What if Mr Spencer doesn't go out?'

'Bound to. It's pay day and he always goes straight to the pub.'

Jimmy narrowed his eyes, 'I've planned this properly you know.'

'Look. There he is on his bike,' Peter whispered as he caught sight of the insurance man. They watched as he called at two houses before the Spencers and then breathed a sigh of relief when he went into the house. 'Right, round the back. You keep watch while I go down the entry.'

Peter watched nervously as Jimmy set off down the narrow entry. It was a cold night but he was sweating. Jimmy reappeared minutes later.

'Haven't got it' he said. The pair of them are downstairs necking on the couch.'

Peter's relief was undisguised, 'Thank goodness, let's go home, you can't go in if they're sitting downstairs.'

'We could go and watch them,' suggested Jimmy, 'might be worth it.'

Peter nodded in agreement and they made their way to the back yard of the Spencer's house. Peering in through the kitchen window they could clearly see Mrs Spencer and the insurance man kissing passionately on the couch.

The boys gazed in awe as the insurance man unbuttoned Mrs Spencer's blouse and the sight of her exposed breasts caused a sharp intake of breath from them both. 'Just look at that,' Jimmy whispered.

'I am,' Peter replied.

After a brief discussion on the merits of Mavis Johnson's teenage breasts as opposed to Mrs Spencer's impressive form the boys were forced to crouch down quickly as the lovers suddenly left the couch and moved upstairs.

'Quick, get back to the top of the entry.' Peter did as he was told and signalled that it was all clear. Jimmy seemed to be back at his side in no time at all, triumphantly clutching his passport to Mavis courtesy of the insurance man.

'How much did you get?'

'What I wanted, five pounds. This way he'll have no idea where he lost it.'

Peter looked at Jimmy in admiration. He may not approve of Jimmy's activities but he had to hand it to him. He was smart and he had nerve.

'You'd have thought they'd have locked the door' Peter said.

'How on earth did you know they hadn't?'

'I didn't 'til I tried it but I reckoned they had other things to think about.' Jimmy gave his friend a knowing wink, threw back his head and laughed.

That Friday Jimmy took Mavis for a Chinese meal followed by a visit to the cinema. Mavis was impressed with Jimmy's nonchalant negotiating of the menu, proof of Jimmy's theory that forward planning paid off. He had been to study the menu at length in the restaurant window before collecting Mavis.

Her admiration grew when Jimmy, on sighting the long queue for the cinema stalls, strode up to the booking office and bought two tickets for the circle.

As the film got under way Jimmy hesitantly snaked his arm around Mavis's shoulders and was gratified that this appeared to be what was expected of him. As this was his first date with a girl he was a little unsure of how to proceed, but his natural confidence soon overcame his initial shyness. He allowed his hand to fall gently down onto Mavis's right breast, so gently that it took her a minute to register what had happened. Mavis pushed his hand away and gave Jimmy a dark look.

'Sorry,' he mumbled.

Later as they waited for the bus home, Mavis reached for Jimmy's hand. 'You can hold my hand you know.'

'About the pictures,' said Jimmy, 'I thought you might be expecting me to do something.'

Mavis smiled, 'Plenty of time for that Jimmy. Just don't rush things.' Jimmy took that as a promise of good times to come and was content for the moment to clutch Mavis's hand as they stood in the bus queue.

The following day Jimmy regaled Peter with tales of his visit to China town and the cinema. Peter was sorry Jimmy's hand had been knocked away.

'Bit disappointing after all you'd spent on her,' he said.

'All in good time. You don't rush these things. I'm seeing her again next Friday, same time after she comes out of work.'

'Does that mean more money?'

'Certainly does and I'll need your help again.'

'Oh come on. I didn't mind once but I don't want to keep on doing it. You're bound to get caught.'

'No chance. You could drive a bus past those two and they wouldn't notice.'

Reluctantly Peter agreed to keep watch one more time and the following Thursday night Jimmy repeated his performance. Against Peter's better judgement this became a weekly occurrence as Jimmy's dalliance with Mavis gathered momentum. Peter took to warning Jimmy, pointing out that to continue stealing at the same time in the same place was certain to lead to trouble. But Jimmy, bound by the lure of the increasingly generous Mavis's sexual favours, ignored him.

It was a typical Thursday night. Peter once again had been cajoled into keeping watch. 'You won't be able to keep this up much longer you know, the nights are getting lighter now' Peter warned.

'What's that got to do with it?'

'There'll be more people about.'

'Well I'm not going to worry about that now. Right, keep watch' and with that Jimmy disappeared down the entry. Peter looked up and down the street nervously. He had helped Jimmy half a dozen times but was growing uncomfortable about his friend's forays into crime.

After waiting several minutes for Jimmy to reappear, Peter began to feel anxious. Jimmy had never taken so long before. Peter knew that if Mrs Spencer and her paramour were still downstairs, Jimmy would have called him and they would have watched through the window until proceedings moved upstairs.

'Jimmy,' Peter's call was unanswered. He decided to make his way to the Spencer's back yard and found the entry door open as Jimmy had left it to make good his escape. Peter edged up to the kitchen window as far as he dared. Mrs Spencer and the insurance man were standing to the left and to the right a stranger was holding onto Jimmy's arm. Peter's legs felt weak as the realisation that the man must be the police occurred to him. Jimmy must have been arrested.

3

'Mr Challoner? I'm Detective Constable Roberts, Liverpool CID. Your son here has just been arrested for stealing money from an insurance collector.'

Mr Challoner gripped the door as ashen faced he motioned to the burly detective to come into the house.

Mrs Challoner looked up as Detective Roberts strode into the kitchen with Jimmy and Mr Challoner following closely behind. Instinctively she knew that her son was in trouble. Her worst fears were confirmed when Mr Challoner said in shocked tones, 'It's our Jimmy, the detective says he's been arrested for stealing money.'

'No,' Mrs Challoner cried out, 'There must be some mistake.'

'I'm sorry Mrs Challoner, there hasn't been any mistake,' Detective Roberts spoke gently to the distraught women.

'Let me explain,' he went on. 'Every Thursday night an insurance collector, a Mr Taylor, calls at the home of Mrs Spencer. Now he's been in the habit of leaving his coat, with his wallet, in the kitchen while he and Mrs Spencer were otherwise occupied. He noticed that his insurance money was often five pounds short and he also knew that the only place that his jacket had been left unattended was at the Spencer's house. Last Thursday he and Mrs Spencer kept watch through the back bedroom window and sure enough they saw someone, your son Jimmy here, enter the back yard and leave again after a couple of minutes. Mr Taylor reported the matter to the police and tonight I was waiting in the Spencer's hall when Jimmy walked into the kitchen all set to steal the money.'

'Oh Jimmy. How could you?' Mrs Challoner's eyes filled with tears.

'Now don't go upsetting yourself' Mr Challoner said quietly before turning to Detective Roberts. 'What happens now officer?'

The detective explained that a new scheme called the Juvenile Liaison Scheme had been started in Liverpool. This meant young offenders could be given a caution from a senior police officer instead of going to the Juvenile Court. DC Robert's tone softened 'In my opinion your son would qualify for this scheme and it will be my recommendation that on this occasion young Jimmy receives a caution.'

'I appreciate it officer and I can promise you one thing. He will never steal again while he's under my roof.'

After taking down the necessary details, DC Roberts left, saying that they could expect to know if a prosecution would be going ahead in a day or two.

The blow from his father threw Jimmy across the room and he was left in no doubt about his father's anger as he fled upstairs. Ordered to stay there he sat on the end of the bed and reflected on the night's events. He had been so certain that the insurance man wouldn't dare to report him. But, he thought that was lesson number one, never assume anything. Lesson number two was to never steal to a pattern, Peter had been right.

When Peter realised that Jimmy had been caught he quickly made his escape reasoning that nothing would be achieved by him staying. Even so he felt guilty at leaving his friend and his sleep was fitful that night. Peter was glad to see the morning and was round at Jimmy's house as early as he dared. He was surprised when Mr Challoner opened the door as normally he would have been at work.

'Jimmy won't be going to school today,' Mr Challoner looked grim.

'Is he ill?'

'You'll find out soon enough so I might as well tell you myself. Our Jimmy has been arrested for stealing.'

'Is he in prison?'

'No, nothing like that. But he can't go out just now and he can't see anybody.' Mr Challoner sighed, 'I don't suppose you know anything about this do you?'

Peter shook his head vigorously.

'I thought not. You've got more sense.'

It was Monday before Peter heard the full story from Jimmy. He was relieved that Jimmy approved of him making himself scarce when the policeman had caught him. Jimmy appeared unchanged by his ordeal even laughing when Peter said 'Well I hope this has taught you a lesson.'

'You're right there. It's certainly taught me a thing or two. One thing it's taught me is that girls cost money. When I called to tell Mavis I wouldn't be able to meet her Friday night she must have thought I couldn't afford to. Anyway she said not to bother calling again.'

'How did you get out of the house?'

'Dad went to work after dinner and me mam had to do the shopping so I nipped up to where Mavis works,' Jimmy's face looked glum at the memory.

'Not all girls will be like that,' Peter said.

'I'm afraid they will, the ones I fancy anyway.'

When the Challoners heard that Jimmy was going to escape prosecution, they were all grateful to the police. Although Jimmy received a strongly worded caution, it paled in comparison to the lecture he received from his dad. He promised he would never steal again but silently assured himself that next time he'd make certain he wasn't caught.

Shortly afterwards Jimmy told Peter that he was leaving school that summer and going to work on the docks like his dad.

'Wouldn't it be better to stay on for the School Cert.?' Peter said.

'No point. Besides, I want a bit of money in my pocket now.'

'What did you mum and dad say?'

'Haven't told them yet so keep quiet.'

Jimmy talked his parents into letting him leave school and he started work as a stevedore on the docks. The physical nature of the job suited Jimmy and he quickly learned the various dodges. He became a member of a cargo broaching scheme which meant that along with the other members he took a share of any cargo that had been broached. They each took a percentage of part of the contents of various cargos, which could range from spirits to tinned fruit. Jimmy soon discovered that there were always 'traders' on the docks who were willing to pay for these goods and surprisingly none of the dockers considered this to be theft. It was thought to be a perk of the job and to Jimmy it meant that he was now able to indulge his growing admiration of the opposite sex.

School for Peter was never the same again with Jimmy gone. Homework kept him indoors in the week and ensured he only saw Jimmy at weekends, but they still went down to the river each Saturday morning. Jimmy still liked to watch the traffic on the Mersey in spite of working there all week. In the afternoon they invariably went to a football match.

Apart from these weekend rituals Peter found that he and Jimmy had less in common. Although Jimmy always invited Peter along when he went out with friends from work, Peter soon felt too uncomfortable to go.

It made him feel awkward that they had money and he didn't. Jimmy, with his newfound circle of friends and girlfriends, didn't miss Peter's company and Peter felt more and more isolated.

Peter had always planned to go to university but gradually it dawned on him that he wasn't prepared to commit himself to the years of further study. He had always enjoyed English at school and was more than happy when he successfully applied for the position of cub reporter on The Liverpool Daily Post.

When he met Jimmy the following Saturday afternoon he told him about the job and his promised wage packet of two pounds weekly.

'You must be mad to work for that. Why don't you come down to the docks? You'd start on four pounds a week but the perks double that.'

'I don't want to work on the docks. Money isn't everything you know.'

'Not afraid of hard work are you? You're as big as me, you'd manage easily.'

'It's not that. It's just not what I want to do.'

'Well it's not what I want either' said Jimmy, 'but it'll do for now. You just wait 'til you take a few girls out. You'll soon see why you need money. By the way, did I tell you I'm getting a motor bike after my birthday?'

'They cost enough don't they?'

'I'll just nick what I can't afford'

'Not that again. I thought you'd have been bright enough to have given up those ideas now.'

'Don't worry, I won't be soft enough to get caught again.'

Jimmy had absolutely no intention of giving up his dream of owning a motor bike. He had been shocked to discover that even second hand ones were too expensive for him. There was only one solution but this time he wouldn't make mistakes.

There were times when Jimmy considered himself to be one of life's philosophers. Crime, he reasoned, was like life itself. To be a success you had to be prepared to grab opportunities when they arose.

Jimmy knew that he needed at least seventy five pounds to buy a motor bike and set out to make owning one become a reality. The opportunity came just as Jimmy had known it would. One lunch hour he was walking back to Huskisson Dock with some work mates when one lad broke away and approached a man standing just inside number two gate. Jimmy was curious. He watched his friend hand the man what appeared to be a piece of paper and when he returned Jimmy asked him what he had passed over. He was told that the man was a bookie's runner collecting bets from the dockers. This was illegal but, as with a number of things that went on at the docks, the authorities appeared to turn a blind eye.

For the next week Jimmy spent his lunch hour studying the bookie's runner. He estimated that in the course of the hour two hundred bets must have been placed and they would amount to about one hundred pounds. Jimmy knew that this was the opportunity he had been waiting for. He decided to wait until the following Thursday as that was pay day for the dockers, when collection was likely to be at its highest.

Thursday came and Jimmy went to see his foreman and requested an hour off work in the afternoon to attend a family funeral. He felt confident that the foreman wouldn't see anything of his dad as he worked at the other end of the docks.

Jimmy, armed with a seven pound hammer from his work box and a balaclava helmet, which was standard issue to all dockers, positioned himself where he could watch the bookie's runner unseen. Jimmy estimated that within an hour the runner had collected three hundred bets from the dockers. As soon as the hooter sounded the end of the lunch break he left the dock estate through number two gate out into the Dock Road. Jimmy followed at a discreet distance.

He had intended to approach the man when the moment was right, threaten him with the hammer and steal the money. The runner was a puny specimen and Jimmy didn't anticipate much resistance from him. Dock Road itself was busy with traffic either entering or leaving the docks. Jimmy had to continue trailing the man in the hope that he would eventually turn into a side street. After over half a mile the runner finally turned off the main road into a deserted street. Jimmy pulled on his balaclava and ran up behind the runner, pulling the hammer from under his jacket. The bookie's runner turned in alarm at the sound of Jimmy's footsteps and he tried to escape. Jimmy soon caught up and to his great surprise the little man stopped and turned to face him. Jimmy saw the knife in the runner's hand and his mind went blank.

In panic Jimmy hit out at the man and the blow struck him across his cheek, causing him to stumble. With the second blow from the hammer the man fell to the ground but to Jimmy's surprise he started to stagger to his feet. Jimmy hit him again with the hammer and watched as the runner slid drunkenly to the ground before lying still. Jimmy searched his victim's pockets, took all the money he could find and fled in the direction he had come from. A woman coming out of her house and confronting the bloody scene started to scream, the sound echoing in Jimmy's ears as he ran. He ripped off his balaclava and panicked momentarily when he realised that he had dropped the hammer at the scene. Jimmy decided he was safe, the hammer hadn't been customised and so could only be traced to the docks, not to an individual. The police would only be able to establish that it was similar to the type issued to dock workers but there were over twenty thousand of those.

Curious to find out how much he had taken Jimmy went into the lavatory to count the money. The bulk of it was in ten shilling notes and came to a final total of eighty pounds.

'Come on lad, there's been a robbery with violence down by the docks.' Brian Bellis, crime reporter with the *Liverpool Daily Post*, was already throwing on his jacket as he called to Peter. He had been teamed with Peter to give the new boy an insight into crime reporting. Peter himself had been somewhat disappointed to discover that most of a crime reporter's duties involved sitting in the courts for hours on end.

This was Peter's first real assignment and he was thrilled to be going with Brian, who was a respected reporter.

'What's happened?' asked Peter.

'The ambulance crew are on their way to Slater Street. Apparently a man has been badly beaten in a robbery.'

Peter was relieved to hear that the victim would have been taken to hospital by the ambulance crew before their arrival.

When they drew up in Slater Street Brian got out of the car and went over to the Detective Inspector, who he seemed to be on very good terms with. Peter moved over to where a group of onlookers were standing and saw that a pool of congealed blood had been circled on the pavement. Sickened, he turned away. Brian told him the victim was a bookie's runner who had been attacked and robbed by a young athletic man wearing a balaclava and carrying a docker's hammer.

'They're sure the attacker must be a dock worker, but it could be one of thousands,' Brian said.

'What happens next?'

'Well I've got all the details we need from here so we'll go on to the Infirmary. The witness wasn't much use as she didn't see the actual attack, but I've taken her name and address so that we can mention her in the article.'

To Peter's relief they were informed at the Infirmary that the victim hadn't been too seriously injured and was being kept in for observation.

Back at the office Peter thought about the events of the day as Brian wrote up the article. His mind was drawn back to the conversation he'd had with Jimmy Challoner when Jimmy had said he would steal in order to buy a motor bike. Jimmy was a docker, he was also young and athletic and he had stolen before. Peter wondered if Jimmy would resort to violence, he hoped not but he couldn't help thinking that Jimmy might be responsible for the attack. He considered telling Brian but on reflection decided against it. After all, he didn't want to be responsible for drawing attention to Jimmy if he was innocent.

'I see the bookie's runner who works the docks was beaten up and robbed,' said Mr Challoner, looking up from his copy of the Liverpool Daily Post. Jimmy and Mrs Challoner were sitting at the table eating breakfast.

'How bad was it?,' Jimmy asked.

'Not that bad, he's just been kept in for observation.'

'Have they got anyone?' Jimmy was perfectly calm as he asked.

'No, but they reckon it might be a docker.'

'Well they've plenty to choose from.'

'Aye and there's plenty down there who'd do it,' Mr Challoner shook his head as he turned the page.

Jimmy was relieved that the police didn't appear to have a good description of him and for the first time since the attack, he realised that he hadn't really cared whether he had hurt the man or not. He knew now that he was capable of violence and if circumstances warranted it he would resort to it again.

4

'Peter, Jimmy's here,' shouted Mrs Turner from the bottom of the stairs. Peter was in his bedroom putting the finishing touches to his article on the Quarter Sessions that had taken place that day. He was puzzled as to why Jimmy should call round in the week.

'I've got something to show you' Jimmy motioned excitedly to Peter to follow him outside. There, at the top of the entry, Peter could see a brand new Norton five hundred cc motor bike.

'Is that yours?' he said quietly.

Jimmy nodded. Not for the first time Peter felt a stab of envy.

He longed for a motor bike but knew that it was an impossible dream on his wages.

'It's a beauty' he said at last.

'It is isn't it? I only picked it up today so I'm still getting the hang of it.'

'It must have cost a packet.'

'Just over a hundred.'

'In that case I think I know where you came by the money.'

'I know you do, told you I was going to nick it,' Jimmy was unabashed.

'You never said you were going to beat up an innocent person to get it though.'

'I don't know what you're talking about, I didn't beat anyone up' Jimmy replied.

'Look Jimmy, I may not be able to prove anything, but you and I both know it was you who robbed the bookie's runner.'

'Like you said, you can't prove it and I'm not admitting it so why don't we just forget about it?'

'I can't forget about something like that. Beating someone with a hammer is a whole lot different to stealing the insurance man's fiver.' Peter's distaste for his friend's actions was etched in his face.

'I told you years ago I was going to be rich and if crime is what it takes then crime it is.'

'Start again Jimmy. Maybe the army will knock some sense into you' Peter added hopefully.

Peter and Jimmy didn't see much of each other after that. The attack had changed everything.

Shortly before his eighteenth birthday Peter received instructions to report to the Army Recruitment Office for his medical. He had opted to serve his two years national service in the army and hoped it would be in the Royal Signals Regiment.

His aim was to gain valuable experience in communications as his initial enthusiasm for reporting had waned and he hoped new skills would lead to a new career on his release from the army.

Shortly afterwards Peter met Jimmy Challoner and his first question was, 'Got your call up papers yet?'

'Well I got them but I won't be going. I failed the medical,' Jimmy said.

'Come off it. You're as fit as me if not fitter!'

'It seems I'm not. Remember that bout of rheumatic fever I had when I was eight? It weakened my heart apparently. They won't take me.'

Peter looked at his old friend in disbelief. He knew Jimmy had looked forward to his national service and felt a wave of sympathy for him.

'Is it serious?' Peter asked.

'Not according to the medical officer. He said I'd got a slight heart murmur but that it shouldn't stop me having a completely normal life.'

'Well that's good to hear anyway. But I'll be honest it would have been great if we could have joined together.'

'It certainly would, but that's life for you.'

A few weeks later Peter was told to report to Catterick Camp in Yorkshire for his basic training. At the end of the training period he was disappointed to learn that because of a lack of vacancies in the Royal Signals he would be joining the Military Police.

With Peter gone and most of his other friends now doing their national service, Jimmy now found himself without male company of his own age. He spent long hours riding his motor bike, sometimes alone, sometimes with one of his many girlfriends. His bitterness at the army's rejection grew daily and eventually his thoughts turned to crime. This at least would satisfy his craving for excitement and he started looking around for opportunities ripe for the taking. He reasoned that being alone would be an advantage and greatly reduce his chances of getting caught.

Sitting in the cinema some weeks later, it occurred to Jimmy that the girl he had thought so mesmerising an hour earlier was in reality boring the life out of him. As soon as the film ended he lost no time in putting her on the next bus home with a half hearted promise that he 'would be in touch.'

He decided to go for a Chinese meal as it was too early to call it a night and made his way to the Pearl City, a busy, popular restaurant in the heart of Liverpool's China town. Not only had Jimmy discovered a liking for Chinese food, he had grown to respect the Chinese as a race. They were a close community and they kept themselves very much to themselves.

Leaving the restaurant after his meal Jimmy crossed the street to establish where the sound of music was coming from. He found himself going up the stairs of a small club over one of the restaurants. On the landing sat a bored looking Chinese man sitting behind a small table. He asked Jimmy if he was a member and, when he said he wasn't, told him that the entrance cost was five shillings. Jimmy's curiosity got the better of him and he gave the man the money and went into the tiny room that passed for a club. There were a few chairs and tables in the room surrounding the smallest dance floor Jimmy had ever seen. The music Jimmy had heard in the street was coming from a record player placed behind the bar. Looking round the dimly lit room he saw that he and three other men were the only customers and ordering a drink from the English barmaid he struck up a conversation with her.

'Not very busy,' Jimmy said.

'Not in here we're not but it's early yet' she replied pleasantly.

'Is there another room then?'

'Yes, through there,' she pointed to a door in the corner.

'What goes on in there then?'

'Gambling, what else would the Chinese do?'

'What sort of gambling. Cards and that?'

'They'll gamble on anything. You name it they'll be playing it.'

'And how long does this go on 'til'?, Jimmy's interest was growing.

'Oh about two in the morning, maybe later on a Saturday.'

'Who runs the gambling side of things?'

'To be honest I don't know. The club is run by Mr Wong but I know he isn't the owner'.

'He must be worth a few bob.'

'Oh I'm sure he is. Most of the Chinese lose heavily but there are a couple who play every Saturday night who always seem to win.'

When Jimmy asked how she could know that she replied, 'I see them counting their winnings.'

Jimmy sat by the bar for an hour and watched as about fifteen people entered the back room of the little club. This, thought Jimmy, was the opportunity that he had been waiting for. He made the decision to return the next night and have his own share of the winnings.

The following night he went back to the club and was relieved to discover that his five shillings of the previous night apparently covered his membership for life. Talking to Sonia, the barmaid, he discovered that she herself was married to a Chinese man and that she worked most nights at the club. She drew his attention to the two Chinese men who she said always seemed to win and Jimmy noticed that they were both very smartly dressed. In appearance they both looked more like businessmen than the regular Chinese clientele who all seemed to be in the catering business.

Jimmy left the club at 2am. He had been careful not to tell Sonia anything which might later identify him and he had drunk sparingly. He decided to take his position early in case the gamblers left the club earlier than he had anticipated. Returning to the side street where he had parked his motor bike he collected his balaclava and a heavy monkey wrench. The latter he concealed in the waistband of his trousers and the balaclava was slipped into his pocket. He found a good vantage point in a small recess in the wall of the building opposite the club where he could watch the entrance without being seen himself. Only the occasional shouts of late night revellers broke the silence as Jimmy began his vigil.

He watched several people leave the club but chose to ignore them, preferring to wait for the two men. At quarter to four they appeared accompanied by two further men.

Realising that he couldn't tackle four men Jimmy cursed his bad luck. Then, to his relief, the two men he hadn't expected turned and walked off in the direction of the town centre. Jimmy pulled on his balaclava, took out his money wrench and silently crossed the street and followed his prey as the two men started to walk away from the club. They were completely oblivious to Jimmy's presence and chatted as they approached a parked car which Jimmy rightly guessed to be theirs. Jimmy came up behind them brandishing the money wrench and simultaneously their hands shot up as though it was a gun.

'Just give me the money' Jimmy barked. Neither man said a word, both silently handed over bulging wallets to him. Jimmy was amazed that robbery could be so simple. He snatched the wallets, ran back up the deserted street and when he was sure he wasn't being followed went down the side street to where his motor bike was parked. Having dropped the empty wallets down the nearest grid Jimmy started his bike and made for home. He was stunned on counting the money to discover that it amounted to two hundred and fifty pounds. Jimmy was tempted not to go to work on Monday but he reasoned that he would be wiser not to change his routine in any way thus avoiding drawing any unwanted attention to himself. He clocked in as usual and halfway through the morning the foreman approached him to inform him that someone wanted to see him at Number Two gate. Jimmy couldn't imagine who it could be. It couldn't be anyone official or they would have gone to the manager's office he mused as he made his way to the gate. Two 'heavies' were standing together waiting for him and Jimmy was so sure that a mistake had been made that he strode confidently over to them saying, 'You want to see me?'

After establishing that he was Jimmy Challoner one of the men took Jimmy firmly by the arm and said, 'Come on, you're coming with us.' As Jimmy opened his mouth to protest the other man silenced him with, 'You can either walk or be dragged, make up your mind because either way you're coming.' Jimmy knew when he was beaten. One of these gorillas would be a match for him, two would kill him. He did the sensible thing and went with them. They escorted Jimmy across the Dock Road towards a Jaguar car where a man was waiting on the back seat. The car door was opened and Jimmy was ushered inside.

'So you are Challoner?' said the man in the back of the car.

'That's right,' Jimmy felt a frisson of fear now.

'Well Challoner, you owe me some money' said the man quietly.

Jimmy breathed a sigh of relief, they obviously had the wrong man.

'There's been a mistake, I don't owe anyone anything.'

'You're right, a mistake has been made but it's you who made it Challoner,' the man's tone was menacing.

'No I mean it, I don't owe money to you or anybody else' repeated Jimmy.

'Oh I think you do, I think you owe me exactly two hundred and fifty pounds.'

As the penny began to drop Jimmy's confidence nose dived.

'I don't know what you're talking about.' Even to himself it didn't sound convincing.

The man turned in his seat to face Jimmy, 'Look Challoner, don't mess me about any more. You took two hundred and fifty pounds from two friends of mine and I'm here to get it back for them.'

He wasn't a big man but Jimmy sensed a ruthlessness about him that made his blood run cold. He suspected that if he wasn't very cautious he could end up getting seriously hurt.

'Why should I give it to you?' Jimmy said.

'Because if you don't you'll never walk again,' replied the man. Jimmy believed him.

'I haven't got it with me.' Jimmy had now abandoned all hopes of bluffing his way out of his dilemma.

'I didn't imagine that you had. Bring the money, all of it, to the club tonight at ten o'clock. With that Jimmy was dismissed.

He made his way back to where he had been working with his gang and was approached by the foreman.

'What did Spicer want with you?'

'Who the hell is Spicer?'

'He's only Mr Big, the Liverpool Mafia,' said the foreman. 'Take some good advice kid and don't get mixed up with the likes of him, he's bad news.'

Jimmy shrugged as the foreman walked away.

That night Jimmy took the stolen money from its hiding place in his bedroom and gave thanks that he hadn't spent any of it. He arrived at the club just before ten o'clock and was surprised to see that the room was full of Chinese people. Spicer was standing by the bar flanked by the two heavies who had accompanied him earlier in the day. They were talking to the two men that Jimmy had threatened and robbed.

Jimmy walked up to Spicer and held the money out.

'That's the smartest thing you've done recently,' Spicer said turning slightly to pass the money on to the two Chinese men. The sickening realisation that he had robbed two men who were part of Spicer's protection racket suddenly became clear to Jimmy. He had heard rumours about a big protection racket in Liverpool. Now he knew who was running it.

'The thing is Challoner, you've got to learn not to interfere in things that don't concern you,' Spicer said as he nodded to the two heavies. As if given a signal the Chinese patrons moved back forming a circle. Whatever was about to happen they had obviously seen it all before and Jimmy felt his legs go weak as realisation dawned. One of the heavies grabbed Jimmy from behind and pinned his arms behind his back. The other systematically and professionally beat Jimmy Challoner much to the enjoyment of the crowd. The last thing that Jimmy saw before he lost consciousness was a sea of grinning Chinese faces who were being shown just what their money bought for them.

When Jimmy came round it was in a hospital ward. Every part of his body ached and throbbed, every movement caused him to wince in pain.

'Good, you're back with us' said the nurse at the end of his bed.

'You're in the Royal Infirmary. Don't worry, nothing is broken but you'll be in for a couple of days. You've taken quite a beating.'

'Yes I know, I was there,' Jimmy grimaced.

The following day two detectives from the CID paid Jimmy a visit and asked Jimmy what had happened to him.

When Jimmy replied that he had no memory of the attack one of the detectives said, 'Come on son, you were beaten up and dumped just outside the Infirmary. Only one person in the city works like that, Tony Spicer.'

'Never heard of him,' Jimmy replied.

The detectives left knowing that Jimmy was lying but unable to get him talking on the subject of Spicer. It was something they were getting used to.

Jimmy was in hospital for a week and off work for a further week. He had ample time to reflect on his chance meeting with the head of the biggest criminal syndicate in the city. Jimmy knew now that Tony Spicer was the man he would have to replace if he was ever to become Mr Big in Liverpool.

When he returned to work the foreman gave him a note which simply told Jimmy to telephone the number printed on the piece of paper. During his dinner hour Jimmy rang the number and a female voice answered. She asked Jimmy to hold and the next thing he knew he was talking to Spicer.

'Challoner, I'm busy right now, meet me tonight at the Adelphi, OK?' said Spicer.

'OK,' was all Jimmy could say. The telephone went dead before he could ask Spicer why he wanted to see him. His first thought was not to go. He was only just recovering from one beating and didn't relish the thought of another. He decided to go to the Adelphi when he reasoned that even Spicer wouldn't invite him to the best hotel in Liverpool to beat him up.

At seven that night Jimmy Challoner walked through the swing doors of the Adelphi Hotel and entered the foyer. His confident demeanour didn't betray his astonishment at the grandeur of his surroundings and he strode up to the reception desk to ask where he might find Mr Spicer. Spicer was alone, taking coffee in the lounge and on Jimmy's approach he indicated that he should sit down.

'You look well Challoner. Must have good powers of recovery,' Spicer said.

'No thanks to you that I'm here at all.'

'That is where you're wrong. If I didn't want you around you wouldn't be around,' Spicer said matter of factly.

Jimmy instinctively looked around the room.

'Don't worry, they're not here tonight, I didn't imagine that I would need them.'

Jimmy started to breathe a little easier on hearing this.

'Why do you want to see me then?' he said.

'I've asked you because I'm impressed with you. You know when to keep your mouth shut and I like the way you show initiative. I think you've got all the qualities that I'm looking for in an employee and I'd like to offer you a job.' For probably the first and only time in his life Jimmy was so taken aback he was lost for words. His bewilderment was so obvious that Spicer laughed loudly and chortled, 'Well I can see you didn't expect that.'

'What exactly would I be doing?'

'The truth is,' Spicer continued, 'I've taken a liking to you Jimmy. I can see a lot of myself at your age in you and I feel you will make an excellent personal assistant. I'll pay you fifty pounds a week and you'll be given a car.'

'Fifty pounds. I'd be a fool to refuse.'

'Yes you would. Not only would you be earning five times more than the docks can offer you, I would help you to develop your full potential.'

'It's a deal,' Jimmy said thinking to himself that here in front of him was the very opportunity he had been waiting for. A chance to break into the big time but more importantly, an opportunity to learn his trade from the very man he intended to usurp.

'Tell me one thing,' said Jimmy, 'How did you know it was me?'

'Simple, Sonia remembered you had dated a cousin of hers,' Spicer grinned.

5

From the start Jimmy was impressed with Spicer's organisation. Spicer wasn't exaggerating when he said that he controlled every major racket in Liverpool. In addition to the protection racket he ran sixteen brothels. He ran a laundering service for 'hot' money which he recycled through the Isle of Man and he fenced all the major stolen property within the North West. Spicer possessed a natural flair for business and Jimmy felt that he would have succeeded at whatever he turned his hand to. Added to his illicit businesses were several legitimate enterprises which included a property development company and a number of licensed clubs. It was from one of these clubs that Spicer ran his empire.

Spicer was equally impressed with Jimmy and gradually introduced him to his various endeavours. The last and probably the most lucrative that Jimmy was shown was the Casino which was run from Spicer's flagship, the River Club. It puzzled him at first just how Spicer was able to run a gambling business in the city centre. Jimmy soon discovered that Spicer had a number of influential figures on his payroll including senior members of the city council, magistrates and senior police officers.

Jimmy thought it prudent to be sparing with the truth when telling his parents about his new job. He said that having helped a man who was being robbed he had been offered a job as bodyguard to that same man. Although they were delighted that Jimmy appeared to be earning a vastly improved salary, they were concerned when he announced that because of the demands of the job, he would be moving into a flat nearer to the city centre.

Soon after moving into his new flat Jimmy took and passed his driving test and Spicer bought him his first car. Jimmy Challoner was nineteen and on his way.

After twelve months he was put in charge of the protection and prostitution side of the business. It was a well established business and all

Jimmy had to do was to manage it and collect the cash. It was inevitable, and no surprise to Jimmy, that certain people would try to take advantage of him when he first took over. They soon learned that he was every bit as ruthless as Tony Spicer, maybe even more so.

After one or two ill advised people found themselves in hospital the business settled down and almost ran itself. It was at about this time that Jimmy met up with Peter Turner again. Both had been independently to watch Everton playing Burnley at Goodison Park and Peter was making his way home when Jimmy's car drew up alongside him.

'Hi Peter. Want a lift?' Jimmy grinned as Peter did a double take.

'I don't believe it, is it really Jimmy Challoner?' Peter said in mock disbelief.

'Stop mucking about and get in.'

'This is very nice,' said Peter, as he got into the car. 'What have you done this time, robbed a bank?.'

'Better than that, I work for this property tycoon who treats me like a son. I'm his personal assistant and he's showing me the business.'

'Is it above board?'

'Course it is. Tell you what, Mr Spicer owns a few clubs in the city. Why don't you be my guest at the River Club tonight?' Peter agreed. It would be good to catch up with Jimmy again.

Peter couldn't miss the flashing red neon sign of the River Club. He was met at the door by a giant of a man who looked decidedly ill at ease in his smart dinner jacket and bow tie. Peter took in the man's features at a glance. He had a square face that looked as if it had been carved out of granite and didn't appear to have a neck at all. His slightly hunched shoulders held the promise of an awesome power. Peter could well understand why he'd got the job, it would take a brave man or a complete imbecile to tangle with him.

As he made his way across the foyer Peter noted with admiration the plush surroundings. This was nothing like the clubs he frequented around the army towns while doing his national service. 'This place has class,' thought Peter to himself. As he went through the double doors of the club's interior Peter was approached by an attractive blonde.

'Peter Turner?' she asked. Peter nodded.

'Hello, Jimmy's waiting for you. I'm Maureen by the way, Jimmy tells me you're a policeman.'

'Well the Military Police anyway, I'm doing my national service.'

'Ah that sounds more like it, I couldn't imagine Jimmy with a real policeman as a friend,' Maureen giggled.

Peter was puzzled by her remark but at that moment they arrived at one of the tables where Jimmy was sitting along with two other men.

Jimmy stood up at Peter's approach and said 'Peter, I want you to meet my boss Mr Spicer.' A short thick set man stood up and extended his hand. 'Call me Tony,' he said, 'Welcome to my club, I hope you enjoy your evening.' Jimmy then introduced the second man as Mike Hanlon and niceties were exchanged before Spicer and Mike Hanlon resumed their conversation. It sounded to Peter as though they were discussing business although he couldn't hear their exact words. Jimmy explained that Hanlon was Spicer's solicitor and dealt with all legal matters concerning Spicer's business interests. Peter enjoyed a first class meal followed by a classy cabaret, all at Jimmy's expense, and just for a while allowed himself to relax and believe that Jimmy was legally and gainfully employed. He listened as Jimmy regaled him with tales about his new flat and his numerous girl friends, the latest of which was Maureen. It was around midnight that his suspicions were tweaked when Spicer interrupted their conversation to say to Jimmy, 'Time you went to collect the rent.' Jimmy turned to Peter and told him to order whatever he wanted and charge it to him. He told Peter he would be about an hour and during his absence Peter thought about the remark that Spicer had made. He wanted to believe that the remark referred to Spicer's own premises, but instinct told him otherwise. Jimmy, true to his word, was back within the hour and after telling Spicer that the bag was in his office he slipped into his seat next to Jimmy.

'What on earth have you been getting up to at this hour?' Peter said.

'Oh just business,' replied Jimmy in a tone that suggested that the matter was now closed.

When Peter got up to leave he and Jimmy shook hands and both knew that this was the parting of the ways. Jimmy was now in a different league and mixing with people that Peter suspected that he wouldn't want to know.

During the next twelve months Jimmy consolidated his position as Spicer's right hand man. Spicer had virtually handed over the running of his illegal activities to Jimmy. He himself concentrated on his legitimate ventures and establishing himself as a prominent member of Liverpool society. This suited Jimmy. He was content for the time being to act as

Spicer's managing director. He was earning excellent money and learning the business from the master. He knew though that this feeling of contentment wouldn't last forever.

One evening Jimmy was present at the River Club when Spicer made his weekly payment to the CID. One of the detectives speaking to Jimmy said, 'You know a Peter Turner don't you?'

'Yes I know him. We grew up together. Why what's he done?'

'He's joined the local force as a uniformed constable,' the detective replied.

Jimmy was nonplussed at this piece of news, although on consideration he realised that it was a natural progression for Peter from the Military Police. He wondered momentarily if it would be worth trying to cultivate Peter in the same way as the detectives he was helping to entertain. Surely better to help a friend than someone you don't know, he reasoned. He knew though that Peter would need to be a member of the CID if he was to be of any use to him and that could take three or four years. Jimmy thought a little help in the right quarters would probably shorten this apprenticeship.

Over the next twelve months Jimmy sensed that one or two of the rival concerns were flexing their muscles, possibly with a view to a take over bid. Jimmy suggested to Tony Spicer that they should consider employing some more muscle themselves.

'That's all very well, but where would we employ them? I don't pay people just to sit around in case of trouble,' Spicer said.

'Well if we ever needed to confirm just who's boss it could be dodgy at the moment.'

'Who do you think might push their luck then?'

'There are two outfits that worry me. The Jacksons who I reckon should be our first concern, and then there's Walsh who is mustering ex national service lads.' Jimmy went on. 'The Jacksons have sewn up all the rackets in the black quarter of Toxteth and I reckon they are about ready to move out towards the city.'

'And that means us?'

'Who else? But I reckon we could avoid a gang war if we strengthened our staff now.'

'Well as far as I'm concerned a gang war is a no win situation for everyone. But tell me, how would you go about recruiting new staff yourself?' Spicer leaned forward and waited for Jimmy to answer.

'My plan is to kill two birds with one stone' Jimmy said eagerly, 'I'm sure I could persuade Walsh and his outfit to join us and if he did, Jackson would back off. He's not stupid and he'd accept that we would now be just too much for him to take on.'

'Brilliant,' Spicer laughed, 'I knew you were bright Jimmy, but I hadn't realised you were a strategist too.'

'I've also thought about what to do with Walsh,' added Jimmy. 'The city could use a professional squad of bouncers. All the clubs and dance halls are having trouble with fighting on the premises and I'm certain they'd pay well for the right type of protection.'

'You're right, placed throughout the city they could join forces if necessary. They'd be a force to be reckoned with Jimmy.' Spicer was delighted with his protégé.

'You handle Walsh and then we'll pay the Jacksons a visit, if you know what I mean,' Spicer looked at Jimmy.

'I'd already planned to leave him my calling card,' Jimmy said.

That evening Jimmy, accompanied by two colleagues, went to the Mariner's Club on the Dock Road where he had a good idea they'd find Walsh. Jimmy had known Walsh for a number of years, they had worked in adjacent gangs on the docks until their call up. Walsh had been out of the army for two years now, had gathered together a small team and was making a reasonable living from petty crime, but Jimmy had a feeling that he would be open to a good offer. He was right. After listening to Jimmy, Walsh and six of his cronies agreed to join Spicer's organisation.

Within a few weeks of their recruitment Walsh and his team had been placed as bouncers throughout the nightspots of Liverpool. Although they met with a certain amount of resistance they soon established control and a calm settled on the city's clubs and dance halls.

Jimmy decided then that a call on Jackson was due. Brian Jackson was an unknown quantity to Jimmy. He had grown up in Bootle, just outside Liverpool, and had been indoctrinated into a life of crime from birth. Brian and his three brothers had graduated from approved school to borstal, much as the aristocracy follow in their predecessors' path through the likes of Eton and Harrow. Their education had proved to them that crime did pay, providing you knew your trade. The Jackson's trade was violence.

They intimidated and took what they wanted when they wanted it. As an indication of their prowess, they had taken control of all the illicit gaming houses and shebeens that had formerly been run by the black members of the Toxteth community. A feat that Jimmy appreciated had not been easy.

Jimmy, together with Walsh and eight hand-picked men, all armed with pickaxe handles, visited the Jamaican Club the headquarters of the Jacksons. The first indication of trouble to the club's patrons was the terrified screaming of the doorman. He had made the mistake of offering Jimmy some resistance and Walsh and the others following him were forced to step over the prostrate form of the unfortunate man. Jimmy's eyes quickly acclimatised to the gloom of the club and he saw the Jackson brothers and three of their gang start to get up from the table where they had been sitting. The customers made for the exit as quickly as they could. None of them wanted to be part of the bloodbath.

Jimmy made straight for Brian Jackson and started attacking him with the pickaxe handle. Jackson instinctively raised his arms to protect himself but the hardened piece of wood smashed into his wrists. The sound of bones splintering accompanied the steady thud of the axe handle as Jimmy systematically beat Jackson into unconsciousness. He looked round in satisfaction and noted that Walsh and the other men had all completed their set tasks in a similar manner. Jimmy was satisfied. The Jacksons would think twice now about expanding their business interests in the direction of Spicer's territory. It would also serve as a warning to anyone else who had ideas above their station.

6

The first three months of Peter Turner's service as Constable 84A of the Liverpool City Police were spent at the Home Office Training School near Warrington. Peter felt it was almost like being back in the army since nearly all his fellow students were ex-service men.

Eight similar training centres served the police forces of the number one district. This was made up of the police forces of Cheshire, Lancashire, Cumberland and Westmorland plus all the City and Borough Forces that were part of those counties. The work was demanding and required the students to learn the basics of English law during the thirteen weeks training course. They were examined monthly and Peter was pleased with his progress and with his final position on the course. He finished third in the final examination, which ensured that he received a good report to be sent to the Chief Constable of his force.

The first two years of any police officer's service are spent on probation which means if he doesn't measure up he is advised to leave. Peter worked hard and discovered he liked the challenges of police work. He received good assessments from his superior and after two years his appointment was confirmed.

Liverpool in 1957 was a thriving port with its large docks complex fully employed. Being a large city it had various crime related problems and the fact that it was an international port meant it had a higher than average proportion of violent crimes.

Peter was posted to A Division and worked from a police station called Rose Hill. This division was considered to be the busiest of the force's seven divisions and was the ideal placement for an ambitious young constable eager to learn his trade. Peter was intent on becoming a detective in the CID, although he appreciated it wouldn't be easy. Proven ability as a good uniformed officer was essential and he knew that the more arrests, (or 'collars' as they were called), the greater his chance of selection for the detective branch. His personal record of arrests was reasonably good but Peter knew that it needed to improve. He needed to make arrests for crimes that had been committed off his own beat and this would mean the use of an informer but Peter didn't know anyone likely to be of any use to him.

Arriving on duty one evening Peter received an anonymous telephone call. A muffled male voice confirmed his identity and then proceeded to inform him that the previously night a robbery had taken place at a tobacconist's shop on Scotland Road. The voice continued 'All the stuff is at Flat 22A Ormonde Gardens, got that?'

'Yes, but who is this?' Peter asked.

'Let's just say I'm a friend who will pass you information now and again.' With that the line went dead.

'Well I hope that wasn't a personal call' the sergeant said as Peter replaced the telephone.

'No, I don't think it was. Someone who wouldn't give his name, he just gave me some information,' Peter replied. When he passed on the message to the sergeant Peter was told to pass it on to the CID upstairs. The sergeant remembered reading on a crime report that there had been a break in at the newsagents the previous night. Confronted by the news that an unknown caller had contacted Peter the detective on duty was not impressed.

'I've got news for you Turner, we don't go getting a warrant to search someone's house on the strength of an anonymous 'phone call. Get back downstairs and tell your sergeant we're not interested.' Peter had expected more from the CID and he returned to the sergeant feeling disappointed and disillusioned with the detective branch.

'Can't say I'm surprised,' the sergeant said, 'Ah well, if the jacks don't want to know you'd better just get out on your beat.'

The following night Peter took yet another muffled 'phone call.

'Constable Turner, why didn't you act on the information I gave you?' the voice asked.

'I had to pass the information to CID and they didn't want to use it,' Peter replied.

'I might have known. They were probably all out drinking,' the caller said.

Peter expressed surprise that the caller claimed to know so much about the CID

'It's my business to know', the voice said 'Anyway you're in luck, all the stolen property will be moved from that address I gave you at four o'clock tomorrow morning. You won't need the jacks, just be there yourself.' With that the caller rang off.

When Peter told his sergeant, he suggested that they find out for themselves just how good the information was.

At three thirty in the morning, Peter, his sergeant and four uniformed colleagues were waiting in Ormonde Gardens. Ormonde Gardens was a circular block of tenement flats made up of four floors. On each floor there was a balcony. It was an easy matter for the officers to conceal themselves and still keep watch on Flat 22A. Almost exactly on the stroke of four, a van drove up and Peter saw two men get out. One went up the stairs and one opened the rear doors of the van. Peter's mouth felt dry and he was filled with a nervous excitement. His mind went back to the last time he had felt like this, when he kept watch as his pal Jimmy was stealing the insurance man's money. Peter's mind quickly refocused when he spotted three men coming down the staircase carrying cardboard boxes. The sergeant had instructed them that no one was to move until something was safely in the van. He stressed it was essential that they had proof that the property had actually passed into the possession of the receiver.

The surprised men, seeing the show of strength from the police, offered very little resistance. In total fifty thousand cigarettes and several pounds of tobacco were recovered from the flat. When the night detective was called out and the premises were searched professionally further stolen property from other crimes was recovered.

'That'll teach those jacks not to turn down good information when they're told it,' the sergeant looked delighted. Peter sensed that he regarded the night as a personal triumph.

Peter continued to receive regular information from his mystery caller and now the CID acted on everything he passed on to them. His informant never gave wrong information and the CID were at great pains to discover the identity of Peter's benefactor. Peter too was intrigued by the calls but he made no move to try and uncover the caller's identity.

It was a source of amusement to Jimmy that he was passing on news of fellow criminals anonymously. It didn't concern him that he was breaking the criminal's code of never informing on a fellow criminal, for these were small fry who were of no consequence to Jimmy. The intrigue involved appealed to the showman in him.

Jimmy was pleased with the way the business was flourishing and he allowed himself to take full credit for this situation. Spicer had become merely a figurehead while Jimmy ran the syndicate. He often felt he didn't really know Spicer at all. Unlike himself Spicer never sought female company which led Jimmy to wonder exactly what Spicer's sexual preferences were.. All that Jimmy knew was that Spicer was unmarried and lived in what Jimmy assumed was some splendour on the Wirral, an area largely reserved for the wealthy.

Eventually the day came when Jimmy, anxious to speak to Spicer, was forced to ring him on his personal number as a last resort. To Jimmy's surprise Spicer instructed him to visit him at his home. Spicer's house was at the end of a long tree lined drive and Jimmy was vaguely disappointed when Spicer himself opened the door. He had been half expecting a butler to usher him in. Jimmy stepped into a large oak panelled hallway and looking up he could see a galleried balcony around a spacious landing. Spicer smiled in greeting as he led Jimmy into a book filled library off the hallway. He laughed as Jimmy gazed around the room. 'Don't be too impressed, the books came with the house. I haven't actually read any of them.'

Urgent business concluded, Spicer said, 'Now you're here you had better meet Geraldine.'

'Who's Geraldine?' replied Jimmy in surprise.

'Geraldine is who I live with,' said Spicer opening the door into a large sitting room. A girl rose to meet them from the chair where she had been reading as Spicer introduced the two.

Jimmy thought she was the loveliest thing he had ever seen. The revelation that Spicer was living with this beautiful creature left him speechless with surprise. She stretched out her hand and said warmly, 'Hello Jimmy, I'm pleased to meet you at last.' Jimmy stammered, 'Hello Geraldine' and silently cursed himself for sounding like a schoolboy. He couldn't believe it, lost for words because of a woman. Geraldine had a natural easy manner but Jimmy's brain didn't appear to be working in conjunction with his mouth. He took his leave as soon as decency would allow and drove away relieved that his ordeal was over.

Driving back, Jimmy's head was filled with thoughts of Geraldine. He was puzzled as to what such a classy lady was doing with Spicer. Easy to see why Spicer was with her. She was his passport into society.

The next time Jimmy met Geraldine was at Aintree for the Grand

National. Tony Spicer had taken a hospitality tent and had sent out invitations to selected guests.

The Thursday before to the race meeting, Spicer sent a message to Jimmy saying he wanted to meet him at the Adelphi that night.

'Sorry if it all sounded a bit melodramatic, but I wanted to speak to you before I introduce you to a very good friend of mine. He'll be one of my guests on Saturday.'

'Sounds as though he's important,' Jimmy said.

'Jimmy, as you become more involved in the business I'll be introducing you to one or two people in the same line as us but who operate in other areas. You'll find that these contacts are invaluable. My friend, and I'll only introduce him as Sam, is one of my contacts. He operates in Leeds and we owe each other a lot. Now Sam is having a few problems on his own patch. He's reasonably optimistic that he can withstand a takeover bid when he's on site as it were, but he feels vulnerable away from home. He accepted my invitation this weekend on the understanding that I would guarantee his safety while he's down here.'

'Got it. My job is to be his minder.'

'Precisely. But there's a little more to it than that,' Spicer continued. 'I know something Sam doesn't. Someone's going to take a pop at him while he's at the National on Saturday.'

'Any idea who's involved?'

'I know it's gone out to contract and to a London hit man. I'll admit it's a long shot but I've a good idea who it will be.'

'Well that gives us a fighting chance.'

'It will be your job Jimmy to see that Sam comes to no harm while he's my guest. Do I make myself clear?'

'As crystal,' Jimmy replied understanding only too well that if anything happened to Sam his own position would be threatened and he wasn't ready yet to challenge Spicer. It didn't promise to be an easy weekend. Jimmy had never come up against a professional killer before and he knew he would have to pull out all the stops to ensure Sam's safety.

'When do I meet Sam?'

'Soon' came Spicer's reply followed by a lengthy description of the man he suspected of being the hit man hired to kill Sam. From the detailed picture that he drew Jimmy felt sure that Sam had used the hit man's services himself. 'You obviously know this man. Why haven't you warned him off?' Jimmy asked.

'Too late. I tried but he'd already left London. Which is why I'm convinced it's him.'

'Sam, come and sit down. Meet Jimmy Challoner, my right hand man,' said Spicer to the small, balding man who was approaching their table. Jimmy noted that Sam was expensively tailored, something that Jimmy now appreciated having graduated to the personal services of his own tailor.

'Good to meet you Jimmy, Tony speaks very highly of you,' said Sam, holding out his hand.

'Likewise. And welcome to Liverpool,' said Jimmy.

'Thank you. Sorry to burden you with my domestic problems.'

'Not at all. What are friends for if not to help out in a crisis?' Spicer said. Jimmy sat back and allowed the two old friends to chat. He had known that in Spicer's business it was sometimes necessary for political reasons to be seen to be totally unconnected with certain events in your own area. For this reason an outside agency was employed and Jimmy had often wondered who had been Spicer's contact. Now he knew.

Jimmy excused himself from the table, telling Spicer he had some business to attend to. Spicer knew what the business was and merely murmured to Jimmy, 'Just get back in a couple of hours.'

Jimmy went straight to the River Club and sent for Mick Walsh. He had taken to Walsh and considered him to be his number one.

Jimmy outlined to Walsh the gist of what Spicer had told him and asked Walsh to hand pick a team of their best men for Saturday. He told Walsh that he would brief the team personally and then returned to the hotel in order to spend the rest of his time before the race meeting with Sam.

While they were together Jimmy and Sam talked at length and Jimmy warmed to the little man. Sam explained that he hadn't always been involved in crime. He was once a successful businessman but having gone bankrupt, he had then taken on similar rackets to Spicer although now, like Spicer, he fronted legitimate businesses.

'It was while I was reasonably successful before the crash that I became good friends with Geraldine's parents. You've met Geraldine haven't you?'

'Yes, but only recently,' Jimmy answered.

'That's right, Tony keeps her away from business. She's a lovely girl, my god-daughter you know,' said Sam proudly. Things fell into place now for Jimmy, Tony must have met Geraldine through Sam. He reflected that Sam must think a great deal of Spicer to allow his god-daughter to become involved with him.

As Saturday drew nearer, Jimmy sensed Sam was becoming apprehensive and tried to reassure him. 'Don't worry about the races. I've got a first class team standing by. They'll look after you.'

'I appreciate that but I can't help thinking it was a mistake to leave Leeds. I've left myself wide open.'

'The point is, if we look after you as I know we can it's bound to give you more street cred back home' Jimmy said confidently.

'True enough. If an attempt's made and fails then my problems in Leeds should be a thing of the past.'

'Keep this between the two of us,' Sam went on, 'but I've got a hunch that a professional hit man will be looking for me this weekend. It's what I would do.'

'You've no evidence though,' Jimmy said, glad Sam didn't know that Spicer had already come to the same conclusion.

'No, but it's not often my intuition's wrong.'

'Don't worry, if there is a professional hit man he'll be up against me, and I'm no amateur,' Jimmy tried to sound reassuring.

'I don't doubt it. But don't underestimate the professional. They're usually very good,' Sam said.

That evening Jimmy met two of the senior police officers retained by Tony Spicer. He outlined the information he had about a possible hit man and let them know Spicer would expect them to add their weight to the protection of Sam.

'We'd like to help but Aintree's not our patch,' said one of the detectives.

'What do you mean? It's only just up the road,' Jimmy said.

'Yes but it's in the Lancs. County area.'

'All we can do is tell the county lads,' the second detective chipped in.

'No, forget it. I'll handle it myself,' said Jimmy. 'By the way, either of you two know a friend of mine, Constable Turner?'

'Yes. As a matter of fact he's just been appointed to the CID,' said the senior of the two detectives. 'He seems to be doing well and a lot of it is down to an unknown informant who has been supplying him with some excellent stuff. To be frank I've just realised who that informant might be,' he stared at Jimmy. Jimmy kept quiet, he wasn't going to admit anything but it struck him as amusing that Peter's success was directly attributable to himself.

The following morning, the day of the National, Jimmy rose early and was out of the hotel before Sam was up. He briefed his men again and instructed them to tell him if they saw the hitman. He was reasonably confident that his team, who were to be positioned at each entrance to the course, would be able to identify the hired killer.

Returning to the hotel for breakfast with Sam, he suggested they leave immediately afterwards for Aintree. He wanted to avoid the crowds on the road. Sitting in a car in slow moving traffic would not be ideal for Sam. Arriving at the course he was pleased to see that two of his men were already in position at the main entrance.

It was early but the crowds were already arriving. Mick Walsh joined them and they made their way to the hospitality tent Spicer had hired. At noon Spicer arrived with Geraldine. She was wearing a simple pale green silk shift and heads turned admiringly as she walked over to where he was standing with Sam.

'Uncle Sam, lovely to see you again,' she said as she stepped forward into Sam's embrace. Jimmy watched as Sam kissed her on the cheek and wished it was him, not Sam who was holding her.

'Everything set?' said Spicer quietly to Jimmy.

'Everyone's in position. Mick is outside in the enclosure, he's going to be with Sam and me when we go out on the course.'

'I hope you're going to take good care of Uncle Sam,' Geraldine said.

Tony leaned forward before Jimmy could answer and said 'I've told Geraldine that hoodlums could cause trouble for Sam but nothing for us to worry about.'

Jimmy's opinion was that it would have been better if Tony hadn't said anything to Geraldine but wisely he didn't voice this opinion.

'Of course I will,' Jimmy smiled at Geraldine.

'That's good. I'll be with you both for most of the day.'

Jimmy couldn't believe his luck, a day spent with Geraldine was a bonus he hadn't expected but he was uneasy at the thought of her being so close to danger.

He took Tony to one side and said 'I don't like this idea much, things could get nasty. Where does that leave Geraldine?'

'This hit man knows the score. He knows what the consequences would be if Geraldine came to any harm. The same consequences there would be if anyone tried to come between Geraldine and me.' Tony stared hard at Jimmy.

Just before the first race at two o'clock Jimmy got word that Mick Walsh wanted to see him at the entrance to the main stand. Jimmy made his way over to where Walsh and two of his men were watching a man they recognised as the hired killer.

'Give me the gun,' Jimmy said to Walsh. Mick Walsh took the revolver from his inside pocket and handed it to Jimmy. Jimmy moved silently up behind the man and said, 'I've got a gun pointing at you because I know who you are and why you're here. Do what you're told and I won't have to use it. Just walk nice and quietly over to the exit and keep your hands by your side.'

'I don't know what the hell you're talking about. Is this some sort of joke?' the man asked.

'I work for Tony Spicer and he doesn't joke.'

'What are you going to do?'

'We're going somewhere quiet so we can have a little chat,' said Jimmy. The hit man, having already spotted Mick Walsh and the other two men, realised he was in no position to argue. He walked off the course slightly ahead of Jimmy. They took the hired killer in Mick's car and drove him to a quiet country lane in a nearby village. 'You're a lucky man. I'm not going to kill you. Tony says you've been useful to him in the past.

'You can tell Spicer I didn't know that the contract was a friend of his. I'd never have taken it if I'd known.'

'I'll remember to tell him,' said Jimmy nodding to Walsh. He then watched with clinical detachment as Mick and his men beat the hit man to merciful unconsciousness. Returning to the racecourse Jimmy stopped off to make a call for an ambulance.

Sam was visibly relieved to see Jimmy return. 'Jimmy there's always a job for you with me should you tire of Liverpool,' Sam said in a jocular tone but Jimmy knew that it was a serious offer. The tension having lifted Jimmy was left free to enjoy the remainder of the day. Geraldine's relaxed manner, together with Spicer's generous quantities of champagne, combined to untie Jimmy's tongue. He delighted in making Geraldine laugh with his many anecdotes and the afternoon sped by.

At the end of the race meeting Spicer invited people back to the River Club for a meal and to his surprise Jimmy was amongst them. Although Spicer held Jimmy in high regard as an employee, his largesse didn't normally extend to social functions. Jimmy nursed a secret hope that the invitation had been at Geraldine's request but he later learned that it had been Sam who had insisted on his presence.

At dinner Jimmy monopolised Geraldine and Spicer, much to his annoyance, could see she had no objections. After the meal Spicer indicated to Jimmy that he should follow him into the office. Looking Jimmy directly in the eye Spicer said, 'Look I gave you a warning this afternoon. You haven't taken any notice so now I'll spell it out. Stay away from Geraldine, understand?'

'I was only being polite,' said Jimmy.

Don't make the mistake of treating me like an idiot. I know you're attracted to her. Why wouldn't you be? She's a very beautiful girl, but she isn't for you. Do I make myself clear Jimmy?' Jimmy nodded. Spicer left the office and Jimmy followed him to rejoin the other guests. He sat down next to Sam who turned to him and said, 'I think I know what all that was about. Believe me Tony isn't too pleased with you. Leave her alone Jimmy. He'll kill you if you don't.'

'Thanks for the warning Sam, but it'll never come to anything even though I'm crazy for her.'

'Everyone can see that. Just be very careful.'

Towards the end of the evening Spicer went to his office and immediately Geraldine came and sat beside Jimmy.

'Jimmy I'm sorry if I got you into trouble before. It's just that I was having so much fun. Most of Tony's friends are so much older than me that it went to my head having you to talk to. I'm sorry if I embarrassed you.'

Jimmy looked at her intently, 'You could never embarrass me.'

'Really?' she whispered.

Jimmy felt his body moving towards her and had to force himself to remember that Spicer was in his office only yards away.

'I have to see you alone, we need to talk,' Jimmy said.

'I don't see how we can.'

'Do you want to?'

'You know I do.'

'That's all I needed to hear. Leave it to me.'

7

Peter Turner had just four years service in the Liverpool City Police when he became a detective. He was posted to Prescott Street Division for six months as an aide to the detective branch. After this preliminary six months, if everything went well, Peter could expect a permanent position. He was confident this would be the case due largely to the continued help given by his informant.

It was the custom in Liverpool for all newcomers to the CID to be put with an experienced detective who was responsible for teaching them the basics of detective work and the skills of investigation. Peter was attached to DC Dave Roberts, a man in his forties with fifteen years of experience as a detective. His track record was well known inside and outside the force. Peter was only too aware that he was something of an encumbrance as far as Dave was concerned. An aide on attachment couldn't be taken to haunts best kept private and Dave treated Peter with disdain. Peter didn't take it too personally as he had been warned.

Peter was relieved when his contact followed him on to his new station. Now that he was in the CID Peter was able to act on much of the information himself. As always it was sound and Peter was grateful because now more than ever he had to maintain a good arrest record.

The turning point in Peter's relationship with Dave came shortly after they had been sent to investigate a particularly vicious attack on a rent collector. The man was close to death after a savage beating with an iron bar. Dave found himself unusually disturbed by the crime as he couldn't tie it in with any of the known villains. He was under pressure from his Chief Inspector who in turn was under pressure from Headquarters to finish the case quickly. On the fourth day after the attack Peter received a telephone call from his informant.

'That was him,' Peter nodded in the direction of the telephone, 'He gave me two names.'

'Are you sure it's the same one who's been so reliable in the past?'

'Certain. And he hasn't been wrong yet.'
'Who does he finger for this job?' Dave asked.
'Two out of towners from the north east. They're lodging in Bootle.'
'No wonder we weren't getting anywhere,' Dave said, 'We'd better go and tell the Detective Inspector and see how he wants to handle it, Bootle isn't in our force area.'

When the Detective Chief Inspector was convinced he rang his counterpart in Bootle and ordered Dave and Peter to report to Bootle Police Station. When they arrived they were to be given help from Bootle Borough CID and indeed they found the CID waiting for them with a search warrant.

Pitt Street reminded Peter of the street where he had been brought up and where his parents still lived. He had moved into a flat nearer the city centre three years ago. The Detective Sergeant from Bootle sent his two Detective Constables round to the back of the house and then waited while they positioned themselves. He then went with Dave and Peter to the front door which was answered by an old lady. Peter looked from her to Dave and back again and for the first time he began to doubt the accuracy of the information had had been given. To his great relief he saw one of the Bootle detectives appear behind the old lady to announce that two lads had been arrested trying to escape through the back entrance. When their room was searched the money from the robbery was found along with the rent collector's satchel. The Bootle detective also found several wallets which were identified as the property of seamen who had been robbed in a series of violent attacks.

Peter received a commendation from his Chief Constable and from then on Dave treated him as an equal. When Peter was confirmed as a full member of the CID Dave asked for him as his regular partner.

It was during the investigation into the attack on the rent collector that Peter met Jean. Within twelve months, she became Mrs Turner. Jean had been a nurse in charge of the ward where the rent collector had been treated and Peter found that he was still visiting the hospital on the pretext of checking up on the unfortunate man long after it was necessary for his investigation. Peter and Jean moved to Allerton and Jean encouraged Peter to study for his promotion examinations to sergeant.

Dave and Peter formed a formidable partnership and their detection rate was well known. However when a squad of elite detectives was formed by HQ to combat the ever growing problem of serious crime in the city,

Peter was not surprised when Dave was chosen to serve in it. Peter had mixed feelings. He was pleased that Dave had been shown the recognition, but sorry to see him leave Prescott Street.

Peter himself was glad that he had persevered with his studies when he passed the qualifying exam. This in itself didn't bring automatic promotion, but it did mean all qualified candidates vied with each other when vacancies came up.

Peter was delighted when only two months after passing his promotion exam he heard that he too had been selected to serve on the Serious Crime Squad. He was even more delighted when he once again found himself teamed with Dave Roberts.

Peter discovered that as well as investigating serious crime, the squad were required to investigate potential criminals who were deemed to be involved in major crime. Each pairing on the squad was given a name, a target criminal and it was then their duty to gather together as much evidence about that criminal as they could. Peter caught his breath at the name of their target criminal, James Arthur Challoner.

'An interesting choice,' Dave said, 'but he's got corrupt policemen on his payroll. We'll have our work cut out to nick him.'

'I think I should tell you that Jimmy and myself were brought up together. We used to be good mates,' Peter explained.

'I'm glad you told me, although I did know. I arrested Jimmy years ago for stealing money from an insurance collector and I knew too that you were looking out for him,' Dave smiled.

'Why didn't you arrest me as well?'

'I knew you'd only been helping out a mate. Also I believed Jimmy when he said he wouldn't steal again so I couldn't see the point of dragging you into it all. I reckon I was half right, don't you?'

Jimmy Challoner was beginning to lose his patience with Tony Spicer. He felt the business needed to keep up with changing times. The protection racket was not as strong as it had been, business in the Chinese quarter had changed considerably and many of the smaller businesses had stopped trading. The prostitution and the club protection rackets were still lucrative but Jimmy felt that they needed support from new sources. Tony was only interested in expanding his legitimate interests and this added to Jimmy's frustration. He knew he would be well supported within the organisation if he attempted a takeover bid. What he couldn't gauge was the amount of support Spicer would be able to command from outside Liverpool. Jimmy already knew of Sam and he guessed there must be others like him who would support Spicer in a crisis. He was well aware that any hasty action would result in a bloodbath and that he stood to lose. Jimmy believed that a possible compromise might be reached if he started his own firm. Providing, of course, that Spicer was agreeable.

He also let his thoughts dwell on Geraldine. He was pretty certain that Spicer was keeping her away from anywhere they would be likely to meet. He also knew that since Spicer had warned him off Geraldine, she had been accompanied by a minder in the shape of his chauffeur. Jimmy longed to see her again but it was proving impossible.

Then Jimmy, as he had so often in the past, had a stroke of luck from out of the blue. Tony Spicer was being driven by his chauffeur when the Jaguar hit a lorry that had jack knifed immediately in front of them. The chauffeur did all he could and although they were kept in hospital they both escaped with relatively minor injuries.

Jimmy immediately telephoned Geraldine and offered to take her to see Tony in hospital.

Geraldine was near to tears for most of the journey. 'I may not love him anymore, but I do still care about him,' she said quietly. Jimmy smiled in what he hoped was a sympathetic way and silently prayed that Spicer's injuries wouldn't reignite Geraldine's feelings for him. Both Jimmy and Geraldine relaxed when they learned that Spicer had only broken ribs and his right leg.

'What are you here for?' said Spicer to Jimmy.

'I heard about the accident and I thought you'd like to see Geraldine,' replied Jimmy.

'Just make sure that's the only favour you do for me,' Spicer said.

Jimmy didn't bother to reply but sensing that his presence wasn't welcome at Tony's bedside he excused himself and told Geraldine he would wait for her in the car.

After the hospital visit Jimmy drove Geraldine home. He was taken aback when she didn't invite him in.

'Don't make the mistake of thinking that Tony wouldn't know,' Geraldine said. 'If I meet you it must be in the daytime and not in this area.'

'How about a hotel in Chester?'

Her eyes gave her answer and Jimmy silently gave thanks for Spicer's timely indisposition.

The following morning Jimmy telephoned the hotel, booked a suite of rooms and arranged for a champagne lunch to be served. He had never felt so nervous but when he saw Geraldine walking towards him, his happiness overtook his nerves and he determined to just enjoy the moment.

The conversation flowed naturally on the twenty mile journey to Chester, but while Geraldine tried to block Spicer from her mind the fact that he would make a dangerous enemy only heightened Jimmy's growing excitement.

The champagne was chilling in its bucket by the buffet when they arrived at their suite.

'Do you want to eat?' Jimmy asked.

Geraldine shook her head and Jimmy smiled as at last he took her in his arms. His senses reeled as he breathed in the warm musky scent of her skin. Kissing her softly at first as they backed towards the bed and then more urgently as they fell laughing and kissing onto the four poster. They undressed still kissing. Neither wanted to break away.

As they ate a late lunch Geraldine told Jimmy how she had met Tony while on a cruise. He had charmed both her and her parents and before long she found herself as Tony's girlfriend. The fact that Tony showed no interest in marrying had upset her parents a little. Geraldine herself had been content with the arrangement but now she had reached a stage where she was disenchanted with Tony. He appeared to be determined to foil all her attempts to leave him.

'What you're telling me changes everything,' Jimmy said, 'you must get away. It'll be different now. You'll have me.'

'No Jimmy, I know him so much better than you do. He'll kill you before he'll let us be together.'

'Spicer doesn't frighten me. I know how to handle him,' Jimmy murmured into her hair.

'But you wouldn't know who he would hire to kill you. Jimmy don't ask me to be responsible for your murder.'

'Geraldine I wanted you from the first moment I saw you. Believe me I'll find a way out of this.'

'It was the same for me,' said Geraldine reaching out her hand. As she did so her robe fell away. 'Can we leave the coffee Jimmy?' she whispered, but by then coffee was the last thing on Jimmy's mind.

Later that night Jimmy went to collect Geraldine from her home and was surprised to find Michael Hanlon, Spicer's solicitor standing in the hall.

'What brings you here?' Jimmy asked.

'I'm here to accompany Geraldine to see Tony and to pass on a message to you.'

'Oh, and what's that?'

'Tony wants you to concentrate on the business and not waste time taking Geraldine to see him. He's arranged for Geraldine to stay at the Adelphi during his hospital stay.'

As Geraldine came down the stairs, suitcase in hand, Jimmy asked if Hanlon had told her what was going on.

'Yes. I'm off to the Adelphi. I'm sure Tony's right, it will be much more convenient for me.'

'Well if Mike is taking you to Liverpool I'll get back to work,' Jimmy replied trying hard not to let his elation at the news he had just heard creep into his voice.

Jimmy couldn't believe it. Was Spicer losing his grip? With Geraldine at the Adelphi he would be able to see her every night until Spicer was discharged.

'Let's hope he has a relapse,' Jimmy said to himself. He made his way to the River Club where the manager reported that there were no problems. It was a Thursday evening and the Casino was particularly busy. Jimmy went into the Casino and as he had expected the club was full. This was a side of the business that Spicer managed himself and Jimmy rarely had reason to visit the Casino. As with the River Club, Spicer ensured that the clientele were hand picked. All of the gaming tables were packed and Jimmy saw plenty of chips being lost by the unlucky punters. This place must be worth a fortune to Spicer, he thought. No wonder he doesn't want to expand his criminal activities. At eleven o'clock Jimmy told the club manager he was leaving and told him to cash up and leave the money in the office safe. Having given the casino manager the same message, Jimmy then left the club and took a taxi to the Adelphi.

Jimmy decided to ring Geraldine from reception and was surprised when a female voice that was not Geraldine's answered.

'Is Geraldine there?' Jimmy asked impatiently.

After a moment Geraldine came on the line. 'Hello, who is it?'

'It's Jimmy. Who the hell was that?'

'Oh Jimmy, nice of you to call about Tony's progress. He's so much better you'll be pleased to know.'

Jimmy gathered from her tone that she couldn't speak freely. Geraldine continued, 'Tony has arranged with Michael Hanlon for his secretary to stay with me, he didn't want me to be lonely. Isn't that thoughtful of him?'

'What a crafty bastard.'

'Yes it is sweet of him isn't it?' Geraldine said stiffly.

'Can I see you tomorrow?' Jimmy said getting increasingly frustrated.

'It's so kind of you to offer me a lift tomorrow Jimmy, but Tony has seen to that too. One of his staff is going to drive me everywhere.'

'OK, I've got the message, but listen to me. I won't give up that easily you know. I love you and if it takes me forever I'll make sure we're together soon. Your days with Spicer are numbered.'

8

'How much do you know about Challoner?' Dave Roberts asked Peter as they sat in the Serious Crime Squad office.

'Like I said, we grew up together. But I don't in all honesty know him well at all now.'

'Do you still feel loyalty towards him?' Dave asked.

'No worries on that score, I'll nick Jimmy as fast as anyone.'

'Fine, but it had to be asked,' Dave grinned to show that he hadn't really wanted to ask and Peter nodded to show he understood and there were no hard feelings.

They had been building up a picture of Spicer's organisation and saw the protection racket as a weak spot. This of course was the section of Spicer's business directly under Challoner's supervision. The Chinese, who were the primary targets of the protection racket, had been established for many years in the city. Through sheer hard work they had formed a number of successful business ventures, the strongest of which was their hold on the restaurant trade. They had always been an insular community and it was almost unknown for the police to be called in to deal with incidents of lawlessness within Chinatown. Dave was convinced that before the Chinese community would be prepared to give them information, he and Peter would need to build up an atmosphere of trust. They took to spending a good deal of their time eating and being seen in the Chinese quarter.

One evening a row broke out between a waiter and two local men in a restaurant where they were eating. The argument appeared to be over a bill and within minutes a fight broke out. Dave and Peter quickly took charge of the situation and peace was restored. They advised the men to pay up and waited by the till while they did so.

The next day Dave and Peter were again eating a meal in one of the Chinese restaurants when they were joined by Mr Wong. Both detectives were aware that Mr Wong was the most respected and influential member of the Chinese community.

'I apologise for my intrusion, but I want to thank you for your help last night,' Mr Wong looked at both men in turn.

'Happy to be of service,' Dave said.

'All the same, not everyone would have done what you did,' Mr Wong replied.

'Well we're not everybody, we're police officers,' Dave confessed.

'Yes, I'm aware of that and I can't imagine why you spend so much time in our community.'

'We're hooked on your food,' Peter smiled.

'I wonder,' said Mr Wong, looking far from convinced as he bid them goodbye.

After finishing their meal Dave attempted to pay but the waiter brushed his notes aside. From that day onwards the two detectives found that they were unable to pay for another meal in Chinatown.

During event visit Mr Wong always made an appearance and chatted with them.

'I think it's time to ask Mr Wong about the protection rackets,' Dave said after a few weeks.

'You're right. If anyone can tell us anything it'll be him,' Peter replied.

The next time that Mr Wong joined them Dave said, 'The reason we're spending so much time here is that we want to prove that a protection racket is operating in your community.'

'I suspected you were,' Mr Wong said.

'Without the assistance of your people we can't do a thing,' Peter chipped in.

'I know, and I think I know you well enough to trust you now. Besides, many of my friends are struggling to pay this protection money.'

'How much do they pay?' Dave asked.

'Usually about ten pounds a week.'

'Why pay it to them?'

Mr Wong sighed, 'It's often easier to pay than having trouble with the people who collect it.'

He went on to explain that every Friday night a Mr Challoner visited the Blue Lagoon club and picked up all the protection money himself. It would have been collected for him by Tony Yen and would amount to about one thousand pounds.

'So who's this Tony Yen?' Dave asked.

'He's the waiter at the Blue Lagoon. And no, he doesn't work for

Challoner. He is just made to get the money together for him.'

Armed with this information, Dave and Peter planned to watch the Blue Lagoon the following Friday and hopefully arrest Challoner with the protection cash. They didn't tell anyone about their plans.

On the Friday evening Dave and Peter sat in the restaurant opposite the Blue Lagoon club and from their vantage point had a clear view of the entrance. At about eleven they saw Challoner's car draw up outside and watched as Jimmy got out and entered the club. The two detectives left the restaurant and went to stand by his car. Jimmy stopped when he got back and found them waiting for him but quickly recovering he grinned and said, 'Hello Peter, didn't know you came down here. I can recommend the Pearl City if you're after a good restaurant.'

'The only thing we're after is you,' Dave said.

'Me? What am I supposed to have done?'

Dave walked up to him and took the leather satchel he was carrying. He opened it and showed it to Peter. It was crammed full of paper money.

'Challoner, you're nicked,' said Dave.

'Nicked. What for?'

'For extorting money.'

'I don't know what you're on about. This is payment of a gambling debt.'

'Who have you collected it from?'

'I'm saying nothing more until I've seen my solicitor,' said Jimmy, as he stared at Peter.

Challoner was taken by the two detectives to the Main Bridewell in Cheapside. He was charged with blackmail and put in the cells.

Word spread around the force that Jimmy Challoner had been arrested and was in custody. Dave and Peter had gone to the squad office and were preparing the file of evidence for court the following day. They were stunned when their Detective Inspector came in and asked why they had allowed Challoner to have bail.

'Bail? What are you talking about? He's at the Bridewell in custody,' Dave said.

'That's not what I've been told,' the inspector replied. Dave, believing the inspector to be mistaken, telephoned the Bridewell sergeant who confirmed that Challoner had indeed been released on bail. He had received a call allegedly from Dave telling them that Challoner could be released on bail until the following morning. Dave slammed the 'phone down in temper and frustration saying. 'Well we knew Challoner had friends in the force, now we know what we're up against.'

The following morning Challoner appeared before the Magistrates' Court. He was represented by Mike Hanlon. It was useless asking the court to remand Challoner in custody as the police themselves had already granted bail. After giving evidence of arrest Dave had to reluctantly agree to Challoner being bailed again.

After court the two detectives went straight to the Chinese quarter to get the statements of evidence needed to support their charges against Challoner. The first thing they did was to find Mr Wong so he could act as an interpreter. His news shocked them. No one would make a statement.

'I don't understand,' Dave said, 'why?'

'Spicer's men have been calling and threatened them,' Mr Wong said.

'We'll give them protection,' Peter said.

'That's impossible. Sooner or later Spicer would get them.'

'Isn't there anyone who'll make a statement?' Dave said.

'Can you proceed with just one statement?' Mr Wong asked.

'The case would be a bit thin but yes, one witness would be enough to go ahead.'

'Then I'll do it. After all I've been paying these people longer than most.'

The detectives took down Mr Wong's statement and told him that any attempts to bully him into not giving evidence must be reported.

Blackmail was an offence that could only be heard by a judge sitting at the Assize Court. It was necessary to have a committal hearing before a Magistrates' Court to ensure that there was a case to answer. Two days before the committal proceedings Dave and Peter heard that Mr Wong had been taken to the Royal Infirmary having been found unconscious in the street. They went to see him straight away and were told his condition was serious. He had taken a severe beating. When Mr Wong briefly regained consciousness they were allowed in to see him. The look of abject terror in his eyes confirmed their worst fears, Mr Wong would not be giving evidence. At the committal hearing the police had no choice but to offer no evidence against Challoner and he walked from the court a free man. Mr Wong was later released from hospital and, although the two detectives continued to visit him, it was clear he remained a very frightened man.

Within three weeks of the hearing Dave and Peter were transferred from the Serious Crime Squad back to divisional duties.

'Someone in authority is very worried that we got too close to nailing Challoner and they obviously didn't like it. Whoever Spicer has in his pocket must be very senior to be able to split us up like this,' Dave said. Within weeks Dave was posted back to Prescott Street and Peter was promoted to Detective Sergeant and transferred to Essex Street.

'Promise me something,' Dave said, as they were about to leave the office. 'Don't give up on Challoner. You're young Peter, time is on your side. Be patient and you'll get him.' Peter had decided that already.

It wasn't long after his posting to Prescott Street that Dave retired from the force. He never seemed able to motivate himself after the Challoner incident. Peter had no choice but to carry on. He had a wife and now a child as well to support. It was ironic thought Peter. He owed his promotion to the Challoner incident. But whoever it was that wanted Dave and himself removed from where they could investigate Spicer's activities had cleverly arranged for Peter to be promoted to account for his removal from the Serious Crime Squad. To have transferred Peter, who thanks to his informant had an impressive record of arrests, without good reason would have raised awkward questions. His promotion had been a shrewd move because it was perfectly normal to transfer an officer on promotion.

Peter wasn't very happy with his posting to Essex Street, but it was a busy station and he had little time to dwell on past events. He hadn't noticed at first but several weeks after he had taken up his appointment at Essex Street he realised that his informant hadn't been in touch. Peter realised that there had been no contact since Challoner's arrest.

Peter took advantage of his time at Essex Street to study for his promotion exam. He and Jean now had a baby daughter as well as a toddler son and the extra money that went with the position was needed more than ever. In 1965, having passed his exams he was posted as Detective Inspector to the number One Regional Crime Squad. The RCS as it was referred to, was a new innovation introduced to the police service by the Home Office. It was made up of squads of proven detectives who were stationed in regions throughout England and Wales.

The objectives of the RCS were to concentrate their resources and to target major and travelling criminals. In the same way the travelling criminal knew no boundary the RCS were not hampered by having to operate within a specific police force area. Peter's first task on taking up his appointment at the Liverpool branch office of the RCS was to identify James Arthur Challoner as the branch target criminal.

Jimmy Challoner had been shocked to find himself arrested and had been grateful when Spicer had arranged for his release from police custody. Spicer had also arranged for the lone Chinese witness to be silenced and Jimmy realised that it had been a close call. If he had been convicted of blackmail he could have expected several years in prison. He knew he owed Spicer but couldn't help thinking that he was also the one to blame for his being in that particular predicament.

He had been arguing with Spicer for months to drop the protection racket. It was only yielding a thousand a week now, which was peanuts to Spicer. Jimmy had been unable to convince him and it had almost been his undoing.

Since Spicer had left hospital Jimmy had felt that his relationship with him had deteriorated and Spicer had made absolutely certain that Jimmy had no reason to come into contact with Geraldine. Geraldine was undoubtedly the crux of the problem between them. Spicer knew Jimmy had designs on her, which clearly unsettled him. Jimmy had tried several times to 'phone Geraldine but someone else always answered the telephone. He was more convinced than ever that he had to break with Spicer. Their working future together was doomed because Spicer no longer trusted him but he was having doubts about the wisdom of trying to persuade Spicer to let him start his own business. Jimmy came to the conclusion that Spicer's main concern would be the threat of instability in his camp which could lead his rivals to think he was vulnerable and encourage them to make a bid for his empire. He decided to seek Sam's advice and arranged to meet him at his home on the outskirts of Leeds.

'If I can be of assistance without betraying Tony then I'm happy to give my advice,' Sam said handing Jimmy a scotch.

Jimmy outlined his plans to break from Tony, telling him he intended to start from scratch and had no thought of taking any of Tony's business.

'Well that's good. Any alternative ideas and you'd have been dead my friend' Sam said.

'Quite,' replied Jimmy with a wry grin.

'In all honesty the last thing Tony wants is trouble. He has been meticulous in recent years to cultivate his legitimate business profile, keeping well away from any direct criminal involvement. He could think that you leaving the firm might give the impression that there's a weakness in the organisation. There again, Tony's no fool. He must know you're unhappy and that a break up is on the cards. He could decide to let you go and at the same time save face by giving the impression that the parting is entirely amicable. The best advice I can give you is to approach Tony and be straight with him.'

'Thanks for that Sam, I hadn't considered honesty, but I reckon you've got a point.'

'Just out of interest, where does Geraldine fit into all this?' Sam said.

Jimmy looked directly at him, 'Oh she fits into my future, no question about that Sam.'

'I suspected she might. Does she know about this?'

'Naturally. She's been unhappy with Tony for a long time now.'

'I had no idea,' Sam said frowning, 'though to be frank I was never reconciled to the idea that they were an item.'

'Well I'll admit I did find it strange that you had introduced them,' Jimmy said, 'until Geraldine told me it had been a chance meeting.'

'No, it's not a match I would have chosen for Geraldine and to tell you the truth neither are you Jimmy.'

'At least I love her and would never hurt her.'

'You wouldn't intend to Jimmy, I know that. But your lifestyle is not what anyone would wish for a very dear god daughter,' Sam sighed.

On the journey back from Leeds Jimmy mulled over what Sam had said. It could have been worse. The fact that Sam disapproved of Spicer's relationship with Geraldine could still prove useful. He went straight to see Spicer and had a hunch that Spicer was expecting him. Sam had probably spoken to him already he thought. Jimmy decided to employ Sam's suggested tactics and plunged straight in.

'Tony, I'm not going to dress this up, I'll get straight to the point.'

'Always a good idea,' Spicer replied thoughtfully.

'I'm sure you've realised that I haven't been altogether happy lately. I think the time is ripe for me to make the break and set up on my own.'

'I must admit,' Spicer said slowly, 'I had been waiting for this.'

'Naturally I wouldn't expect to take any of your business with me but I will be asking Mick Walsh and his team if they want to come with me.'

'Does that mean that you'll be taking over the club protection?' Spicer raised his eyebrows.

'Well I figured that as I'd nurtured the entire racket it was more mine than yours anyway,' Jimmy replied.

'Fair point. I'll agree to you leaving and taking the club protection provided Walsh wants to go with you. If he doesn't, it stays with me.'

'Agreed,' Jimmy said confidently.

'I'll announce it personally,' Spicer said. 'Neither of us can afford to give any of the upstarts in this city any ideas that they can muscle in.'

'Obviously I'll support you if anyone else makes a move.'

Spicer looked curious. 'Just out of interest, what are your plans?'

'My first priority will be to make my mark and to do that I'm going to have to pull off a job that will make me some serious money. As to where I will go, I'm not entirely sure yet.'

'It won't be easy, but if anyone can do it I reckon it's you Jimmy, but,' and Spicer's tone changed, 'don't imagine that I'll give Geraldine up as easily.'

Jimmy heard the threat but dismissed it. Whatever the risks he intended to take Geraldine away from Spicer one day.

The break went smoothly. Tony made the announcement in such a way that it didn't arouse the hopes of his rivals. Mick Walsh and six of his team readily agreed to join Jimmy and Mick became Jimmy's number one. His priority then was to find a suitable headquarters, a legitimate business front for his dealings. Jimmy went to see Mike Hanlon about buying a pub, a club being beyond his present finances. As he worked for Spicer Mike thought it prudent not to take on Jimmy as a client, but he was only too happy to recommend a young, ambitious solicitor called Kenneth Armstrong who had just broken away from a business partnership and had set up his own practice. Jimmy outlined his proposition to Armstrong and told him he wished to invest five thousand pounds in a pub. Armstrong rang Jimmy two days later and told Jimmy that he had an option on a pub in the Dock Road. The property was run down but Jimmy felt sure it had the potential to be his flagship, for the time being at any rate. Once Armstrong had arranged purchase a brother of one of Walsh's men, who had run a pub in the past, was installed as landlord of the refurbished Admiral. Within three months Jimmy and his team were established in their own headquarters.

Jimmy consulted Mick Walsh on how they intended to operate and both agreed that their immediate problem was cash, or lack of it. After dismissing most of their ideas on just how to get it they finally agreed the solution was to rob a bank.

9

'What type of bank job do you think we should pull?' Mick asked Jimmy. Jimmy looked thoughtful. He was sitting with Mick in their office, the back room of the Admiral.

'Not an armed robbery, there have been too many of those.'

'What about walking in and asking for the cash?' Mick grinned.

'Well with a bit of planning and some original ideas it should be possible to do it without any risk.'

Jimmy frowned. They discussed various possibilities but they were all rejected for one reason or another. Suddenly Jimmy banged his fist on the table. 'Mick I must be slipping, it's been staring me in the face.'

'Well come on then, let me in on it.'

'We don't rob a bank, we break into the safe deposit vault.'

'Safe deposit vault, what are you on about?'

'It's a new system that Martin's Bank started about a year ago,' Jimmy went on, 'They hire out safe deposit boxes to customers who don't want anybody else to know what they own. The boxes are kept in a vault at the bank and only the customer has a key so you can imagine what some of them must hold.'

'How come you know so much about them?' Mick said.

'Tony Spicer has got one and he explained the system to me when I went to the bank with him one day. I didn't go downstairs to the vault so obviously I haven't actually seen them.'

'Then how do we find out what the set up is? We'll have to know what the lay out of the vault is like.'

'That's the reason I'll pay the bank a visit tomorrow and open a safe deposit box account.'

'You'll need to do a really good job of casing the vault area. Estimate thickness of the steel doors, identify the alarm system. That kind of thing.'

'Just tell me what I should be looking for' said Jimmy. Warming to their theme they sat and discussed the answers they would need to the questions posed by Mick Walsh on the bank's security system. They were convinced that the plan was workable provided the security wasn't too sophisticated.

The following morning Jimmy was shown in to see the Assistant Bank Manager who, he had been told, was in charge of the safe deposit box section.

'May I enquire how you came to hear of our service, Mr Challoner since it isn't an area we've advertised at all' the assistant manager asked.

'It was through a business colleague,' answered Jimmy, deliberately not revealing Spicer's name.

'I see. Thank you Mr Challoner. Now let me explain how the system works' he said. He told Jimmy that for an annual charge the bank would provide a confidential means of keeping secure whatever the customer wished to store in a small metal box. He emphasised that nobody other than the customer was present when putting in or taking out articles from the deposit box so that complete privacy was assured.

'I think this is just what I'm looking for,' said Jimmy 'I'd like to start renting a box immediately if that's possible.'

'Of course sir, there are just a few forms to fill out,' the man smiled, pleased with his salesmanship. After the forms had been completed the assistant manager gave Jimmy a key and said, 'Now if you would care to accompany me down to the vault I'll show you how the system operates.' He led Jimmy down a flight of stairs which ended in a metal barred gate. The assistant manager unlocked it and took Jimmy into an empty room. Seeing the puzzled look on Jimmy's face the manager said, 'This room is just an ante room. The boxes are held in the strong room through that door.' He indicated a door at the far end of the room. 'Whenever you wish to use your safe deposit box you will enter the strong room alone while the bank official who accompanies you will remain in this ante room until you come out.'

'Thank you,' Jimmy said, 'I'd like to use my box now if that's possible.'

'By all means sir, I'll unlock the door for you.'

Jimmy noted that when the door opened it triggered a switch mechanism which turned on the electric light inside the strong room. He went in and closed the door behind him. Jimmy had been told that the light would only remain on for ten minutes. Once inside he saw that the strong room housed rows of small metal boxes, each of which was numbered. Jimmy opened number 234, which had been allocated to him, and as the front of the box dropped down on a hinge he was able to gauge that the interior was about twenty inches long, twelve inches wide and four inches deep. He spent a few minutes looking around the strong room before opening the door and returning to the ante room.

'Did you find the box to your satisfaction Mr Challoner?' the assistant manager asked.

'Perfect, thank you. But I would just like to go over the security arrangements if you don't mind.'

'Yes of course. As you can see the only access to the vault is through the metal barred gate which is fully alarmed and also operates a timing mechanism, opening during banking hours only,' the main explained.

'What about the vault itself?'

'The door leading to the strong room is on the same security system as the barred gate.'

'Is the vault alarmed?'

'No but because the only access to the strong room is through the gate and door I can assure you that our security arrangements are sufficient to guarantee you complete protection.'

'That is very reassuring' Jimmy said as they made their way back up the stairs.

When he left Jimmy walked around the perimeter of the building and discovered it was in a corner position. The front and both sides of the building were detached but the rear butted onto another building. A brief investigation told Jimmy that it was a Barrister's chambers and was not alarmed.

Feeling very satisfied with his findings Jimmy went back to the Admiral and told Mick what he had discovered. 'I should think we'll be able to enter the bank through the rear and if my calculations are right, we'll be able to tunnel into the vault itself.'

'How do we do that? We can't knock a hole in the wall of the bank.'

'That's exactly what we will do except that we'll be going in through the dividing wall between the bank and the barrister's office' Jimmy explained ignoring Mick's sarcasm.

'Are you sure that the wall between the bank and the office is the one that leads into the vault?' asked Mick.

'Yes. The back wall of the vault will be the wall between the bank and the office.'

'It's bound to have a reinforced metal grill at the back of the boxes and it could be alarmed.'

'It's bound to have some form of protection, but it's not alarmed. I checked with the manager. The only alarms are fitted to the doors.'

'How many boxes are stored there?'

'There are five hundred altogether and from the signs of wear around the locks about three hundred are in use.'

'Do you really think they'll contain what we're after?' Mick looked doubtful.

'Look, people don't rent one of these things for nothing. I suspect we're going to be pleasantly surprised.'

'Well we'll have to get them first.'

Jimmy and Mick then worked out what they would need to do in order to enter the back of the bank. It was open until noon on Saturday mornings and then closed until nine on Monday mornings. Neither of them believed they could get in within a day and a half. They decided that they could enter the barrister's chambers on the Friday night, as they didn't work on Saturdays, and begin work on the dividing wall through Friday night until the bank opened on Saturday morning.

Once they had worked out the basic plan Jimmy began work on the details. He was confident that a week end would give them sufficient time to break into the bank, assuming that the back of the boxes weren't reinforced with heavy metal. He didn't think that oxacetyl burners would cut through that type of defence in the time they had and this was Jimmy's main worry. He had no way of knowing until the night of the actual job what type of reinforcement was in situ between the bank and the barrister's chambers and he hesitated to go in blind. The solution to this problem came the following day when Mick mentioned that in the army he had seen engineers using a new type of burning tool. It was called a thermic lance and generated about ten times more heat than the usual oxyacetylene torch. Consequently it was much quicker.

'With a thermic lance we'd be through the wall in no time whatever the type and thickness of the plating,' said Mick.

'That sounds ideal, but where do you get that sort of equipment?' Jimmy asked.

'As far as I know we don't but it is used in naval shipyards.'

'We haven't got any of those in Liverpool though.'

'No, but we have got Cammel Lairds in Birkenhead and they build ships for the navy.'

'That shouldn't be too hard to check. You nip over there and see what you can come up with.'

When Mick returned a couple of hours later he announced to Jimmy that not only did Cammel Lairds have the equipment but that he had arranged for two fitters to steal the equipment for collection by Mick that night. It would cost a hundred pounds, but they would soon have the burning equipment they needed.

Jimmy made the decision that they would do the job the following week end and he chose a team of four to accompany himself and Mick Walsh. On the Wednesday before the planned break in Jimmy received a telephone call from Tony Spicer asking him if he would call round at the River Club. Intrigued Jimmy went to find out just what Spicer wanted to see him about. The call brought back bittersweet memories of Geraldine and it crossed Jimmy's mind that she might be the reason Spicer had called.

Spicer didn't mince his words, 'I'm having problems with two troublemakers who are trying to muscle in on the prostitution racket Jimmy.'

'Nothing you can't handle is it?'

'Of course, but I was hoping you might deal with it for me. I don't particularly want to be associated with trouble in the city especially after the Chinese business.'

'No problem.' said Jimmy

The two men, Tony explained, were brothers who had come over from Nigeria ten years ago. According to him they were regulars at a shebeen in Parliament Street.

'I'll see to it tonight with a couple of my lads,' Jimmy said as he rose to go.

'Be sure to come round and have a drink with me afterwards,' said Spicer smiling broadly.

On his way back to the Admiral Jimmy felt that he was missing something. He didn't believe the nonsense that Spicer had told him about not wanting involvement in this particular trouble. This wouldn't even register on Spicer's scale of trouble. There had to be more to it, but just for the moment Jimmy couldn't figure out what. It did cross his mind that Spicer might be trying to set him up and possibly the Spenser brothers were lying in wait for him at the shebeen with a gang of followers. He dismissed the thought knowing that Spicer, should he ever decide to deal with Jimmy, would arrange something a little more subtle and personal.

However he had promised he would take care of the problem and so together with Mick Walsh and two of the team he went to the shebeen at ten that night. Jimmy had decided that on this occasion a public warning would be enough. He entered the small clubroom, in reality the basement of a house, and saw that there were perhaps a dozen people inside. Jimmy went to the bar and asked where he could find the two Spenser brothers. The barman indicated two men sitting at a table in the far corner of the room and Jimmy went over to them followed by Mick and his men.

'You called Spenser?' Jimmy asked.

'Who wants to know?' said one of the men, rising to his feet. He was well over six feet tall and broadly built. His stance was menacing and a roomful of expectant black faces turned towards Jimmy and waited for his reaction.

'I asked you a civil question, now let's just have a civil answer' said Jimmy. He heard the sound of chairs and tables being moved and saw that the rest of the customers were starting to circle Mick and his two lads. Jimmy sensed that the time had come to exert his own authority. 'Pass it to me,' he said to one of his two men. With that the man took a sawn off shotgun from under his coat. Jimmy took it, pointed the gun at the crowd and said 'I think you'd better all sit down now.' Support for the Spensers faded fast and quietly everyone returned to their seats.

'Now,' said Jimmy, 'We'll try again. Are you the Spensers?' The man who was seated pulled his brother back into his chair saying, 'We are the Spensers.'

'Good. You've got some brains anyway, pity you haven't been putting them to good use.' He pointed the gun directly at the two brothers who sat perfectly still. With a quick jerk of his wrist Jimmy raised the shotgun and fired it into the ceiling. Both the Spensers almost jumped out of their skins.

'That was a warning, now keep away from the girls otherwise the next shot's for you,' Jimmy said. Neither of the brothers moved or spoke but their eyes followed Jimmy and his team as they left the club in silence. Outside Jimmy left the others and went alone to join Spicer in his office at the River Club. He saw that Spicer had a bottle of champagne chilling in an ice bucket.

'You shouldn't have any more hassle with the Spensers,' Jimmy said, opening the conversation.

'Thanks Jimmy, I was confident you'd deal with it' Spicer said. 'Now let's have that drink I promised you. Champagne alright?'

'Champagne will be fine but the job wasn't that difficult.'

'No, the champagne's is for something quite different. It's to celebrate my engagement to Geraldine. We're getting married.'

Jimmy was speechless.

10

As planned on the Friday evening Jimmy, Mick and four hand picked members of the team were dropped off in an entry that ran along the back of the barrister's chambers. They unloaded all their equipment, the thermic lance and its burners, lump hammers, chisels, two pickaxes, a sledge hammer and several electric drills. They also had enough torches and provisions to last throughout the weekend and sleeping bags. One of the men climbed the wall into the yard of the chambers, unlocked the entry door and let the others through to the yard. The same man then forced the rear door of the office and they were all relieved to listen to the silence that followed which confirmed the building wasn't alarmed.

Jimmy and Mick found the door that led to the basement and together they went down the stairs.

'If my geography of the bank is right that's the wall we need to go through,' Jimmy said, pointing to the back wall. Mick went over and struck the wall a heavy blow with a lump hammer he'd brought. There was a heavy thud indicating that the wall was solid. He struck the other walls in turn and each gave off a more hollow sound.

'Guess you're right,' Mick grinned. They called the other men down and in shifts of two worked for an hour at a time. They chipped away at the bricks between the office and the bank until by midnight they had removed sufficient bricks to reveal a solid metal sheet.

'You were right Mick the back of the boxes has been reinforced,' Jimmy said.

'Do you want me to start burning now or wait 'til tomorrow?'

'We night as well make a start, we don't know how thick that screen's going to be.'

Mick set up the thermic torch and began the burning operation. It was a painfully slow process even with the thermic lance. By three in the morning they had only managed to cut a five foot length of the metal sheet.

'Let's call it a night,' Jimmy said. 'This room is like a furnace and it needs to cool down. Nobody was sorry to hear him suspend work for the time being. They were exhausted from the work and the tremendous heat.

'We'll start again after the bank closes at mid day,' Jimmy said and with that they all went upstairs to a small windowless room, unrolled their sleeping bags and promptly fell asleep.

At twelve exactly Jimmy ordered that work start again on the metal screen. They were now refreshed, having eaten and slept soundly. They resumed work with new energy and discovered that the thermic lance was easier to handle with experience. Progress proved faster even though they often had to leave the room to allow the smoke to clear. By eight that night they had cut out a piece of the metal screen which gave them access to the back of one of the rows of safety boxes. The metal plate that they had burned through was exactly one inch thick. It had been Mick's suggestion that they cut just enough space to allow them to crawl through a section of the safety boxes into the vault. This would minimise the burning of the box contents which was inevitable with the lance. There was little or no resistance from the metal of the boxes, the lance cut through it like a knife through butter. Once they had all crawled through into the vault Mick ran a power cable back into the barrister's offices to which he connected several power points to run the electric drills from. With four drills being used on the locks of the boxes they were soon opened so that one by one they revealed their contents.

'Only take cash and jewellery,' Jimmy said. By midnight on the Saturday night they had opened over half the boxes. Jimmy then ordered everyone to get some rest and once again they went upstairs to the offices to snatch some much needed sleep.

The following day they continued the work and by two o'clock in the afternoon had opened the last of the boxes. They were all chronically tired but all were re-energised when they realised just how much money and jewellery they had amassed. Jimmy gave instructions that the money was to be placed in canvas sacks and the jewellery to be placed in the holdalls that they had brought with them.

While this was being done, Jimmy idly went through the contents of the boxes that were left. They were mostly deeds, legal documents or wills. He noticed that one of the boxes contained pornographic photographs of an elderly man with two young boys. Jimmy stared hard at the man's rather distinguished features and felt certain that he knew him from somewhere. He pocketed the photographs feeling sure he would remember in time who the man was.

They took the bags of money and jewellery up into the daylight of the offices and started counting up the cash while they waited for darkness to fall. Even Jimmy was stunned when the money totalled two hundred and fifty thousand pounds. He estimated that the jewellery was worth much the same amount.

'I wonder how much belonged to Spicer?' Jimmy said to Mick.

'A fair amount I should think.'

'Let's hope it was a bloody fortune.'

When it grew dark their transport from the Admiral came to collect them as arranged.

In common with the rest of Liverpool, Peter Turner learned of the robbery at Martin's Bank on Monday morning. The news broke at shortly after nine o'clock and was the talk of the town. Peter sat and read the early edition of the Daily Post and hoped that the Regional Crime Squad would be called in to help with the case. This was a drawback to being in the squad. They had to wait to be asked to assist, they couldn't turn up uninvited which could be frustrating. Peter had read that it was safety deposit boxes that had been broken into and he rightly thought that the true contents would never be known to anyone other than the thieves. The cash involved was probably a tax fiddle, he thought to himself.

On Wednesday morning Peter was called for by his detective chief inspector and as he went along to his office he hoped that it was to be told that the squad had been requested to help with the bank job. It was the biggest crime in the city for years and Peter and his team desperately wanted to be in on the action.

'Peter, the City Division have requested our help with the bank job. I want you and three of your section to help with the enquiry,' said Chief Inspector Hughes from behind his desk.

'Not before time,' said Peter, 'we should have been called in from the outset, not when the trail is two days old.'

'I understand how frustrating it is but we can't go in until we're asked. Let's hope the RCS can help solve this one.'

'We'll do our best but I can't help thinking the trail is cold or else we wouldn't have been called in,' Peter said. Secretly he was pleased to be going in on this crime, but for appearances sake he felt obliged to have a little moan. He selected three detective sergeants and went down to the City Division to get together with the detective inspector who was in charge of the investigation. After being briefed Peter found that his fears had been well founded. There were no leads to follow up and he discovered that the division had made little progress. He took his team to the bank and they began by taking statements from members of staff. Peter interviewed the bank manager and asked for a list of the customers who had been holders of the safety deposit boxes. He was surprised when on being handed the list he saw that it totalled two hundred and twenty names and there were some who held three or more boxes.

'What were the contents of the safety deposit boxes?' Peter asked, knowing full well the answer.

'I don't know. When we rent the boxes for the customers we guarantee complete confidentiality. Only the customers know what the boxes contain,' the manager said.

'Yes and I'll bet I don't get the truth out of most of them.'

Nevertheless he had to interview everyone on the list of box holders in order to get as full a description of the stolen property as he could. He was optimistic that he would at least get a good description of the jewellery that had been stolen but he was not so naïve as to believe that any of the customers would admit to storing cash. He knew that it was likely to be money that the owner did not want anyone else to know about.

Running down the list of names he was surprised at the number he recognised, two of whom he took particular interest in. Jimmy Challoner and Tony Spicer. Peter had a hunch that he had just received his first lead.

'I'm interested in two names on this list, a Mr Challoner and a Mr Spicer.'

'I know Mr Spicer well, but who did you say the other name was?'

'James Arthur Challoner.'

'No, it doesn't ring any bells. Perhaps he's a new customer,' the manager frowned, trying to recall the name.

'I need to know when both of those people began their rent agreements with you.'

'I can tell you now that Mr Spicer has been a customer since the scheme began over twelve months ago, but I'll need to check our records to see when Mr Challoner began his agreement.'

'Do that right away if you don't mind. It could be important.'

The manager left Peter in his office and went out into the front of the bank. Within minutes he was back holding a hard backed book. 'Here it is Inspector, Mr Challoner opened his rental agreement two weeks ago,' the manager informed Peter. Peter instinctively felt that Jimmy Challoner was mixed up in this job. It had all the hallmarks of being planned and executed by the target criminal of the RCS. Now he needed to prove it.

After the exhausting weekend spent working in the cramped conditions of the bank vault, Jimmy was pleased to be able to relax at home on Monday morning. At lunchtime on his way to the Admiral he stopped to buy an early edition of the Liverpool Echo. The break in at the bank made headlines as he had expected and he was interested to read that the police had no clues as to the identity of the offenders. Initial reports estimated that over two hundred people had rented deposit boxes at the bank and it was thought the thieves had got away with jewellery worth thousands of pounds. Jimmy was pleased. He knew he couldn't take the newspaper article too seriously, but they must have some idea of the amount stolen. When he read in a footnote at the bottom of the article that deposit box holders should visit the bank as soon as possible he decided to go round there straight away.

On arrival he was shown into the manager's office where he was told that the box contents could be checked but that nothing must be touched as the police were still asking questions. Jimmy went through the motions of checking his box although he knew of course that there had never been anything in there anyway. He saw a number of other customers doing the same thing, most of them clearly distressed when they realised that nothing of value had been left.

Jimmy made his way upstairs and informed the manager that the contents of his box had been stolen, but that he wasn't going to report the loss. The manager understood perfectly. As Jimmy was leaving he bumped into Tony Spicer.

'Hello Tony, I didn't expect to see you here,' Jimmy said.

'Why ever not? You knew I had deposit boxes here which is more than I knew about you. I presume that's why you're here.'

'Yes I followed your example and put my money into one of these boxes thinking it would be safe,' Jimmy gave a wry grin 'How wrong I was.'

'How much?'

'Enough.' Jimmy didn't bother to ask Spicer since he knew what the answer would be, but he suspected it must be a tidy sum as Spicer was visibly upset. While he was talking to Spicer he saw a man walking towards the bank who he recognised as the man in the photographs that he had taken from the bank.

'Good day your honour,' Spicer said.

'Good afternoon Mr Spicer, I presume you are one of the unfortunates as I am myself,' said the judge, raising his hat.

'Yes, I'm just going to check my boxes but I don't expect to find anything.'

'I hear they haven't bothered to take anything that they didn't consider to be valuable,' the judge said, walking on into the bank.

'Who's that?' Jimmy asked.

'That's Judge Brown,' Spicer answered. Jimmy remembered now. Judge Brown was the resident judge at the Liverpool Assize Court.

Interesting, very interesting thought Jimmy.

As Spicer walked away Jimmy smiled to himself. Even Spicer hadn't realised that he had done the break in. He was just about to walk away when he spotted Spicer's Jaguar parked further down the street. Thinking that Geraldine might be waiting in the car he approached it, catching his breath when she suddenly opened the door and got out.

'Hello you,' he said, smiling.

'Hello Jimmy.'

They looked at each other, both remembering their last encounter.

'I hear congratulations are called for?'

'Yes. I knew Tony had told you, I wanted to contact you but there was no way,' Geraldine said.

'Well I must admit I think I'm owed an explanation.'

'You don't understand Jimmy. There's no way out for me.'

'I know you don't have to marry someone if you don't want to. Why don't you leave him?'

'I can't Jimmy. Wherever I went and whoever I went with he would track us down and kill us.'

'Well this could be our opportunity. Maybe he's lost his money in the bank raid.'

'Not Tony, he's much too shrewd to have all his eggs in one basket. He's lost enough but not enough to make a difference to him.'

'When are we going to see each other then?'

'Are you going to the Mayor's Charity Ball next week?'

'I am now if you're going to be there.'

At that point Spicer emerged from the bank and returned to his car.

'Jimmy,' he said as he approached, 'we've both lost a packet in this break in and so have quite a number of my personal friends. As we're all anxious to recoup our losses, I suggest working together to find out who is responsible, what do you say?'

'Yes alright, but I'll be honest, I reckon they're outsiders,' Jimmy said.

'Rubbish, whoever did this job isn't a million miles from here,' Spicer said looking hard at Jimmy. He wondered if after all Spicer did suspect him. Jimmy said goodbye to Geraldine as Spicer ordered her back into the car. Before he drove away he reminded Jimmy, 'Don't forget, whatever you hear about this job, I want to know.'

11

When the RCS had interviewed all the people on the list of box holders, they were able to make a comprehensive list of the property that had been stolen. Jewellery valued at two hundred and fifty thousand pounds had been taken and as Peter suspected, it was the main item of property that people had admitted to keeping in their boxes. Five thousand pounds in cash had been reported as stolen but apart from legal documents no other claims had been made by the box holders. Peter was interested in the fact that some of the box owners had been concerned about the property left behind by the thieves and were anxious as to when they would be able to recover it. He failed to imagine what was so important about a few legal documents.

Detective Inspector Turner followed his instincts and directed his squad to keep Jimmy Challoner under surveillance. He didn't have any hard evidence to connect Jimmy to this job and it was true that he didn't have any previous history of this kind of crime but Peter knew that Jimmy was innovative and he had an undeniable gut feeling about the case. Unfortunately the surveillance on Jimmy Challoner was revealing nothing useful. He simply came and went between his flat in Sefton Park and the Admiral on the Dock Road. Neither Challoner nor his breakaway group were spending money, which was the usual custom after a job like this and after several more days proved fruitless Peter Turner was forced to abandon the surveillance.

As part of their routine enquiries the RCS circulated a description of all the stolen jewellery to the local jewellers. They weren't very hopeful of any of the property being sold but it was worth a try. Exactly two weeks after the break in the squad received a call from a jeweller who had a shop in London Road to say that he thought he might have a brooch that was part of the stolen property from the bank. He was paid a visit and he told the detectives that he'd bought the brooch the previous day for twenty pounds. On closer examination he had come to the conclusion that the stones he originally supposed to be glass were in fact genuine diamonds. The brooch was taken by the detective back to the RCS office where Peter examined it against the description given by one of the complainants who had lost property in the break in.

'It looks very much like the stolen brooch,' Peter said to his detective sergeant.

'It sure looks like the real thing and the jeweller reckons it's now worth nearer two thousand.'

'There's only one way to be sure, show it to the complainant.'

As soon as she was shown the brooch the woman concerned immediately identified the brooch as her property and a part of the jewellery that had been stored in the safety deposit box.

'This is the break we've been waiting for.'

'I've got a first class description of the man who sold the brooch,' the sergeant said taking out his pocket book.

'Let me see that description?' Peter reached for the book.

'No, that doesn't tally with any of Challoner's men.'

'That's what I thought.'

'Go down to criminal records,' Peter said, 'See what they come up with. Whoever he is he must be a thief.'

Within a couple of hours the sergeant was back at the squad office with the names of three possible suspects. After studying the files on them Peter said 'I can't believe any one of these three could have been in on the bank job. All the same we'll go and show these to the jeweller. You never know.'

'That's the man, no doubt about it,' the jeweller recognised the man who had sold him the brooch instantly.

'Are you absolutely sure?' Peter said.

'Couldn't be more certain.'

Peter thanked the jeweller for his co-operation and arranged for him to make a statement to one of his sergeants. He went back to the squad office where he opened the file on one Raymond Jackson and started reading his criminal history.

'He's just a petty thief. Most of his previous offences are sneak ins,' Peter said to his sergeants who were assembled in his office at his request.

'The jeweller was certain though wasn't he?' said one of the sergeants.

'He was in no doubt whatsoever, so whether we think Jackson was on the bank job or not he's got to be arrested. Ready?'

Within an hour Jackson had been arrested at his home and he immediately admitted that he had sold the brooch to the jeweller. He denied that he'd been on the bank job and claimed that he had stolen the brooch from a house in Francis Street. This Peter could believe. It fitted Jackson's previous form but the puzzle was as to how the brooch had come to be in Francis Street. As far as Peter could recall none of Jimmy's organisation lived in such an unfashionable part of town, but he still hung onto the belief that Jimmy was behind this job. Jackson couldn't remember the number of the house he'd stolen the brooch from but felt he could point it out to the detectives. He was taken to the street and immediately pointed out number twenty one. Before obtaining a warrant to search the premises Peter made enquiries to find out the name of the occupier. 'I don't believe it, it's just too good to be true,' he said delightedly to his sergeant on discovering that a Mrs Margaret Foster lived alone at number twenty one.

'What is? The name Foster?' the sergeant asked.

'That's right,' exclaimed Peter 'One of Challoner's gang is called Reggie Foster.' He called the whole of the squad together and briefed them on the result of the enquiries they had made. Peter ordered search warrants to be obtained for the homes of every member of the Challoner syndicate including the Admiral Pub. Meanwhile he arranged for Mrs Foster to be brought in for questioning. As Peter suspected Mrs Foster was only able to tell them that her son Reggie had given her the brooch as a gift a few days earlier.

The following morning as dawn was breaking the RCS were at the homes of the Challoner syndicate.

Jimmy's immediate problem wasn't the break in but securing a ticket for the Mayor's Charity Ball. He hadn't realised how difficult they were to come by but as usual with Jimmy's dogged determination, he went to the ball.

Jimmy arrived in good time, anxious not to miss a potential minute with Geraldine. Searching the sea of faces he spotted Judge Brown seated next to the Lord Mayor. Jimmy looked at him with disgust, glad he had the means to make the Judge pay for his perversions. Convinced after an hour that Geraldine couldn't be coming, Jimmy's heart leapt when he finally saw her following Spicer into the packed ballroom. She towered above Spicer in her high heels and her simple but exquisitely cut dove grey ballgown only served to make every other woman in the room look tacky and over dressed. Jimmy went over to her.

'Geraldine, you look lovely.'

'Why thank you Jimmy, how nice to see you in a dinner suit,' replied Geraldine, a mischievous smile playing round her lips.

'Hello Jimmy, didn't expect to see you here. Bit out of your league isn't it?' Spicer asked, looking annoyed with this new turn of events.

'On the contrary, if a place is good enough for you Tony, then it's certainly good enough for me,' Jimmy said, staring Spicer directly in the eye.

'Well just remember what they say about a sow's ear Jimmy,' Spicer spat the words as he took Geraldine by the arm and led her to their table. He was hosting a table of local dignitaries all of whom had been invited for their potential assistance in furthering Spicer's social ambitions. Jimmy waited for a few minutes and then approached Geraldine and asked her to dance. She turned to Spicer to ask if he minded and although he was obliged to say, 'Not at all,' his thunderous expression betrayed his true feelings.

Pulling Geraldine close Jimmy whispered, 'I must see you, just tell me where we can meet and I'll be there.'

'Haven't you forgotten something Jimmy? I'm getting married in three weeks.'

'No, I haven't forgotten anything,' Jimmy paused, 'I mean it Geraldine I have to see you again.'

As the music came to an end Geraldine made her way back to Spicer, but not before she had quietly said 'The station, Wednesday, eleven.' Spicer made sure Jimmy didn't have any further opportunity to get close to Geraldine for the rest of the evening, but the thought of Wednesday sustained him.

Jimmy was early on Wednesday morning and the thought that Geraldine might not come caused him actual physical pain in his chest. He ran forward in relief when she finally emerged from the bustling crowds of commuters.

'How long have you got?' were Jimmy's first words.

'Tom thinks I'm at the hairdressers in Church Street and he's picking me up at one o'clock.'

'Good, that gives us two hours. But how are you going to explain your hair?'

'I did it myself after Tony left this morning. Don't worry, he won't notice.'

'He must be mad' Jimmy said, taking her hand as they walked the short distance to the Lyceum Restaurant where they found a quiet corner table.

'We've got no time to waste,' Jimmy said after they had discussed a hundred theoretical solutions to their dilemma, 'As I see it the only way is for me to buy a house, somewhere out of town, where you will be safe until after the wedding date.'

'But Tony will know I'm with you.'

'No, I'll stay on in my flat. I'm sure we can keep your whereabouts from him.'

'It all sounds very simple but I know him and it won't take him long to find me.'

'I just need time to stop the wedding, after that I'll think again. Don't ever doubt that eventually we'll be together.'

Jimmy explained that as Spicer would be watching his every move they wouldn't be able to see each other for some time.

'I don't mind anything as long as you are safe,' Geraldine said softly.

'It'll work, believe me,' Jimmy took Geraldine's hand and gently kissed her finger tips.

'First I'll have to get my solicitor on the case. We'll need a house within three weeks.'

'But surely a solicitor can't work that fast.'

'Mine can,' Jimmy said, grinning.

After saying his goodbyes to Geraldine, Jimmy went straight to his solicitor's office and told him that he wanted a secluded house in the Southport area and that the sale had to be completed within two weeks. Once he had established that payment would not pose a problem Kenneth Armstrong told Jimmy that he didn't foresee any hiccups and he left the offices feeling optimistic. The break in had gone well and once the jewellery had been disposed of he would be in a suitably strong financial position to take on Spicer. He had been very strict with the proceeds from the bank, none of the money had been allowed to circulate and he had taken both cash and jewellery to his maiden Aunt's house. Telling her he was storing a friend's belongings while he was in Australia, he had left the haul in a locked suitcase in the spare bedroom of the little terraced house.

The morning after his meeting with Geraldine Jimmy was surprised at six o'clock by the Regional Crime Squad looking for the proceeds from the break in at the bank. They left, as he knew they would, empty handed. Knowing that everything was at an address that the police would not connect with him or other members of his team, Jimmy was puzzled when he heard that the homes of every one of them, as well as the Admiral, had been searched. He called a meeting at the Admiral and it was here that Jimmy learned of Reggie Foster's arrest.

'I don't believe it,' said Jimmy, 'He must have pocketed it when he was emptying one of the deposit boxes.'

'I had no idea he was that stupid.'

'Well he's one of your original team, is he likely to talk?'

'He might have been stupid, but he won't talk. He'll give the usual spiel about buying it from an unknown person in the pub, rest assured the police won't break him.'

'Well that's something. But you realise we'll have to make an example of him,' said Jimmy.

'Yes, it will be expected.'

'What concerns me most is that the fool has brought us to the attention of the Regional Crime Squad,' Jimmy grumbled.

Fortunately for Jimmy the police were not able to break Foster's story and with no evidence against him they were forced to release him. After his discharge Jimmy and Mick met him as he left the court and drove him in a stolen car to the beach at Ainsdale.

Reggie talked for the entire journey. He pointed out to Jimmy that the police had been unable to break him and no harm had been done. Jimmy sat staring silently out of the window while Mick drove. As the car came to a halt Jimmy turned to Foster.

'Shut it Reg, you're starting to annoy me.'

He pulled Foster out of the car and with Mick's help dragged him fifty yards further into the cover of the sand dunes. Foster was making a low moaning sound but not struggling. He seemed to be resigned to his fate or too traumatised to act. Even when Jimmy and Mick threw him face down in the sand Foster didn't move. He didn't move when Jimmy cocked the gun by his ear. Foster knew when he was beaten.

'Bury him', Jimmy said before walking back to the car.

As soon as Mick had buried the body they drove back to Liverpool leaving the car in the same place they had taken it from hours earlier.

Driving home Mick said, 'Stupid little bugger.'

'Yeah.'

Now that he had been brought to the notice of the Regional Crime Squad Jimmy felt obliged to get rid of the stolen jewellery earlier than he had intended. In a moment of greed one man had nearly jettisoned the entire operation. Foster, Jimmy reasoned, had had it coming.

Two days after Foster's arrest Peter got a call from Tony Spicer asking him to visit him at his club. Peter was surprised to hear from him but hoped that he might have picked something up along the grapevine about the break in at the bank. After all, Spicer himself had been a victim. At the River Club Peter was shown into Spicer's office. Spicer stood up as Peter entered, 'Inspector, good to see you, you've come a long way since our last meeting.'

'Thank you for coming so promptly,' he went on, 'I'm interested in Reggie Foster's arrest, do you believe his story?'

'I don't believe I'm hearing this. Did you call me out here to ask questions about a police enquiry?' said Peter, still standing.

'Sorry, I phrased that badly. What I meant to say was if you suspect that Foster was involved in the bank break in then I may be in a position to help you,' said Spicer, sitting down again.

'You seem to forget that I'm not one of your bought police officers. I don't discuss details of my investigations with anyone from outside the force.' Peter said, heading for the door of Spicer's office.

'Don't leave Inspector. My apologies for asking what might appear to be impertinent questions. I was trying to find out if you really are as straight as I'd heard.'

Peter had no idea what he was talking about and was still most put out that Spicer felt that he could summon him to his office and expect him to discuss details of a police enquiry.

'Calm down,' said Spicer. 'Now I'm sure I can talk to you in confidence,' Spicer leaned forward..

'You can, but don't expect anything from me.'

'No no, I think I may be able to help you with the bank break in. I hadn't really thought about Challoner being involved, but when you arrested Foster it all fell into place. Now I'm sure he did that job I've tried to imagine what his next move will be.'

'Well he's doing very little at the moment. Certainly not acting like a man who has pulled off one of the biggest jobs we've ever known in Liverpool.'

'Don't you see, that's exactly what Jimmy is so good at. He never does the obvious, that's why I'm surprised at the Foster incident. Jimmy would have had no knowledge of Foster helping himself to that brooch.'

'Yes, I'll buy that.'

'Now it's the jewellery I think I can help you with. Jimmy will want to get rid of it soon and there aren't many who handle jewellery of that value.'

'Do you include yourself in that number?'

Spicer chose to ignore Peter's remark and continued 'Like the police I have my contacts and I reckon only three people would be prepared to handle this type of jewellery. I've made enquiries and none of them has been approached yet.'

'Well, that's all very interesting. But why tell me? I'm not one of your paid policemen.'

Spicer looked a little taken aback at Peter's remark but again he ignored it and continued, 'That's precisely why I'm telling you. If I can bribe them, so can Challoner.'

Reassured by the truth of that remark, Peter said 'Right, now from your experience which of the three would Jimmy be most likely to approach?'

'Jimmy has only met one of them so I think we can assume with confidence that it will be him.'

'How will Jimmy make the contact?'

'Initially by telephone when a meeting will be arranged,' Spicer was visibly relaxing now that he had Peter's interest.

'Looks like I'll have to watch Jimmy day and night.'

'If you'll pardon my saying so, that wouldn't be a good idea. He'll be very careful when he's in possession of the jewellery and believe me he's well versed in anti-surveillance methods.'

Peter wasn't too happy to hear this from Spicer but as a professional he realised it was the truth. Spicer continued, 'I think I can help you if you are prepared to co-operate.'

'I'm not prepared to make any kind of deal with you.'

'Wait 'til you've heard what I've got to say first. The receiver is prepared to tell me where he'll meet Challoner, provided he has your assurance that he will not be arrested.'

'I can't do that.'

'No, Your Regional Co-ordinator can though.'

Peter looked across the desk at Spicer and wondered just how much he knew about how the police service operated. He was right, the Regional Co-ordinator, who was the senior police officer in charge of the number one RCS, did have the authority to give an amnesty to a criminal if he considered that the circumstances warranted it. Peter believed that he could be persuaded and he told Spicer that he would make the request.

'Good, but do it quickly. I have a feeling Jimmy will be making contact pretty soon.'

Peter returned to the squad office and discussed what had taken place between himself and Spicer with his detective chief inspector, who was the officer in charge of the Liverpool Branch. It was agreed that Peter should seek the approval of the Regional Co-ordinator and an appointment was made to see him at his office in Manchester. Peter had met the Co-ordinator on several occasions and judged him to be a first rate detective. After discussing the matter with him Peter received his assurance that no action would be taken against the receiver. However, if the meeting took place outside the number one area then the Co-ordinator would need to contact his colleagues from the appropriate area.

Peter returned to Liverpool and paid another call on Spicer to tell him that his terms had been approved by the Regional Co-ordinator. Spicer then gave Peter the details of the receiver, who he said came from Birmingham.

Jimmy knew there was nobody locally who was capable of handling jewellery of the quantity and quality that he had stolen. He did recall that Spicer had once introduced him to a dealer in Birmingham, who according to Spicer, could handle any amount of stolen jewellery. Jimmy looked up his name in the file he had kept of useful contacts and found Max Cohen, together with his telephone number. He gave Cohen a call and a brief description of the jewellery he wanted to dispose of. Cohen expressed his interest and a meeting was arranged half way between Liverpool and Birmingham at Trentham Gardens, Stoke on Trent for ten thirty the following morning.

Later that day Armstrong telephoned Jimmy to tell him that he had found a house he hoped might be suitable. It was at Blundellsands, about twelve miles from Southport and Jimmy arranged to meet Armstrong there immediately.

Jimmy fell in love with the house straightaway and was pleased he was able to buy it fully furnished.

'How soon could I move in?' he said.

'In a matter of days,' replied Armstrong, 'The owners have already moved out.'

'This deal has got to be hush hush you understand. I don't want anyone knowing I've bought this place.'

'I understand,' said Armstrong, avoiding Jimmy's gaze.

On his return to Liverpool Jimmy telephoned Geraldine and told her about the house.

'Jimmy that's wonderful, but are you certain that nobody knows why you're buying it?'

'No one at all apart from Armstrong. Why?'

'It's just that Tony is acting rather strangely, almost as though he knows what we're doing.'

'He can't. It must be your imagination. Try not to worry, I'll have you out in a day or two.'

'Be careful Jimmy, I'm sure Tony is plotting something.'

'I'll be OK, I've just got a bit of business to see to tomorrow and then I'll be in a better position to take on Spicer.'

True to his word, Spicer telephoned Peter and told him that Challoner had been in contact with the receiver from Birmingham and a meeting had been fixed in the car park opposite the main ballroom of Trentham Gardens. Peter told the Regional Co-ordinator who later informed Peter that it had been arranged for him to meet with the detective inspector of number four RCS, in whose area the meeting was to take place.

The next day Jimmy set off from Liverpool at eight o'clock. He didn't want to rush the journey and allowed himself ample time. He had collected the suitcase the previous night, making sure that then as now, he wasn't being followed. It was a perfect day and he enjoyed the drive in his new Ford Zephyr Zodiac, arriving at Trentham Gardens at ten o'clock. He drove into the car park and settled down to read through the newspaper while he waited for Cohen to arrive.

He had been waiting for about five minutes when he saw several cars, each holding two men, closing in on him from each of the entrances to the car park. He knew instinctively it was the police. He also knew it was pointless to try to escape so he merely sat tight and was not surprised when the man who approached him was Peter Turner.

12

'Jimmy, you know who I am. This is official, I have reason to believe that you have stolen property in the boot of your car,' Peter said.

'I don't know what you're talking about.'

'Then you won't mind opening the boot.'

'Open it yourself, here's the key,' said Jimmy passing it through the open car window. Peter gave the key to one of the detectives and told him to open the boot and bring the contents to him.

The detective returned carrying a holdall which he handed to his inspector. Peter looked inside the bag and said, 'James Arthur Challoner, I am arresting you for being involved in the break in at Martin's Bank in Liverpool and stealing cash and jewellery.' He went on to caution Jimmy. Jimmy Challoner looked at his boyhood friend and said 'What do you expect me to say Peter, it's a fair cop or something? For the record, I don't know where the jewellery came from.'

'Get out of the car. You'll be driven back to Liverpool where you will be charged with this offence' Peter said.

'What about my car? It's brand new. I don't want to leave it here.'

'One of my officers will drive it back.'

'Well tell him to be careful, it's still being run in.'

Peter and Jimmy travelled back to Liverpool in separate cars and on arrival Jimmy was formally charged.

Peter charged Jimmy with breaking and entering Martin's Bank and stealing jewellery to the value of two hundred and fifty thousand pounds. Jimmy didn't reply to the charge but he did allow himself a wry smile when he heard the supposed value. The following morning Peter arranged for Jimmy to appear before the Stipendiary Magistrate, where much to Peter's surprise, Jimmy appeared without his solicitor. Mr Armstrong had seen Jimmy from about nine o'clock and Peter was at a loss to know why he wasn't making application for bail on Jimmy's behalf. The prosecutor outlined the details of the arrest and asked the magistrate to remand

Challoner in police custody whilst further enquiries were made. The application was granted and Jimmy didn't even question the decision. He was placed back in the cells while arrangements were made for the jewellery to be identified by the victims of the break in.

Later that afternoon Peter went down to the main Bridewell where Jimmy was being held and arranged to interview him.

'Jimmy I'm going to ask you some questions about how you got hold of this jewellery which has now been positively identified as coming from the break in at the bank.'

'I'm saying nothing, we both know I was set up.'

'Oh yes and who would do that?'

'Spicer of course. Who else?'

'Are you saying that Spicer arranged for your arrest?'

'You know what I mean Peter.'

'I couldn't help noticing,' Peter went on, 'that this morning in court you weren't represented by Mr Armstrong. He did see you earlier, didn't he?'

'That double crossing bastard. He won't be representing me anymore'

'What went wrong?'

'It's private. Nothing to do with the police.'

'Fair enough. But you can request another solicitor if you want one.'

'Can I make a telephone call instead?'

'Depends who it's to.'

'It will be to my business associate, Mick Walsh.'

'OK, I'll arrange it for you,' Peter grinned at Jimmy's reference to Walsh.

Peter instructed the Bridewell sergeant to allow Challoner to make the telephone call. He simply asked Mick Walsh to visit him as soon as possible and he appeared within the hour.

The next day a solicitor by the name of John Wakefield arrived at the Main Bridewell and said he had been sent for by a Mr Challoner. Peter knew Wakefield as a young solicitor who had recently opened his own practice in Liverpool. He was already building himself a reputation as anti-police, taking every opportunity he had to suggest to the courts that they had acted outside the law. He had won a couple of battles and because of this his name was becoming popular amongst the criminal fraternity. He was allowed to see Challoner and spent an hour with him. Although Peter questioned Jimmy on several occasions during the three days he was remanded in police custody he always refused to answer.

At the next remand hearing Challoner was represented by Wakefield and despite the case put by the prosecution to keep Challoner in custody, Wakefield managed to convince the court that his client should be granted bail. Peter was none too happy seeing Jimmy walk from the court but as the Stipendiary Magistrate had granted bail, there was nothing Peter could to. Jimmy was delighted with the way Wakefield had handled himself in court and remained convinced that Armstrong had betrayed him. On the drive back to Liverpool he thought about the events leading up to his arrest. It had to be Spicer who had set him up. He would have realised that it would be Cohen that Jimmy contacted, having introduced them. Geraldine had been right to be suspicious of Spicer but what Jimmy couldn't understand was who had put Spicer on to him. He concluded that Armstrong must have mentioned his new house to Spicer's solicitor and he had reasoned it out for himself. Jimmy was unable to contact Geraldine and when he confronted Tony Spicer at his River Club and demanded to know where she was, Spicer laughed in his face.

'Nowhere you'll find her that's for sure.'

'That's just where you're wrong, you can't hide her forever.'

'Well be honest, you won't be much use to her where you're going.'

'I guessed it was you. From now on this is war.'

'My thoughts exactly Jimmy. Now get out,' Spicer said holding his office door open.Jimmy left the River Club and went straight to the Admiral to see Mick Walsh.

He told Mick to have the entire team at the pub before eleven that night. Jimmy told them they were all about to pay Spicer a visit and no-one questioned what he meant.

At midnight Mick Walsh and six men entered the River Club. It took three of Jimmy's men to render the bouncer unconscious and as they walked into the main clubroom, they saw that it was packed with customers. Jimmy scanned the faces as they turned towards him and failing to see Spicer among them he went over to the office. Spicer was talking with two of his employees when Jimmy burst in. Realising what was about to happen Spicer's men lunged at Jimmy, who neatly stepped aside and left them to Mick Walsh and the rest of his men. Jimmy himself had gone over to the desk where Spicer had started to get up. Jimmy pushed him roughly back

'Not yet Spicer. I'll tell you what we're going to do first.'

'What do you mean?'

'It's such a lovely night, I thought we'd go for a little drive,' Jimmy said quietly.

'You must be mad, I'm not going anywhere with you,' Spicer's voice was still trembling. Without warning Jimmy's clenched fist suddenly caught Spicer squarely on the jaw.

'Now we can either do this here, smash the place up and upset all those nice customers, or you can come with me like I said.'

Outside the club Spicer was bundled into Jimmy's car and Mick took the wheel.

'Where to?'

'The car park off Linden Road.' Spicer sat on the back seat ashen faced and shaking.

The drive took less than ten minutes. When Mick had parked the car Jimmy got out and removed a sawn off shotgun from the boot. Spicer started to plead, 'No don't kill me.'

'Give me one good reason why I shouldn't?'

'I'll leave Liverpool, you can have the lot, just don't kill me,' Spicer said whimpering like a child.

'There's only one thing I want from you. Tell me where you've taken Geraldine.'

'If I tell you will you let me go?'

'You,' Jimmy said poking the gun in Spicer's chest, 'are in no position to bargain. Tell me where she is and then I'll think about it.'

'Alright, she's with Tom, my chauffeur at my cottage in Barmouth.'

'The one you took me to last summer?'

'Yes,' replied Spicer, almost inaudibly.

'I don't know why but I'm going to let you live.' But seconds later Spicer's eyes widened in terror as Jimmy raised the gun. He screamed in agony as Jimmy discharged both barrels into his legs. Jimmy smiled as he walked away leaving Spicer writhing on the ground.

'Stop at the next kiosk. I think we'd better tell someone that a man seems to be injured on the car park,' Jimmy said to Mick Walsh as they drove away.

The next morning Peter Turner was flicking through the incident report of the previous twenty four hours when he spotted the report of Spicer's shooting. When he realised who the victim was he went to the hospital immediately and asked to see Spicer, but was told that a visit wasn't possible as Spicer was too ill at present. He had lost a leg below the knee and although he wasn't expected to die, he was still very seriously ill. Peter went next to his old station at Rose Hill where he saw his colleague, Detective Inspector Hughes who was in charge of the CID for the area where Spicer had been shot. He cleared it with Bob Hughes so that he could see Spicer and make enquiries into the shooting because he was convinced that Challoner was behind it. The anonymous call about Spicer had been made just after midnight, so Peter reasoned Spicer must have been abducted from his club since he was always there at that time. Peter took three of the squad with him and went to the River Club. Although they interviewed all the staff who were on duty, none of them were prepared to say what had happened.

Peter felt certain that Challoner had shot Spicer in a revenge attack and he cursed himself for not anticipating this. Challoner should have been kept under constant surveillance, but it was too late now for recriminations. He would have to do this the hard way. Peter went to the Admiral and saw Jimmy himself.

'Where were you around midnight last night?' Peter asked.

'Here until about twelve twenty, then I left,' came the answer.

'Now that's interesting, that was the time the police were called to a car park in London Road.'

'Why, what was happening there?'

'Don't come the innocent with me. You know exactly what was going on since it was you in the middle of it all.'

'Look, I don't know what you're on about. Either tell me or get out.'

'Are you trying to tell me you don't know Spicer is hospitalised with gun shot wounds?'

'No, I didn't know, but I won't pretend I'm sorry. I think I'd better make myself clear, I'm getting a little tired of you coming round here every time there's a crime committed. In future make sure you've got a search warrant.'

'I only come when I know you're responsible.'

'Well unless you can prove something and are going to arrest me, get out.'

'I need the names and addresses of those people who I'm sure will remember vividly that they were here with you until twelve twenty this morning.'

'Happy to oblige. Oddly enough they're all here, you can see them before you go.'

Peter went through the formality of seeing them but they all supported Jimmy's alibi. It was three days before Spicer was well enough to be interviewed and it came as no surprise to Peter that he wouldn't make a statement about the incident. The Chief Constable of the Liverpool City Police was anxious that the shooting could lead to a gang war. He told his detectives that he wasn't prepared to see Liverpool turned into another Chicago and the CID must make it their job to prevent it happening.

Peter knew that it would be several weeks before Spicer was released and nothing was likely to happen in the meantime. He reasoned that if Challoner was in prison when Spicer was released the matter would be closed and so he set about bringing the committal proceedings on the bank break in forward. He felt confident that Challoner had no hope of evading conviction on this charge and felt sure that Jimmy would receive a lengthy stretch in prison, which would solve all their problems. On the day of the committal hearing Peter was not pleased to hear that the prosecuting solicitor had agreed with Challoner's defence to drop the break in charge and proceed only on the charge of receiving stolen property. Peter argued that the two charges should remain and since he knew that this was one of the few occasions that the court could return an alternative verdict from the same set of circumstances, he couldn't understand what the prosecution were up to.

'I have an undertaking that if we proceed only on the receiving charge Challoner will plead guilty,' the Prosecuting Solicitor said.

'Have you got that in writing?' said Peter.

'No, of course not. But I feel sure the agreement will be honoured.'

'And pigs might fly. Challoner won't plead guilty to anything believe me.'

'It's too late for arguments. I've given my word and since I have to take account of long trials and consider the expense incurred during those trials, I have to accept every opportunity from the defence when they intimate that a guilty plea is in the offing.'

'What people like you don't take into account is the cost of investigating someone like Challoner. My squad have spent precious hours trying to bring him to some kind of justice and frankly we're not happy when you do deals with your legal colleagues without even consulting us.'

'I trust you're not implying that anything improper has taken place.'

'The only thing I'm implying is that you've made it that much easier for Challoner to be acquitted,' Peter replied.

'The strongest evidence is that relating to the receiving charge and it's that charge we'll commit him on.'

'I don't doubt that we'll commit him since we only need to prove a prima facie case. What concerns me more is whether we'll convict him now. Don't forget you have restricted the amount of evidence we can give against him.'

'You really are defeatist inspector. Have confidence in me. After all I am the qualified lawyer,' he replied as he turned to leave.

Peter knew that further argument was futile so he let the matter drop.

13

Jimmy Challoner was expecting a visit from the police after the shooting incident and he had carefully rehearsed his alibi with members of the organisation. That Spicer hadn't talked was obvious by his non-arrest. This came as no surprise but Jimmy was aware that one day Spicer would deal with the issue in his own way.

Once Peter had left him Jimmy sent Mick to Barmouth with instructions to collect Geraldine and bring her back to the Adelphi, where he would meet her later. Jimmy went to see John Wakefield to establish how far he was from finalising the purchase of the Blundellsands house. He had put his own plans to move into the house on hold, safer to sort out the Spicer problem first, but he was anxious to install Geraldine there. This would keep her safely away from the violence that Spicer was doubtless already plotting from his hospital bed.

Jimmy decided to walk the distance between the Admiral and Wakefield's office in the city and was pleased he had. It had given him the opportunity to sort things out in his mind so that he was clear on several issues that would need his attention by the time he arrived at Wakefield's office.

'I'm glad you've called, I was just about to ring you,' said Wakefield.

'If you approve, I'm going to engage Mark O'Rourke to represent you at the Assizes.'

'Is he any good?'

'Probably the best on the circuit. Put it this way, we couldn't do better.'

'Good, then let's have him. What do you think my chances are?'

'Much better since the prosecution agreed to drop the break in offence, now all we have to worry about is the handling and since you never admitted to knowing the property was stolen, I reckon Mark O'Rourke will get you acquitted,' Wakefield smiled.

'I have to say I'm impressed with the way you convinced the prosecutor to drop that charge against me. How did you manage that?'

'I just told him that you would plead guilty to the receiving charge if he did.'

'And he believed you? He must be very gullible. The other thing is the house that Armstrong was purchasing for me. Have you been able to take the case over?'

'Yes, everything's ready. I only need a signature and the house is yours,' Wakefield said, sliding some documents over to Jimmy.

'Just sign at the foot of each page,' he continued. Having signed them Jimmy asked 'How soon can I have the keys?'

'I'll exchange contracts tomorrow and then you can move in as soon as you like.'

Jimmy then took a taxi to the Adelphi where he booked a suite of rooms, all of which he instructed were to be filled with white roses, Geraldine's favourite flowers.

When Mick Walsh finally delivered Geraldine to the hotel she looked tired and drawn from the journey. 'Oh Jimmy, I'm just so relieved to see you,' she sobbed into his shoulder.

'It's alright now, it's over. We're together now,' Jimmy murmured.

After thanking Mick he took Geraldine's cases from him and they made their way to their rooms.

Once in their suite the full story of Geraldine's ordeal at Spicer's hands came tumbling out as Geraldine began to relax. When she had been bundled off to Barmouth she had believed she would never see Jimmy again. 'Tony won't give up though Jimmy, I know him,' she said, shivering at the thought.

'Well he'll have to for a while. Someone shot him in the leg and he's in hospital.'

'No. When did it happen?'

'Last night, I heard.'

'It was you wasn't it Jimmy? I'd wondered how you knew where I was.' Geraldine began to cry.

'Will it make any difference if it was me?' said Jimmy.

'It should, I know it should but it's hard to feel sympathy when he's put me through such hell.'

When they finally fell into an exhausted sleep it was four in the morning and dawn was beginning to break. It had been a long day for them both.

Jimmy woke to the sound of running water. He found Geraldine stepping into the deep foam filled bath she had just run and he walked up behind her. 'Better now?' he whispered. 'Much,' Geraldine smiled as she tried to pull him into the water. 'No need to use force,' Jimmy said as he slid in next to her.

They didn't leave their suite for the next two days, and all thoughts of Spicer were submerged in their obsessive need for each other. They preferred instead to create their own world. Reality was too hard to think about, reality and Spicer.

When Jimmy finally took Geraldine to their new home she was shocked that he wouldn't be staying with her.

'Darling, I can't. Not until the trouble's sorted.'

Geraldine nodded. She knew he was right.

Jimmy heard from John Wakefield that the prosecution had brought the committal hearing forward.

'Not that it makes any difference. I've discussed the case at length with O'Rourke and we won't be challenging any of the evidence at the committal stage.'

Is he still confident he can get me off?' asked Jimmy.

'Yes he is but he wants a pre-trial conference with us once the committal hearing is out of the way,' Wakefield said.

The Committal hearing was a simple enough affair. Since the defence were not challenging any of the evidence each witness came into court and agreed his statement which was read out to him. The whole procedure was a waste of time, thought Jimmy. At the end of the hearing he was committed to the next sitting of the Liverpool Assize court before his Honour Mr Justice Brown. Interesting thought Jimmy to himself.

At the pre trial meeting with Mark O'Rourke, Jimmy was very satisfied with the choice of barrister. O'Rourke was a confident man who told Jimmy that their defence would be one of not knowing that the jewellery was stolen property. It was agreed that Jimmy would say that he had been paid the sum of £100 by an unknown man to take the jewellery to the meeting point at Stoke on Trent. He hadn't looked in the bag and therefore had no knowledge of the contents. It all sounded highly plausible to Jimmy and he believed that with Mark O'Rourke's help he would be acquitted.

'One problem, the prosecution have retained Simon Wheeler to represent them and if there's one man who can convince a jury, it's him,' said O'Rourke.

Jimmy began to feel a little less confident, 'You don't think he can get a jury to convict me do you?'

'Not on the balance of the evidence, but you can never be certain how juries will react.'

Jimmy felt that in the light of what O'Rourke had said it would be wise to take out further insurance. The Saturday before to the trial found Jimmy calling on his Honour Mr Justice Brown. The judge made it clear that he wasn't pleased to see Jimmy, 'I can't see you now, I'm due to hear your case on Monday' the judge said to Jimmy.

'Actually that's exactly why I'm here. Perhaps you'd better invite me in.'

'I most certainly will not invite you in. Now I suggest that you leave immediately before I am call the police.'

'You do just that. I'm sure they'd be interested in some photographs I have. The one of you spanking two little boys' bottoms is particularly good, don't you think?'

'What are you taking about. Utter nonsense,' the judge said.

'Maybe it will save time if I show you one of the photographs,' said Jimmy, taking a snapshot from his inside jacket pocket. Judge Brown paled.

'You had better come into my study,' the judge said quietly.

'That's more like it,' said Jimmy, 'I knew you would understand when you saw the evidence.' The judge led the way down the hall and into a room on the left.

'Well what is it you want? I presume you intend to blackmail me.'

'That's an ugly word, let's just say I'm expecting you to do me a small favour.'

'And what might that be?' the judge said wearily.

'You can make bloody sure I'm not convicted.'

'That's completely out of my hands, it's the jury who convict. I merely sentence you.'

'Oh come on judge. I know the score. You can influence a jury should you choose to.'

'And if I refuse? What then?'

'Easy. I contact the News of the World.'

'Yes, I'm sure you would. Well I'll do what I can but if the jury find you guilty I can't help you.'

'That's where you're wrong. If the jury find me guilty you will then give me a very light sentence.'

'I understand, but when will I get my photographs returned to me?'

'Just as soon as the trial is over and you've delivered the goods.'

As soon as Jimmy was satisfied that Judge Brown understood exactly what was required of him Jimmy made his way home to a pleasant weekend with Geraldine. Jimmy was of the opinion that finding the photographs had been quite a stroke of luck for him, if not for Judge Brown.

When Peter Turner heard that Jimmy had retained Mark O'Rourke to defend him at his trial he started to worry. He knew O'Rourke to be one of the best barristers on the Liverpool circuit and he believed in a case of this importance the prosecution would be well advised to appoint someone just as able. He made an appointment to see the prosecuting solicitor and hoped that their recent difference of agreement wouldn't influence him in deliberately blocking the request he was about to make.

'Good morning Inspector, do sit down,' said the prosecuting solicitor as Peter was shown into his office. 'Now I understand from my secretary that you want me to retain a particular barrister to represent the prosecution in the case against Challoner.'

'That's correct, I'd like to request that we retain Mr Simon Wheeler.'

'Why him?'

'I've had experience of cases where Simon Wheeler has been involved and I know he's thorough and competent.'

'I couldn't agree with you more and for what it's worth, in my opinion Simon is the only barrister on the circuit who is any opposition to O'Rourke,' the prosecuting solicitor said.

'Will you retain him for the prosecution then?'

'I'll arrange it today.'

Peter was relieved. At least he knew that the case would now be prosecuted professionally and Simon Wheeler would not allow Mark O'Rourke to ride rough shod over the witnesses for the prosecution, as was his reputation.

True to his word the prosecuting solicitor did retain Simon Wheeler and, as is usual with the better barristers, Simon Wheeler asked Peter to visit him in Chambers to discuss the prosecution case. Wheeler asked Peter why the prosecution had withdrawn the break in offence from the indictment against Challoner.

'It was on the authority of the prosecuting solicitor,' Peter said.

'Apparently the defence indicated that they would plead guilty to the receiving charge if the break in offence was withdrawn.'

Wheeler raised his eyebrows, 'That isn't the impression I got from my conversation with O'Rourke.'

'I said at the time that I couldn't see Challoner pleading guilty to anything.'

'Pity. I would have liked the opportunity to tell the court all the facts about the break in at the bank. I'll be restricted now because I can only mention those facts directly concerned with the receiving charge.'

The fact that the eminent Simon Wheeler agreed with his own judgement was of some small comfort to Peter, but in the circumstances he didn't derive much pleasure from it.

'This case isn't going to be easy inspector. The prosecution, needs to prove to the satisfaction of the court that Challoner had guilty knowledge with regard to his possession of the stolen jewellery.'

'Yes, I know what you mean. Challoner has never once admitted knowing that the jewellery was stolen,' Peter said.

'Exactly,' said Wheeler, ' and if I know Mark O'Rourke that will be the way he'll defend the case. I have to say that if the prosecution can't rebut that defence we will lose hands down.'

'You sound as if we've lost already,' said Peter glumly.

'I have to be practical. That's why I'm annoyed at the break in charge having been withdrawn. My submission to the court would have been that Challoner's recent possession of the stolen jewellery soon after the break in would have been evidence of his guilt,' said Wheeler.

'Well I guess we'll know soon enough, I see the trial is listed for hearing in two weeks before Judge Brown.

When Peter had heard that the case was to be heard before Judge Brown he wasn't entirely sure that the judge was eligible in law to hear the case since he himself was a victim of the break in. However he argued with himself that the judge knew the technicalities of the law better than he did. And besides, he might just show leniency towards the prosecution. His meeting with Simon Wheeler only confirmed to Peter that they would need all the help that they could get.

The day of the trial dawned and from the outset it was evident that Challoner's defence was that he didn't know that the jewellery which he was found in possession of was stolen property. As the second day's hearing drew to a close Simon Wheeler asked to see Peter.

'Peter I'm very much afraid we're going to lose this case. I need to be able to produce evidence to show that Challoner knew that the jewellery was from the bank.'

'Just what would be acceptable evidence to prove his guilty knowledge of where the jewellery came from?' asked Peter.

'Anything to connect Challoner with the original break in would be good,' Wheeler replied.

'We might just be able to provide that,' Peter said. 'We arrested a petty thief for selling a brooch which had been stolen from the deposit boxes in the bank. He admitted stealing it from the home of a Mrs Foster, mother of Reginald Foster who was a member of Challoner's organisation.'

'And did Mrs Foster tell you how she acquired the item of jewellery?'

'Yes. She was given it by her son Reggie, but naturally he bought the brooch from an unknown man in a pub.'

'If the judge were to allow that evidence we would certainly be in with a chance. The jury hopefully would make the correct assumption in spite of Foster's story. Can you provide me with the statements from the people involved so that I can make a submission before the courts?' asked Wheeler.

'Certainly,' said Peter, 'but I'm afraid I can't get a statement from Reggie Foster, nobody has seen him since the incident.'

'I'm of the opinion that under the circumstances it would be useful if we had the actual witnesses in court tomorrow morning in case Judge Brown wishes to hear the evidence directly from them.'

The following morning Peter arrived at the court with Raymond Jackson and Mrs Foster. He left them in the witness room and went into court to tell Simon Wheeler that the witnesses had arrived. Peter remained in court as Wheeler rose to make his submission to Mr Justice Brown and listened as he told the judge that the prosecution had new evidence. Judge Brown said that he would require further details of the new evidence. He would hear the submissions in open court but not in the presence of the jury and he discharged the jury to their room for a short recess. This was normal procedure when a point of law needed to be discussed between the legal representatives. It simply stopped the jury from hearing any evidence which may be prejudicial to the accused and which after legal submissions may not be allowed to be given at the hearing. Once the jury had cleared the court room Simon Wheeler outlined to the judge the substance of the evidence that he wanted to introduce to the court. Mark O'Rourke made the expected objections of the defence but the arguments were merely routine. O'Rourke was clearly of the same opinion as Wheeler, that the evidence was pertinent and would therefore be allowed by the judge. Both barristers were sitting down after having put forward their respective cases and were waiting for a decision from Mr Justice Brown. The judge was reading his copy of Archbold Proceedings, the legal bible used by both lawyers and judiciary as their book of reference. After several minutes reading Mr Justice Brown addressed Wheeler who dutifully stood up.

'Mr Wheeler, I have listened to your submission and have weighed the balance of your argument against those in R v Hennesy as reported in the All England Law Report. This was summarised in Archbold's, page 1032, where it was agreed that evidence of the nature that you seek to introduce is not acceptable as evidence of guilty knowledge. Do you wish to comment?'

'Your honour, I have read the legal submissions in Hennesy and it is my humble submission that they do not apply in this case. Unlike the facts in Hennesy, in this instance the item of jewellery in question has been positively identified as being part of the stolen property' said Wheeler.

'I have taken that fact into consideration, but I cannot see that it influences the decision in Hennesy. Therefore in the interest of justice, I rule that the evidence you wish to introduce cannot be admitted.'

Wheeler sat down, he was obviously shocked at the judge's ruling. O'Rourke was just as surprised and he realised that victory was now well within his grasp. Within half an hour Challoner was acquitted by the jury on the judge's instructions that the prosecution had failed to establish their case against him.

His acquittal came as no surprise to Jimmy and outside the court he shook Mark O'Rourke's hand.

'Don't thank me, my job was made easy by the inexplicable decision of Judge Brown not to allow the evidence of the stolen brooch. If he'd allowed that evidence we would have lost.'

'Maybe the good judge realised I wasn't guilty.'

'I hardly think so. But whatever it's not the sort of decision you would normally expect from Judge Brown,' said O'Rourke as he took his leave of Jimmy.

The following day Jimmy received a call from Judge Brown requesting the return of the photographs. Jimmy informed him that he had changed his mind, that he was keeping the photographs and despite the judge's pleas Jimmy refused to hand the photographs back.

Later that day Jimmy received a visit from John Wakefield.

'Have you seen the evening paper?' he asked.

'No, why?'

'Here, read the headlines,' said Wakefield handing Jimmy the newspaper.

Jimmy read the headlines 'Judge Brown found shot dead at his home.' Jimmy read on but his face betrayed no emotion.

'Appears he shot himself accidentally while he was cleaning his gun,' said Jimmy.

'Seems very strange. He was an experienced man when it came to guns and had been president of the local gun society for a long time,' John Wakefield said.

'Guns are funny things, even the most experienced of people can have accidents.'

'Perhaps he was losing his mind slightly. That would explain his strange decision in court.'

'Maybe, but there's nothing we can do about it so let's quit worrying. Just be thankful he didn't have this accident before he made the right decision as far as I'm concerned.'

'All the same, I find it very odd.'

'Anyway,' Jimmy changed the subject, 'I'm glad you called, can you do anything about the harassment I'm getting from Peter Turner?'

'We could write to his Chief Constable.'

'No, that wouldn't do any good. It might stop him for a while but he'd soon be back persecuting me.'

'I thought you had ways of dealing with people who got in your way?'

'Normally it wouldn't be a problem. Call me sentimental if you like but I can't bring myself to deal with him.'

'Have you tried to bribe him?'

'Turner is one of that rare breed, he's incorruptible.'

'I see. Well there's only one other way then.'

'What's that?' Jimmy started to look interested.

'It's something I've done before with considerable success. We'll open a bank account in Turner's name and make regular monthly payments into it. When there's a fair amount in it we'll write to the Chief Constable and let him know that one of his officers is receiving bribes.'

'Sounds easy enough. But will the Chief Constable do anything?'

'He would have to since we'd send him the bank statements and when Turner couldn't come up with an explanation he would at the least be dismissed from the force and might possibly be prosecuted.'

'Sounds ideal, but can you open a bank account in somebody else's name?'

'You can open a bank account in any name you like.'

The next day Jimmy opened a bank account in the name of Peter Turner giving the address as that of Peter's parents. He deposited £1,000 and made regular deposits of £500 every month.

With Challoner's acquittal fears of gang warfare in Liverpool were a major concern of the local police and particularly the Regional Crime Squad who had been given the task of monitoring the situation. Peter knew Spicer was still in hospital but being aware of his track record felt that he couldn't afford to be complacent. Although he suspected that things wouldn't start happening until Spicer was discharged, the squad were put on full alert.

Peter believed that Spicer would have been as disappointed as he was to have witnessed Challoner's acquittal, especially as Spicer himself had taken the trouble to set Jimmy up. He wondered if Spicer was now reflecting on the high price he had paid. He had lost Geraldine to Jimmy and also lost his leg. Peter was convinced that whatever Spicer had planned for Jimmy he would want to administer it himself.

He decided to visit Jimmy and warn him against any outbreak of violence between his organisation and Spicer's. Jimmy was undoubtedly taking the situation seriously because he had now recruited two solid looking individuals who accompanied him wherever he went. During their conversation Jimmy said, 'When are you going to give up this crusade against me? You're like a bloody praying mantis waiting to strike.'

'I've no intention of giving up until I've seen you convicted and sentenced' Peter replied.

'Oh come on. You know that's never going to happen. Why not give up while you can?'

'I trust that isn't a threat?'

'More of a promise,' said Jimmy, not smiling.

Peter wondered just what Jimmy had in mind. He would need to be extra vigilant although he found it hard to believe that Jimmy would ever condone an act of violence against him.

When Spicer was finally released from hospital Peter called on him at his home.

When Peter commented on how lovely his house was Spicer said bitterly, 'This house means nothing without Geraldine. Nothing.'

Peter's heart sank as he realised that Spicer's need for revenge was as strong as ever.

'I've seen Challoner and warned him what will happen if you two keep this aggravation going. Now I'm giving you the same warning,' Peter said.

'You could have saved yourself a trip, I've no intention of carrying anything on between Challoner and myself. I tried to set Jimmy up and he reacted in the only way he knows how. You could say I had it coming. I assure you inspector, as far as I'm concerned the incident is closed.' Spicer then struggled to stand as he said goodbye to Peter. On the drive back to Liverpool Peter felt a sense of foreboding. He had not been fooled by Spicer's apparent acceptance of the situation and he had already decided that he would need to keep a close watch on both Challoner and Spicer.

The following day Peter had just left the Liverpool Magistrates' Court and was making his way to the Bridewell in Cheapside when he met the bank manager from the local branch office. Peter stopped to speak to him.

'What brings you into the big city?' he asked, smiling at the bank manager.

'Since my promotion and transfer I'm here every day.'

'I had no idea you've moved. Congratulations anyway. Where did you move to?'

'I'm at the main Church Street branch. Surely you know that with you changing your account to my bank?'

'I think you might have made a mistake,' said Peter, 'my account is where it's always been.'

'I don't understand. It's an account in your name and what's more it's in a very healthy state.'

'Exactly how long has this account been open?' asked Peter.

'Only a few weeks. Are you suggesting that the account isn't yours?'

'I'd be grateful if you'd keep this conversation strictly confidential. Something is amiss and I need to take advice,' Peter said.

'Rest assured, anything between a bank manager and his client is always confidential.' Peter suspected he was being set up in some way and went straight to the office of his Regional Co-ordinator. He told him what he had just learned and was told in turn that the matter would now be taken over by the Co-ordinator's office.

Some time later the Regional Co-ordinator sent for Peter and told him that they had been monitoring the account and had seen James Challoner making two deposits, each of £500.

'Why haven't you arrested him for bribery?' asked Peter.

'You obviously aren't thinking straight Peter. Challoner hasn't committed any offence. Anyone can open a bank account in any name that he chooses.'

'What's he playing at?'

'We'll just have to wait and see,' replied the Co-ordinator. Some weeks later Peter was visited at his office by a uniformed superintendent who informed him that he had been ordered by the Chief Constable to investigate an allegation that Peter had been receiving sums of money from a criminal source.

'Where's the information come from?' Peter asked.

'Well the original information came from an anonymous letter, but the rest I've checked on,' the superintendent said.

'I think it best if you have a word with my Regional Co-ordinator, he'll be able to tell you more about this.'

Several days later Peter was again summoned to the superintendent's office and told that once the circumstances surrounding the bank account had been confirmed by the Regional Co-ordinator the superintendent had interviewed Challoner. He had denied writing the anonymous letter and although he admitted opening an account in Peter's name he claimed it was to avoid the attentions of the Inland Revenue. The superintendent explained to Peter that Challoner couldn't be charged as they had no evidence to support a criminal offence. It was a very relieved Detective Inspector who sat in his office and reflected back on the chance meeting with his bank manager. Any explanation he gave would not have been believed especially once the superintendent's investigations revealed the relationship that he and Jimmy had had as boys. It would have been suggested that Challoner's acquittals at court were due to Peter's influence in return for cash payments. Peter knew that his promising career would have come to an abrupt end.

14

The visit by the police superintendent left Jimmy feeling uneasy. He was at a loss to know how the police had known it was him who had opened and deposited cash in the account. He had been so taken aback at the visit that he had only been able to give a hurriedly made up story about evading the income tax in answer to why he had opened the account. Thinking it through he decided that it must have been Peter who somehow found out about the account. Peter was becoming a force to be reckoned with and the thought didn't please Jimmy one bit.

Jimmy thought that it was high time that the direction and shape of the syndicate was thought through. He was happy with the start they had made, the cash from the break in had been invested legitimately, through John Wakefield, into a property development company and was showing signs of being very rewarding. The organisation was still providing a service to the clubs and dance halls but it wasn't giving Jimmy the challenges he sought. He still craved excitement and his mind turned to the avenues of crime that he could exploit.

During a discussion with Mick Walsh about the future of the syndicate the craze that was sweeping the country was mentioned. It was 1968 and in addition to 'Beatlemania,' which had the country's youth in its grip, there was pot. 'Everyone seems to be using it, hippies, youngsters, we should get involved,' Mick suggested to Jimmy.

'What you mean?' said Jimmy.

'Well since the early sixties a lot of youngsters have been smoking hashish. The drugs have to be smuggled into the country so the suppliers are making a fortune.'

'What the hell is hashish anyway?'

'It's what they call cannabis or marijuana, it's like tobacco only stronger and the kids hallucinate on it. Tripping out they call it.'

Jimmy's brain was starting to kick into action, 'You say these drugs have to be smuggled into the country from abroad, but what do we know about that sort of operation?' asked Jimmy.

'We learn, we take over what's already been started. According to my enquiries Liverpool's drug scene is managed by those two Spenser brothers and I reckon we should muscle in.'

'You mean that pair of black lads we had to put the frighteners on over Spicer's girls?'

'The very same, they're only into it in a small way but everything they bring in the country sells very quickly,' Mick said.

'Are these drugs dangerous?'

'Probably but we're going to supply them not take them. Don't start getting a conscience, if we don't someone else will.'

'Yeah right. OK set up a meeting with the Spensers.'

It had been twelve months since the shooting incident involving Spicer and Jimmy was puzzled that no revenge attack had been mounted. On the contrary, Spicer had been busy expanding his interests in club ownership and developing his property business. It was as though his involvement in a myriad of criminal activities had never been. He had completely abandoned his control over the prostitution racket and apart from handling stolen property through his network his only other unlawful activity was the gambling casino which barely rated the description of criminal.

Jimmy had been surprised by this reaction of Spicer's and at first he had been guarded and suspicious. Eventually he began to believe that maybe Spicer had given up the stress and danger of his criminal life. This belief led him to move into the Blundellsands house on a permanent basis.

His naturally suspicious nature meant that Jimmy was not entirely convinced that Spicer had given up all thought of revenge. It made him uneasy that Spicer hadn't released any of his syndicate members. This bothered Jimmy since he knew full well how Spicer detested employing staff who were not fully employed.

Since Jimmy was keeping such a close eye on Spicer he couldn't fail to admire the way in which Spicer had risen to the challenge of his disability. In a short space of time, through intense personal effort, Spicer had graduated from crutches to an artificial leg. Jimmy told himself that it was perhaps because of the way in which Spicer had adapted to his artificial leg that he had decided to close the incident between Jimmy and himself.

Although he remained watchful for any signs of possible aggression from the Spicer camp Jimmy did become sufficiently relaxed to start taking Geraldine out in public. The first major social occasion they attended together was the Mayor's annual charity ball, ironically the same event at which Jimmy had vowed to take Geraldine from Spicer the year before. At first Jimmy had a certain amount of difficulty persuading Geraldine to attend the ball.

'I just don't know if I can do it, Tony is sure to be there.'

'It doesn't matter whether he's there or not, we don't have to have anything to do with him.'

'In all honesty it won't be easy, I haven't seen him since his accident.'

'I really don't know what you're worrying for. Look it's something I have to go to and I'm fed up with going to these functions on my own.'

On the night of the ball Geraldine remained apprehensive about a possible meeting with Spicer. Jimmy waited downstairs for her while she tried on and then discarded most of her wardrobe. Finally she was satisfied and the look on Jimmy's face confirmed that the choice of her favourite little black dress had been the right one. Jimmy stood up as she entered the room, 'Going somewhere?' he laughed. Geraldine started to laugh and the tension between them vanished as Jimmy took her in his arms and kissed her gently on her mouth. 'See, there's nothing to worry about.'

'Unless you take that lipstick off I think there might be.'

The evening passed without incident and when Spicer came over to their table the conversation flowed naturally. 'How about coming to the opening of my new club next Saturday,' Spicer said 'no use bearing grudges and I can promise you a good night.'

'We'd love to come wouldn't we?' Jimmy said turning to Geraldine.

'Yes, we would and I'm so pleased your clubs are doing well Tony,' Geraldine smiled.

'Great, I'll send you a couple of tickets in the post,' Spicer said before returning to his own table.

'I think you may be right, I think Tony has buried the hatchet.'

'He knows when he's beat,' Jimmy said, trying to hide what he really felt. He had sensed that Spicer hadn't forgiven or forgotten anything and instinct warned him that he would be wise to be on his guard. Even so he wasn't going to let Spicer spoil this first night out with Geraldine. He was determined to make the night memorable for her and masked his unease for her sake.

Shortly after the ball Mick Walsh arranged for the two Spenser brothers to meet Jimmy at the Admiral. Jimmy raised an eyebrow as he watched them arrive with a squeal of brakes in their flashy American car wearing expensive but equally flashy suits. It must be true thought Jimmy, Mick was right when he had said these Spenser boys were coining it in. Mick had already explained to them about the syndicate's interest in the drugs scene and how they were anxious to help them to expand their business interests. Once they were all seated in the back room of the Admiral, Winston the elder of the two brothers and, in Jimmy's opinion, the brains of the outfit, was asked to explain how they operated.

'Once a month Desmond or myself flies to Nigeria where one of our cousins has a suitcase of hashish ready for us to bring back to Liverpool. We break it down into deals which we sell in the coffee bars and pubs.'

'Don't you ever get stopped by customs?'

'Not so far, they only seem to be interested in flights from the continent.'

'What sort of profit are you clearing?'

'About £1,000 a month after expenses.'

'What do you reckon the potential market is in Liverpool?'

'I think it's infinite,' Winston shrugged, 'We can't satisfy anything like the demand we have.'

'I think that with my help and backing you could expand this business beyond your wildest dreams, are you interested?' Jimmy looked directly at Winston, but it was Desmond who replied.

'We don't want anything to do with your organisation, we're doing nicely on our own.'

'Hold on brother. I think we should consider this before we make any decisions.'

'Your brother's making sense. Go away and think about it. But think on this too, with or without you I'm going into the drugs business and you know better than most what happens to people who get in my way,' Jimmy's voice was soft but the threat was unmistakeable.

'Right, let's meet again at this time tomorrow,' Winston said as he rose to usher his brother out of the pub before he did something to upset what he considered a very good offer. Winston had already foreseen the possibilities for expansion under Challoner, but he had no illusions as to who would be in control. That night Winston talked Desmond into accepting the proposed merger.

The next day he told Jimmy that they accepted his offer and they sat down and discussed how the operation would function. Jimmy told Winston that he had already appointed several couriers from his own organisation who were standing by to fly to Africa.

'I think we should seriously consider other avenues for importing this drug into the country,' Jimmy said.

'What other avenues? More couriers?'

'Not necessarily, I think we should diversify, doesn't do to put all your eggs in one basket.'

'Well I understand that but I don't know of any other way to bring the drugs in.'

'We need to import in bulk so surely we can capitalise on all the trade there is between Africa and Liverpool.'

'Sounds good but doing it is another matter.'

'Leave it with me,' Jimmy said, 'there must be a way, it's just finding it.' He considered a variety of methods but none proved feasible until one day the means of bringing the drugs into Liverpool presented itself to him quite by accident.

It was while he was at home with Geraldine and their next door neighbour, Jean, called to ask them if they would take delivery of a packing case that was expected from Kenya. Jean's husband was still in Kenya where they had both lived until recently. When they had decided to return to England Jean had come on ahead to reopen their home while her husband tied up the loose ends of his business interests. Geraldine said that of course she would take the case and a couple of hours later the delivery firm dropped off a large packing case. Jimmy was intrigued and immediately read the consignment note that had been left with the case. It stated that the contents of the case were the personal effects of Mr and Mrs Blake. On Jean's return Jimmy carried the case round to her house and casually asked her if sending items in this way was straightforward. Jean insisted that it was the simplest method of transporting anything they had found.

'What about customs, you surely don't want them rummaging through your personal items.'

'We've found that they never seem to bother checking the contents. The paperwork seems to be all they're interested in.'

That evening Jimmy went over the idea of using the same method to import drugs and decided he had found a workable system. He telephoned Winston, told him what he had decided and they arranged to meet the following morning.

At the meeting the next day Jimmy told Winston that he should fly to Nigeria himself and arrange for the drugs to be crated and consigned to Mr John Bolton at 32 Woodyear Road, Atherton, Liverpool. He was to telephone Jimmy as soon as the drugs were loaded with full details of the ship's name and its date of arrival in Liverpool. In the meantime Jimmy would arrange with his former workmates on the docks to off-load the crate and place it to one side until it was collected by one of the syndicate. With everything arranged Winston left for Africa.

Jimmy felt a growing sense of unease about the invitation to the opening of Spicer's new club. In a reversal of roles Geraldine persuaded him to go.

'I think you're worrying about nothing, look how Tony was at the Mayor's Ball,' Geraldine said putting her arm round Jimmy's shoulder as she sat on the arm of his chair.

'I just have this gut feeling that something's afoot and I don't want you involved if it is.'

'Well I shouldn't think Tony will mar the grand opening to indulge in scrapping with you.'

'I guess that's right although I've played safe by not ordering a car for tonight. I thought we'd ring for a taxi.'

'No don't do that. I'd love to drive. It will be a good opportunity to take my new car out and I'm quite happy to stick to orange juice.'

Spicer's new club was at the opposite end of the city to the River Club and was called the Mersey Club. The style was opulent. It was clear to Jimmy as he made his way through the foyer that Spicer had spared no expense on the launch of his new 'baby.'

In spite of his misgivings Jimmy enjoyed the evening and was pleased to see that Geraldine was relaxed and enjoying herself. As the other guests started to drift towards the door around midnight Jimmy asked Geraldine if she was ready to leave.

'I'm ready,' she said, 'but I'm glad we came Jimmy, it's been a wonderful night.'

As Jimmy was helping Geraldine into her coat Spicer strolled over to them. 'I must apologise for not coming over earlier but things have been hectic. I do hope you enjoyed yourselves.'

'We've had a lovely time Tony,' Geraldine said.

'Yeah, nice place, let's hope it stays that way.' Spicer chose to ignore the implied threat and said 'Is your car waiting or can I call you a taxi?'

'I'm driving thank you and my car is parked just by the door,' Geraldine replied.

'Which way will you go?'

'I think I'll take the route along Stanley Road and through Crosby.'

'I thought you might be doing that,' Spicer said, 'The reason I asked is that I believe there's been a serious accident along Stanley Road and the road will be closed for a while yet.'

'In that case I'll take the Dock Road. There isn't much difference in either route but thanks for warning us.'

'I wonder what the hell that was about,' Jimmy said as they walked away.

'What do you mean?'

'Why was Spicer so interested in our travel arrangements?'

'Because of the accident of course. Come on Jimmy, you're becoming paranoid.'

'I'm not so sure about that,' Jimmy said lowering himself into the passenger seat.

As they drove off Jimmy said, 'You know I'm still not sure about Tony, he seems friendly enough but ....'

'Let's not talk about him, did you enjoy yourself?'

'Always do when I'm with you.'

'I love you so much,' Geraldine said glancing towards Jimmy.

'And I love you Geraldine,' Jimmy paused, 'Will you marry me?'

'Is that a proposal Jimmy?' Geraldine laughed.

'It's the best I can do in a car.

'Then I accept but I shall expect something more formal when we get home,'

'No problem, just ...,' Jimmy never finished what he was going to say. Geraldine screamed and he looked up to see a lorry driving directly towards them. He felt the car swerve as Geraldine turned the car away from the oncoming lorry. Then the crash of metal on metal filled his head as the lorry ploughed into them.

'Peter, wake up, the telephone's ringing,' Jean Turner said giving her husband a shake.

'What? The telephone. Who on earth?' Peter said as he attempted to wake himself up.

'It's probably the office. Go and answer it quickly before it wakes the children,' Jean said.

'I don't know why the hell the force won't pay for a bedroom extension. It's usually the middle of the night when they call,' Peter said as he made his way to the hall where the telephone's shrill tone echoed eerily in the darkness.

'Yes?'

'Inspector Turner?'

'Yes,' said Peter struggling to wake.

'Sorry to disturb you sir. The night detective, Constable Taylor, has asked me to inform you of an accident that has just occurred on the Dock Road,' the control room officer said.

'Not one of my squad?'

'No sir, it involved a car and a lorry.'

'Then why the hell are you calling me, don't you need the traffic inspector?'

'DC Taylor thought that you'd want to know that the occupants of the car were Jimmy Challoner and his girlfriend.'

Immediately alarm bells started ringing in Peter's brain and he understood why the night detective had made sure that he was told.

'How bad?'

'The women's dead and Challoner's not expected to live.'

'Tell Taylor I'll meet him at the scene. You'd better give me the exact location.'

Having made sure where the accident had taken place Peter explained what had happened to Jean as he dressed.

'Good morning sir,' said DC Taylor as Peter approached the mangled remains of Geraldine's white BMW.

'Good morning Bill, this looks quite a mess.'

DC Taylor was on the third night of his week as night detective. Liverpool City Police had begun the night duty detective roster two years ago. Each detective throughout the force had to take a weekly turn at being on duty between 10pm and 6am. The duty only came round about twice a year and the whole of the CID liked the scheme. It meant that the night detective would deal with all routine CID matters and the arrest of prisoners during the night, eliminating the need for divisional detectives to be called out of bed.

'I thought you would want to know,' Bill Taylor said.

'Yes, thanks for the call. You obviously don't have it down as a routine traffic accident then?'

'No I don't. The lorry didn't stop and has been abandoned half a mile away, I've discovered it was stolen from a haulier's yard in Bootle.'

'No traces of the driver I suppose?'

'No such luck, but if you examine the scene the only skid marks are from the BMW. The lorry made no attempt to brake and was definitely on the wrong side of the road. I'm sure this was a deliberate act intended to kill or seriously injure Challoner,' Bill Taylor said pointing out the skid marks made by the BMW.

'I think you're right. Who was driving?'

'The woman and if she hadn't swerved they would both have been killed.'

'Just how bad is Challoner?'

'Very bad sir, he has internal injuries and is not expected to make it through the night.' Peter made sure Taylor had covered everything that he needed to at the scene of the accident and then went with him to examine the stolen lorry. As he had expected the lorry had been wiped clean of all fingerprint evidence. Peter was sure now that this was not an accident enquiry. They were looking at a murder enquiry. Peter's next task was to go to the hospital to find out what had happened to Jimmy. The report wasn't good and when Peter discovered that Mr and Mrs Challoner hadn't been contacted he went to tell them himself. They were devastated at the news, especially to hear that Geraldine had been killed.

After taking the shocked couple to the hospital, where they began their vigil at Jimmy's bedside, Peter returned to the Crime Squad office. He tried to puzzle out what had happened and where Jimmy and Geraldine had been that evening. It certainly hadn't been the Admiral. While the pub was on the Dock Road it was beyond the scene of the accident. Besides Peter knew that Jimmy would never have taken Geraldine there. He reasoned that since the accident had been stage managed someone had known that they would be driving along the Dock Road and more to the point they knew exactly when. He didn't have to stretch his imagination too far to come up with Spicer's name. Like everyone else he had been lulled into a false sense of security over the feud between Spicer and Challoner. Twelve months had passed since the shooting and although the peace was an uneasy one, Peter had hoped that with the passage of time it would prove to be a permanent one. How wrong he had been and how crafty Spicer had been to fool everyone, including it seemed Challoner himself. Peter was convinced that it was Spicer who had arranged the accident, but one nagging doubt disturbed him. He was sure that Spicer would have had no compunction about killing Jimmy, but would he really be prepared to kill or harm Geraldine? Perhaps, thought Peter, his need for revenge had extended towards Geraldine too. All that Peter had to do now was to prove the case was murder and the murder had been arranged by Spicer.

At eight o'clock that Sunday morning Peter Turner called in the members of the Regional Crime Squad and briefed them as to what had happened. He told them they must discover exactly where Challoner had been the previous night and suggested that Mick Walsh would probably be a good source of information. His next task was to arrange for one of his squad to wait at Challoner's bedside in the hope that should he regain consciousness, even momentarily. He may just say something to help them with their enquiries. The rest of the squad were sent to the Admiral and to the homes of the known members of the organisation. Peter went to see Mick Walsh. Walsh lived with his girlfriend in a new block of luxury flats in Crosby. He answered the knock on the door bleary eyed and dishevelled.

'What the hell do you want at this time in the morning?'

'I've got some bad news.'

'You'd better come in, I don't want to give the neighbours anything to tittle tattle about,' Mick said as he opened the door to let Peter pass.

'Early this morning Jimmy and Geraldine were involved in a traffic accident on the Dock Road. I need to know where they had been.'

'Accident? Are they alright?' Walsh was suddenly wide awake.

'Geraldine is dead, Jimmy's not expected to make it.'

'No it can't be true.'

'I'm afraid it is true. Where did Jimmy go last night, do you know?'

'They went to the opening of Spicer's new club in town.'

'Are you sure they intended to go to Spicer's club?'

'Yes, Jimmy wasn't keen but Geraldine wanted to go so he went to please her.' Mick paused and then went on, 'Was it Spicer who fixed this?'

'We don't know the full facts of the accident yet but we believe it was a deliberate act.'

'It was no accident, I'll bet the other vehicle was nicked wasn't it?'

'Yes the lorry involved was stolen.'

'It's got to be Spicer, his name is written all over this one.'

'I must warn you that this enquiry is being investigated by the police and I don't want you or any of your organisation getting involved.'

'You've no chance proving anything against Spicer and if Jimmy dies I'll see to Spicer.'

Peter returned to the squad office where all the squad members confirmed the fact that Jimmy had been to the opening of Spicer's new club. It was now beginning to make sense. Spicer would have known exactly what time Jimmy and Geraldine left the club. All that would have been necessary would have been a telephone call to the lorry driver to say that they were on their way. It was time to interview Spicer and Peter decided that the interview would take place at the police station. He sent two of his squad to pick Spicer up. Before the officers arrived back at the station with Spicer, Peter was informed that Hanlon, Spicer's solicitor, had arrived and was asking to see him.

'Good morning Inspector, I understand you have arrested my client Mr Spicer.'

'You understand incorrectly, Mr Spicer has been invited to the police station to assist me with my enquiries into a case of murder.'

'Murder?'

'Murder set up to look like a traffic accident.'

'And just when did this alleged act of murder take place?'

'At approximately twelve thirty am this morning.'

'In that case I fail to see why Mr Spicer has been sent for. I can verify, along with a number of people of some standing in this area, he was at his new club,' Hanlon said.

'Well I wouldn't expect Spicer to do his own dirty work, but he will have arranged it.'

'I would advise you to exercise a little caution before you say any more Inspector.'

'For the record Hanlon an innocent woman was killed in the accident so don't you tell me what I can or can't say. I know your client arranged this so called accident and I'm going to do my damndest to prove it.'

'I want to see my client before you question him.'

'You can see him when I say you can and not before,' Peter said and started to walk away from him.

'Inspector, I will report your conduct to your Chief Constable,' Hanlon shouted at the retreating back of Inspector Turner. Peter learned that Spicer had arrived and was in the interview room. He made his way to the room and found Spicer sitting behind a table on one of the two chairs that completed the furnishings.

'Inspector, why have I been brought here?' Spicer asked.

'You are here to answer questions about a fatal road accident which occurred on the Dock Road earlier today,' Peter replied.

'A fatal traffic accident, what can that have to do with me? Surely you realise that since my own accident I don't drive anymore.'

'Well for a start this accident was no accident, it was a deliberate act of murder.'

'I still don't understand why I'm being questioned about something I know nothing about.'

'Are you aware who was involved in this accident?'

'No idea at all, why should I have?'

'I think you know very well but for the record I'll tell you that it was Jimmy Challoner and Geraldine Graham,' said Peter watching Spicer intently for even the slightest reaction. Spicer didn't blink.

'How did the accident happen?' he asked.

'They were hit head on by a stolen lorry which failed to stop.'

'I'm sorry to hear that Geraldine was killed, but I can't pretend to be similarly disturbed by news of Challoner's demise.'

'I haven't said who was killed,' Peter said watching the colour drain from Spicer's face.

'Oh I just presumed they had both been killed. Are you saying Geraldine is still alive?'

'No, she was killed, but Challoner is still alive.'

Spicer had now gone white as the realisation of what Peter was saying sank in. Geraldine was dead but Challoner was still alive. In spite of a lengthy interview Spicer said nothing to incriminate himself in any way and Peter reluctantly was forced to let him leave the police station.

After a long day at the office analysing what small amount of evidence he had Peter called it a day and drove wearily home. No sooner had he arrived than the telephone rang. It was the detective at the hospital to tell him that Challoner had regained consciousness. Peter went immediately to the hospital where he found Jimmy's parents. He felt for them, the shock of their only son's accident seemed to have aged them in the space of a few hours.

'Have you seen him?' Peter asked.

'Yes, but he's so poorly Peter,' sobbed Mrs Challoner. Peter put his arm round her frail shoulders and said, 'Your Jimmy's a strong lad, if anyone can make it he will.'

'Yes I think you're right and Jimmy is a fighter, but nothing can bring poor Geraldine back,' she said, tears streaming down her face. Peter patted her arm saying, 'I'll just see if he can speak to me' and left them outside the side ward while he approached Jimmy's bedside. The nurse told him he could only stay for a few minutes as Jimmy was very weak. Peter didn't waste time.

'What happened Jimmy?' he asked, pulling up a chair so he was close to Jimmy's face.

'I don't know. Geraldine was driving and I heard her scream. I looked up and saw this lorry bearing down on us. There was a crash, Peter I can't remember anything else.' Jimmy's voice was barely audible as he strained to speak, 'Geraldine, where's Geraldine? no one will tell me anything. Do you know anything Peter, for pity's sake tell me if you do?'

'Geraldine's dead, I'm sorry mate. She didn't suffer, it was quick.'

Jimmy cried silently, tears coursing down his face and Peter was transported back through the years. For a few moments Jimmy was just his boyhood friend again and Peter shared his pain. A few minutes later the doctor on duty came to Jimmy's bedside and asked Peter to leave. Outside the ward he said, 'I'd meant to warn you not to tell Mr Challoner that his girlfriend is dead, but I gather I'm too late.'

'Why don't you want him to know?' asked Peter.

'To be honest we felt that he might lose the impetus to carry on if he knew.'

'Oh believe me, the contrary will be the case with Jimmy.'

'Well I hope you're right because his own strength of will is all that will save him.'

Peter left the hospital reassured. If the difference between life and death for Jimmy was his mental attitude, he was convinced that Jimmy wouldn't allow himself to die. Not with such a personal score to settle.

15

One of the first things that Jimmy Challoner remembered after the warning scream from Geraldine was waking in hospital to find Peter Turner at his bedside. He had wanted to know about the accident but even more he had wanted to know about Geraldine. He had vague memories of asking the nurse and the doctor and of being fobbed off with platitudes. Jimmy knew that in spite of all that had happened he would be given the truth from Peter. The news that Geraldine was dead was like a physical blow and he was grateful to Peter for his instinctive understanding.

Jimmy felt guilty. He knew that Geraldine had deliberately swerved the car so that her side would receive the brunt of the impact and in doing so had saved his life at the expense of her own. He remembered gripping Peter's hand so hard that the pain from his own injured hand was agonising. Wanting to suffer in some small way for what he had allowed to happen to Geraldine. After Peter had left the ward with the doctor the temptation to lie back and just die was almost too great. The one thing that kept him alive was the knowledge that Geraldine had sacrificed her life for him. There was no way he was going to let her death go unavenged. He was satisfied that he knew who was responsible for Geraldine's death and his mind went back to the last conversation they had with Spicer. Spicer must pay for Geraldine's death.

In spite of protests from the hospital that he was not well enough to go to Geraldine's funeral, Jimmy refused to listen. John Wakefield had made all the arrangements and had contacted Geraldine's parents. On their arrival in Liverpool they visited Jimmy in hospital and met him for the first time. 'I'm so sorry we have to meet like this,' said Mrs Graham, tears filling her deep blue eyes that were so reminiscent of Geraldine's, ' we want you to know Jimmy that Geraldine had never been happier than she was in these last months with you.'

'I just don't know how I'll manage without her, we were going to marry you know. I proposed to her just before she died.' Jimmy's voice trailed off and he fell into a fitful sleep while the Grahams sat beside his bed drawing comfort from this last link with their daughter.

Jimmy attended the funeral travelling first by ambulance and then by wheelchair. It was a miracle the doctors had said that he had not broken any bones in the accident. Although very weak he followed the coffin into the small church for Geraldine's funeral only giving way to tears of despair when he tried to stand but failed. It was Sam who stepped forward at this point to push the wheelchair and Jimmy saw his own grief mirrored in Sam's stricken face. The church was full but even so Jimmy noticed Peter amongst the throng of mourners. He wondered whether Peter was present in his official capacity or as a friend for old times sake. His mind strayed back to the hospital ward when Peter had shown him such kindness and he wished that their paths had not taken such diverse directions. That the gulf between them was not so wide.

After the service Jimmy went straight back to the hospital ward. The funeral had exhausted him and he craved the solitude of his hospital bed where he could be alone with his grief. As he was being helped into the ambulance Sam knelt beside the wheelchair. 'Jimmy, I know what you're thinking but promise me one thing. Before you take any action against Spicer come and see me first. Don't forget that I loved her too,' he whispered. Jimmy looked up and nodded, too heartbroken to speak.

Once Jimmy had made the decision to live he astounded the medical staff with the speed of his recovery. He was discharged from hospital three weeks after Geraldine's funeral and returned to his flat in Sefton Park. Jimmy was well aware that the Liverpool underworld were expecting him to blast Spicer's brains out, but although thoughts of revenge were uppermost in his head, Jimmy knew that he must be patient.

He made arrangements for the house in Blundellsands to be cared for until he decided what he was going to do with it. For the present it held too many painful memories.

He returned to work and was reassured by Mick Walsh that everything was running smoothly. Winston Spenser had sent the first consignment of drugs from Lagos and they had arrived in Liverpool just one week ago. The arrangements at the docks had gone like clockwork and the collection had taken place without any undue attention from the authorities. The half ton load had been dispersed to users through Desmond Spenser and they had made a clear profit of £150,000.

Within a few days of Jimmy's return to work Winston arrived back in

Liverpool and informed Jimmy that he had arranged for a weekly delivery of half a ton of cannabis to be shipped from Lagos to Liverpool. Added to this regular supply was the suitcase full of cannabis which the couriers brought in weekly and yet even so the demand was not being met. Jimmy, not being keen to work to a regular pattern, called Winston and Mick to the Admiral to discuss what further methods could be used to import the drugs.

'Why change a winning system. It's established now and everybody knows what they're doing?, Winston said.

'How long do you think it will take for Customs to wonder why so many people are shipping their belongings from Lagos to Liverpool' Jimmy asked.

'You're right, no sense in going on too long,' agreed Mick.

'Exactly, we can't afford to work to an obvious pattern so we must think up some other ways of importing the stuff,' Jimmy said standing and stretching himself. 'Anyone want another drink?' Both declined the offer and Winston said, 'It might be a good idea if you and I visit Lagos to see what opportunities there are at that end to ship the drugs out.'

'I might just do that,' Jimmy said 'I could do with a holiday, but first I must do something I've been putting off for far too long.'

Remembering the promise that he had made to Sam at the funeral Jimmy decided that he must drive to Leeds to hear what Sam had to say. They met in the lounge of the Queens Hotel. Sam greeted him warmly and said, 'I'm so glad that you came to see me before taking any action against Spicer Jimmy.'

'I said I would.'

'What happened to Geraldine was tragic and definitely out of order.'

'You're so right.'

'I don't underestimate what you must be feeling. I loved her too and that's why I want you to let me deal with Spicer.'

'No way, Spicer's mine. This is going to cost him his life.'

'Just because Spicer let his personal feelings cloud his judgement I don't want you making the same mistake.'

'You're not suggesting I let Spicer get away with this are you?'

'Yes in a way I am.'

'Forget it.'

'Look Jimmy, I owe you my life for what you did for me at Aintree and it goes without saying what Geraldine meant to me. Let me repay you both by taking care of Spicer myself.'

'I know what you're trying to say but no, this is just something I've got to do myself.'

'Think about it,' Sam reasoned, 'Everyone is waiting for you to make your move. You'll be arrested in no time. Spicer's still got some very important people in his pocket and they're ready and waiting for you to act. What good will a life behind bars do you?'

'I'll have the satisfaction of knowing I killed Spicer that's good enough for me.'

'Spicer will still be taken out, you have my word on that but with one difference, you won't be involved. Let me as your friend do this one for you Jimmy.'

'It won't matter who kills the bastard, I'm always going to be the number one suspect so I might as well do it myself.'

'No we'll arrange for you to be out of the country. You must have a water tight alibi and so must all your organisation.'

'How will you do it? I'd want to know that he was going to suffer.'

'We can deal with him and it won't be pleasant I can assure you.'

'Alright Sam, I must admit what you say makes sense. I've been arranging a trip to Africa so I'll bring it forward and go next week.'

'Perfect and now arrange with Mick for all your syndicate to be together during the entire evening ten days from now.' Jimmy said that he would and shook hands with Sam as though sealing a business agreement.

On his return from Leeds Jimmy briefed Mick Walsh exactly as Sam had requested and then met Winston Spenser.

I've decided to take a little holiday before meeting up with you in Lagos. I'll be leaving next week, any ideas where I should go?'

'Only one place I'd go, Mombassa in Kenya,' Winston replied. Taking Winston's advice Jimmy made a reservation for one week at the White Sands Hotel in Mombassa. He left Manchester Airport four days later. Exactly ten days after his conversation with Sam, Jimmy Challoner threw a party for his fellow guests at the hotel making certain that everyone of them would be able to vouch for his presence.

The following week he met Winston in Lagos. He also met Winston's large extended family who were all only too eager to assure him that they could supply all the ganga, cannabis, that he could take. It seemed that all the farmers in the region were now committed to growing this most lucrative of weeds.

'I want you to come down to the docks with me tomorrow. I think I may have found what we've been looking for,' Winston said.

'You sound pleased with yourself, have you found a new angle on things?'

'I think so but I'd like you to see it for yourself.'

The next morning they went down to the dockside where Winston pointed out a ship being loaded with sacks of cargo.

'See those sacks? They contain cocoa beans being shipped to Liverpool.'

'Right, I think I know what you have in mind. How often do these ships visit Liverpool?'

'This is one of three that make the trip regularly.'

'What enquiries have you made this end?'

'No problems here. I've seen the loaders and for a backhander they will load a few extra sacks.'

Jimmy said nothing for a moment, he thought over Winston's idea. It was a good idea and he had to admit, Winston had impressed him.

'It looks promising. We'll have no trouble at our end, I can arrange for the sacks we're interested in to be looked after. I like this one Winston, let's go for it!'

'Well the ship will take about three to four weeks to reach Liverpool so we might as well start right away.'

'How many sacks of cannabis do you intend shipping?'

'I thought about a ton at a time. I reckon we can get it into twenty sacks.'

'A ton every three weeks. Are you confident we can shift that amount, I don't want to be stuck with the stuff?'

'Well let that be the least of your worries because we can get rid of that amount in Liverpool alone. I've been considering expansion to other cities like Manchester and Birmingham. What do you think?'

'Listen I'm happy to leave this one to you, you seem to know what you're doing,' Jimmy said giving Winston a hearty slap on the back to show his approval. Jimmy made travel arrangements to return to Liverpool to supervise the arrival of the cannabis when it reached its destination. He was also interested to learn of Tony Spicer's fate. If it had gone as he expected there would be some serious re-organising to be undertaken. He would need to establish himself as head of Spicer's organisation and the sooner he did that, the easier life would be.

When Jimmy Challoner was discharged from hospital Peter Turner ordered his squad to keep surveillance on him and Tony Spicer. He fully expected that Jimmy would take his revenge as soon as he had the chance. Much to his surprise Jimmy merely settled back into his old routine. He moved back into his Sefton Park flat and did very little other than travel between the flat and the Admiral. The squad had been surprised at the association that had sprung up between Jimmy and the Spenser brothers. Peter instinctively knew that this relationship spelled trouble. It was unheard of for the city's white and black criminals to mix. Knowing Jimmy as he did he guessed that the Spensers were providing Jimmy with something that he couldn't get anywhere else. Peter knew that finding out what the Spensers were up to was vital. As far as he knew they were minor criminals who ran one or two little rackets in the black quarter.

The surveillance on Jimmy and Spicer wasn't achieving very much but on the other hand it might just be preventing the two factions coming to blows. Peter decided that he would continue it for the time being. Over the next weeks the squad followed Jimmy to Leeds and witnessed his meeting with Samuel Jacobs, described by the Leeds crime squad as their most notable criminal. This piece of intelligence was placed in Challoner's target file. Days after his return from Leeds the squad watched Jimmy depart from Manchester Airport bound for Kenya and Nigeria. Peter wondered whether the trip to Africa and Jimmy's growing association with the Spenser brothers were connected. It didn't take Peter long to come to the conclusion that the recent influx of drugs into the city was the link between them.

During Jimmy's temporary absence from the country Peter heard of the apparent suicide of Tony Spicer. He was told that the body of Spicer had been found by a milkman at five thirty am at the foot of the block of flats in Everton. He asked for the official police report which he read and found it suggested there were no suspicious circumstances surrounding the death and the case was being dealt with as suicide.

'Bugger suicide,' Peter said aloud. He lifted the telephone on his desk and dialled the number of the Detective Inspector who had reported the death.

'Tom, Peter Turner here, I'm interested in the alleged suicide of Tony Spicer.'

'Nothing alleged about it, it's a straight up and down suicide,' Tom Watson replied.

'You do know the history of Spicer don't you and the business with Challoner?'

'Yes of course I do. But I also know that Challoner's in Africa so that even if the death was suspicious, which it isn't, it can't be pinned on Challoner.'

'I can't see Spicer taking his own life. What are the circumstances?'

'The circumstances are straightforward. He jumped from the balcony of the tenth floor where we found several cigarette ends. He had probably been up there some time, maybe just trying to get his nerve up. There are no witnesses of course and no note, but the post mortem only revealed injuries consistent with a fall. As far as I'm concerned, suicide it is.'

It didn't make sense. It could be argued that he was finding life difficult with his disability, but in reality Spicer gave every appearance of having adapted to his prosthetic limb exceptionally well. No Peter thought, it has got to be murder. 'Tom, I think Spicer was thrown from the balcony, he didn't jump of his own accord.'

'You can think what you like, it's going down as suicide. I'm not having an undetected murder on my books because even if you were right this job was done by a professional and we'd have no chance of clearing it up.'

'All the same I'm not happy that the case isn't even going to be investigated.'

'Look Peter, this is a divisional matter, nothing for the squad to get excited about. Why don't you concentrate on something else?' Tom said, hanging up on him. Peter replaced the handset and knew that whoever had killed Spicer was going to get away with it. It was clear Tom Watson was taking the easy way out and treating the death as suicide. He knew from the surveillance log that his squad had completed for the previous evening that Mick Walsh and all the remainder of Challoner's organisation were alibied. Whoever had murdered Spicer didn't come from Liverpool. Peter knew it would be impossible for him to make his own enquiries and Tom Watson had made it clear enough that he didn't want or need the assistance of the Regional Crime Squad.

Peter found that he was the only police officer in Liverpool who didn't accept Spicer's death as suicide. He came to the conclusion that this must be the perfect murder. He was certain that somehow Challoner was behind it but he had been very clever and had distanced not only himself but his entire organisation from the incident. He suspected that Challoner's meeting with Jacobs in Leeds had some bearing on the case but he knew that any enquiries that he made would have to be very discreet. If it became known that he was asking questions he would be in serious trouble. Even so Peter felt that he couldn't allow the matter to drop without some investigation. He had requested from Leeds branch of the RCS a copy of their file on Samuel Jacobs and after reading through the contents he was more convinced than ever that Jacobs was linked in some way with Spicer's death. Looking at Jacob's photograph Peter felt that he had seen him before and after a couple of minutes it dawned on him that he had been one of the mourners at Geraldine's funeral. Any doubts that Peter had about Jacob's involvement in Spicer's death evaporated. It made perfect sense. With Jimmy out of the country and the rest of the syndicate completely alibied they were beyond suspicion. How typical of Jimmy thought Peter to plan a murder with such ingenuity and imagination. Even though Peter was absolutely certain that Spicer had met his death at the hands of Jacobs or more likely a member of his syndicate, he was fully aware that he had no chance of proving it and kept it to himself.

Returning to Liverpool Jimmy Challoner went immediately to see John Wakefield his solicitor. As always Jimmy was ushered in to see the solicitor straightaway. Wakefield stood as Jimmy entered, 'Nice to see you again Jimmy. You certainly look well, the holiday has done you good.'

'Yes I feel much better than I did a few weeks ago.'

'John, I want you to arrange for me to buy the River Club. I take it that since Spicer's untimely death it will be up for sale.'

'I had an idea you'd be interested in that particular property so I've already spoken to Hanlon about buying it.'

Jimmy was impressed, he liked the way Wakefield anticipated events.

'And what's the score?'

'Well it seems that Spicer hadn't made a will. Surprising don't you think if he was planning suicide?' he asked looking at Jimmy with raised eyebrows. Jimmy stared back at him, it wasn't wise to trust anyone completely.

'It could be said that the decision to take his own life was unplanned and happened in a moment of mental instability,' replied Jimmy. Wakefield was clearly amused by this and laughed.

'Where did you get that from?'

'From a book I took on holiday,' Jimmy chuckled. 'Now we're straying from the point, is the club for sale or not?'

'It will be but Spicer's estate has got to be sorted through probate and that might take a little time.'

'And what happens in the meantime, a club like that won't run itself?'

'Too true. I have suggested to Hanlon that you, as a prospective purchaser, should act as caretaker of the club until the legal formalities are sorted out. Hanlon was only too happy to agree. In fact I'd say it's taken a weight off his mind.'

'Good, I can move into Spicer's office right away then can I?'

'Yes, I've already got the keys from Hanlon. We've agreed that until the club is sold you will receive five per cent of the takings as your commission for running the club,' Wakefield said as he opened the drawer of his desk and handed Jimmy a bunch of keys.

'That will do for starters. I'll get over there now and see what sort of state it's in,' Jimmy said as he rose and said goodbye to Wakefield. Jimmy left the office and walked the short distance to the nightclub. The two managers were there and Jimmy explained to them that he would be taking over on a temporary basis until the legalities could be sorted out. He invited them to continue in their previous capacities and made the same offer to the rest of the staff. They all agreed to stay on which didn't surprise him in the least. He then called Jim Burrow, the manager of the casino, into what was once Spicer's office and which now Jimmy intended to use as his own.

'Just how much does the casino take in a week?'

'On average approximately £50,000,' Jim answered.

'Can that be increased?'

'Sure it can. Tony insisted the punters be given a three to one chance of winning, but we can easily reduce that to four to one.'

'Then do it. I'm not as interested in pleasing punters as Spicer was, I have no ambitions to climb any social ladder.'

He dismissed Jim and sitting in Spicer's chair in Spicer's office he recalled the early days when he worked for him. To be in this position had been his ambition since day one, but Jimmy knew that he wouldn't be satisfied until he owned it outright. He lifted the telephone, dialled the Admiral and asked Mick Walsh to join him at the club. A short time later Mick was sitting in the office with him.

'What's the mood in the city since Spicer's death?' Jimmy asked.
'Very uncertain, everyone expected you to kill him, now they're not sure.'
'Is anyone making a move for Spicer's business?'
'There have been one or two murmurings, but we've put ourselves about a bit and dampened things down. Now you're back I doubt anyone will be foolish enough to make any serious attempts.'

Jimmy nodded and then explained to Mick about the latest method of importing the cannabis. He revealed that the first batch was already on its way and also that from now on the River Club was to be the headquarters of their operations.

The following day Jimmy went down to the docks and looked out an old work mate. He found out exactly what he wanted to know. Where the cocoa beans were unloaded and more importantly, who was in charge of the gang of dockers who off loaded the African ships. He made his way down to Huskisson dock and found Pat Riley, the foreman. Jimmy introduced himself and Pat said, 'I know you, what on earth do you want with me?'

'I want to make you a rich man.'

'Forget it. I'm not into fiddles, at any rate not the sort of fiddles you're mixed up in.'

'Why don't you hear me out before you decide.'

Pat sighed, 'Go on then, tell me.'

'I need twenty bags of special cargo taken off the African ships and put on one side until they're collected.'

'And just what does this cargo consist of?'

'Tobacco that's all.'

'That's a Customs fiddle, I don't touch anything involving that lot.'

'Customs don't check on cocoa beans do they?'

'Not as such but they're always sniffing around, you don't take chances with them.'

'I'd make it worth your while.'

'How much?' Pat asked showing more interest now that there was a mention of money.

'A hundred pounds for you and twenty each for your gang.'

'And we don't have to deliver, just take them from the ship and store them?'

'It's as easy as that,' Jimmy said, hoping that he had convinced Pat that the deal was as simple as he had painted it, although he was pretty sure that Pat wouldn't have agreed to anything if he had known the true contents of the bags.

'OK, we'll give it a go. When is the first lot due?'

'In a fortnight's time and then once a week.' Having established with Pat how he could be contacted Jimmy left the docks feeling decidedly pleased with himself. With over a ton of cannabis being imported each week his profits from the drugs business would net him five hundred thousand pounds per week. That was the sort of money that gave you real power Jimmy thought to himself.

16

Within a few months of returning to England from Africa, Jimmy Challoner had completed the takeover of Spicer's empire. He now owned the River Club outright and like his mentor before him he had made it the seat of his operations. He was acknowledged as Merseyside's number one criminal, a position that he had strived for and believed he now deserved. He thought about the events of the last few months. The shipments of cannabis from Lagos were now arriving more or less weekly and as he had anticipated there hadn't been any trouble when the cargo arrived in Liverpool. Pat Riley was a very experienced docker and his gang was able to separate the sacks of cannabis from the main cargo of cocoa beans without arousing the suspicion of the authorities. However Jimmy always ensured that once Pat rang to tell him the consignment had arrived, it was collected immediately and wasn't left on the dockside for a moment longer than necessary. Winston had returned from Africa and had taken control of the cannabis distribution. He now sold to two dealers in Manchester and Leeds, disposing of a quarter of a ton to each. While this meant a slightly reduced profit margin, it did eliminate half the risk associated with the storage. As far as Jimmy was concerned this more than compensated for the reduction in profits. Jimmy was pleased with the way that Winston managed the drugs side of the business and for this reason alone made sure that Winston was rewarded for his efforts.

Taking a leaf out of Spicer's book Jimmy started to entertain people who held positions of authority, people who were able to do him, 'a favour.' He was making regular cash payments to council and police officials which if nothing else ensured that his gambling operation was allowed to function.

There was no doubt that Jimmy was feeling pleased with the way that life was treating him. The one lack in his life was the love and companionship he had known with Geraldine. Not that Jimmy felt ready to form another close relationship, the memory of Geraldine and the tragic circumstances of her death were still too vivid for that. He saw numerous girls on a temporary basis but none retained his interest until the morning.

It came as a shock when Mick brought Jimmy the news that Pat Riley had been arrested for smuggling cannabis.

'When did it happen?' Jimmy asked.

'About an hour ago, the African ship had just docked. Pat and his gang had gone down to the hold and were in the process of separating the cargo when the Customs pounced.'

'Where are they now?'

'They've been taken to the Custom House.'

'In that case you had better go and warn Winston. I don't think Pat will talk, but just in case tell Winston to move any stock he has.'

'Pat doesn't know where Winston keeps the gear so even if he did talk he couldn't tell them anything.'

'Pat knows that his contact man besides me is Winston so if he tells Customs about Winston they'll turn over all the addresses he has, understand?'

'OK, see what you mean. I'll go and give Winston the nod.'

As Mick left his office Jimmy picked up the telephone and dialled Wakefield.

'Hello John, Jimmy here. I've just heard that Pat Riley and his gang have been nicked by Customs. I want you to go down to the Customs House and do what you can for them.'

'The Customs House, is that where they're being held?'

'That's what I've been told.'

'I'll get onto it right away.'

'Good, keep me informed won't you. I need to know what, if anything, Pat has said to them.'

'Sure, I understand. Leave it with me and I'll call you later.'

Jimmy replaced the handset and leaned back in his swivel chair.

'Damn, how the hell did they get onto Pat?'

He reflected on the impact Pat's arrest would have on the business. Now he would have to find another smuggling route into the country and that would take time to establish. Time which would mean a loss of money which didn't please Jimmy at all. The current operation had worked well for the past twelve months and had netted him a personal fortune. What he needed was to talk to Winston and fast. Jimmy was still deep in thought when a couple of hours later his telephone rang and for a moment the shrill ringing startled him.

'Yes?'

'You sound glum Jimmy, something happened that I don't know about?' John said.

'No no, I'm just a bit edgy over losing my importation route.'

'Well I can appreciate you must be concerned. Anyway the news from Riley is good. He hasn't said a word to Customs and since I've spoken to him and the rest of his crew they're in better shape.'

'How do you mean, in better shape?'

'Well I've told them what to say. It seems to me that Customs jumped in too quickly.'

'What are you getting at?'

'It's simple enough, Pat and his lads were in the hold of the ship shortly after it docked. They were actually sorting out your bags from the cocoa beans when the Customs arrested them. Now what I've told them to say is that they had gone down to the hold to start the unloading exercise when they noticed some strange bags. They were in the process of sorting these from the cocoa beans when the Customs arrested them.'

'Sounds good, will it work?'

'I suspect it will. I've just had a word with the Chief Customs man and he isn't too pleased now he knows what our defence is going to be.'

'Where will they be taken to, they can't keep them at the Customs House can they?'

'No you're right. They have to take them to the Main Bridewell where they will be charged. In view of the cock-up they now realise they've made, they're not going to oppose bail.'

'Nice one John, send me the bill and I'll take care of it.'

'I planned to anyway, I don't think Riley could afford me.'

John Wakefield was proved correct. Customs realised that they had jumped the gun and at the first Magistrate's hearing they offered no evidence against Pat and his crew. Since there were no criminal charges against them the Mersey Dock Board had very little choice other than to reinstate them. Jimmy saw Pat and made one final payment to him. From now on he would be of no use to the Challoner organisation. Jimmy's own reputation on the docks flourished as he had known it would. The fact that he had looked after Pat Riley and his crew had stood him in very good stead and Jimmy was delighted.

The drugs problem was becoming widespread, not just throughout Merseyside but throughout the country as a whole. In 1970 the Home Office called on all Chief Constables throughout England and Wales to establish special squads of officers to combat this growing menace. The Chief Constable of Liverpool followed the recommendation and formed a squad in Liverpool. He promoted Peter Turner to Detective Chief Inspector and placed him in charge of the newly formed squad. Peter was delighted, not only with his promotion, but also with the promised challenge of taking charge of his own command. His squad was made up of one detective inspector, four detective sergeants and four detective constables.

Peter Turner called his newly formed squad together for the first of their regular briefing sessions and told them he thought James Arthur Challoner was the man responsible for the importation of drugs into Liverpool. He explained to them how the Regional Crime Squad had observed Challoner and the Spenser brothers, establishing an association between them. He explained in his opinion it meant they could only be running a drugs racket.

'It was significant that when the Customs arrested a team of dockers recently, it was Challoner's solicitor who appeared on their behalf' Peter said.

'Was that the job that Customs made a balls of?' asked one of the detectives.

'Let's not be critical of our colleagues, I'll be frank, I intend to work with them in the future.'

'You can't mean that, they're a bunch of civil servants, they haven't anywhere near the experience that we have,' said one of the sergeants.

'As far as the drug problem is concerned they have more experience than we do. If we pool our knowledge it will be to our advantage and that's a fact.' Peter Turner was determined to seek the assistance and co-operation of the Customs & Excise. He was only too aware that with the limited resources of his squad. He would be restricted in what type of operation he was able to mount and as it was his intention to go after Jimmy Challoner his own resources would not be sufficient. He knew he needed assistance and since he could not approach his former colleagues on the Regional Crime Squad Peter appreciated that his only option was to approach Customs & Excise. He believed that he would have no difficulty in establishing a good case for them to join forces against

Challoner. He intended to explain the association between Challoner and the Spensers and how, since their return from Africa, cannabis had been circulating in the North West. He would remind them that the recent seizure of a ton of cannabis had been made on a ship that had sailed from Africa. Added to this was the arrest of the dockers with their representation in court by Challoner's solicitor, all of which pointed the finger directly at Challoner and his organisation. Peter recalled that when he was in the Regional Crime Squad he had dealings with a member of the Customs Investigation Division. This can be likened to the CID of the Police Service and he decided to ring him to find out who he ought to contact in order to propose his plan for a joint operation.

He telephoned the office of the Customs Investigation Division in London and left a message for Nigel Hunt to ring him on his return to the office. It was the following day before Nigel Hunt returned Peter's call. Peter explained to Nigel what he had in mind and to his delight heard Nigel tell him that he himself was now a member of the drugs team. The two men agreed to meet at a Liverpool pub, neutral ground for both. Peter knew that relationships between the police and Customs were at a low ebb since the Customs had been badly let down in a recent joint venture with the Metropolitan Police. A corrupt police officer had leaked information about an operation being carried out against a team of villains from London. He felt that Nigel was having some difficulty in deciding which side of the fence the newly formed Liverpool Drugs Squad sat. Peter decided that he would be completely honest with Nigel and told him all he knew about Challoner.

'There is one thing I should tell you at the outset, Jimmy Challoner and myself were once the best of friends. We were kids together living in the same street.'

'Well you've certainly been honest with me and I can't ask for more than that. How do you intend to nail Challoner?'

'It will have to be for conspiracy. Challoner is now too big for him to be caught with his own hand in the till.'

'You'll need to explain, we don't charge conspiracy. What needs to be proved?'

'We would have to prove that Challoner was indirectly involved in the importation of drugs,' Peter explained 'in other words that he controlled the operation.'

'Sounds difficult if Challoner is as big as you say.'

'Not really, proof of association and control over the gang will often suffice.'

'And this will be done by surveillance?'

'Exactly. That's why I suggest we work together. I simply haven't got the manpower to mount a surveillance operation.'

'If we were to agree, apart from Challoner, who else would we need to concentrate our resources on?'

'It would be my recommendation that we concentrate on Winston Spenser, I'm convinced that it's him who is arranging the drug shipments from Africa. He originates from there and I suspect still has connections over there.'

'Sounds a good bet to me. Right we'll supply the vehicles and manpower, you supply the local knowledge and together we've got a fighting chance.'

'I'm certain we have. I'll arrange for intelligence files to be sent to you on key members of Challoner's organistaion. Once you have an idea who is involved we can set the operation up.'

They remained talking for another hour, discussing the details of the joint venture. They each felt that the other was trustworthy and recognised in the other a professional commitment to ridding the country of a major drugs trafficker.

Within a month of the meeting with Nigel Hunt, Peter was telling his squad that they would be working in unison with Customs & Excise with immediate effect. After one or two minor teething problems the two organisations settled down and showed every sign of becoming a good working team. Peter and Nigel were pleased with the start of the combined operation. The joint squad divided their resources and concentrated on their main targets, Challoner and Winston Spenser. A written log of the surveillance duties was maintained and it soon became apparent from their many meetings that Winston Spenser and Jimmy Challoner were involved in some kind of activity. Each of their meetings was carefully recorded by the watching squad and three weeks into the surveillance the combined squad felt that they had made their first major breakthrough. Winston Spenser was observed making a travel booking to Lagos for the following week.

Peter and Nigel met to discuss this latest piece of intelligence.

'We've got to know why Spenser is going to Lagos,' Peter said, 'our intelligence suggests that it's not for a holiday.'

'I agree and the only way we'll find out is to follow him over there.'

'That's out of the question for us, the Police Authority wouldn't agree to sending a police officer abroad.'

'I think my people will agree to one of my staff going.'

'If that can be arranged it would be excellent evidence towards our conspiracy charge, particularly if we could confirm that Winston Spenser was over there to set up a drug run.'

'I'll talk to my bosses and see how they react. I'll give you a ring tomorrow and let you know,' Nigel said as he rose to leave.

The next day Nigel telephoned Peter and told him that his senior officers had agreed to a customs officer going to Lagos. Peter was delighted and felt that his decision to involve the Customs in his war against Challoner would prove to be the weapon he had needed. For the first time in a long time he felt optimistic that on this occasion he would achieve his objective.

Jimmy Challoner hadn't been pleased when he heard the news about Peter's promotion and his new posting. He raised the matter with the senior detective officer who was accepting regular payments from him. Jimmy was assured that the squad had only been formed to appease the Home Office and the limited resources allocated made them virtually ineffective. This reassured Jimmy and he became less concerned. His main worry was how he was going to re-establish his methods of importation. Since Riley's arrest he had only been able to deal in the drugs brought in by couriers and while he had stepped up this operation there was a limit to the amount a person could carry in a suitcase. Jimmy summoned Winston and together they agreed that another visit to Lagos was essential. He also decided that he would repeat the trip to the White Sands Hotel in Mombassa before meeting up with Winston in Lagos. Looking forward to the warm sunshine of Kenya, Jimmy made the reservations and left the following week.

17

Having arrived in Mombassa Jimmy spent the first day lazing in the heat and recovering from the effects of jet lag. He was pleased that he had had the forethought to book this extra week, particularly when he recalled the dismal November weather he had left behind. Later that evening he was sitting in the bar of the hotel talking to Abdul, the barman, when he saw an attractive woman walk into the room and sit at one of the tables.

'The usual Mrs Houldin?' Abdul asked.

'Yes please Abdul, that would be lovely,' the woman replied. Jimmy watched as Abdul mixed a dry Martini with ice and took it to the table. On his return to the bar Jimmy asked him who the lady was, expecting to be told that she was the wife of a fellow guest. When Abdul told him that she was staying at the hotel alone Jimmy looked at her with renewed interest. She was about thirty five years old with sun streaked light brown hair that framed a heart shaped face with neat, even features. Her light summer dress revealed a girlish figure and Jimmy felt a stirring of emotions which he had thought gone forever. He picked up his gin and tonic and went over to where she was sitting.

'Hello, I'm Jimmy Challoner. I'm from Liverpool in England, do I detect a British accent?' he asked with a smile.

'Hello, yes I am from England. I'm Jennifer Houldin,' she replied, returning his smile and holding out her hand to Jimmy which he took and held slightly longer than was necessary.

'Do you mind if I join you?'

'Please do.'

'Is this your first visit to Mombassa?'

'No, I've been once before.'

'That's a coincidence, so have I.'

'My last visit was on my honeymoon.'

'And where is Mr Houldin?'

'He died recently, we'd been so happy here that I just wanted to come back.'

'I'm really sorry to hear that, he must have been very young.'

'Cancer is no respecter of age.' Jimmy deliberately steered the conversation to lighter topics and was delighted when Jennifer accepted his invitation to join him for dinner. Over the meal he realised just how much he had missed female company. Jennifer proved to be an intelligent and witty dinner companion, but although the conversation flowed at the end of the evening, Jimmy found that apart from knowing that her home was in Reading he really didn't know anything about Jennifer at all.

After dinner they returned to the bar and stayed chatting for a further hour until Jennifer finally said goodnight and went to her room.

The following morning Jimmy dressed in shorts and a light short sleeved top and went down to the dining room. His eyes scanned the occupied tables expecting to see Jennifer and he felt a pang of disappointment when she wasn't there. He sat down to a solitary breakfast, eagerly looking up as each new arrival entered the room, but there was no sign of her.

It was noon when he next met her. He was sitting on a sunbed alongside the pool when he saw her walking towards him.

'Hello Jimmy, enjoying the sun?' she asked, her wide smile lighting up her face.

'Certainly am, didn't want to waste the opportunity to top up my tan.'

'You sound like a typical tourist.'

'Not too typical I hope,' Jimmy said. Jennifer looked away from him and he knew he mustn't rush things.

'You don't look dressed for sun bathing.'

'No, I've made arrangements with some of the other guests to drive into Mombassa this afternoon,' Jennifer replied. Jimmy felt a stab of disappointment and it must have shown on his face for Jennifer quickly said 'If you're free this evening it would be lovely if I could join you for dinner again.'

'I'll make sure I am, 'I'll see you in the bar around six thirty.'

Jennifer said goodbye and Jimmy settled down to more sun worshipping. The afternoon dragged and he couldn't get thoughts of Jennifer out of his mind.

He was already in the bar when Jennifer entered at six thirty. She was wearing a low cut white dress which accentuated the warm honey tone of her skin and clung enticingly to her curves. Jimmy rose to greet her and as she sat down Abdul appeared from nowhere with her martini. 'You look wonderful,' Jimmy said. Jennifer blushed and again sensing her feelings Jimmy lightened the mood. They took their coffee in the bar after their meal and Jimmy asked her how much longer she was staying. He had already decided that if Jennifer was staying beyond his own arrangements he would extend his stay. When she said she was leaving the day after next Jimmy picked up a sense of regret in her voice. Encouraged he said 'In that case we must make the most of tomorrow.' Jennifer seemed pleased and agreed to spend the day with him. As she rose to go to her room she leaned over to Jimmy and kissed him lightly on the cheek.

The following morning Jimmy was up early to arrange for a hire car with the hotel. When he went in for breakfast he was surprised to see Jennifer already there. 'You're not the only early bird,' she laughed.

After breakfast they set off to explore the local area.

During the day Jennifer asked Jimmy about himself. He told her that he was a property developer, that he owned seven night clubs but was careful not to reveal anything of his true profession. Jennifer sat quietly while he struggled to tell her about Geraldine and the accident. Silently she took his hand and squeezed it gently.

'How long is it since you lost David?' he asked and felt her grip tighten on his hand as she answered.

'Just over a year, but he was very ill for much longer than that.' Jimmy longed to hug her tight but he knew she wouldn't have welcomed such a display of intimacy at this stage. Instead he continued to hold her hand and let her talk.

'We had been married for ten years and until David's illness we were very happy. He was a stockbroker in the city and when our daughter was born five years ago we both thought we had it all, how wrong can you be?'

'Where is your daughter now?' asked Jimmy.

'She's with my sister and I really miss her.'

'What do you intend to do with your life now?'

'I'm still not sure. David left me pretty well provided for which means at least I have choice. I was a graphic artist on a weekly magazine, that's a possibility I suppose.' Jimmy felt she didn't sound too enthusiastic at the prospect and changed the subject by asking Jennifer if she would join him for their last night dinner.

During dinner Jennifer seemed quieter than usual and feeling puzzled

Jimmy asked her if the meal was not as good that night.

'No it's not that Jimmy. I'm feeling sad I suppose, I've only just met you and after tonight you'll be gone, just another ending.'

'It doesn't have to end.'

'Be realistic. You're in Liverpool, I'm in Reading,' her voice trailed off.

Jimmy reached out for her hand across the table and whispered 'If you'll let me I'll visit you as often as you'll have me.'

You'll be doing a lot of driving Jimmy.'

'Suits me', Jimmy said, smiling broadly.

After their meal they walked along the beach, arms tight around each other, relaxed and comfortable in each other's company. It was midnight by the time they came back to their hotel, the warm night air was heavy with the scent of Hibiscus and the ocean lapped rhythmically in the distance. 'This is perfect,' Jennifer said softly. 'No,' said Jimmy leaning down and kissing her gently on the mouth, 'Now it's perfect.' As he kissed her again he felt her body arch towards his own as she whispered, 'Stay Jimmy, stay tonight.'

Jimmy waved to Jennifer as her taxi drove her away to the airport. He was surprised at how much it hurt to see her leave and he promised himself that once his business was finished he would see her again in London, where they had agreed to meet on his return to England. Jimmy left Mombassa that day and flew to Lagos where he met Winston. Winston told Jimmy that he had been busy since his arrival and he believed he had found another way to export cannabis to England in bulk. He explained that most of the cargo now shipped to Liverpool was by freight container ships. Once the container was sealed it wasn't opened again until it arrived at the customer's address.

'What about Customs, they must check it before it's sealed?' Jimmy asked.

'Not a problem. They can be easily bribed this end and unless they have suspicions about a container they never open one in England.'

'We can't very well list the drugs on the ship's manifest so how do we get round that one?'

'Simple, you will need to form an import company dealing in some kind of merchandise between Lagos and Liverpool.'

'Sounds easy, just what exactly do we trade in?'

'I've established a contact in the import and export business. I'd like you to meet him tomorrow and he'll explain how easy it is to export goods.'

Jimmy agreed to the meeting and then, tired after his journey went straight to bed where he slept until morning.

The following day Winston took Jimmy to the docks at Lagos. Jimmy was introduced to the import and export merchant who explained to him that he would export regular consignments of cannabis to whatever company Jimmy set up under cover of a legitimate product. However Jimmy wasn't entirely happy with this arrangement sensing that if the Customs in England ever became suspicious about one of the consignments it would lead directly to him.

It was while he was mulling over the pros and cons that Jimmy found himself watching a container ship being loaded. His interest was caught by two containers that appeared to have been placed on one side. Jimmy asked the merchant why these containers had been isolated from the rest. He was told that often there was insufficient cargo to fill all the containers a ship could carry and it was the custom of shipping companies to have empty containers returned to the home port.

'The two containers that you see will be empty and will be returned to Liverpool.' Jimmy asked how often empty containers were returned like this and was delighted when the answer was, 'On most trips.' He turned to Winston and said 'This is how we'll get the drugs to Liverpool, in empty containers.' He chuckled at the simplicity of the method. Winston grinned but said, 'How's it going to work?' Jimmy sensed that Winston was not entirely convinced.

'It's very simple, our friend here loads the cannabis into an empty container which is being returned to Liverpool. Then he telephones us with the name of the ship and the serial number of the container. We do the rest in Liverpool.'

'Do you think you can fix things in Liverpool?'

Jimmy looked offended and replied, 'Of course.' Chastened, Winston didn't pursue the matter any further. He knew Jimmy had made up his mind.

That afternoon Winston took Jimmy to three plantations where acres of cannabis were being grown. They were at various stages of growth and Winston pointed to those ready for harvesting. They were approximately six feet high with green foliage. At the top of each plant was a beautiful white flower.

'I didn't realise how lovely these plants are when they're growing like this,' Jimmy said.

'You know it's just the leaves and the flowering tops that are used.'

'No, I had no idea. So the stems are no use?'

'No use at all.'

Winston next took Jimmy to a series of huts where he saw the now dried and harvested plants being bundled into manageable bales.

'How much would you say one of these freight containers could hold?'

'About a ton I reckon. The bales are quite bulky so they'll take up a fair amount of space.'

'Why don't they compress it?'

'Easy, they haven't got any presses.'

'I suspect it's high time we introduced some modern technology into this operation.'

'You mean equip them with presses?'

'Yes, that's exactly what we should do, how many suppliers do you use?'

'Just the three we've seen today.'

'Right when you get back to England buy three presses and get them sent out here. Then our containers should be able to carry about a ton and a half instead of a single ton.' Winston couldn't help admiring Jimmy's ability to immediately identify the strengths and weaknesses of the proposed operation. Even though he felt slightly embarrassed that he hadn't identified either, he still marvelled at the fact that in just a day Jimmy had identified a plausible importation route as well as potentially doubling the amount of cannabis each container would carry.

That night Jimmy telephoned Jennifer and arranged to meet her in London. He was feeling content, having established a safe and satisfactory method of importing cannabis would mean an early resumption of the most lucrative side of his business, and Jimmy felt a certain amount of relief. His call to Jennifer went well and he was pleased to hear a note of enthusiasm in her voice that matched his own. He had feared that on her return to England she might have felt differently towards him. Reassured on all counts he left Winston to deal with the finer details of the operation and flew back to Heathrow.

Jennifer was at the airport to meet him and Jimmy felt his spirits lift when he saw her. Jennifer had booked them into the Cumberland Hotel at Marble Arch and they took a taxi there. Once inside their room Jimmy took Jennifer in his arms and kissed her hungrily. She in turn returned his kisses with an urgency and passion that matched his own.

They spent three perfect days together and before parting Jimmy felt confident enough to invite Jennifer and her daughter to spend Christmas with him in Liverpool.

Returning to Liverpool Jimmy knew he was in for a busy time. Priority was to re-open the house at Blundellsands which had been closed since Geraldine's death. Until now Jimmy hadn't wanted to return to the empty house which held so many memories and reminders of Geraldine. He hoped that with Jennifer it would become a home again.

He arranged an early meeting with Mick Walsh and was satisfied after a briefing on the state of his business. Jimmy explained to Mick the new plan for importing the cannabis.

'It sounds a simple method, do you reckon it will work?' Mick asked.

'Simple methods are usually the best. Yeah it should work but first we'll need to find out what happens when the ship is unloaded at this end.'

'That will mean going down to the container base won't it?' asked Mick.

'We'll go down in the morning and watch one or two ships being unloaded,' Jimmy suggested.

The next day Jimmy and Mick Walsh were standing on the dock at Seaforth container base. This was a part of the dock complex that was previously unknown to Jimmy for he had only worked on the docks known locally as 'Liverpool.' Mersey Docks & Harbour Board owned the docks, but for easy recognition the docks had been sub-divided into three areas. They were named after the town through which they ran so the largest section, referred to as the Liverpool docks ran into the middle section known as Bootle & Bootle docks ran into the final section which was now the Seaforth container base.

As a former docker himself Jimmy found himself engrossed in watching the speed at which the ships were now unloaded. One operator handling the massive overhead custom built crane was the only worker necessary to unload the containers from ship to shore. He mentally calculated the tonnage of the cargo and then compared the number of men it would have required in his time on the docks to unload that amount of cargo. It didn't bear comparison and Jimmy thought it was no wonder that the dock labour force had been reduced from over fifty thousand men to five thousand in just a few years. Jimmy couldn't help feeling relieved that he had escaped the docks especially as he came from a family that had traditionally been dockers for generations. Over the years dockers had been careful to create strong family ties. Since 1948 when the agreement had been signed for the protection of jobs for life in the case of dockers, unless you were a member of a family actually employed on the docks your chance of finding a job was virtually nil. Together the dockers and the unions had forced a closed shop syndrome and this Jimmy now felt had been a contributory factor in the end of Liverpool as a thriving port.

Jimmy watched the unloading process with close interest, noting particularly where the crane driver deposited the two containers he had identified and believed to be empty. They were placed in a small compound adjacent to the dockside. There were no security measures in operation and Jimmy was satisfied that his planned operation stood every chance of success now that he had looked over procedures at the journey's end. Under cover of darkness a container placed in this compound could be quickly unloaded and transferred into a vehicle without arousing undue attention. The crane driver would need to be bribed and Jimmy left that detail to Mick Walsh.

The distance from Seaforth to Blundellsands was only two or three miles so Jimmy had decided that since he was close he would visit his house to ensure that everything was ready for Jennifer and her daughter Debbie.

He found the house as he had left it and was relieved that he had employed a couple to keep the place habitable. He stood in the garden for a few minutes allowing the happy memories of Geraldine to flood his mind. Letting himself in through the front door he felt immediately the tranquillity that had first attracted him to the house. It still had an aura of calm that he had never found in any other house and he asked himself why he hadn't been back since Geraldine died. This house would have provided him with a comfort that his flat never could.

After he had checked over the house he telephoned Jennifer and arranged for her to arrive the following week. Talking on the telephone was all very well, but not to be compared with seeing her and being with her. The thought suddenly struck him that he would have to buy Christmas decorations and presents and what's more, fast. After all this year he was going to play Father Christmas for Debbie. Jimmy grinned at the prospect.

18

Peter Turner was sitting in the drugs squad office impatiently awaiting the arrival of Nigel Hunt. He had telephoned to say he was on his way over to update Peter on what had occurred in Lagos. Peter knew that Jimmy had returned and that several days later Winston Spenser had also arrived back in Liverpool. Peter had immediately resumed surveillance on Challoner and had noted with interest his visit to the container base at Seaforth. Peter knew the visit was significant and obviously connected with the trip to Africa and he was hoping that Nigel would be able to tell him what the connection was.

Nigel arrived alone and just by the look on his face Peter knew that the news was good. After a few moments of polite chat Nigel said 'I think the visit to Lagos was a resounding success. Firstly they had no idea they were being observed so my man was able to get very close.' Peter was anxious to ask umpteen questions, but decided to sit down, shut up and let Nigel give the details in his own time.

'Before Challoner arrived in Lagos, Spenser made several visits to the docks and spent a lot of time talking to import and export dealers. He had obviously made up his mind which dealer he wanted to use because when Challoner arrived he took him to meet the dealer. 'Now this dealer,' Nigel continued, 'exports almost anything to anywhere but, and this is the interesting part, he always uses containers as his method of shipment.'

Nigel leaned back in his seat and looked at Peter to make sure that the significance of the information had registered with him. It had but his face remained impassive.

'We've had a chat among ourselves,' Nigel said 'and we believe that Challoner will form a company that will import from Lagos. We know who the exporter is. All we need to do is monitor the ships trading between Lagos and Liverpool, checking on all consignments shipped in by our pal from Lagos, until we identify the name of the company Challoner is using.' Nigel looked pleased and obviously expected an enthusiastic response from Peter. It wasn't forthcoming and Peter appeared to be deep in thought.

'Well you might at least look pleased. Don't you see, we'll have Challoner bang to rights, which is what you want isn't it?' Nigel asked.

'Sorry, I was just thinking,' Peter said, 'I'm puzzled, why would Challoner and Walsh go down to the container base as soon as Challoner returned to Liverpool if the drugs are to be imported as cargo?'

'Perhaps he wanted to know how the container traffic was handled.'

'No, Challoner would know that already. He never, never does anything unless there's a reason.'

'Well whatever the reason he had for going there it doesn't alter the fact that we've identified his route of importation.'

'I'm not entirely convinced. Challoner would know, however well he tried to disguise a new company, an investigation would eventually lead back to his door. He just wouldn't be that stupid.'

'He wouldn't exactly be expecting to get caught.'

'You are absolutely right, Challoner wouldn't expect to get caught because he weighs up every eventuality. That's one of the reasons he's never been convicted, he plans too well and identifies any potential weakness before it occurs.'

'I can't help wondering if in your quest to convict Challoner you may just have over estimated his abilities.'

'I failed to convict him in the past because I didn't give him enough credit, there's no way I'm making that mistake again.'

'Well, what do you suggest?' asked Nigel.

'Believe me I'd love to think you're right, that Challoner did form a company to import the drugs. That way we know we would have a case against him, but since I don't believe that will happen we still need to establish exactly how he intends to bring the drugs in.'

'It's got to be by means of containers.'

'Yes I don't think there's any doubt about that.'

'Good, well we're agreed on that at least.'

'The problem remains though, how does he intend to do it?'

'I'll leave you with that one since I don't think there is a problem and in the meantime I'll monitor container trade between Lagos and Liverpool. We'll soon see who's right.'

After Nigel left Peter sat and thought. He asked himself repeatedly if he was giving Jimmy too much credit. But the answer always came back to no. He was missing something, his professional instinct told him so, but try as he might he couldn't identify what. However he knew that Challoner must have had a reason to visit the container base so soon after returning from Africa. Peter decided that he would make a similar visit.

The following day he went to Seaforth and spent several hours simply watching the containers of cargo being off loaded. He found himself fascinated with the speed of the operation and with the skill of the operator of the huge custom built crane that lifted the heavy containers with such ease. After watching two ships being unloaded he felt he needed to ask a few questions about some of the containers. Peter found the base manager and introduced himself.

'I'd like to know why a few containers are isolated when a ship has been unloaded?' Peter asked.

'It's more than likely from the circumstances you describe that the containers will be the empty ones,' the manager replied.

'Does that happen often?'

'Almost every ship will carry one or two empty containers.'

'What happens to them?'

'We place them in a compound to be collected by the shipping companies as and when they are required for cargo.'

'I'd like to see that compound.'

The manager took Peter to a small yard that was surrounded by a wiremesh fence. Peter noticed that the yard had no security checking system and remarked on this to the manager.

'Who would want to pinch an empty container? It's the full ones we have to worry about.' Peter felt confident that he had discovered how Challoner intended to import the drugs. It was beautifully simple and almost foolproof, it would have appealed to Jimmy from the outset. All he needed to ensure was that the crane driver was on his payroll. After that his own men could empty the containers without any chance of detection.

On his return to the office Peter telephoned Nigel Hunt and told him what he had discovered. Nigel was suitably impressed and agreed that it seemed probable that Challoner was planning to use the method that Peter had suggested. They agreed to meet the next day to discuss the situation in more detail.

The following day Peter took Nigel to the container base and showed him the compound where the empty containers were housed. Nigel was stunned at the simplicity of using this method to import contraband. He had to admit he'd never heard of any previous seizures being made on anyone using this simple but almost foolproof system.

'It looks like we'll have him as soon as the first consignment arrives.'

'I doubt it.'

'What now, you're not suggesting Challoner won't use this method now are you?'

'Oh too right he'll use it, but I don't think we'll have sufficient evidence to prove a conspiracy against him.'

'Why the hell not? All we need to do is identify which of the empty containers has the drugs in it and then sit here and wait for him to collect it.'

'That's the point. Challoner won't come anywhere near the drugs, he'll send a couple of his organisation and we'll have the same problem that you had with the cocoa beans. No evidence to tie Challoner in with anything.'

'I see what you mean, since it's Challoner we want from that point of view this will be a wasted exercise.'

'Not entirely,' Peter said, 'what we need to do is use the situation to force Challoner into making a mistake.'

'How do we do that?'

'Can your department identify which of the containers will be carrying the drugs?'

'Yes I can arrange for one of my men to watch the unloading of all the ships trading between Lagos and Liverpool. There won't be many, perhaps one a week. He'll be able to tell by the operation of the car crane if a full container is being picked up and then dropped as an empty one.'

'Excellent, then he'll be able to alert us and we can watch the compound and arrest whoever Challoner sends to collect the stuff.'

'But how do we use this situation to arrest Challoner?'

'We hit him where it hurts, in his pocket. Challoner will expect to make at least a million from each container load. Every seizure we make will annoy him and eventually force him to change his importation methods. That's when I'm banking on him making a mistake.'

'I thought this Challoner guy didn't make mistakes.'

'Normally he doesn't,' said Peter choosing to ignore Nigel's sarcasm, 'but Challoner is primarily motivated by greed and the loss of such huge profits will hopefully rattle him enough to force him into making a mistake.'

'OK, I'll buy that. As from today I'll arrange for every ship from Lagos to have it's unloading very carefully monitored.'

Two weeks later, just before Christmas, two tonnes of cannabis were seized while in the process of unloading a so called empty container that had arrived in Liverpool from Lagos and three of Challoner's organisation were arrested. Jimmy learned of the seizure of his drugs by HM Customs from Mick Walsh. Whilst he was annoyed at the loss of the consignment and the arrest of three of his staff, he wasn't unduly worried. He considered it an occupational hazard and believed the Customs had simply struck lucky. His mind was preoccupied with the plans for Jennifer and Debbie's imminent Christmas visit and he had transformed the house with decorations and a huge tree in the hallway. He had spent a long time choosing suitable gifts for the unknown little girl he already felt affection for and for Jennifer, after much deliberation, he settled on an elegant pearl choker.

On the day Jennifer and Debbie were due to arrive Jimmy was at Lime Street Station in plenty of time to meet their train. When at last he spotted them walking down the platform to meet him, Jimmy was unsure for a moment how to greet Jennifer in front of her small daughter. He settled on a chaste peck on the cheek at which Jennifer smiled approvingly as she introduced him to the wide eyed five year old at her side. Debbie was a pretty little girl with her mother's colouring and she chatted happily to Jimmy when he asked her about the journey as they walked to his car.

The ten mile journey to Blundellsands passed quickly and that evening all three of them decorated the Christmas tree, Debbie shrieking with delight as the lights were finally persuaded to work. After Debbie had been asleep for an hour and all the debris cleared away, Jimmy and Jennifer sat in front of the log fire relaxing with a drink. 'Tell me,' Jimmy said, 'I'm curious, what did you tell Debbie about me?'

'I told her that we had become friends on holiday and that you had asked us to spend Christmas with you.'

'I take it we're in separate rooms?'

'Yes, it's much too soon for Debbie to see me in bed with you. I don't want to rush things and spoil everything.'

Jimmy assured her that he understood and oddly enough he did, happily tip toeing out of Jennifer's bed at five o'clock the next morning.

Christmas was a great success and Jimmy was delighted with how things had turned out. He was particularly thrilled with the silk tie that Debbie gave him and to her obvious delight wore it throughout the holiday. Jimmy took pleasure in showing them all the local sights and Debbie had been thrilled with a visit to the pantomime. He found her enthusiasm captivating and it was with a heavy heart that he sat holding Jennifer close to him on their final night.

'This has been the happiest Christmas I've known Jennifer, the two of you have made me realise just how empty my life's been.'

'Believe me, it's been wonderful for us too. Debbie has really taken to you and I know she doesn't want to leave.'

'She's a lovely little girl and what's more I love her nearly as much as I love her mother.'

'And we love you too.'

'Don't go back to Reading, why don't you both stay here with me.'

'No it's just too soon yet. Let Debbie get used to you gradually, I'm sure it won't take long.' Jimmy reluctantly agreed.

The following morning Jimmy saw them off at the station. As the train drew out of the station he felt a loneliness engulf him which was only made bearable by the knowledge that he would see Jennifer again in two weeks time.

In the meantime Jimmy turned his attention to business matters.

19

As Jimmy had left specific instructions with Mick Walsh that he wasn't to be disturbed over Christmas he was unaware that another consignment of drugs had been seized by HM Customs. Also that a further three members of his organisation had been arrested.

'I don't like this one little bit,' Jimmy said to Mick Walsh.

'I didn't imagine you would.'

'I can't believe that Customs could be so lucky twice in a row.'

'Particularly in an area where they've never shown any previous activity.'

'Someone's tipping them off, got to be.'

'But who, apart from you, me and Winston nobody else knows what the set up is?'

'Two other people know, the exporter at Lagos and the crane driver at Seaforth.'

'I'd forgotten about those two.'

'I can't see it being the exporter, he's hardly likely to work with British Customs, so it has to be the crane driver'

'But how will we know if it's him for sure?'

'We don't ever know for sure but we have to put the matter right and fast, all this is costing me money.'

'What do you want doing?'

'Is it too late to cancel the next consignment?'

'Yes it will have left Lagos by now.'

'Right let's suspend the operation until this is sorted. Cancel all further loads and when this load arrives just leave it. It's no use losing any more men.'

'You'll want me to watch it arrive, right?'

'Yes, I want to know if Customs seize this load as well. What I can't understand is why we haven't had a visit from police or Customs, they're bound to know that the lads they've arrested work for me.'

'Not necessarily. The police would know but Customs won't know everyone who works for us,' Mick said.

'True but knowing Turner I can't believe he doesn't know what's going on.'

Ten days later Mick Walsh watched the unloading of the ship containing the next consignment of drugs. As he watched he observed another man who appeared to have an equal interest in the unloading. 'Customs,' said Mick to himself. Two days later he read in the Liverpool Echo that Customs had seized two tonnes of cannabis at Seaforth Docks, no arrests had been made.

Before leaving for Reading to spend a few days with Jennifer, Jimmy called a meeting with Mick Walsh and Winston Spenser. They went over the events of the last few weeks. The loss of three consignments of drugs which Jimmy estimated had cost him six million pounds. Winston agreed that it was unlikely that the leak had been at the Lagos end and Jimmy decided that it had to be the crane driver.

'You know what you have to do.'

'Yeah will it be partial or complete?'

'Complete of course.'

Mick then set his fertile mind to work on how to make the death of the crane driver appear to be accidental.

Jimmy told Winston to meet him at Heathrow in five days time when, after visiting Jennifer, he would return to Lagos and think again about the method of importation. Jimmy was annoyed that things hadn't gone according to plan. Aside from the loss of cash he was annoyed that he needed to set up the whole operation afresh. He was sure he wouldn't be able to find such a simple method a second time and cursed the greed and stupidity of the crane driver who had wrecked the operation for what Jimmy guessed was a pittance of a reward from HM Customs. Serves him right that he won't live long enough to spend his blood money Jimmy muttered to himself.

However, on the train journey to Reading he put all his business worries aside and looked forward to his weekend with Jennifer. She was there to meet him at Reading Station and he laughed when Debbie broke away from her mother and ran towards him. He dropped his suitcase and gathered her up in his arms. As Jennifer reached them he bent to kiss her.

'It's good to see you,' he whispered and Jennifer nodded, her eyes filling with happy tears.

Jennifer lived in a cottage in the village of Hook, just a few miles outside Reading. The weekend was perfect but all too soon it was time for Jimmy to leave for Heathrow where he had arranged to meet Winston. When Jennifer wondered why he was going to Africa he told her that he was interested in developing property and had business interests in Lagos that he needed to visit.

Jennifer had insisted on driving him to Heathrow airport and he had accepted her offer simply so that he could prolong their time together.

'You know I've been talking to Debbie about you and I really think she's starting to think of you as her new daddy,' Jennifer said.

Jimmy was silent, he hadn't really thought of Debbie being a daughter to him. He turned the idea around in his head and realised how much it appealed to him.

'You're very quiet,' Jennifer said.

'Sorry, I'd seen us all together but hadn't thought I'd be a daddy.'

'And now you have?'

'I'll love it. I only hope I'm up to the job because I adore that little girl.'

'Well that's all it takes; you'll be fine.'

Nigel Hunt was sitting with Peter in the drugs squad office in Liverpool. They had been discussing the latest seizure of cannabis which they knew had been destined for Challoner. It had been decided at the outset that in spite of the arrests of Challoner's men they would make no attempt to approach Challoner. Peter knew that it would have been a waste of time because the only link they would have been able to establish between the arrested men and Challoner was that he employed them in his clubs. As expected they hadn't given any useful information to the Customs.

'Why do you think that Challoner didn't attempt to collect the latest consignment?' Nigel asked.

'He'll have known that his importation method was blown and after the second seizure he'd really have been on his guard.'

'What happens now?'

'We just keep watching. I know he'll be bothered by all this and trying to work out a new way to get the stuff in.'

'Do you think he'll make another trip to Africa?'

'More than likely.'

'I'll keep my guy on stand by then.'

Peter was taken by surprise the following day when he was told the surveillance team had followed Challoner to Reading where he had been met by a woman with a young child. He had accompanied them to a cottage just outside Reading where he was staying with them. Peter wondered who the woman was and more to the point what was her connection to Jimmy? From the description he'd been given she didn't sound like the usual type of person that Jimmy would use as a courier. Needless to say his team would discover her identity and also her connection with Jimmy. He was relieved when after three days Challoner was driven by the woman to Heathrow Airport. He was seen meeting Winston Spenser and boarding a flight to Lagos with him. Peter hoped that Nigel's man was on the same flight.

He was deep in thought when the telephone on his desk rang and startled him back to his senses.

'Peter? Albert Hughes speaking,' said the voice on the other end of the line.

'Albert, what can I do for you?'

'You can tell me why you were sniffing round the container base and asking questions about empty containers.'

'Not until I know why you're asking.'

'Right, I'm investigating a suspicious drowning. A man called O'Reilly who worked at the base as a crane driver.'

'What's that got to do with me?'

'Quite a lot I'd say. Firstly I hear that you're asking the depot manager questions, then I hear Customs have made a number of seizures of cannabis. The drugs were in what should have been empty containers and surprise surprise the dead man was the crane driver who off loaded each of those containers.'

Peter realised instantly what had happened. Challoner must have suspected the crane driver as the cause of the leak that had led to the Customs seizures. No wonder he was dead thought Peter, Challoner would believe that O'Reilly had cost him about six million pounds.

'Albert, I'll come over and see you, I think I know what the connection is between O'Reilly's death and the drug seizures.'

Having spoken to Albert Hughes, Peter learned that O'Reilly had been found floating in the dock at Seaforth. The post mortem revealed that death was due to drowning and no marks of violence had been found on the body. Peter hadn't expected to hear anything else. He knew how thorough Challoner was. After telling Albert Hughes all he knew, the

Superintendent said, 'I knew this wasn't a straightforward drowning, but we both know I'll never prove anything else.' Peter nodded in agreement, this was more proof of Challoner's ruthlessness.

On arriving in Lagos, Jimmy Challoner, together with Winston, made contact with their exporter. He was surprised to see them again so soon and had been wondering why the export of the cannabis had been halted. Having spoken to him Jimmy was happy that the leak wasn't at this end therefore he must have been right about the crane driver. No doubt justice would now have been done. Jimmy was coming round to the view that Winston was suggesting again, which was to form his own company and to risk importing the drugs that way. He couldn't see an alternative in the circumstances, Jimmy suspected that now Customs were aware that drugs had been shipped to England in supposedly empty containers they would be checking them more thoroughly and so he had to abandon this method. He believed that in spite of not being visited by the authorities over the arrest of his staff they knew that it was his organisation responsible for the importation. Jimmy thought they would be watching all cargo between Lagos and Liverpool with interest, intent on establishing a link with him. If he formed his own company and imported the drugs through that company it wouldn't take the police and Customs long to tie him in with the importations. Was he prepared to run the risk? It was while he was pondering on this dilemma that he noticed a cargo of cocoa beans being loaded out of one container into another.

'What's going on there?' Jimmy asked.

'The container has been damaged so the shipping company won't handle it. The cargo has to be transferred to a good container, it happens now and again,' the exporter explained.

'What happens to the damaged containers?'

'It's taken back to Liverpool where they repair it.'

Jimmy smiled. Winston looking at him, knew intuitively that his boss had found his new method of importing the cannabis.

Jimmy didn't say anything to Winston, who was dumbfounded when Jimmy announced to the exporter that he had decided to form a company dealing between Liverpool and Lagos.

'What do you suggest I trade in?' Jimmy asked the exporter.

'Well a very profitable line would be machinery that needs to be shipped to England for repair.'

'Right, I'll start a small engineering company as soon as I return to

Liverpool. In the meantime get those orders rolling in.'

'And which of the consignments do you want the stuff hidden in?'

'In none of them, this company is going to be completely legit.'

'I don't get it.'

Jimmy grinned as he looked at Winston's puzzled face. 'I want the drugs taken out in a damaged container on the same ship that's carrying my machinery.'

Winston's face creased into a wide smile.

'I see it now, while Customs are sniffing round the machinery we'll be off loading the cannabis right under their noses,' Winston laughed.

'Got it in one,' said Jimmy.

Not wanting the operation to run into teething troubles at the African end in the early stages, Jimmy arranged for Winston to stay on until he was satisfied that things were running smoothly. Jimmy returned to Liverpool and told John Wakefield to find a small engineering firm that the organisation could take over. Within a week Jimmy was the major shareholder in Simpsons Engineering Company.

'Peter?' Nigel speaking. Sorry I can't get over, but I just want to have a word.'

'No problem Nigel, what's new?'

'Quick update on Lagos. Our two chums arrived and made contact with the same exporter as before. Challoner left after a day or two but the Spenser guy stayed on. My lad got him talking and discovered that he's about to form a company and will be exporting machinery to workshops in England for repair work.'

'That's tremendous news, so Jimmy has been forced into forming a company. You realise what this means Nigel?'

'I hope it means that we'll soon be feeling Jimmy's collar.'

'How soon can we find out the name of the company?'

'I'm leaving a man in Lagos. He'll find out where the machinery is going and once we've got the address I'll get the VAT squad to visit the company and find out what Challoner's connection is.'

'I reckon this time we'll have Jimmy exactly where we want him.'

'Behind bars,' was Nigel's parting shot.

Peter reflected on the information that Nigel had just given to him. It was exactly what he'd been waiting for, indeed it was what he had planned for. With the seizing of the drug consignments sent in the so called empty containers, Jimmy had been forced to change his system or else abandon the trade altogether. Peter knew Jimmy too well to imagine that he would abandon such a rewarding enterprise; and now he was being forced to conceal drugs in legitimate cargo.

Peter was only too aware that he must be patient. There must be no action taken against Challoner until it was absolutely beyond all doubt that his connection with the new company could be established and a conviction was a certainty. All he could do now was wait to hear from Nigel's man in Lagos and force himself to keep his growing excitement in check.

Fortunately within three weeks Nigel's colleague in Lagos had reported that a container addressed to Simpson Engineering Ltd, Liverpool had been shipped. Nigel telephoned to say he was on his way to Peter's office to update him on the situation.

'The VAT team have done us proud,' Nigel said with a self satisfied smile in Peter's direction. 'They've been to Simpson's on the pretext of a VAT examination and have come up trumps.'

'In what way?' Peter asked. He was sitting across the desk from Nigel who was thumbing through a file of documents.

'Simpson's is a small family firm dealing in ship's engine repairs. With the decline in shipping over the years they've been forced into repairing all types of machinery and even then struggling to make a profit. Two weeks ago Challoner Enterprises took the firm over and, here's the good news, Challoner himself is a director.'

'I can scarcely believe our good fortune, it does surprise me that Challoner has become a director though.'

'Vanity, you said he always had grand ideas.'

'Well that's true enough.'

'Unfortunately I have had to bring my man from Lagos back so we aren't going to know when consignments will contain cannabis.'

'That's a shame, but it's the same everywhere, the pressures don't get any less do they?'

'Yes you're right, my bosses were fine about the trip but only until we found out the name of the company.'

'How are we going to know which of the containers will be carrying the drugs? We can't just take pot luck and search everyone. Once we make a search Challenor will know we're on to him so our first strike has got to be the one that counts.'

'I realise that, but without specific information we're never going to know.'

'There's only one way to find out, we'll have to resort to old fashioned police work.'

'Which is?'

'We will need to follow every container destined for Simpson's Works and wait until one is diverted elsewhere. I can't believe that Challoner will allow the drugs to be taken to the company's premises, even though he owns them now.'

'That's what we'll do then. I'll monitor the containers from the ship's manifesto and we'll follow each one.'

'Let's hope there aren't too many.'

'In view of the number of seizures we've made against him, I suspect Challoner must be desperate to import another bulk load.'

During the next three months the police and HM Customs followed three containers from Seaforth Docks to Simpson Engineering and not one of the loads deviated from its route to the workshop.

'I don't get it. We know Challoner is receiving cannabis in bulk from the amount available on the streets. How the hell is he getting hold if it?' Peter asked Nigel as they sat in the bar of a local pub.

'Beats me. We've even witnessed the unloading of the last container and all it contained was machinery.'

'I thought things were too good to be true, nothing is that simple with Challoner.'

'I'm beginning to grasp what you mean about Challoner's ability, the bugger's got me beat.'

'Unless,' Peter leaned forward to emphasise what he was going to say, 'the company is just a front to stop us looking too closely at the rest of the cargo. Somehow Challoner must have found another method of importation, but I'm willing to bet it's on the same ship as the machinery.'

'We're still examining all the empty containers so we know that isn't the route.'

'No he wouldn't do that again.'

'Then there's only one other way, he must have formed a second company. I'll start checking the manifesto of the last three voyages and see if there's a second firm that can be linked to Challoner.'

'It certainly needs checking out, but you know I've a sneaking feeling it will be something much simpler.'

20

Having established the import of machinery through Simpson's, Jimmy now had to decide what happened to the damaged containers once they arrived in Liverpool. Mick Walsh was sent to Seaforth Docks and reported back to Jimmy.

'All damaged containers are taken for repair to a firm called Liverpool Container Repair.'

'Have they got the monopoly?'

'Yeah, there's no competition.'

'Who and where is this firm?'

'It's owned by a Cyril Bell and operates from a yard just off the Dock Road in Bootle.'

'Is that Cyril Bell who used to deal in scrap metal?'

'He dealt in scrap metal before going into containers. Why? Know him?'

'Yes, I know Cyril, come on we'll pay him a call.'

Jimmy and Mick drove the short distance to Bell's yard.

'Hello Jimmy, long time eh? What can I do for you then?' Cyril asked sounding surprised at Jimmy's sudden appearance.

'I've come to talk business,' Jimmy replied, avoiding entering into any social chit chat.

'How can I help you? I'm not into scrap any more so I don't handle stolen property.'

Cyril Bell was a big man who, although thirty years Jimmy's senior, was still relatively fit and felt confident he could take care of himself if necessary. However he knew Jimmy's reputation and feared him which Jimmy sensed.

'Relax Cyril, I'm not here to do you any mischief. All I need is to use your services once in a while.'

'In what way?'

'From time to time a damaged container will arrive in Liverpool in which will be of interest to me. Before it comes to your yard it will need to stop off en route.'

'That doesn't sound a problem.'

'It won't be,' Jimmy stared at Cyril, 'so long as you and your driver do as you're told.'

'My driver knows how to keep it shut.'

'Good, well that's very good. All settled then, I'll telephone you when my container arrives and tell you where to take it.'

'What's in it for me?' Cyril asked, greed overcoming his fear.

'I wondered when you'd ask.'

'Well I'd expect something for my trouble,' said Cyril as he shifted from foot to foot.

'You'll get five hundred pounds for every container you move for me.'

'Sounds like easy money,' said Cyril risking a grin.

'It is,' said Jimmy, his unsmiling face looking straight at Cyril, 'but breathe a word of this arrangement and you won't live to spend it.'

Cyril watched as Jimmy and his henchmen left the yard. He had a good idea what would be in the containers but he knew better than to probe. He and his driver would simply carry out Challoner's instructions.

Three weeks later Jimmy roared with laughter when Mick told him that the first consignment of cannabis had arrived without a hitch, but that the container with the machinery inside had been discreetly followed by a small convoy of unmarked police cars.

It was during Jennifer's second visit to Liverpool that Jimmy proposed.

'Jimmy I'd love to marry you. I honestly never felt I would want to live with anyone again, but you've changed everything. The real bonus is that Debbie adores you too.'

'And I adore her,' said Jimmy 'I just can't wait for this wedding.'

They sat late into the night making plans. The wedding would be in June so that in just four months Jennifer and Debbie could move in and make their home with Jimmy in Blundellsands. When Debbie found them sharing Jennifer's bed the next morning she laughed and promptly jumped in beside Jimmy for a hug.

Over the next three months Jennifer was like a whirlwind supervising and overseeing all the wedding arrangements as well as the redecorating and refurbishment of the house. Jimmy assured her that cost was not a problem, but even so she was left speechless when Jimmy presented her with an exquisite emerald and diamond ring.

As the house was transformed Jimmy felt that in Jennifer's hands it was coming alive. Life thought Jimmy, was damn near perfect. His business was ticking over nicely, the new importation method working like a dream and he was soon to marry. What more could a man wish for?

Peter Turner was at a loss. He couldn't fathom how Challoner was getting the cannabis into Liverpool. Informants confirmed that there was a good supply of high quality cannabis on the streets and Peter's colleagues had proved it to be of African origin. Peter hadn't considered any other person to be responsible for the drugs now being pushed, such was his conviction that Challoner was behind the upsurge. Try as he might he hadn't been able to discover how Challoner was getting the stuff into the country. Nothing had come of Nigel's investigation of the other companies shipping goods alongside Simpson's and Customs were certain that Challoner hadn't formed a second company.

In an effort to impress on his squad the urgency of finding out how Challoner was importing such a large quantity of drugs Peter called a conference. He discussed methods past and present which Challoner and other drug smugglers had used over the years and in passing mentioned Challoner's suspected involvement in the death of the crane driver at Seaforth Docks.

Tim Crawford, one of the detective constables, said,

'I don't know whether you know boss, but the new crane driver at Seaforth used to be a bouncer at one of Challoner's clubs.'

'Are you sure about this?'

'Saw him myself when I was at Seaforth a couple of weeks ago.'

'Who is he? Do we know anything about him?'

'I only know him as Nick Beatty, but he's worked on the docks before as a crane driver.'

After the conference Peter sat alone in his office mulling over this latest piece of news. There must be a very good reason why Challoner had put one of his own men into the vacant position created when the crane driver died. In that case, Peter said to himself, he must still be using empty containers, although he knew this had been ruled out since Customs checked them on a regular basis. Somehow Challoner must have discovered another method, one that needed a crane driver at Seaforth.

The next morning Peter called on the manager at Seaforth and although he wanted to lay his cards on the table Peter thought it prudent to be cautious. It was impossible to guess just how far Challoner's influence extended.

'Is there any other reason, other than cargo or empty containers being returned, why a ship might carry containers?' Peter asked.

'No, shipping costs are very high these days so even empty containers are kept to a minimum. The available space on a ship costs money and is only cost effective when it's filled with loaded containers,' the manager told Peter.

'Yes, I understand that but it doesn't help me.'

'If I knew what it was you're interested in I might be able to help you further.'

'I'm just interested in methods that could be used to smuggle property into or out of the country.'

'Wait a second, there might be another way and it wouldn't arouse interest.'

'Tell me?'

'Now and then, but not often, there's why I've only just thought of it, a container gets damaged. Usually because of incompetence or lack of proper lifting facilities at foreign ports. Anyway it's shipped back to this country for repair. Now providing the damage isn't too bad, goods could possibly be hidden in one of these containers.'

'What happens when it arrives in Liverpool?'

'It's put on the dockside to wait for collection by the repair firm.'

'Do you have any idea how many repair firms there are?'

'Only one, I think it's called Liverpool Container Repair.'

Peter thanked the manager for his help and returned to his office to telephone Nigel and arrange a meeting.

He told Nigel what he had discovered and that the likelihood was that this was the method being used by Challoner.

'You have to be right. It's as good if not better than using an empty container. I can see now why he wanted his own guy in charge of the overhead crane.'

'Exactly, but we still have the problem of connecting Challoner with the drugs.'

'I knew there would be a catch somewhere.'

'This repair firm is owned by a man called Bell. He's an ex scrap metal dealer who's never been renowned for his honesty.'

'Is he likely to be part of Challoner's organisation?'

'I think not. Challoner would have used this method right from the start if that had been the case. I reckon Challoner will simply use Bell each time a damaged contained arrives.'

'So you think the container will be taken to Bell's premises?'

'I don't know, but there's only one way to find out. We'll have to follow the container and see where it goes.'

'How are we going to know when it's arrived? We can't watch every ship coming in from Lagos.'

'I should think the container will always be on board the same ship carrying the stuff for Challoner's engineering firm. Otherwise Challoner would have no reason to invest in all this machinery, it has to be his smokescreen.'

'Right, I'll check on the ship's manifesto and tell you when the next consignment is due for Simpson's. Just one point, my bosses won't allow a container load of drugs to leave the docks without us seizing the drugs first.'

'What do you mean?'

'We have instructions that we can't allow drugs to leave our jurisdiction just in case we lose them.'

'How the hell can we lose a container.'

'Listen, I don't make the rules, I just have to obey them.'

'Unless we allow the drugs to run we won't get Challoner.'

'I know, but if we could substitute the drugs with bales of peat we could still get the evidence we want.'

'Replace the drugs with peat? Are you mad? Challoner would know the container was being interfered with, don't forget the crane driver is one of his.'

'Well that's the only way we can allow the container to run.'

'Then the only thing we can do is not tell our bosses until after the arrests.'

Several hours of hard talking later Peter finally managed to persuade Nigel to allow the drugs to continue without interference from them.

'God help us if this goes belly up,' Nigel said when he realised that he was committed to Peter's course of action.

'Don't worry, nothing will go wrong and if it did we just won't admit it,' Peter had said. Nigel was less than happy, he had never had to deceive his superiors before.

Two weeks later Peter, Nigel and their respective squads were discreetly watching the unloading of the ship that Nigel had confirmed was carrying machinery destined for Simpson Engineering. They had seen all the containers, except one, lifted off and placed together on the quayside. The remaining container was lifted off and placed on the quayside some distance from the others.

'Looks promising,' Peter said to Nigel.

'All we want now is for Liverpool Container Repair to collect the thing,' said Nigel, 'I hope they don't keep us hanging around.'

'I shouldn't think so, Challoner will have arranged an early collection. The longer the drugs are on the quayside the greater the chance of someone finding them accidentally.'

Peter had been right, within half an hour the lorry from the Liverpool Container Repair was loaded with the damaged container.

'All mobiles stand by. Charlie One, you take the lead and report when you have eyeball. The rest stay in position until Charlie One starts his commentary,' Peter said over the car to car radio system.

'Charlie One to all mobiles, I have eyeball, the subject is leaving the dock estate and heading towards Bootle,' Peter told his driver to move off and said, 'All mobiles take up positions in the surveillance.'

He replaced the radio handset and listened as Charlie One gave a commentary on the progress of the container lorry.

As taught in their surveillance training the convoy alternated their positions, each taking eyeball of the suspect vehicle as and when they felt they might have been noticed. It quickly became apparent to Peter that the lorry was not making for the repair yard. He lifted the radio handset and said, 'The vehicle isn't making for home base. Under no circumstances let it out of your sight.'

The surveillance continued along the Dock Road towards the city and then headed south. Although the driver didn't appear to be aware of being followed the pursuing vehicles took no changes and kept their system going.

'Bravo Two to all mobiles, the subject has turned into the industrial estate. Do not, repeat do not follow. Peter immediately sensed that the lead car was concerned that the presence of the rest of the surveillance entering the industrial estate might arouse the suspicion of the driver.

'Hold your present positions,' he said.

'Bravo Two to all mobiles, suspect vehicle stopped outside warehouse premises, we will have to drive on.'

Peter was not concerned that they didn't now have the lorry under surveillance, but he couldn't risk sending in any of the other vehicles. He would have to hope that the lorry had entered the warehouse premises that Bravo Two had seen him stop at.

'Bravo Two, what is your position now?' Peter asked.
'We're at the bottom end of the estate,' came the reply.
'Can you see the premises in question?'
'Only the side view.'
'Can you see the lorry?'
'Negative.'
'I want you to drive back past the warehouse and report what you see.'
'Bravo Two to Oscar One, no activity at the warehouse, vehicle can not be located.'
'Hell, we've lost it,' Nigel said in panic.
'It's shit or bust now,' Peter replied lifting the handset into which he said, 'All mobiles converge on suspect premises.'

Peter's car was third to arrive at the warehouse and he immediately saw two large double doors that were closed. Alongside the double doors was a small wooden door.

'We go in through there,' Peter said indicating the smaller door. One of the officers tried it and discovered it was locked.

'Who has the key?' Peter asked.

'Here boss,' replied one of the detective constables. Peter looked up and saw that the detective was carrying a sledge hammer which was always referred to in the Drugs Squad as the 'key."

'Right, open up.'

The door, though quite substantial yielded under several blows from the sledge hammer and Peter and his squad entered the warehouse.

His trained eye immediately took in the scene before him. The warehouse was empty except for the lorry and container that they had just followed from the docks. The rear of the container was open and on the floor of the warehouse at the side of the container were several bales of cannabis. Four men were unloading the container.

'We're police and customs officers, stay where you are.'

It was apparent from the expressions on the faces of the warehouse crew that the rapid entry of the law had taken them completely by surprise. Little or no resistance was offered and the four men, together with the lorry driver, were placed under arrest.

They were all taken to the local police station at Speke where they were individually interviewed by a member of the Drugs Squad, together with a member of HM Customs & Excise. In the meantime Peter and Nigel Hunt arranged for the removal of the cannabis to one of the customs warehouses where it was weighed and found to amount to two tonnes.

On their return to Speke Police Station Peter and Nigel listened to the report of the interviewing officers. None of the arrested men had said anything other than to give their personal details but Peter wasn't surprised. He hadn't expected anything else. From their own intelligence of the Challoner organisation, the drug squad were able to identify the four arrested men. Enquiries revealed that the warehouse where the drugs were seized had been rented by Challoner's company.

'I think we've enough evidence to arrest Jimmy Challoner now,' said Nigel to Peter.

'Yes I agree, but is it enough to convict him?'

21

Jimmy Challoner was sitting in his office at the River Club with Mick Walsh waiting for a telephone call to tell them that the drugs were safely locked away in the warehouse at Speke. He tended to spend most of his time at the office when Jennifer was in Reading, throwing himself into his work because he missed her so much.

When the telephone rang Jimmy was surprised to hear the voice of a detective chief inspector. He collected regular cash payments from Jimmy in return for inside information on police activities.

'I don't know if you've heard but the Drugs Squad have just arrested four of your men and seized a haul of cannabis.'

'Where are they?'

'As far as I know they've been taken to one of our divisional stations at Speke.'

'Anything else?'

'No but expect a visit.'

Jimmy replaced the receiver and turned to Mick, 'Turner has nicked the team and seized the drugs, he's on his way here.'

'How the hell did he get on to us?'

'Buggered if I know, but I'd better get Wakefield over here in case.'

He called Wakefield and told him to get down to the River Club as soon as possible. Minutes after replacing the receiver his secretary announced that Detective Chief Inspector Turner wished to see him.

'Show him in,' Jimmy said. 'Peter how nice to see you again. Is this a social call?'

'No it's not,' Peter said, 'This is Mr Hunt from HM Customs & Excise and we're here to arrest you for conspiracy to import drugs.'

'Are you joking? I don't deal in drugs. I'm a legit business man.'

'Get your coat, let's go.'

'Tell Wakefield what's happened,' Jimmy said to Mick as he was led out of the office by Peter. Turning to Peter he said, 'You know you're making a big mistake, this silly vendetta has got to stop.'

'We'll see who's made the mistake.'

Jimmy sat in the back of the car, Peter was driving and Hunt was in the front passenger seat. There was no conversation which gave Jimmy time to think. He knew that none of those arrested would say anything that would incriminate him and he felt reasonably confident that Wakefield would sort things out and fix his release.

As Jimmy looked out of the car window he realised they were heading for the docks.

'Where are we going? This isn't the way to the Bridewell.'

'No. We're not going to the Bridewell, we're going to the Custom's office.'

'If I'm arrested you have to take me to a police station.'

'Not so,' answered Peter, 'this is a joint operation with HM Customs so we're entitled to take you to a Customs office for interviewing purpose.'

Jimmy said nothing. He was concerned that John Wakefield wouldn't know where he was and would head straight for the Bridewell where he doubted the police would be generous with information concerning his whereabouts.

They arrived at the Customs House and Jimmy was taken into a small office where he was told to sit down. Both Peter and Nigel sat down opposite to him. Jimmy saw a telephone on the desk and said

'I'm entitled to make a telephone call.'

'You're entitled to nothing unless I say so.'

'Then you'd better telephone my office so that they can instruct my solicitor as to where I'm being held.'

'You can have your solicitor when I say so and not before.'

'Then I'm not prepared to say anything until I've consulted my legal adviser.'

'Please yourself, but I'm still going to ask the questions.'

'Let's start by saying why you have been arrested. Earlier today we arrested four of your employees in the act of unloading two tonnes of herbal cannabis from a container which had recently arrived on board a ship from Africa.'

'What's that to do with me? What my staff do in their own time is no concern of mine.'

'The container was being unloaded in a warehouse leased to you.'

'Not leased to me, leased to my company, there's a difference.'

'The drugs were shipped from Lagos, you were recently in Lagos.'
'On business.'
'At the container base at Seaforth the crane driver employed to off load the container of drugs is one of your men.'
'Used to be one of my men, he wanted to leave and I arranged for him to return to the docks where he worked before.'

Jimmy looked across at his former friend and sensed that his confidence was weakening after hearing his replies. Jimmy on the other hand felt his confidence growing.

'Bit of a coincidence that you're so closely linked to this container load of drugs,' Peter said.

'It's merely circumstantial, you've got nothing positive against me.'

'Most murderers were convicted on circumstantial evidence.'

'OK if you have the evidence then charge me,' Jimmy's tone was openly challenging. He knew he had Peter worried and when Peter left the office with Nigel Hunt, Jimmy was confident that his release from custody would be a certainty.

Outside the small office being used as an interview room, Peter turned to Nigel and said, 'He's got us over a barrel. His answers offer an alternative to everything we had hoped to prove against him.'

'Yes, but his answers are only an alternative, a Jury may not accept them.'

'They would when it's being put to them by a clever barrister and Challoner will employ the best you can depend on that.'

'Are you suggesting we let him go?'

'We have no choice unless we can get some more evidence against him.'

'Perhaps he'll confess eventually.'

'No chance, we could keep him here for ever and he wouldn't confess,' Peter paused, 'unless of course, he wanted to.'

'From all you've told me and from what I've seen of him myself, I can't imagine any reason why he'd want to confess.'

'There is just one thing which might prompt him to admit his involvement in the importation.'

Intrigued Nigel asked, 'And what's that?'

'To protect someone he wouldn't want to be involved in this.'

'We both know that there's no such person.'

'We know that yes, but we could suggest to Challoner that we would involve his new girlfriend. That might just tip the scales in our favour.'

'We couldn't do that, it's not ethical.'

'Ethics my arse, I'd use any device I could to nail Challoner.'

'Well I don't want to be a party to such an activity.'

'Suit yourself, I'll interview him myself. But if he does confess I'll want you to corroborate his confession otherwise it will be my word against his.'

'I'll corroborate his confession only if there is no reference as to how it was obtained.'

Peter agreed. He had to although he was a little surprised at Nigel's reluctance to support him wholeheartedly.

He then asked to be alone so that he could give some serious thought as to how he would conduct the interview with Challoner. He would need to convince Jimmy that he would arrest and charge Mrs Jennifer Houldin unless he confessed to his part in the cannabis importation.

'Where's your mate?' Jimmy asked Peter as he re-entered the office alone.

'What I'm going to say to you is between us and us only,' Peter declared.

'You're not coming the old pals act are you?'

'In a way I am, I want to do you a favour.'

'Forget it, I don't need favours from you. You've got nothing on me and you know it.'

'You're right, unless of course you admit your guilt.'

'Why would I do that?'

'To protect a lady maybe?'

'What are you on about. Protect what lady?'

'Mrs Jennifer Houldin.'

Jimmy couldn't believe his ears but he knew he had just heard Peter mention Jennifer's name. How did he know about her? The bastard has been following me thought Jimmy. He suspected it was probably a bluff on Turner's part, but he would need to tread carefully. He wouldn't risk harming Jennifer.

'Jennifer has nothing to do with my business interests.'

'Really? I could suggest otherwise.'

'You know you couldn't convict her of any crime, she's just not involved.'

'You are so right, I wouldn't get a conviction. But I could still charge her and oppose bail for a while.'

'You can't just arrest her for doing nothing.'

'It wouldn't be for nothing. I know that she was in Africa recently and I know you visited her before you left for Lagos. I know that the drugs are from Africa. I know that she is very friendly with you and I know that four of your men were arrested unloading those drugs. How does that sound?'

Jimmy was stunned. Put like that Peter could make out a case against Jennifer and Jimmy knew that Peter would do it to get at him. He needed to talk this over with Wakefield, Jimmy knew he needed some sound legal advice.

'I need to discuss this with my solicitor.'

'Nothing doing. Either you confess or I'll send two of my staff down to Reading and you know what that will mean.'

'I need time to think about this.'

'Fair enough, but don't take too long. I'm not prepared to wait all night,' said Peter as he made his way out of the room.

Jimmy knew he was between a rock and a hard place. If he confessed he would be facing a prison sentence and where would that leave him as far as Jennifer was concerned? She would doubtless wash her hands of him. Alternatively he could say nothing and take the risk that Peter would carry out his threat. If Peter arrested Jennifer he knew that at the very least Turner could keep her in custody for two or three days. In his heart Jimmy knew the matter was settled, he couldn't subject Jennifer to such an ordeal nor deprive Debbie of her mother.

When Peter returned in ten minutes, Jimmy said, 'I'll never forget this Peter, it was way below the belt even for you.'

'I take it you want to make an admission to the importation of drugs.'

'Yes, but I'm putting nothing in writing.'

'Deals off then.'

'You're really going for your pound of flesh aren't you?'

'I merely want to ensure that you don't wriggle out of this one in court. Even you will find it difficult to dispute the facts when they're written down in your own statement of admission.'

'You leave me no choice, but remember I'm not going to forget this.'

Peter made no reply but rose to open the door and asked Nigel to come into the office.

'Mr Challoner has decided to admit the charge and wishes to make a written statement about it.'

Peter could hardly believe his luck. He actually had in his possession a signed statement from Jimmy Challoner in which he admitted smuggling cannabis into the country. Peter had been slightly disappointed that Jimmy hadn't named anyone else, but on reflection he had much more than he had ever expected.

'We'd better take him back to the Bridewell and get him charged and locked up,' Peter said to Nigel.

'Tell me,' Nigel asked, 'Would you have arrested Challoner's girlfriend?'

'I would have done whatever I needed to.'

Peter knew himself that he wouldn't have arrested a person he knew to be completely innocent, but it wouldn't do Nigel any harm to wonder.

'Mr Wakefield is here, he's been waiting hours to see you sir,' the Bridewell Sergeant said to Peter as he entered with Challoner. 'Tell him I'll see him when I've charged Challoner,' Peter replied.

Peter formally cautioned and charged Challoner for conspiring with others to import a controlled drug into the UK. Challoner made no reply to the official charge but that didn't concern Peter. He had the signed confession. He still couldn't really believe that Challoner had succumbed. He must think a great deal of this Mrs Houldin.

Leaving Challoner in the charge of the Bridewell staff who would complete the formalities before placing him in a cell, Peter went to find John Wakefield.

As he entered the solicitor's room reserved for their use, Peter saw that Wakefield was very angry.

'At last, do you know how long I've been kept waiting?'

'I didn't ask you to come.

'You know very well why I'm here, I want to see my client.'

'Who would that be?'

'You know damned well who.'

'I suggest you calm down before you see anyone.'

'You have already exceeded your duty Chief Inspector, don't make it worse by being impertinent as well.'

'Exceeded my duty, in what way?'

'By keeping my client from seeing me.'

'But you can see your client as soon as you wish.'

'Look he's been in custody for several hours. Where has he been?'

'He was detained at the office of HM Customs & Excise.'

'You're a police officer, you should have brought him to a police station.'

'Tell me where it says that?'

'I shall be making a strong protest to both your Chief Constable and to the courts about your conduct.'

Peter grinned to himself as he watched Wakefield heading for the Charge Office whose staff would arrange for him to see his client.

'If he's mad now just wait until he hears that Challoner has made a written statement of admission,' Peter murmured.

'Jimmy what the hell has been going on?' Wakefield said when Jimmy was brought into one of the interview rooms.

'Hasn't Turner told you?'

'Not in any detail.'

'Well just after I telephoned you Turner and the Customs guy arrested me and took me to the Customs office.

'That was a diabolical trick by Turner to keep me from seeing you.'

'You didn't say anything did you?'

'I'd better start at the beginning and tell you everything.'

When he had finished Wakefield sighed and said, 'It was just a trick to make you confess, he'd never have arrested Jennifer.'

'I couldn't chance it.'

'There's still a chance that we can get the statement dismissed at court.'

'Dismissed? How? I signed it don't forget.'

'If we can argue that the statement was made under duress then under the Judges' Rules, the court, if satisfied, can dismiss its admissibility.'

'It sounds a bit of a gamble, but it's better than nothing I suppose.'

'Without the statement the prosecution would not be able to substantiate a case against you.'

'It's our only hope then.'

Before he left Jimmy arranged for John Wakefield to telephone Jennifer and tell her that he had been called abroad on business. He didn't want Jennifer to know about his arrest and for the time being at least it would be as well if she thought he was out of the country. It would explain his inability to get in touch with her if he was remanded in custody.

The following morning Jimmy appeared at the Magistrates' Court with the other four men who had been arrested at the warehouse. John Wakefield had warned him that he wouldn't get bail at the first hearing and he didn't intend to make an application. The Magistrates remanded

Jimmy in custody for three days. The prosecution made no objection to the bail of the other four men and they were all released.

After the court hearing John Wakefield saw Jimmy before he went back to his cell.

'Did you telephone Jennifer?'

'Yes, she did wonder why you hadn't telephoned yourself, but I told her that you left in a hurry and you were rushing for the plane.'

'Thanks John, she'll be wondering why I haven't called, I always do even if I'm abroad.'

'Not a lot we can do I'm afraid, the police aren't going to let you make a telephone call.'

'What are my chances of bail next time I appear?'

'Not great. With that statement of admission the prosecution are in a strong position.'

'Bloody statement and bloody Turner.'

'What are you going to do about Turner? He does seem to have it in for you.'

'Believe me Turner will get what's coming to him, no danger.'

Jimmy was very disappointed when on his second appearance his application for bail was turned down by the Magistrates. He was remanded in custody to Risley centre and before leaving he saw John Wakefield briefly.

'What the hell is going on? Why can't you get me bail?'

'That statement you made that's why. If you hadn't done that we wouldn't have a problem.'

'You've given me an idea. If my statement went missing, could Turner carry out his original threat to arrest Jennifer?'

'No, no chance.'

'Then get a message to Detective Chief Inspector Hindley and tell him to visit me in Risley.'

Two days later one of the wardens at Risley said, 'Challoner, there's a police visitor for you this afternoon, they've just telephoned to make an appointment.'

'What time?'

'Two o'clock.'

Jimmy knew it would be Bill Hindley. Hindley was one of several police officers in Liverpool who Jimmy made regular payments to as bribes. Hindley was the most devious of all of them and that was why Jimmy had chosen him for the job he had in mind.

At two o'clock Jimmy was sitting opposite Hindley. It was a common occurrence at Risley for police officers to interview remand prisoners and nobody was surprised at the visit.

'What is it you want to see me about?'

'I want you to destroy the statement that I made to Turner.'

'I see, well I'll need to find it first,' Hindley said, not showing any sign of surprise.

'Surely you know where to look. Where would you keep it?'

'In my desk drawer.'

'Well there you are then.'

'It isn't going to be easy. I don't work at the same nick as Turner. If I'm found in the Drugs Squad someone will ask questions.'

'Then don't get caught.'

'Alright, I'll do what I can'

'It'll be worth a grand,' Jimmy said knowing that for that sum Hindley would succeed.

22

Peter Turner was feeling happier than he had for a long time.

Challoner was where he had always wanted him, in custody. Even though the custody was only on remand it was depriving Challoner of his freedom and once the trial was over he fully expected Challoner's imprisonment to be of a more permanent nature. He was whistling to himself as he entered his office but stopped abruptly when he saw that his desk had been broken into. The drawers had all been forced and the contents strewn on the floor. With a sickening feeling he knew immediately what the intruder had been after. His suspicions were confirmed when he found that the only item missing was Challoner's signed statement. Peter cursed his own stupidity in leaving the only real piece of evidence he had against Challoner in a place where it could be stolen.

He telephoned the prosecuting solicitor's department and made an appointment to see the principal solicitor, Mr Keen. Peter knew that he had to tell the solicitor's department immediately about the theft. He also started making his own enquiries into the theft. Peter already had a good idea which of the force's police officers Challoner had in his pocket and going through them in his mind he narrowed the names down to two as being the most likely to have turned his office over. Hindley or Nicholson, it had to be one of them Peter thought.

He went downstairs to the enquiry office and asked to see the records of prisoners who had been detained overnight. Jimmy reasoned that since neither Nicholson nor Hindley worked from the police station they would have needed an excuse to visit since neither would have been stupid enough to try and sneak in. It was very common for detectives to visit other stations to talk to people under arrest about offences they may be responsible for elsewhere. If a visit had taken place then the name of the officer and his division would be recorded on the prisoner's apprehension sheet. Peter scanned the sheets and found what he was looking for.

Recorded on the sheet of a prisoner who had been arrested for robbery was an entry signifying that the prisoner had received a visit from Detective Sergeant Jones from F Division. Peter knew that Hindley was in charge of F Division and that he would have arranged the visit. He was also sure that Hindley would have been clever enough to cover his own presence by accompanying his sergeant who would doubtless deny that his superior officer had been with him.

Peter returned to his office still very annoyed. It was difficult enough taking on criminals outside without having to be concerned with so called colleagues inside. He telephoned Hindley and said, 'I just want you to know Hindley that what you did last night was about as low as even you can sink. I just hope you can live with yourself,' Peter gave Hindley no opportunity to reply as he slammed down the receiver on hearing Hindley start to protest. He knew that there was nothing further that he could do, making an official report was pointless as it could never be proved that Hindley was responsible. At least he felt better now that he had told Hindley that he knew it was him.

After his interview with the Prosecuting Solicitor, Peter's spirits were raised. Although the absence of the statement per se was a set back, the solicitor had explained that he could give evidence on what the statement had contained. This would be as if it had been a verbal admission by Challoner and with Nigel Hunt giving evidence of corroboration the solicitor was reasonably optimistic that they could still convict Challoner. He stressed to Peter that it would be prudent not to oppose bail at the next hearing.

Jimmy Challoner found himself once more in the police cells beneath the Liverpool Magistrates' Court. He was waiting to be called into court and he was a little impatient to climb the steps that would take him directly into the dock of court number one. He had been told by John Wakefield that the prosecution were not opposing bail. He had also been told by Wakefield that the prosecution had informed him that the statement he had made to Peter Turner had gone missing.

Two hours later outside the courts, Jimmy looked down Dale Street and took in the familiar sights. He breathed in the clean tasting air and although he had only been in custody for one week, these were the things he had missed most. The week had strengthened his resolve to ensure that whatever it took in the future to keep out of prison would be done.

After leaving court Jimmy went directly to his flat where he showered and changed his clothes. Refreshed he telephoned Jennifer, told her he was back and that he wanted to see her as soon as possible. Nothing was said, but he sensed that she had been hurt that he hadn't contacted her while he'd been away. He hoped that once they were together he could smooth things over.

That weekend he met Jennifer and Debbie at Lime Street Station and was almost bowled over as Debbie hurled herself at him on the platform. He picked her up and swung her squealing excitedly in his arms. Putting her down he turned to Jennifer and kissed her on the lips. He sighed as he held her close, unwilling to let her go and Jennifer looked at him with a puzzled expression.

'Is anything wrong?'

'No nothing. I've just missed you that's all.'

'You must go away more often if this is what happens.'

On the drive to Blundellsands Jimmy listened to both Jennifer and Debbie as they brought him up to date on what they had been doing. As they swept into the driveway Jennifer asked about the business trip and he promised to tell her about it later that evening. The rest of the day was spent inspecting the progress of the decorators.

After dinner that evening when they were alone Jimmy turned to Jennifer and said 'Jennifer, do you really love me?'

'I knew something was wrong, what is it Jimmy?'

'In a way something is wrong and because it might affect our relationship I'm afraid.'

'Well whatever it is I'll still love you Jimmy, why don't you tell me and stop worrying.'

'Well last week I wasn't abroad, I was in prison.'

'In prison, whatever for?'

'It's a long story so I'll start at the beginning. As a boy I grew up with a friend who is now a policeman. At one time we were inseparable, but when we grew up we just seemed to drift apart. As far as I was concerned my attitude towards Peter never changed but sadly his towards me has. I suspect it's jealousy because I've attempted to make something of my life. He has a kind of vendetta against me and on occasion uses his position as a policeman to harass me. Arresting me on trumped up charges, none of which are true of course. I've always been completely exonerated, but it's not pleasant.'

'Is he allowed to that?'

'Oh he's clever, he always manages to conjure up enough false evidence to make a case against me and while it's a nuisance in the past I haven't been too concerned. Obviously now I have you I couldn't bear this kind of thing to come between us.'

'You mean he's arrested you again?'

'Yes.'

'And the charge was trumped up again?'

'Yes, some people who work for me have been caught up in smuggling drugs into the country. Apparently they were using one of my warehouses when they were caught. On the strength of them being my employees and using my premises, Turner, the policeman I grew up with arrested me and charged me with being involved.'

'Did your men say you were involved?'

'Don't be silly, they know I'm not.'

'It seems unbelievable that you can be arrested on such flimsy evidence.'

'Tell me about it. Thing is Jennifer, it's always been like this.'

'What happens now?'

'There'll be a court case and I'll be freed as always.'

'Why did you imagine that this would affect us?'

'I was afraid you might think there was some truth in Turner's lies.'

'Jimmy I'll only ask you once. Were you involved in any way in this?'

'I give you my word, I knew nothing about it.'

'Then what are you worrying about?'

'I just couldn't bear to lose you Jennifer.'

'Now it's you who's being silly,' Jennifer whispered as she put her arms around Jimmy, holding him tightly.

Peter Turner had heard that Challoner was to be represented at the Crown Court by Mr Robert Fox QC. Mr Fox had the reputation of attacking the prosecution evidence in an effort to discredit the police with the Jury. His methods had met with a great deal of success and of all the defence barristers on the circuit Mr Fox was the most feared by the police. Peter knew full well that he was in for a tough time when he entered the witness box to give evidence against Challoner. However the prosecution had retained Mr Richard Brown to prosecute the case, a choice Peter approved of. If anyone could match Mr Fox in a courtroom drama it was Richard Brown.

On the first day of the trial Mr Brown outlined the prosecution case. He informed the Jury that the police and HM Customs & Excise had observed the unloading of a freight container. This had been shipped as empty and in a damaged condition from Lagos, Africa to Liverpool. It was this container that was suspected of containing a quantity of drugs. Mr Brown told the Jury that an experienced crane driver would have known instantly that the box container wasn't empty. The fact that the crane driver made no mention of this to his employers may strike you as strange until I tell you that until very recently the crane driver was employed by Mr Challoner.

'Good point,' muttered Peter to Nigel Hunt. Mr Brown continued by telling the Jury that the container had been followed to a warehouse at Speke where the police had arrested the four men, who are alongside Challoner, in the act of unloading two tonnes of cannabis. He continued by telling the Jury that the men and the warehouse were part of the Challoner organisation. The Jury were also informed that when interviewed by the police Challoner had made a voluntary statement which had been taken down in writing. This statement, Mr Brown had told them, amounted to an admission of Challoner's own guilt in this conspiracy. Brown then went on to explain the statement had gone missing and could not be produced in court. He told them the evidence would be given informing them of what the statement had said and that they were perfectly entitled to accept that evidence. In conclusion he informed the Jury that the prosecution would endeavour to prove to them that James Arthur Challoner, together with the other accused, conspired together to bring illegal drugs into the country.

It is the rule of the British Legal System that witnesses for the prosecution are not allowed to be present in court while other witnesses are giving evidence until after they themselves have given their evidence. Peter and Nigel were about to leave the court when Mr Robert Fox QC rose to his feet and said to the Judge. 'Your Honour, it's at this point that I wish to address the court on a point of law.'

Jimmy had persuaded Jennifer to postpone their wedding until after the trial. She had been reluctant to agree initially, but he eventually convinced her that he wouldn't be able to enjoy the occasion with the court case pending against him. This wasn't the real reason, in reality he didn't want to be distracted from his immediate priority, securing his acquittal. He had spent considerable time with John Wakefield and although Jimmy had wanted to contest the case at the committal proceedings, John had convinced him to reserve his defence for the Crown Court.

Jimmy had sufficient knowledge of the legal system to know that certain cases can only be dealt with by a Judge and Jury. His case was such a one. He also knew from past experience that before a case can be passed to the Crown Court it had to be heard by an examining Magistrate to ensure that there was a case to answer. The defence has the right to fight the case at that stage in the hope that the examining Magistrate will find insufficient evidence to commit the case for trial. John Wakefield's argument had been that if they fought the case at the committal proceeding and lost, the prosecution would have knowledge of their defence strategy which Wakefield had said was best kept for the Jury.

John Wakefield had engaged Mr Robert Fox QC, a barrister who Jimmy knew by reputation to be highly successful at getting people off charges. Often against the seemingly overwhelming odds of the prosecution evidence. He didn't come cheap, but that was of no consequence to Jimmy. He asked Wakefield why he hadn't retained Mark O'Rourke again since he had done such a good job the last time. Wakefield explained that this case warranted a QC and Mark was just an ordinary barrister. At their first case meeting Jimmy was impressed by Fox and he outlined to Jimmy the basis of his defence tactics which he was confident would result in an acquittal.

On the first day of his trial Jimmy was required to arrive by nine thirty a.m. and to surrender himself to the court officer in accordance with his bail condition. He was familiar with the routine and after reporting in he was taken downstairs to the court cells to await his trial. At ten twenty five a.m. he was taken up to the court and placed in the dock. Shortly afterwards the other four accused were brought into the court and put in the dock alongside Jimmy. Jimmy didn't speak to any of them and sat impassively waiting for the case to begin. He watched with interest as twelve members of the Jury were sworn in and while the defence had the legal right to challenge a particular Jury member and have him or her replaced, Mr Fox made no such objection.

Once the Jury had been sworn in, the Judge entered and the trial began. The clerk of the court read out the charge to each of the accused and they were asked whether they were guilty or not guilty. Jimmy answered 'Not Guilty' in ringing tones.

The prosecution barrister then made a speech which suggested that Jimmy was the ringleader and organiser of the incident. When he had finished addressing the Jury, Mr Fox rose and told the Judge that he wished to address the court on a matter of law.

Peter stood at the back of the court while the Jury filed out. If the trial Judge agrees to hear an application by one of the barristers on a point of law he does so in the absence of the Jury. This is so that things can be said which if the Jury had been present might prejudice them either way. Peter made his way to one of the court benches and sat down. Satisfied the Jury had all retired the Judge invited Mr Fox to begin.

Your Honour, you are aware that in this case the prosecution were to have produced a written statement which they were to allege was, a voluntary confession made by my client, Mr Challoner. It is said this statement went missing from the desk of Chief Inspector Turner, an issue I find difficult to comprehend. However it is still the intention of the prosecution to give evidence of the existence of the statement and its contents by means of verbal evidence. It is this issue that I make my submission Your Honour. Peter looked at Nigel and whispered, 'He's going to challenge the way we took the statement.'

'Don't worry, I complied with the Judge's Rules, we'll be ok,' Peter murmured.

Mr Fox continued, 'The Judge's Rules state quite precisely that before an alleged confession can be given in evidence, it must be proved to the satisfaction of the court that it was given voluntarily. Without inducement from fear or favour. It is my submission that the alleged confession by Mr Challoner was not obtained voluntarily, but was induced from him by fear,' said Fox sitting down as he finished speaking.

'Mr Brown do you have any observations to make?' the Judge asked.

'It is the prosecution's contention that the confession was given freely and without inducement and therefore is in accordance with the guidelines laid down for our instruction in the Judge's Rules,' Mr Brown replied.

'Mr Fox, how do you intend introducing evidence to convince me that the statement made by your client was not voluntarily given?' the Judge asked.

'By asking, Your Honour, to allow me to call the police officer who took the statement so that I may cross examine him and elicit from him the manner in which the statement was given.' Mr Fox replied.

'Very well Mr Fox, I will allow your application.'

'I'm obliged to Your Honour. Call Detective Chief Inspector Turner,' said Mr Fox.

'Here we go, a trial within a trial,' Peter whispered to Nigel as he stood up to make his way to the witness box.

'Before I ask you to take the oath officer, may I ask that if Mr Hunt, the Customs Officer, is in court then would he kindly leave.'

Mr Fox turned and watched as Nigel left the room.

'Now officer you will be sworn in.'

Peter took the testament in his right hand, held it up and read the oath from the card handed to him by the clerk of the court.

'Now tell me officer,' began Mr Fox 'when you arrested my client, Mr Challoner, you took him to an office of the Customs & Excise. Why did you not take him to a police station?'

'I felt it would be more expedient to interview him at the Customs Office rather than the police station,' Peter replied.

'Oh really, why was that?' Mr Fox asked. Peter glanced across the court and saw a sea of expectant faces, all listening intently, sensing that the hearing was about to ignite. As it was a joint venture with HM Customs, I felt that either venue would suffice for the purposes of the interview.'

'But you're a police officer are you not?'

'Yes I am.'

'Then why didn't you take my client directly to a police station?'

'As I have said on this occasion, because it was a joint investigation, I didn't believe that it was necessary to take him to the police station.'

'Tell me officer, are there any facilities at the Customs Office for the reception of prisoners?'

'No.'

'Just as I thought. In that case you knew that you would be duty bound to take my client to a police station eventually didn't you?'

'Yes.'

He knew exactly where the line of questioning was leading, but couldn't do anything to divert it.

'Wasn't the reason not to take Mr Challoner directly to a police station simply to deny my client his constitutional rights as a citizen to the services of a solicitor?'

'No.'

'You did hear Mr Challoner instruct his business colleague to inform a solicitor that he had been arrested didn't you?'

'Yes.'

'Did you make any comment at that time as to where you intended to take Mr Challoner?'

'No.'

'Then would you not agree that the natural assumption would be to imagine that Mr Challoner was on his way to the police station?'

'Yes.'

'Exactly,' said Mr Fox, 'you knew that Mr Challoner's solicitor would go to the police station and would receive a negative response to his enquiry as to Mr Challoner's whereabouts didn't you?'

'I hadn't really given any thought to it.'

'That is not the truth officer, you deliberately took my client to the Customs Office knowing that his solicitor wouldn't be able to trace his whereabouts.'

'No, that wasn't the reason.'

'I suggest to you officer that it was the reason and you effectively denied my client the right to legal representation.'

'No.'

'Let us move on to the interview itself. We can see from your deposition that Mr Challoner started the interview by denying any involvement in the charge of importing cannabis. Is that correct Inspector?'

'Yes that's correct.'

'Are we being asked to believe that after a short interview with you he made a confession?'

'Yes that is perfectly correct.'

'Tell me officer, is the deposition you have produced to the court the full account of your interview with Mr Challoner?'

'Yes,' Peter said starting to feel uncomfortable knowing that there was no mention of Mrs Houldin in the deposition. Surely Jimmy wouldn't want her mentioned in court, he had wanted to protect her at all costs.

'I put it to you officer that the deposition is not a full account of the interview.'

'It is a full account of the interview, but we did have a conversation which I didn't record,' Peter admitted hoping to salvage something from the wreckage that loomed ahead.

'Oh I see,' said Mr Fox, 'you only recorded that part of the conversation which you believed was relevant to the prosecution's case.'

'No I recorded the whole of the conversation that was relevant to the case.'

'I don't see any reference in the deposition to a threat made to Mr Challoner.'

'I didn't threaten Mr Challoner.'

'Oh I see, perhaps it was more of a promise then.'

'I don't understand.'

'Allow me to explain. My client recalls you telling him that unless he made a confession you would implicate an innocent woman who means a great deal to him. Is that true or not?'

'I do remember talking to Mr Challoner about his new girlfriend, but I didn't make any threats to involve her.'

'Chief Inspector, that is a lie. You made a threat to my client knowing that he would make any kind of confession to avoid this woman being harassed in the manner in which you have harassed Mr Challoner.'

'No there was no threat made to Mr Challoner, his confession was entirely voluntary.'

'I put it to you Chief Inspector. The reason you took my client to the Customs Office and not to a police station was simply to keep him from his legal right to see a solicitor. This enabled you to force him into making a confession by threatening him with the involvement of the woman he hopes to marry shortly.'

'No,' said Peter.

With that Fox sat down, his job done well. Peter was under no illusion that the confession that Challoner had made would now be eliminated from the evidence.

Nigel Hunt was called into the witness box. He did his best to corroborate Peter's evidence, but was forced to admit to the court that he wasn't present for the entire interview. He had left the interview room when Challoner was denying his involvement and had only re-entered when Challoner had been ready to make a confession.

It was as Peter had expected. Little more than a formality after Nigel had given his evidence. The trial Judge delivered his judgement by saying, 'Mr Fox, in view of the matter you have raised, it is evident that Mr Challoner was denied his right to consult with a solicitor. Since you have raised a doubt as to how the confession was obtained, I cannot allow the confession to go before the Jury. It must be struck from the evidence.'

Mr Brown had to stand before the court and offer no further evidence against Challoner, who once again was formally acquitted.

23

To celebrate his acquittal Jimmy Challoner held a celebration party at the River Club. He entertained everyone who had helped him during his trial for he was in no doubt that conviction would have meant a lengthy prison sentence. He had telephoned Jennifer with his good news and arranged to take her and Debbie to Paris that weekend, as a celebration of his freedom.

The following day he met Mick Walsh and said that the syndicate must stop trading in cannabis. In order to make the profits which would render the venture worthwhile, the drugs had to be imported in bulk. Jimmy felt that the risks were just too great and although it was hard to give up a scheme that netted so much profit Jimmy didn't intend to give up his freedom. Both were only too aware that cannabis importation had easily been their biggest profit maker. Other areas of the business were in a healthy state financially, but the profit margins were simply not as high. The amount of stolen spirits and cigarettes that were disposed of through the chain of clubs was steady and netted a regular income. It was the same story with the property development, that too was steady. Jimmy's inside information from corrupt officials meant that he was able to buy up large developmental sites at give away prices. All good business thought Jimmy, but dull. More than anything Jimmy craved excitement, an element of danger combined with the opportunity to outwit his old friend Peter Turner.

Jimmy turned to Mick, 'What else do these druggies use?'

'They seem to use whatever's available. It'll be interesting to see what happens when we drop our cannabis supplies.'

'Keep your ears to the ground and let's be quick to pick up on whatever it is they want.'

'There's always heroin but it's pricey and besides I don't think the druggies will go for it at the moment.'

'Right, I'll leave you to research the market, just let me know where we should concentrate our energies.'

'No problem. What about Winston Spenser, now you're not importing the cannabis, will you bring him back?'

'Didn't I tell you, he's staying on there. With the money he's made he has decided to start his own business.'

'Doing what?'

'Haven't a bloody clue, but knowing Winston nothing legal.'

After Mick had left Jimmy considered his options. Without the input from the drugs the next most lucrative section of the business was prostitution. Over the years this side of the business had changed considerably. There were still 'street girls' who served the needs of the seamen, but the real money now came from the hostesses who were employed in the organisation's clubs. These girls were specially chosen for their charm as well as their figures and were very successful with the affluent clientele who visited the clubs. As with all the prostitutes working for the organisation a percentage of their earnings was paid direct to the syndicate.

Jimmy had never really understood how John Wakefield and the company accountant recorded the various enterprises which made up the business of the syndicate. What he did know was that the annual turnover was a multi-million pound operation and that much of the money from the criminal activities was invested in off-shore dealings. The remainder Jimmy had invested himself and that went towards his private fortune which had been growing steadily over the years.

The next day as he drove down to Reading, Jimmy put all thoughts of business from his mind. He was collecting Jennifer and Debbie en route for Paris and business had no place in his immediate plans.

The break proved to be a resounding success and Jimmy returned feeling considerably happier with life. Even though Jennifer had assured him of her complete trust in him Jimmy had sensed a certain doubt. He believed that his acquittal had finally convinced her of his innocence.

His complacency was ruffled somewhat when Jennifer announced that she would prefer to postpone the wedding and simply live together as a family.

'I don't understand. We'd agreed on the wedding for next month.'

'I still want that Jimmy, just not so soon. We've only known each other for a short time. I'm sure it will be better for all of us if we take things at a slower pace.'

'Is it my arrest that has done this?'
'I can't pretend it's not one of the reasons.'
'Then you still think I was involved.'
'No, I'm certain you weren't. The fact remains it does highlight the fact that I know nothing about your business, about vast areas of your life.'

Jimmy was silent. He had been shocked that Jennifer wanted to postpone the wedding, but on reflection decided maybe she had got it right. It was true that they didn't know a great deal about one another and Jennifer had to consider Debbie after all. Swallowing his pride Jimmy told Jennifer that although he couldn't pretend he hadn't been hurt by her suggestion, he understood. He would wait until she was ready.

It was agreed that Jennifer and Debbie would move up to Liverpool as soon as possible. Jimmy had wanted to sell Jennifer's house, but she had persuaded him that keeping it would be the better option. They would be able to use it as a weekend cottage or when they visited London.

Taking John Wakefield's advice Jimmy enrolled Debbie at a local private school.

'I have to warn you they might insist you go on the waiting list for twelve months,' John had said. Jimmy smiled, he had no intention of going on anyone's list, although even he felt slightly intimidated by the formidable Miss Tatlock as she peered over the steel rim of her spectacles.

'Mr Challoner, you must realise that girls have their name down from birth for St Mary's,' she had said scathingly when Jimmy had arranged an interview with a view to enrolling Debbie. Sensing that things were not going his way and aware of how Jennifer had set her heart on this school for Debbie, Jimmy swallowed his growing anger. Smiling broadly he placed his cheque book on the desk between them and proceeded to write a cheque for ten thousand pounds. Pushing it towards Miss Tatlock he said, 'Now Miss Tatlock, do you or don't you have a place for Debbie next term?'

Wordlessly Miss Tatlock picked up the cheque and having inspected it carefully, folded it and placed it in her desk drawer.

'Mr Challoner, I see no reason why St Mary's cannot accommodate young Debbie in September. Rules after all are there for the breaking are they not?'

'Oh indeed they are Miss Tatlock, indeed they are.'

Peter Turner's resolve to convict Jimmy Challoner was still unshaken, but with every acquittal Challoner was becoming more confident, Peter more despondent. Challoner's burgeoning fortunes enabled him to distance himself from the crimes that he was involved in and Peter realised that it would be a waste of time trying to convict him. He had come to the conclusion that his only hope of cornering Challoner was through his involvement with drugs. This was the only area where Jimmy required assistance. He needed people who knew more about drugs trafficking than he did. Peter knew from experience that drug traffickers in general tended to be less reliable than the average criminal type that Jimmy was accustomed to. All Peter had to do was wait until Challoner resumed his dealings in drugs and he was confident that it wouldn't be too long. Peter was relying on the fact that nothing would bring in the massive profits for Challoner that drugs did and he was certain that Challoner's innate greed, coupled with an insatiable demand for drugs on the streets, would tempt Challoner back into the ring.

Challoner's arrest had resulted in a sharp rise in break-ins at chemists' shops and doctors' surgeries. The lull in the cannabis supply drove users to seek out replacement drugs and Peter knew Jimmy wouldn't be able to resist such an easy target.

24

With his domestic life settled into a happy routine, Jimmy felt able to turn his attentions to his business. He had begun monthly meetings with Mick Walsh who had day to day control of events, but Jimmy liked to keep everyone aware of who had the final say.

It was at one of these meetings that Mick suggested that they get back into the drugs scene.

'It's too soon, isn't it?' Jimmy said.

'I don't reckon it is.'

'Aren't we still being watched?'

'Well Customs might still be watching the docks, but I know the Drugs Squad have stopped their surveillance of us.'

'That's the docks out then.'

'With what I've got in mind we don't need to import, so we wouldn't have Customs sniffing round.'

'There's still Turner's mob. But go on, tell me what you've got in mind.'

Mick told Jimmy that the current drugs market centred on manufactured drugs, especially amphetamines. Demand far outstripped supply and the market was ripe for exploitation. He had discovered that a crude form of amphetamine was being distributed in Liverpool. The source was a student who had dropped out of Oxford University and was making up the drugs in a shed in his parents' garden.

If this guy was properly managed the amphetamine business could be worth twenty thousand pounds a month.'

'As much as that.'

'At least.'

'You sure Customs aren't interested.'

'No danger, they're only involved when the drug is imported.'

'In that case I think you and I should meet this budding chemist. Make an appointment Mick.'

Within days the meeting took place at the Adelphi Hotel where Mick introduced Tim Owens to Jimmy. It was evident to Jimmy that Owens was a character after his own heart with the same entrepreneurial spirit. He liked Owens, particularly when it became clear that he was motivated by a desire to make money.

'Let's talk business,' Jimmy said, 'how many amphetamine tablets do you make in a month?'

'About 1,000.'

'How much do they sell for?'

'Fifty pence a tablet.'

'Why not turn out more, the market can take it?'

'Big problem there, I've only got a very basic mould which I made myself. It only makes twenty tablets at a time so making a thousand takes quite a while.'

'Given the right equipment, how many could you make in a month?'

'Fifty thousand I expect. The compound is no problem, it's the tabletting.'

'Why haven't you bought a decent tablet making machine?'

'Oddly enough they're made locally, but the snag is they will only sell to pharmaceutical outlets.'

'I'll get you the machine and then I'll expect you to make fifty thousand tablets a month. I'll pay you a regular sum of ten thousand each month, but you must maintain the fifty thousand target.'

'What about getting rid of them? I can't sell that many.'

'Leave the selling to me, all I want you to do is make the things.'

'Right, you're on, a deal it is.'

'Just one thing, you'll deal with Mick from now on. You and I never met, erase this meeting from your memory,' Jimmy leaned forward, 'understand?'

'What meeting Mr Smith?' Owens said with a grin. Jimmy liked that.

Jimmy arranged for Mick to acquire the tablet making machine and later that night an engineering firm that manufactured the machines was broken into and the latest electrical model, capable of stamping out five thousand at a time, was stolen. Owens was delighted with the new equipment and the monthly manufacture of fifty thousand tablets began.

Jimmy asked Mick how he was going to dispose of the tablets.

'Local dealers will take twenty thousand and I've arranged to sell the other thirty thousand direct to major dealers in the north west.'

'How much will we be selling for?'

'Locally we'll sell at £1.50 a tablet and the bulk sales can go for £1.00 each.' Jimmy did some mental arithmetic. Six hundred thousand a year with no capital outlay or overheads was very satisfactory indeed.

Mick obviously set up the amphetamine distribution well because each month all the tablets that Owens produced were sold as soon as they hit the streets. Just as Jimmy felt that everything was under control Mick announced that he wanted to be a partner in the drugs side of the business.

'I can't agree to that.'

'Why not? I've put a lot of personal effort into it.'

'I'm not arguing with that but if I agreed to it every other head, like prostitution, protection, you name it would be after the same deal. Sorry Mick, out of the question.'

Mick left the office disgruntled and Jimmy made a mental note to keep an eye on him just in case disgruntled developed into disloyal.

Even though he was half prepared for it Jimmy felt a pang of regret when he found out Mick had been in negotiation with contacts in the north west, trying to recruit a team in order to oust Jimmy from the organisation. Acting quickly Jimmy called unexpectedly at the River Club.

Mick's face drained of colour, 'I didn't expect to see you until next week.'

'I'm sure you didn't, but I have a little business matter that needs attention Mick.'

'What's that then?'

'Oh I think you know that already, it's your little recruitment drive.'

Mick's face was ashen as the realisation that Jimmy had discovered his treachery hit him.

'I can explain.'

'That's good, you can explain on the way then.'

'On the way where?'

'We're going for a drive Mick, the car's waiting outside,' Jimmy replied as he led Mick to the waiting car which contained two of the syndicate members who Mick immediately recognised as part of the hit team.

'You're not going to kill me are you?'

'You know the penalty for treason as well as I do.'

Mick looked sick as they made their way to Ainsdale beach. Jimmy knew that it must be conjuring up grisly images in Mick's head, after all he himself had used this venue for similar exercises in the past.

'How am I going to die?'

'You disappoint me Mick, I thought you were my most loyal friend. You let greed cloud your judgement and now it's judgement day.'

'I know, I should've had more sense. For old time's sake make it quick.'

Jimmy said nothing, he was looking directly at Mick, admiring his composure. He clearly thought he was going to die and yet he hadn't screamed and begged. It re-enforced Jimmy's belief that Mick would keep his cool whatever the crisis.

'I'm not going to kill you Mick. In spite of everything I still reckon you can be useful to me, but I hardly need to remind you that this is merely a stay of execution.'

'Thanks Jimmy. Believe me nothing like this will ever happen again.'

'Just to make sure you remember that,' Jimmy said as he nodded towards the two heavies standing either side of Mick. He turned and walked back to the car, but not before hearing a sickening crack and Mick's cry of pain as both his legs were broken.

Peter Turner was concerned, his squad was seizing massive amounts of amphetamine tablets daily. Analysis of the tablets had shown that in spite of their initial credible appearance they were not being manufactured legitimately. He also knew from colleagues in the North West that similar seizures were being made across the region. It was evident that the tablets were being produced illegally and probably from the same source.

A conference was arranged with representatives from drug squads throughout the North West and the police forensic science laboratory at Chorley. At the end of the meeting Rex Peters, a chemist from Chorley, was appointed to deal with all future seizures of amphetamines and to act as laboratory liaison officer.

After the conference Peter spoke to Rex to hear his ideas about the tablets.

'The chemical compound of the tablets is reasonably good and suggests a degree of chemistry know how. In all the seizures I've examined the ingredients have been consistent which points towards just one chemist. But beyond that I can't say.'

'Have you kept a log of the seizures and when they were made?'

'Only on a force area, I haven't broken the seizures down to towns or cities.'

'OK well that should help. Can I look at your records?'

'By all means, though I can't imagine what they will tell you.'

Back in Rex Peters' office Peter checked the totals and noticed that twice as many seizures had been in Liverpool. Although there could be several explanations for this it was probable that Liverpool could be the source city. He mentioned this to Rex and also that, in spite of their efforts over the previous twelve months, his squad had not managed to uncover any information about the source.

'Have you tried starting at the beginning. I mean whoever the chemist is, he has to buy his precursor chemicals from a retail outlet. Why not concentrate your resources on that area?'

'How many retail outlets would we be talking about?'

'Most of the ingredients used to make amphetamines can be bought in photographic shops as they're used in developing.'

'I couldn't hope to keep all those covered.'

'Granted, but there is one ingredient which can only be bought from a specialist retailer. It's a chemical with limited commercial use known as BMK. There are only two outlets in the whole of the North West, one in Manchester and one in Liverpool.'

Peter started his enquiries at the manufacturer in Liverpool. He discovered they sold two litres of BMK on a monthly basis to a young man who always turned up on spec without placing an order. Although there was no pattern to his visits it was over two weeks since his last collection. Peter telephoned Rex with the news.

'It's certainly as big as we thought. He could make about fifty thousand tablets at a time with that amount of BMK. All the best with your surveillance and keep me posted.'

Peter arranged for the squad to keep the outlet under surveillance during opening hours from the following Monday. He also arranged for a policewoman, Louise, to be placed in the outlet so that she could relay a radio message once the man appeared.

Three days passed without incident and to keep the squad alert Peter instructed them to change position regularly. However at eleven o'clock on the Thursday Louise radioed to the squad, 'Suspect now present. Male about twenty two years, fair hair, five feet eleven, dressed in brown trousers and black leather jacket.'

Peter radioed one of his sergeants, 'Bob get out on foot and be ready to take our man when he leaves the premises. No vehicle seen as yet.'

'Roger, we saw him arrive on foot. If he has a vehicle it must be parked somewhere else.'

'Louise to squad, suspect leaving now.'

'Bob to squad, I've got him.'

Bob kept up a running commentary and the suspect was followed to a nearby car park.

'Bob to squad, suspect getting into blue Cortina, ATG814E, now driving out of the car park and turning left.'

The surveillance team followed the Cortina out of the city and towards Lancashire. Although the team used their usual routine to avoid being spotted, the driver of the Cortina seemed oblivious to their presence. They followed him to Prescott and Peter, who was in the lead car at the time, saw him turn down a narrow country lane. He radioed for the third car only to follow and the rest remained on the main road. He listened to the commentary now coming being delivered by Brian in the third squad car. He had no idea where the lane led and was forced to rely on Brian's car staying on the Cortina's tail.

'Brian to squad, vehicle turned right into small farmyard, instructions please.'

'Drive past, turn around in about a mile and return to our position.'

'Brian to squad, re-passing farmyard, vehicle parked and unattended, lane is a dead end.'

Peter went back to the squad office and arranged for a search warrant. He also spoke to Rex Peters at the laboratory and told him what was happening.

'Looks like you've struck gold. When amphetamines are being processed a foul smell is given off, but the farmyard smells would mask that.'

'When we do a bust tomorrow what should we look for?'

'Well if you like I could join you. There shouldn't be any danger if all he's doing is manufacturing amphetamines, but with an amateur chemist you can't be too careful.'

'OK, you'll have to be up early though,' Peter laughed.

At eight the next morning Peter and his squad accompanied by Rex and his assistant entered the farmyard. Peter approached a middle aged man he saw coming out of one of the buildings. He was clearly unnerved to see so many people but Peter quickly explained their purpose and showed him the search warrant. Mr Owens read the warrant and said, 'My son Tim uses the outhouse over there but I don't know what he does. He's doing some experimental work, but I can assure you it won't have anything to do with drugs.'

'Is your son at home?'

'Yes, I should think he'll still be in bed.'

Peter sent two police officers to wake Tim up while he and the others checked the outhouse. Even to his unqualified eye the outhouse looked like a laboratory with bottles and test tubes on every surface. He asked Rex and his assistant to make sure everywhere was safe before undertaking a thorough search. In the meantime Peter turned his attention to Tim.

'Are you Tim Owens?'

'Yes.'

'You know why we're here, do you have anything else to say to me?'

'What can I say except I'm surprised I got away with it for so long.'

Once Rex gave the all clear Peter and his squad set about searching the rest of the premises. The tablet stamping machine was recovered along with a record of the number of tablets made to date. It totalled seven hundred and fifty thousand. Owens' building society book showing regular deposits of ten thousand pounds was recovered, all of which enabled Peter to arrest Tim for the illicit manufacture of drugs.

Back at the police station Peter went over the evidence and reasoned that if Owens was solely responsible for the supply and distribution his profits should have been nearer to fifty thousand a month and the payments would have been sporadic. It seemed likely that he was working with a distributor who was taking the lion's share of the profits. Peter felt instinctively that Challoner was that distributor and he decided to have a chat with Owens.

Owens was open about his part in the business but wouldn't say anything, except that he had been commissioned by a businessman, about the distribution side.

'Why are you protecting this man?'

'I don't see the point in involving anyone else. You've caught me, isn't that enough?'

'The man you're protecting is a villain. He has traded on human misery all his life. Is this really the type of individual you want to protect?'

'How do you know so much? I haven't said anything to identify him.'

'I know Challoner's work when I see it,' Peter said watching Owens carefully. He saw the look of fear that flitted across Owens' face and knew without doubt that he had been right. He also knew that fear would keep Owens from ever naming Challoner as the distributor.

Once again all Peter was able to do under the circumstances was to halt the supply and hit Challoner's pocket. Peter craved more. He wanted Challoner arrested and convicted, but again he had been thwarted in his efforts.

25

The trouble with Mick Walsh had left Jimmy wary. He had always assumed that his employees were totally loyal, but it was clear to him that Walsh wouldn't have contemplated making his move unless he was confident of a sizeable following. It was this suggested disloyalty of not only Walsh but of other unknown members of his organisation that irked Jimmy. Walsh's temporary absence had forced Jimmy to re-think the drugs distribution chain. He had overcome this minor hiccup and it was now progressing as smoothly as it had when Walsh was in charge.

On his return Mick was very subdued. He knew that Jimmy had spared his life and was at pains to prove that his loyalty and dedication were as strong as they had always been. One or two thought that Jimmy's leniency towards Mick meant that he had lost his grip. They were soon discouraged in their attempts to make a bid for his crown when they heard of the hospitalisation of those foolish enough to have tried.

One evening when Debbie was staying overnight with a friend, Jimmy seized the opportunity to broach the subject of marriage. It was nearly two years since Jennifer had moved in with him and Jimmy felt that the time had come for some kind of formal commitment.

Jennifer's eyes widened in surprise 'What's brought this on, aren't we OK the way we are?'

'Well yes, but I'd just like to do things properly.'

'You really mean it don't you?'

'I've never been so serious.'

'Well I know Debbie wants it so let's do it. I'd like it to be a small affair though, nothing glitzy.'

'Anyway you want it is fine by me.'

The following day Jimmy began making the wedding arrangements which included chartering a yacht for a honeymoon to be spent sailing around the Greek Islands.

While he was in town he called to see John Wakefield. His solicitor was concerned he was unable to legitimately invest anymore of Jimmy's money. He explained that he had 'laundered' as much as he could through the legitimate companies which had resulted in the annual turnover rising to over five million. Wakefield explained that while the legal companies had provided a useful cover, the company accountant and himself now believed that investing any more cash would be futile. Top rate tax was being paid on the profits these companies were making.

'My advice is deposit any further excess privately.'

'Trouble is I've already got a dozen or more accounts in different names, I can't cope with any more.'

'How about a safe depository.'

'No chance, I happen to know they're not bombproof as it were.'

'Then how about a Swiss bank account?'

'Are they safe though?'

'Not only safe but the Swiss bankers are very discreet.'

'Sounds ideal, how's it done John?'

'I can make all the provisional arrangements but you'll have to visit the bankers personally before the account can be finalised.'

'How much do you think I should deposit?'

'All the profit from the drugs dealing and the casinos would be my advice.'

'But that's about a hundred thousand a month.'

'I know, but there's no alternative. We can't legitimately account for that sort of cash either through your own private account or through the accounts of any of your companies. The last thing we want to do is arouse the suspicions of the Inland Revenue.'

'Fair enough, you're my legal adviser. Let's do it, open a Swiss account for me.'

'I'll get onto it right away. In my opinion it might be just as well to have ready money available to you outside the United Kingdom.'

'I hope I never need it in the way you're implying.'

'So do I but it's good insurance nevertheless.'

'Right now we've got the business out of the way can I ask you a favour?'

'Ask away, I'll be happy to help if I can.'

'Jennifer has agreed to marry me at last and we'd very much like you to be one of our witnesses.'

'Congratulations, it'll be a pleasure Jimmy.'

Jimmy had known that John would agree to being a witness but he was pleased at his obvious pleasure in being asked.

During the weeks that followed Jimmy was busy with both business and wedding arrangements. Together with John Wakefield he flew to Zurich and finalised the details of his Swiss bank account and even the news of Owen's arrest couldn't dent his high spirits.

'I knew that it couldn't last forever,' Jimmy told a stunned Mick.

Once he was assured that Owens wouldn't talk Jimmy seemed to dismiss the incident from his mind.

The wedding and the honeymoon, for which Jimmy had chartered a luxury yacht to cruise the Greek islands, proved to be the culmination of all Jimmy's dreams. Sometimes he found it hard to believe that he had been given this second chance. He and Jennifer were so taken with the yacht that Jimmy made arrangements to buy a fully staffed yacht of his own. For a generous increase in salary, Michael, the vessel's captain was happy to act as Jimmy's interpreter and p.a. He accompanied Jimmy to the lawyer in Athens as well as organising the recruitment of suitable staff.

Once details had been finalised Jimmy returned with Jennifer and Debbie. They spent two more sun drenched weeks cruising around the islands before finally coming into dock at the moorings he had arranged at Piraeus. As he watched the yacht being secured to its moorings Jimmy nodded in acknowledgement to a sun tanned man of similar age to himself who was standing on the deck of his own yacht.

'Hello to you, I am Antonio Silvana, we are from Milan.'

'Hi there, I'm Jimmy Challoner, Liverpool, England.'

'Oh yes I know of Liverpool, the football team, yes?'

'I support Everton,' Jimmy grinned.

'Ah yes, I hear of them also,' said Antonio returning the grin.

After chatting for a few minutes Antonio invited them all for dinner.

The Silvanas were all sitting out on deck when the Challoners joined them later that evening. Jimmy noted that Antonio's wife, Sylvia, was much younger than him and in sharp contrast to his swarthiness she was fair skinned and blonde. Their daughter Laura, who was Debbie's age took after her mother. The two girls hit it off immediately and disappeared below deck together.

'You all speak English so well,' Jennifer said, 'I'm afraid it makes we Brits feel very inferior.'

'Nonsense,' Antonio replied, 'It's because you British are so superior that the rest of us must learn the English.'

Jimmy noticed the twinkle in his eye and said 'Hang on, it's we Liverpudlians who have the sense of humour.'

'I see I fool no-one,' Antonio laughed.

'Take no notice of him Jennifer. Laura has an English governess and that's the reason we speak English reasonably well,' Sylvia explained.

They all joined in the laughter and the evening proved to be the beginnings of a friendship which encompassed all six of them. When Jimmy heard that the Silvanas were visiting England in two weeks time he invited them to stay for a few days and they in turn agreed.

Two weeks later Jimmy met Antonio and Sylvia at Lime Street Station and drove them to his home at Blundellsands. Antonio had said that he was a director of Inter Milan Football Club and that he would dearly like to visit Anfield. He was delighted when Jimmy arranged a meeting with the players and officials of Liverpool and left clasping Jimmy's hand saying, 'Thank you, thank you, you have made my holiday Jimmy.'

On the eve of their departure Jimmy took the couple to the River Club. After the meal he and Antonio left Jennifer and Sylvia listening to the cabaret while Jimmy showed Antonio over the premises. Antonio was particularly interested in the casino where he tried his luck and naturally Jimmy saw to it that his guest didn't lose.

Later when the two men were sitting up having a nightcap, Antonio said, 'I see the law in Liverpool it is very relaxed about the gambling.'

'It doesn't pay if they're too strict.'

'I understand, I also have similar clubs.'

'What else do you do Antonio?'

'Well to start I am my own man.'

'I never imagined you were anything else.'

'Often people think that because you are Italian you must be also the Mafia.'

'I can understand that.'

'I suppose so. Tell me Jimmy, what are you interested in?'

'Ah no, I already asked you that question.'

'The cat and the mouse eh?'

'If you like.'

'OK. I see tonight that your lifestyle it cannot be supported by the clubs, so I think you too have other, maybe less legal interests, am I right, yes?'

'Might be.'

'I'll be honest Jimmy because with you I think I can be. I am seeking the right person to do business with in England and I think maybe you are that person.'

'What sort of business would that be?'

'Drugs.'

'And what makes you think I'm not already dealing.'

'I think that maybe you are but not with the heroin.'

'No, that's true, not with heroin.'

'Heroin's the drug of tomorrow Jimmy, I am needing someone to distribute it in England. Are you interested?'

'I could be, but I'd need to know a lot more about the set up before I committed myself.'

'Naturally you would. Look it's getting very late and we are leaving tomorrow. Why don't you and I meet very soon and talk in detail, yes?'

'Suits me. Just tell me when?'

'I'll get in touch then.'

'I'll be waiting.'

'I think that Jennifer knows nothing of this side of your business, like Sylvia?'

'Too right.'

Jimmy was excited at the prospect of joining forces with Antonio. The conversation had come at the right time for Jimmy as since Owens had been arrested Jimmy had been at a loss when trying to find a replacement for the production of the Amphetamines. Antonio's suggestion that they might work together seemed to be exactly what he was looking for. He wasn't familiar with heroin, but knowing that it was big in Europe and America Jimmy reasoned that he could create the same demand in England. He fell into an untroubled sleep as soon as his head hit the pillow, satisfied that yet again his fortunes had taken another upward curve.

Peter was made aware of Antonio's visit to Liverpool by Special Branch who in turn had been alerted to his presence by Interpol. On contacting Interpol Peter was informed that Silvana was suspected of major criminal activities and latterly of being involved in the distribution of heroin. Having studied all the intelligence held by Interpol Peter came to the conclusion that Silvana's file was virtually identical to Challoner's and he felt instinctively that the Liverpool jaunt was not solely a social visit.

Jimmy meanwhile was giving his full attention to his proposed new venture with Antonio. He needed to know how heroin was likely to be received by users in the UK and made a mental note to check out Mick Walsh for an informed opinion. Also he needed to clip Peter Turner's wings and with that in mind he summoned the highest ranking police officer that he had on his pay-roll.

'John, I need a little assistance,' Jimmy said looking across his desk at the Chief Superintendent.

'What kind of assistance?' the Chief Superintendent looked suspiciously at Jimmy.

'I want Turner moved from the Drugs Squad.'

'I won't ask why but be realistic. Moving someone with a track record like Turner's just doesn't happen without a good reason.'

'Find one then,' said Jimmy, his tone heavy with menace.

'And if I don't?'

'You don't really want me to spell it out do you?'

'There is one possibility,' the Chief Superintendent smiled in relief as the solution to his dilemma dawned on him.

'And what's that?'

'The head of the regional crime squad is due for retirement and I should be able to arrange it for Turner to take his place.'

'No that's no use, he'll still be hanging around like a bad smell.'

'He won't. The RCS aren't allowed to investigate drug offences and I take it that's why you want Turner off your back.'

'Got it in one. OK, that sounds reasonable,' Jimmy grinned, 'I reckon a fair number of the promotions in this neck of the woods are down to me.'

'I can hardly believe it,' Peter said to Jean as they shared a celebratory meal. 'To be promoted to Superintendent and to get the RCS vacancy is almost too good to be true.'

'You've worked for this, you deserve it darling.'

Privately she had mixed feelings. Although she was proud of Peter she knew that promotion would inevitably mean longer periods spent away from home for him and more having to cope with every domestic crisis as it arose for her. Jean sometimes thought that there might be advantages in being married to a regular nine to five man but she knew in her heart that she wouldn't change Peter even if she could. She smiled to herself, at least this way she would never suffer death by boredom.

On taking up his new appointment Peter met with his co-ordinator, Chief Superintendent Jack Potter. Peter took an instant liking to his new boss and felt confident that a good working relationship had every chance of developing.

'I've been studying the target criminal file for the region and it seems to me there's a distinct lack of material, hasn't Liverpool got any major crime?' Potter asked with a wry smile.

Knowing that he was being facetious Peter replied, 'There's only one major criminal who would be an ideal target but the problem is that he's moved into drugs and is off limits as far as we're concerned.'

'Wrong. All this increased drugs activity involving major criminals has led to each region being allowed to nominate a target criminal who is suspected of major drug trafficking.'

'Well that fits our lad to a T.'

'Tell me Peter, what exactly do we know about Challoner?'

Peter told his co-ordinator all he knew about Challoner including his recent meeting with Silvana.

Potter sat in silence listening intently to everything that Peter said.

'Well Peter, my suggestion is this. We set up a special team to be headed by you. You'll need a detective inspector, four sergeants and four constables. How does that sound to you?'

'Great, it sounds great. Just what we need to nail Challoner. Incidentally, any chance of Jim Atkinson as my DI?'

'Jim as in the best DI on the squad?'

'Take it from me I need the best if we're going to put Challoner behind bars. The other thing we'll need is a cover story for the whole operation.'

'Agreed, any ideas?'

'Only the perfect one. How about putting it about that we're investigating corruption within Liverpool Council.'

'Sounds ideal, I take it that Challoner has previous for bribery?'.

'Anyone and everyone,' said Peter as he rose to leave. 'I'll go and get the wheels in motion if we're agreed then.' He hoped that his eagerness to begin didn't strike his new boss as rude but he was unable to curb his impatience to make a start now that he had been given the green light.

26

On his return from his extended holiday, Jimmy, having finalised the details with Antonio, was anxious to get things moving with his new venture. He met Mick in the River Club and after being briefed on what had been happening in his absence Jimmy said, 'Now what about your enquiries regarding heroine, any joy?'

'You'll be pleased, most of the dealers can still remember back to the sixties when the hippies, tired of cannabis turned their attention to dia-morphine which is heroin based.'

'Where would they get that from?'

'From their GPs.'

'From their doctors, why don't they still get it from them then?'

'Doctors can't prescribe it anymore. Since the late sixties the government stopped ordinary doctors from prescribing dia-morphine because so many hippies became addicted. The drug was so easy to obtain. Now only doctors attached to drug treatment centres where the addicts have to register are allowed to prescribe morphine and then only as a linctus.'

'So what you're saying is that addicts from the sixties can only get this linctus if they're registered otherwise they just get what they can for themselves.'

'Got it. The linctus isn't strong enough for them though.'

'Good, that means there's a ready market waiting for us to provide the goods.'

'I reckon that's spot on.'

'All I want now is couriers to travel to Rome, collect the stuff and bring it back here.'

'What sort of people are you looking for?'

'Well my supplier suggests middle aged women who can double as tourists to Rome.'

'Makes sense.'

'I need about ten, any ideas?'

'I think I might have, an old army mate runs a shop lifting racket from Birmingham. I know he uses women for it, maybe they'll do.'

'Depends on their age, I don't want any kids working for me.'

'Why not meet the guy and see what gives, I'll ring him if you like.'

'OK, but don't tell him what it's about.'

Ten minutes later Mick popped his head round the door of Jimmy's office, 'He's free tomorrow, any good?'

'Fine, arrange a hotel will you, I'm not slumming it at some poxy pub.'

The next morning Jimmy rose early. He wanted to be on the road for nine and he had one or two things needing attention at the River Club before he collected Mick and set off for Birmingham. As he showered he was conscious of feeling below par, but any thoughts he had of postponing the trip were immediately banished. Jimmy was anxious to recruit the new couriers and a touch of flu wasn't going to delay Jimmy Challoner's plans.

Two hours later driving along the M6 Jimmy felt even worse and was thinking about asking Mick to take the wheel. As he turned towards Mick, Jimmy was suddenly convulsed with a violent pain in his chest and the last thing he remembered as the car spun into the oncoming traffic was the look of terror on Mick's face.

The next thing he knew Jimmy was waking up in hospital. Wires running from his chest, nurses and doctors scurrying round him and still that pain, though admittedly not so acute, in his chest.

'What the hell was that?' he asked the nearest doctor.

'You've had a heart attack Mr Challoner.'

'A bad one?'

'We suspect that it was a massive attack that would have stopped your heart. All we can think is that your chest must have hit the steering column in the crash which re-started your heart.'

Jimmy lay quietly as the significance of the doctor's words registered in his head. In effect the crash had saved him.

'Am I going to be OK?'

'We've managed to stabilise your condition and your blood pressure is back to normal so things are looking good.'

Later the doctor explained to Jimmy that his childhood rheumatic fever had a bearing on his present health problems. From now on he must take daily medication and take life at a lower pace. At Jennifer's insistence

Jimmy hired a chauffeur for longer journeys. Bill Williams came from within the organisation and Jimmy was confident he would look after him if needs be.

Two weeks after his discharge from hospital Jimmy and Mick set off for their meeting in Birmingham with Mick's former army friend. In the foyer of the Midlands Hotel in the city centre a tall athletic looking man strode towards them and greeted Mick warmly. Then holding out his hand to Jimmy he said, 'Ray McCann, pleased to meet you.'

'Glad to meet you.'

Mick ordered coffee and they sat down with McCann eager to discover what Jimmy wanted.

'I'm intrigued, what do you want to see me about Jimmy?'

Jimmy studied McCann. He had obviously kept himself in shape since leaving the army and judging by his quietly expensive attire was doing very nicely from his shop lifting activities.

'I'm looking for eight women, middle aged women, who'll do a spot of work for me.'

'Sorry wrong guy.'

'I'm not talking tarts, I know your racket.'

'I've already got the outlets for the stuff my girls steal.'

'If you'll just listen I'll explain.'

'Sorry go on.'

'What I need is eight middle aged women, prepared to go abroad every so often for me.'

'To do what?'

'All they'd do would be to bring a parcel in for me.'

'And what's in these parcels?'

'That needn't concern you.'

'Well I can take an educated guess and that sort of deal is going to cost you.'

'First things first, have you got the type of women I'm after?'

'I've got them alright, they're all real professionals who know how to keep it shut.'

'Excellent.'

'What would you be paying?'

'£500 a trip plus expenses of course.'

'That sounds fair enough and what exactly do I get out of this?'

'If your girls are as good as you say I'm willing to make you a generous offer for them.'

'They're not for sale though. They net me a very nice living thank you very much, why the hell would I want to give that up?'

'I could always take them from you but in all honesty I'd rather not.'

'I realise that, I'm well aware of who you are.'

'Then let's be sensible. I don't want to piss on anyone's parade. Why don't I agree to the women continuing to work for you when I don't need them.'

'Go on,' said Ray, 'I'm interested.'

'I'll pay you £20,000 in cash so long as the women all turn out to be suitable. What do you say? Naturally I'd have first call on their time. What do you say?'

'Naturally,' said Mick sarcastically.

'Well is it a deal McCann?'

'Deal,' said McCann holding out his hand.

Jimmy hesitated for a moment then took his hand and gave it a perfunctory shake, 'Good. Now as soon as Mick has interviewed these women and he's satisfied that they're what you say they are, he'll pay you cash. One other thing, from now on you deal only with Mick.'

'Suits me.'

Jimmy stood up, 'I don't need to remind you to keep your mouth shut do I?'

Before McCann could reply, Jimmy had turned on his heel and was heading for the door. Mick stayed for a few minutes to arrange the interviews with the women and then joined Jimmy in the car.

'Everything set?' Jimmy asked.

'All systems go.'

'OK Bill, let's head for home.'

On his return to Liverpool Jimmy immediately contacted Antonio on his 'safe' line.

'Antonio, Jimmy here.'

'Jimmy, good to hear you, how are you feeling now?'

'Much better thanks, nothing I can't handle. Look I reckon I'll have the women soon.'

'That is good Jimmy, how many?'

'Eight, two over every week which means one visit each per month.'

'Excellent, when do you want to start?'

'As soon as possible, I'll be ready to go in about four weeks time.'

'Right, this is what they must do. They'll be booked into the Henslar

Hotel in Rome. The rooms will be reserved in their names so you will need to tell me who they are in advance you understand. They must wait in their rooms and someone will contact them yes, you understand Jimmy?'

'Perfectly.'

'Good, then I will say goodbye, ring me when you have the names, OK.'

'OK,' Jimmy said as he replaced the receiver.

Jimmy made a quick calculation on his notepad. Two couriers per week each bringing back two kilos of heroin. Sold at ten pounds a gram would net him forty thousand pounds. Twenty thousand pounds would be paid into Antonio's London Bank as agreed which left Jimmy a weekly profit of fourteen thousand pounds after expenses.

'Not bad for starters,' Jimmy said to himself, 'and soon, very soon I'll up the price to £15 pounds a gram.' He smiled to himself as he ripped the calculations into little pieces and then sent for Mick to join him. He had no intention of telling Mick where he was getting his heroin supplies hence the private telephone call.

After informing Mick how the arrangements were going to work Jimmy said, 'One small detail Mick, any ideas how exactly they should bring the stuff in?'

'I'm going to use a similar system to McCann,' Mick replied. 'The women usually use coats with false pockets so I thought we'd just vary the theme a little and get specially tailored corsets with pockets built into them. They'll each take two kilos and all the women have to do is wear them on the flight back.'

'Won't they be uncomfortable?'

'Tough, they'll be well paid remember.'

'Must admit it sounds pretty good, how will they pass the stuff over once they're through Customs though?'

'I'm meeting them at Euston Station where I'll hand them a holdall. They go in the toilets and transfer the heroin to the holdall.'

'Why Euston and not Heathrow?'

'Gives me more time to do my own surveillance on them, just in case they're being followed.'

'I like it Mick, now all we need is to see the women.'

'All fixed for next week.'

Once Mick had interviewed and approved the women shoplifters as suitable couriers, Jimmy telephoned their details through to Antonio and arrangements were made for the first trip. Mick told Jimmy later that the operation had run like clockwork. The women encountered no problems whatsoever and had been delighted with the hotel arrangements made for them in Rome.

'What about distribution? Any problems there?' asked Jimmy.

'I'm supplying it in half kilos.'

'Any idea on how it's selling?'

'Not so far, it's early days as yet.'

'Well if needs be I'm prepared to stockpile it until our market is properly established.'

'Doubt if it will come to that,' Mick sounded confident. He was proved right. Within a few days of the heroin hitting the streets every one of Mick's dealers was wanting more.

27

Peter Turner always made a point, at least once a day, of reading the incident log on the state of enquiry into Challoner. The pace of the enquiry was so great that if he didn't constantly update himself he risked being left behind and Peter was determined not allow that to happen. Flicking through the surveillance intelligence he saw things had been active since Challoner had been discharged from hospital. Casting his mind back to the day of Challoner's accident on the M6 Peter recalled how shocked he had been at his own reaction to the news. He has been horrified at the thought Jimmy might die and as he waited for news Peter realised that his feelings towards this man would always be ambivalent. In his darker moments it sometimes crossed his mind that maybe Jimmy had got it right. After all here was he struggling to maintain a modest lifestyle while Jimmy appeared to live a life conspicuously lacking in money worries.

His colleague interrupted his reveries, 'Reading about the surveillance on Challoner and Walsh when we followed them to Birmingham?' he asked.

'Yes, I've just been reading it through, what do you make of it Jim?'

'Hard to say. We've identified the guy he met in Birmingham as a Ray McCann though.'

'Is he known to the local force?'

'Got a bit of form, nothing major.'

'What's his present caper, do we know?'

'Well apparently he runs a little shoplifting racket.'

'Really, I wonder what interest Challoner could have in this guy.'

'One thing we did discover was that McCann and Walsh were in the army together.'

'Still doesn't explain the Challoner connection Jim.'

'Maybe he just wanted to give the Roller a run out and took Mick as a favour.'

'No chance, Challoner's not into good deeds, he's not that magnanimous.'

'Just a thought.'

'There's got to be a connection. Is this McCann into drugs?'

'Neither deals in them nor takes them.'

'Well I'm certain this meeting was important to Challoner. Ask Birmingham for McCann's intelligence file, maybe that will give something away.'

Two days later Peter studied the file on McCann carefully. He sent for Jim Atkinson and asked him if he'd come to any conclusions.

'Could Challoner be wanting to handle the gear the women steal?' suggested Jim.

'No way. Nowhere near valuable enough for Challoner to touch.'

'In that case I can't see it.'

'I think I can. If we're right in thinking that Challoner and this guy Silvana he's in touch with are aiming to traffic in heroin how will they bring it in?'

'Good question, conceal it somehow.'

'Exactly and what better way to conceal something than about your person?'

'McCann's shoplifters?'

'Makes sense doesn't it? They're all middle aged women, hardly your average drug trafficker.'

'Boss you're a bloody genius, that's it.'

'I really think it could be Jim. If we're correct Challoner is getting ready to start this operation up so we must be extra vigilant from now on.'

Peter was only too aware that his knowledge of Silvana was scanty. He had read Silvana's intelligence file but what he really wanted was to speak to someone with personal knowledge of the man. The officer who had supplied the bulk of the intelligence on Silvana was a Captain Deponeo of the Milan Narcotics Branch. The following day Peter spoke to the Superintendent in charge of the Interpol Office at New Scotland Yard to try and arrange a visit to Milan. Firstly Peter had to obtain the necessary approval from the Foreign Office for him to travel abroad and then within days it was arranged for him to meet Captain Deponeo at the Interpol Headquarters in St Cloud, Paris.

The following week Peter flew into Charles de Gaulle Airport and rather than risk his schoolboy French on the Metro took a taxi to his hotel.

His appointment at Interpol wasn't until the following day and after registering at the hotel Peter had the day to himself. By the next morning he felt sufficiently confident to take the train to St Cloud, a twenty minute journey from Paris. Interpol Headquarters were only a ten minutes walk from the station and Peter arrived in good time for his scheduled meeting.

Mario Deponeo was waiting for him and after introducing themselves the two men were ushered into a small meeting room. They were offered the services of an interpreter but as Mario's English was reasonably fluent they politely dismissed him.

The two detectives immediately recognised in each other a similar professionalism and a dogged determination to succeed when the odds seemed stacked against them. They warmed to each other as they told each other all they knew about their respective subjects. At the end of the meeting they agreed each would continue with their individual enquiries but they would also contact each other weekly in order to keep abreast of any new developments.

On the journey home Peter mulled over the information he had been given about Silvana. There was little doubt that he was a true professional criminal. A big fish and, like his counterpart Challoner, he was going to be extremely difficult to convict.

Six weeks after the arrival of the first consignment of heroin Mick Walsh asked to see Jimmy and they met at the River Club.

'What's the problem?'

'No problem, I just thought it was about time we upped the price.'

'Raise it from £10 a gram?'

'I'd double that, the dealers don't care, they just dilute it with a bit more talcum powder and the suckers on the street still pay up.'

'Do it and tell me, how are the women coping with the trips?'

'Great, no worries, why do you ask?'

'I'm a bit concerned,' said Jimmy, 'they're working to a pattern. I think we should use more than one airport.'

'That makes sense, I'll see how many airports have direct flights to Rome.'

'Not only that, vary the flights back. Say Rome to Paris and then home you know the sort of thing.'

'I'll get onto it now.'

'Another thing Mick, I don't want you meeting the women any more.'

'Why not?'

'Be sensible. It may not be too long before someone starts taking an interest and if they start watching us you'd be caught red handed.'

'Got it. Do I still do the briefing before they go?'

'Yeah, that won't tell them very much particularly now we're going to use different routes back.'

'I take it you want someone from the organisation to meet the women and bring the stuff back to Liverpool.'

'Too right,' said Jimmy, 'and to be on the safe side use a different person each time.'

Driving home Jimmy's thoughts turned to his imminent trip to Switzerland. Antonio and Sylvia were sending Laura to a boarding school there and had suggested that maybe Debbie could join her. Jimmy and Jennifer had been horrified initially but gradually Jennifer had come round to the idea, keen to give Debbie what Antonio and Sylvia considered to be the finest education in the world. Jimmy wasn't entirely convinced. His relationship with his step daughter had come as a revelation to Jimmy. Her readiness to accept him as Daddy and her unconditional love for him still overwhelmed him at times. He felt an almost physical pain when he imagined her flying hundreds of miles away to a place he didn't know. Jimmy rather hoped that the school would be obviously unsuitable. Then they could all shelve the idea, but he knew that Jennifer would be disappointed if they didn't at least view the place.

They met Antonio and Sylvia in Zurich and went on to the school where they were met by the headmistress herself. In spite of his misgivings Jimmy was impressed. By the end of their visit he had to reluctantly admit that it would be an unparalleled opportunity for Debbie to attend such a school with her greatest friend.

The two couples spent the remainder of the week at the Silvana's home in Milan and Antonio took the opportunity to show Jimmy over some of his casinos.

'Things appear to be going well for you.'

'Well Jimmy they are now, but it was not always so. The early days were hard and I have great trouble with Mafia until we finally agree on territory.'

'And have the Mafia respected those boundaries?'

'Let's say we have good working arrangement, I have no trouble. Though I'll admit I do have worries that one day they will want to take over my heroin business.'

'I sincerely hope they don't.'

'No no, not yet but they will one day,' Antonio sounded resigned and in no doubt that this was a fact of life.

'They control the drugs scene in the US don't they?'

'Yes they do, that's why it's how do you say it... inevitable they will come to Europe. It is such a potentially huge market for them.'

'And if they do?'

'I retire, I am too wise to take on the Mafia again, too wise and too old.'

'Wouldn't you miss the money?'

'Oh I think I manage. Ten million in my retirement account help I think. I hope you do the same Jimmy, put something safely away in Switzerland.'

'Of course.'

'Excellent. You never know when you may need money that isn't tied up in your own country.'

Jimmy nodded in agreement, 'Quite.'

Jimmy and Jennifer brought up the subject of boarding school with Debbie once they arrived home. Fully expecting her to be enthusiastic and eager to accompany her best friend they were speechless when Debbie burst into tears at the prospect of leaving them. Jimmy's eyes were suspiciously moist as she ran to his outstretched arms, 'Don't you worry kitten, no-one is going to send you away if you don't want to go.' Jimmy stroked her hair and for the umpteenth time Jennifer marvelled at the gentle understanding of her wonderful husband.

28

It had now become an established routine within the Merseyside Police for the senior CID officers to meet monthly in order to discuss cases of serious crime and current crime patterns that were occurring in the area. It was at one of these conferences that Peter Turner heard his successor in the Drugs Squad tell the meeting that there had been an increase in the number of arrests for the illegal possession of heroin. This phenomenon they were told was also being experienced in other major cities countrywide.

The debate that followed led the delegates to conclude that the spate of street robberies and burglaries that had also increased at a rapid rate were directly linked to the influx of heroin. Peter was asked by the conference chairman whether the regional crime squad would be able to allocate any resources to this particular enquiry. When he said that unfortunately the squad were fully committed to other concerns, he sensed an unspoken yet palpable feeling of relief from certain quarters of the room.

It went against the grain for Peter to be deliberately dishonest, especially at a gathering of his peers, but he suspected that some of those present would have leaked the information straight back to Challoner. He couldn't afford any setback to his enquiry especially now that he was under pressure from his Regional Co-ordinator to bring the Challoner enquiry to a speedy conclusion. Peter had a certain amount of sympathy for his co-ordinator who himself had to justify to a committee of chief constables the allocation of crime squad resources. He knew only too well that the heat was on. The enquiry couldn't continue indefinitely. Soon he would have to come up with a result or be forced to abandon the enquiry altogether.

Peter was certain that Challoner was using the women from Birmingham to smuggle drugs into the country, but knew from surveillance that Challoner wasn't physically involved. Peter knew that whoever was giving the women their instructions was a vital cog in the wheel and one which must be found quickly if the whole thing wasn't to blow up in his face.

It was with this thought uppermost in his mind that Peter called together the whole of his operational squad and gave them a full briefing on the events that had taken place at the conference.

'There's firm evidence that regular heroin supplies are finding their way into the country and we know Challoner is behind it. The thing we don't know is how. I think we can safely assume he's using the women from Birmingham but what we need is the name of the contact between the women and the organisation.'

'You mean Walsh don't you?' Jim Atkinson said.

'I think it has to be him, Challoner wouldn't trust anyone else with this.'

'Do we switch our surveillance from Challoner to Walsh then?'

'No we can't afford to ignore Challoner, but what I want you to do Jim is split the team into two groups. Half to continue with Challoner and the other half to start watching Walsh.'

'No problem.'

The surveillance of Walsh was instantly rewarding as for gathering intelligence was concerned. On the second day of the observations Walsh was followed to Birmingham where he was seen meeting two middle aged women. The two watching police officers were left in no doubt as to why Walsh was meeting the women. He was clearly giving them instructions and he confirmed the officers' theories when he handed over a large brown envelope before he left them.

Hearing the report the team were cock a hoop.

'We've cracked it,' said Jim, 'all we have to do is watch Walsh and make our move when he meets the women on their return.'

'I don't know about that Jim, Challoner always has something up his sleeve in my experience.'

'Even the best slip up now and again.'

'Well let's hope you're right,' said Peter not wanting to dampen Jim's enthusiasm, although he had a gut feeling that Challoner wouldn't make such an elementary mistake.

The surveillance file on Walsh quickly built up and soon a pattern was established. Each week Walsh made a visit to Birmingham where he was seen to meet two women. Although they were all of a similar age he never met the same pair of women two weeks running. Photographs proved that he met with a total of eight women in rotation.

Going over the facts with Jim Atkinson, Peter tried to work out a way forward. He knew that each week two women were bringing the heroin into the country. He also knew that neither Walsh nor Challoner was meeting them, therefore it had to be another member of the organisation. One alternative was to have the women followed. It would enable the women to be caught when they handed the drugs over and would be simple enough to set up. The catch was that it would only disrupt Challoner's operation as Peter knew that neither the women nor the contact who met them would tell him anything that would incriminate Challoner.

Peter's dilemma was very much a moral one. Armed with the intelligence he now possessed he could, by arresting the couriers, prevent further supplies reaching the streets. Ultimately this solution would be counter productive because until Challoner was removed from the equation the trafficking would continue.

Eventually, inevitably, Peter decided to continue surveillance on Walsh and Challoner and wished for the thousandth time that he had never heard of Jimmy Challoner.

Mick Walsh had just returned from one of his weekly trips to Birmingham when he called on Jimmy in his office at the River Club.

'Everything OK Mick.'

'Better than OK that's what I want to see you about. These dealers are pressing for more, can you arrange for any more?'

'How much more are we talking?'

'Three more kilos.'

'That would mean doubling the number of couriers, doubling the number to get caught. I'm not happy on that score.'

'I reckon we can manage with what we have now.'

'But that would mean an extra one and a half kilos each.'

'I was thinking of half a kilo myself.'

'And what about the missing two.'

'We make it up, five kilos of heroin, two of talc.'

'But if the dealers are already doing that we'll get junkies fixing with pure talc.'

'Not our problem, the dealers will get the hassle.'

'Won't they be able to tell?'

'Apparently there's a baby talc in Holland, same colour and texture as heroin. I'll get some of the stuff. Don't forget Jimmy this talc is going to be worth twenty thousand to us.'

'OK I'm convinced. Go ahead and organise it. I'll get onto my contact about the extra kilo.'

'Just one thing. I think we should set up a safe house where the drugs can be taken when our guy collects them from the women. This is even more important now that we'll be cutting the heroin ourselves.'

'Makes a lot of sense. Who's doing the cutting? You?'

'Mick shook his head, 'No, I don't want to go anywhere near the place, but I do want to know it's being done right. I thought I'd get someone in there I could trust to do it properly.'

'Good thinking, tell Wakefield to release one of the company houses over to you.'

'Thanks, I'll see to that then I'll get off to Holland and bring back as much powder as I can carry.'

The telephone was ringing as Peter was unlocking the front door of his home and as he stepped into the hallway he heard Jean say 'Hang on a minute Jim, he's just walked in.'

Taking the receiver he said, 'Yes Jim, what is it?'

'Sorry to mither you at home, but Walsh has been buying airline tickets to Holland.'

'When is he going?'

'Ten in the morning, from Manchester.'

'OK, I'll get in touch with the Dutch police. Can you go home and pack a bag, you're off to Holland tonight.'

'I hope that call doesn't mean you're out again,' Jean said as he replaced the receiver.

''Fraid so, will dinner keep for an hour or two?'

'It'll have to but I know you and your hour or two.'

'This really shouldn't take too long, but I've got to make some important calls.'

'Promises, promises,' Jean said 'I've heard them all before, remember?'

Peter hugged Jean saying, 'Back soon, promise.'

Jim was booked onto a flight to Schipoll airport at eight that evening and Peter rang the Dutch narcotics branch to arrange assistance for him. Surveillance of Walsh by both the Dutch and his own squad from early morning was priority.

It was mid afternoon the next day when Peter heard from Jim Atkinson. 'Just to tell you that Walsh is catching the four o'clock flight home from Schipoll.'

'Has he met the couriers?'

'He hasn't met anyone yet.'

'No one at all? Where is he now?'

'Sitting in the departure lounge at the airport.'

'Does he look as though he's waiting for someone?'

'Not really. He's not taking any interest in anyone.'

'What has he been doing with himself all day?'

'You won't believe this but the only thing he's done is buy some baby talc from a chemist's shop.'

'Baby talc! What the hell does he want with that?'

'Well I could just have the answer to that. The Dutch lads tell me that on occasion this talc has been used as an agent to cut heroin.'

'That's got to be the answer. Walsh wouldn't travel all that way unless he had a very good reason.'

'Can't think why he couldn't buy it in England.'

'Is there anything unusual about the powder?'

'I've no idea but I've bought a tin for you to have a look at. It's called Manitol.'

'Excellent. If Walsh does use it as a cutting agent our forensic lads will need to see some so they have a controlled sample for comparison if any is found in possible seizures.'

'Well that's all I've got for you at the moment.'

'Right, we'll get ready this end to meet Walsh and see where he goes.'

'See you later then.'

'Just one more thing, if Walsh meets anyone at the airport be sure to let me know.'

Peter took part himself in the surveillance on Walsh that followed him from Manchester back to Liverpool. Walsh left the aircraft alone, didn't meet or speak to anyone on arrival at Manchester, merely collected his car from the airport car park where he had left it earlier that day. It was also clear to the watching officers that all he was carrying was the parcel of baby talc. On the journey back to Liverpool he drove along his usual route and drove directly to the River Club where he entered carrying his parcel of baby powder.

Mick Walsh knocked on Jimmy's office door. 'Come in,' shouted Jimmy.

'Just clocking in. Got the first batch, I'll whip it over to the professor later today.'

'Let's have a look at the stuff.'

Mick took a tin out and opened it. He passed the tin over to Jimmy who sprinkled some on his desk.

As he pushed it around with his finger he said, 'You're dead right about this, you really can't tell it from the real macoy.'

Mick's grin grew even broader.

'This is a great idea, all down to you too. I reckon it deserves some sort of financial recognition Mick,' said Jimmy as he handed the talc back to Mick.

'I was hoping you'd say that.'

'No worries, you'll get a good bonus next pay day. Now I've got to move it, I'm baby sitting and I'm running late.'

Later that evening Jimmy was reading the paper while Debbie did her homework. He was shocked when suddenly Debbie's voice piped up, 'Daddy, what's heroin?'

'Heroin? It's a drug. Why do you want to know?'

'It's just that some of the girls at school are buying it.'

'Buying heroin,' Jimmy said in horror, 'Well I hope you're not Debbie.'

'Don't be silly Daddy, I don't need drugs.'

'Oh, and what makes you different then?'

'They take drugs to make them happy don't they? Well I'm happy already.'

Jimmy smiled, thankful for her innocence.

'Tell me,' he asked, 'where do these girls get hold of something like heroin?'

'From this man that comes to school and sells it in the lunch hour.'

'What? 'He actually comes to the school?'

'Well he doesn't come in, he sits outside in his car.'

'Why don't the staff see him off?'

'Because they don't know I suppose.'

'Listen to me kitten, promise me now that you'll never ever take drugs.'

'Not even aspirin?' Debbie giggled.

'You know very well what I mean young lady, I'm serious Debbie, don't touch any of them.'

'OK, I promise but they can't be that bad, loads of girls are using them.'

'Not for much longer,' Jimmy vowed to himself.

This conversation made Jimmy realise just how fast his little girl was growing up. He made a mental note to ask Jennifer to make Debbie aware of the dangers sex could present at this vulnerable stage of her life. Meanwhile he himself would take care of the drugs question. 'Easily done,' Jimmy thought to himself, supremely confident that at least he could control that area.

The day after the conversation with Debbie found Jimmy sitting in his car outside Debbie's school. It was just before noon and he had taken Mick along to make sure he knew exactly where was out of bounds to his dealers. Minutes after their arrival another car drew up opposite the school gates. The driver was a man of about twenty five.

'Know him?' Jimmy asked.

'Yeah I know him. Bit of a surprise though.'

'Why?'

'I thought he was more of a user than a seller. He must sell a bit on the side too so he can buy a bit more for himself.'

'Well here's where his little sideline ends,' said Jimmy getting out of the car.

He walked over to the parked car and tapped on the window. The young man wound down the window and said, 'What do you want?'

'Just you, you little bastard.'

'Why, what am I supposed to have done.'

'Listen carefully,' said Jimmy, 'my name is Challoner and what you've done is sell drugs to school girls. The thing is son, I don't like that, I don't like it one little bit.'

The man turned a sickly grey colour as he realised who he was talking to.

'I didn't know I was queering your pitch Mr Challoner.'

'You're not but my daughter goes to this school.'

'I didn't know that, honest. I'll clear off right now.'

'That's what I'd call a good idea. And think of this as a friendly warning son, next time ....'

'There won't be a next time.'

Jimmy heard the car start up and drive away as he walked back to his own.

'I think his selling days are over,' Jimmy said to Mick.

'I hope you're right.'

'Surely he wouldn't have ignored the warning I just dished out.'

'I wouldn't bet on it, he's an addict don't forget.'

For the next couple of weeks Jimmy took to driving past Debbie's school until he was satisfied that the young dealer had got the message. He was therefore more than a little annoyed when he heard from Debbie that the dealer was back in business at his old pitch.

He immediately telephoned Mick, from his study so that Jennifer and Debbie were safely out of earshot.

'Mick, that druggie's back at Debbie's school. Know where he lives?'

'Sure, he's in a bed sit in Croxteth.'

'I want you to meet me in an hour. We need to pay him a visit.'

'What do you want to do?'

'Blast him?'

'I've got a better way, quieter.'

'Just so long as it's permanent.'

'It will be. I'll get the necessary and meet you at the club.'

When Jimmy reached the club the early evening diners had already started to arrive and the restaurant was comfortably busy. He glanced at the casino and was pleased to see that the tables were also busy. This section of the club never really had a lull, it seemed people couldn't wait to gamble away their money. Even this early in the evening some heavy money was being wagered.

Mick had seen Jimmy arrive and followed him into his office.

'OK Mick, let's have it, what have you got in mind?'

'An accident.'

'What kind of accident are we talking about?'

'A typical one for a druggie. We'll give him a fatal dose.'

'You certain it will work?'

'With what I've mixed, pure heroin and barbiturates it's guaranteed,' said Mick matter of factly.

'Let's do it.'

They found the house where their prey had his bed sit to be typical of the other houses in the area. Large houses that had been converted into flats and were now falling into disrepair. The young man they were after occupied a front downstairs room and in answer to the knock on his private door he opened it and found to his horror that he was face to face with Jimmy Challoner. Jimmy pushed him roughly back into the room and followed him in. Mick quietly closed the door.

Jimmy caught his breath as the stench from the filthy room hit his nostrils.

'What's going on?' stammered the terrified young addict.
'Time to take your medicine.'
'I can explain Mr Challoner.'
'Too late son, you had your chance and you blew it.'
'What are you going to do with me?'
'We're only going to give you what you like best, Jimmy said with a smile.
'I don't understand.'
'Then we'll show you, ready Mick?'
Mick Walsh took a small container out of his pocket out of which he removed a syringe. From another pocket he took a small phial and began to fill the syringe from it.
'What's that?' said the boy beginning to shake.
'Smack,' Mick replied.
'I've had my fix, I'm not due one for hours yet,' the boy began to cry as he realised what was about to take place.
'You can never have too much of a good thing,' Jimmy said as he grabbed hold of the boy from behind. Mick roughly pushed a cloth into his mouth and ignoring the muffled cries, tied a tourniquet around the boy's puncture marked left arm. When he was satisfied that one of the veins was ready for the needle he steadied the boy's arm before plunging it in. The helpless boy could only stare in horror as Mick injected the entire contents of the syringe into his arm.

When he had finished Mick pushed the boy onto the bed and removed the tourniquet and the gag. As the drugs started to take effect the boy's body went limp and his pitiful protests stopped. Mick threw the empty syringe on the floor at the head of the bed, took a cursory look around the room to ensure that he wasn't leaving any evidence behind and turned to Jimmy saying, 'All done.'

Jimmy nodded towards the prostrate body and said, 'How long?'
'He'll go into a coma soon.'
'You happy it's going to look natural enough?' Jimmy asked as his eyes scanned the room.
'The police won't bother too much with an addict who has overdosed, they never do.'
'OK, let's get out of here.'

Later that same evening Jimmy was sitting at home drinking a bottle of wine with Jennifer before going to bed. He mentioned to her what Debbie had told him about a drug addict selling heroin outside the school.

'Jimmy that's terrible. I've been reading about the spread of heroin but I never for one moment imagined it was here under our noses.'

'Don't worry, I've put a stop to his little game.'

'What have you done?'

'I've done what any public spirited citizen would do, reported him to the police,' Jimmy lied.

'Good, let's hope they catch him. And the filth that peddle the heroin in the first place.'

'The filth?' Jimmy raised his eyebrows.

'Yes those evil creatures who import it, they're the real offenders and should be hanged for what they do.'

'That's a bit strong isn't it?' Jimmy was starting to feel distinctly uncomfortable.

'I don't think so, these traffickers have no thought for the misery they spread, all they're motivated by is greed, pure greed'

'I had no idea you felt so strongly,' Jimmy said, shocked by Jennifer's passionate outburst.

'I'm sure every parent feels the same. These scum of the earth exploit children's natural curiosity.'

'Well don't worry about Debbie, she's promised me she won't ever take them.'

'Of course I'm worried about Debbie, teenagers are naturally rebellious and that's what these evil people play on.'

At this point Jimmy suddenly found a topic of great interest in the newspaper and steered the conversation away from the heroin. He was feeling literally hot under the collar and was galled to discover just how hostile Jennifer was towards drug trafficking and more especially towards those who did the trafficking.

29

Peter Turner had been summoned to the Regional Co-ordinator's office in Salford. He knew that the Co-ordinator had just returned from a high level conference and Peter suspected he knew what this meeting was about. The conference had been called to discuss appropriate action in the fight to combat the influx of heroin being sold nationally. As well as the regional and national co-ordinators of the crime squads, the conference had been attended by senior representatives from HM Customs & Excise, senior representatives from each of the police forces and senior members of the Home Office.

Once he was seated in the Regional Co-ordinator's office the Chief Superintendent said, 'You know why I've asked to see you?'

'I think so,' Peter replied.

'Then you'll understand that the Government is very concerned about the present drugs problem and are demanding action from the police. They want the offenders behind bars.'

'Offender.'

'So you keep saying. Personally I find it difficult to believe that Challoner alone is responsible for all the heroin that's on the streets.'

'We know he is, particularly now he's cutting the heroin with Manitol powder. Every one of the seizures made by the Drugs Squads nationwide and examined by the forensics show the presence of this particular baby powder.'

'Alright so Challoner circulates the heroin. What I want to know is how much longer before the guy's arrested?'

'I don't know. I still need more evidence to tie Challoner in with the importations.'

'Let's get real, are you likely to get this evidence?' the Regional Co-ordinator said 'after all you've been trying for over eighteen months.'

'We'll get him alright, but I need to know where the stuff is taken for cutting.'

'I would have thought you would have discovered that from watching Walsh. Where does he go on his return from Holland?'

'Mostly he goes back to his flat, but we know he's not using his own place to cut the drugs.'

'Then you should know from the surveillance what he does with the powder.'

'He always takes it to the River Club, but we don't know what happens next. The drugs won't be cut there, he must use a safe house and get one of the team to take the powder there. Trouble is there's so much coming and going at the club that it's impossible to keep track of them all.'

'Well if you can't connect Challoner we'll have to forget him and get the couriers instead. The Prime Minister wants results, now.'

'But that will be a complete waste of eighteen months of hard work.'

'Not entirely, you'll still be stopping the heroin coming into the country.'

'You know and I know that will only be a temporary solution. How long before Challoner dreams up a new way to get the stuff in?'

'Nevertheless it has been made very clear to me which way to proceed.'

'Is there anyone we can explain the problem to, maybe someone at the Home Office who could buy us more time?'

'I suspect it won't do much good because they were at the meeting too, but the best person to try would be a Mr Steen, I'll arrange something for you.'

As he was driving back to Liverpool Peter attempted to marshal his thoughts into a coherent argument, capable of convincing Steen of the need to tackle the drugs problem at source. He knew that the Home Office was under pressure to show results now that some addicts had been found dead due to the effects of the drug. One such case had recently been recorded in Croxteth where a young user had been discovered with the empty needle still in his arm, apparently from an accidental overdose. What a waste of life that had been thought Peter as his mind conjured up the pathetic sight of the addict lying dead in his sleazy bed sit.

Although the Home Office was just around the corner from New Scotland Yard it was the first time Peter had visited it. The design of the building contrasted sharply with the style of the more conventional government buildings situated in Whitehall. The Regional Co-ordinator who was more accustomed to visiting the Home Office than Peter strode across to reception and presented his ID to the uniformed commissioner.

He then asked the receptionist to inform Mr Steen of their arrival. Peter showed his ID and signed the visitor's book beneath the entry of his Chief Superintendent and within minutes Mr Steen's secretary arrived to accompany them up to his office.

Mr Steen was a senior civil servant attached to the Police Department and as such was an influential figure. It was Steen and his ilk who recommended the candidates for the most senior positions within the police service to the Home Secretary. Peter was pleasantly surprised to discover that Steen, in spite of his exalted position, was very approachable and keen to put Peter at his ease.

'Now then Superintendent, I'm most anxious to learn all about your investigations into the trafficking of this wretched drug which is flooding the country. I've only been told the briefest of details over the telephone so please could you give me the whole picture now.'

Peter did exactly that, giving Steen a lengthy account of Challoner's activities.

As Peter came to the end of his report Steen sucked in his cheeks and drummed his fingers on his desks. 'Most interesting, it seems incredible that one man is responsible for the heroin problem that the country is experiencing. The fact remains that in spite of the sterling work you have done so far you are still not in a position to arrest this Challoner character.'

'No not at present.'

'I can quite see why you would want to apprehend Challoner, but the Government's concern is to stop the heroin supply reaching the streets. Which means I'm afraid that in spite of the obvious need to arrest Challoner, if that cannot be achieved quickly, then we must take the appropriate action to stop the drug supply.'

'I can appreciate your concern and do see that preventing the drug hitting the streets is an attractive option, but as I've tried to explain it would only be a temporary solution.'

'I do understand Superintendent and believe me I would like to give you more time, but I do have to ask myself what is likely to change if you are granted extra time.'

'I know that given time Challoner will slip up but I do accept that it could take some time.' Peter was becoming resigned to what he considered to be the inevitable outcome of the meeting. He was therefore taken aback when he heard Steen saying 'Alright Superintendent, I'll agree to a further three months, but if at the end of that time you are no closer to apprehending Challoner then we must take whatever alternative action is open to us.'

'I'm grateful sir,' Peter said 'I sincerely hope that we can arrest him within that time.'

'Perhaps I can be of help as well, provided the Home Secretary agrees we could intercept telephone calls which I believe could be most useful in this enquiry.'

Peter was speechless, he had thought it a resource only available to the security forces.

'Leave it to me,' said Steen, 'we have a department that will deal with the whole thing. They'll contact you with any useful information they hear. I will need to know which line to intercept though.'

'That will be Challoner's office number at the River Club.'

'Jimmy?'
'Yes, who is it?'
'It's Mick'
'Sorry Mick, it didn't sound like you, what's up?'
'The girls have missed the plane and I can't get them on another until tomorrow.'
'What the hell happened?'
'They were due to fly from Gatwick and their train was two hours late. What do we do, cancel?'
'Not sure, hang on while I make a phonecall.'
Jimmy dialled Milan. 'Antonio, thank the lord I caught you. I'm afraid my aunt has missed her flight and can't make it today.'
'That's too bad. When can she come?' Antonio asked.
'Tomorrow, if that's OK.'
'I'll make enquiries. I might have to change the hotel. Rome is very busy with tourists at the moment.'
'Well it doesn't matter if you can't fix anything. I'll just have to wait until next week.'
'It matters to me,' said Antonio, 'I don't want to be left holding the luggage.'
'Yes, I see, will you ring me back if you arrange something?'
''Just give me a few minutes.'
Within a couple of minutes Antonio was back on the phone.

'Jimmy it's OK for tomorrow. Tell them to go to Le Grand not the Heisler though.'

'Will do, same arrangements?'

'Same arrangements. Look I must go Jimmy, see you soon, yes?'

Jimmy called Mick straight away, 'Hi, they can go tomorrow, but they are staying at Le Grand Hotel, usual arrangements.'

'Fine, I'll let them know when they call.'

'Will the delay give you any problems with the collection?'

'To be honest it will. I know Pete won't be able to make it for the meet. I think I may have to meet them myself. I'm pretty certain everyone else is booked.'

'Won't hurt for once I suppose.'

'Right I'll do the necessary.'

'Excellent, I must report this bloody phone, it does nothing but crackle.'

'Perhaps it's being tapped,' Mick laughed as his replaced the receiver.

Within a few days Peter received confirmation that the listening device had been connected to Challoner's telephone line. Although Peter was impatient for results he was told he would only be contacted if anything of real importance came up. In the meantime, and since he was not allowed to inform his team about the telephone tap, his routine surveillance of Challoner and Walsh continued. It was while he was watching Walsh that Peter received a radio message to contact London urgently.

'What's that likely to be about?' asked Jim Atkinson.

'I'm hoping it's a new informant with news on Challoner.'

'London? What the hell can he tell you about our lad?'

'I'll tell you when I've spoken to him,' said Peter telling the driver to take him back to base.

Ten minutes later Peter joined Jim Atkinson.

'Jim, I think we have lift off at last.'

He picked up the car radio handset and instructed the whole team to return to their operational headquarters for an urgent briefing. Half an hour later Peter walked into the operations room where the assembled team were gathered. Waiting with a sense of suppressed excitement for what they had sensed was important news.

'I've been informed by a reliable source that two couriers will leave Gatwick Airport tomorrow destined for Rome. On their return to Gatwick they are to be met by Walsh himself,' Peter paused to ensure that the significance of his words had registered with his team. It had. 'Right, we can safely assume I reckon that Walsh will go straight to the factory once he returns to Liverpool.'

'I don't understand,' said Jim Atkinson, 'How come we're so sure Walsh is going to collect the drugs himself? That's not how it usually happens.'

'Spot on,' replied Peter 'this is a break with their normal routine and it's down to some hiccup with their couriers. The thing is we all know from past experience it's these hiccups that give us our breaks.'

'It seems a huge coincidence to me. First a new informant comes on the scene and then bingo, Challoner starts cocking things up at the same time.'

'Nevertheless,' said Peter, 'I believe the information to be accurate and we'll need to be at our best to keep Walsh under surveillance twenty four hours a day.'

'What's the plan? Do we arrest Walsh once he's gone into the safe house?'

'Once we're sure it's the factory then yes we'll get a search warrant and go in.'

'And if Walsh leaves before we can get the warrant?'

'Nick him.'

The squad were divided into twelve hour shifts in order to keep a round the clock watch on Walsh. Peter went with Jim Atkinson into one of the interview rooms to draw up an operational order. They agreed that once Walsh had met the women couriers and collected the drugs from them he would be followed back to Liverpool. In the meantime the two women couriers would be arrested and brought back to Liverpool.

'Are you going to tell me who this informant is?'

'I can't Jim. It's best that you don't know, believe me.'

'I thought you and I were doing this together.'

'We are Jim and it's for that reason that I hope you'll take my word for this.'

'OK I won't push it.'

Peter sighed with relief. He didn't want this to become a bone of contention between himself and Jim, but he had been ordered by Steen not to tell anyone else on the team that Challoner's conversations were being recorded. Telephone tapping was considered to be such a sensitive issue that the Government were at pains to keep the knowledge that it was used in Britain under wraps. That way if any of Peter's team were asked if they were aware of it they could answer truthfully they weren't. In the event of Peter himself being asked he had been given specific instructions on what to say.

Peter now had another problem to contend with. The information he was now in possession of would be of great interest to Captain Mario Deponeo of the Milan narcotics squad. Peter and Mario still telephoned each other regularly, but nothing of any significance had happened either in Italy or England. However things had now changed. Peter's dilemma was not really knowing how Mario would react if he were to tell him that the two British couriers would shortly be visiting Rome to collect heroin. If Mario decided to act on the information himself and arrest the couriers in Rome then any hope that Peter had of arresting Walsh and Challoner would go up in smoke. Peter was hoping that Mario would allow the women to collect the drugs and bring them back to England and for Mario to then deal with the Italian end. He had as he saw it, two options. One, to say nothing and two, to take a gamble and tell Mario. He decided on the latter reasoning that Mario as the professional Peter knew him to be, would agree to letting the drugs be carried back to England in order for Peter to make the necessary arrests. He telephoned Mario and was rewarded with his full co-operation in allowing the drug run to complete its intended course.

So far so good he thought. If all went according to plan he would soon be in a position to arrest Walsh and as a result of that arrest he would be able to arrest Challoner and charge him with conspiracy to import heroin. The evidence would be strong enough to convict Challoner Peter thought as he ran through the facts in his mind. Firstly there was the evidence that Challoner had met with McCann and that McCann's women had been the couriers of the drugs. There was evidence that Walsh had made regular visits to Holland to purchase Manitol powder, found to be present in every seizure of heroin that was being made. There would be evidence of Walsh collecting the drugs and the identification of the safe house, which was doubtless a part of the Challoner empire, plus the vital evidence of the drugs themselves. Combined with the evidence that Walsh was employed by Challoner in a senior position the connection of Challoner to the seizure of heroin would be complete.

Peter found it hard to suppress the optimism he was experiencing, it seemed for once things might just be going his way.

30

The day had been hot and Jimmy had arrived home tired and sticky. Now an hour later he was relaxing with the local paper and a glass of wine while Jennifer caught up with some correspondence. Debbie was restlessly flicking through the pages of a fashion magazine.

Jimmy looked up from his newspaper and watched his daughter, he couldn't quite make up his mind whether she was restless because of the heat or whether she was worried about something. Whichever, she would doubtless tell him in her own good time.

A few minutes later Jennifer must also have noticed Debbie's unease for she said 'Anything wrong Debbie, you seem very fidgety tonight?'

'No, I'm fine,' Debbie replied.

'Is the heat getting you down?'

'Not really, I'm just bored.'

Jimmy looked at her over the top of his newspaper and this time sensed that Debbie had something on her mind.

'Fancy a stroll kitten, it's a lovely evening and I for one could use a bit of exercise.'

'Don't mind,' Debbie shrugged.

Choosing to ignore her mood Jimmy pressed on, 'Come on, let's leave your mother in peace while she's writing.'

It was a perfect summer's evening now that the fierce heat of the afternoon had died down. As they strolled down the tree lined cul de sac Jimmy said, 'Something bothering you? Is it the heat? It's killing me.'

'No.'

'Is it school then?'

'In a way it is.'

'What way is that?'

'I think I'd like to go to that school in Switzerland with Laura.'

Jimmy was lost for words for a minute, it was the last response he had expected as Debbie had always been adamant that she didn't want to leave home.

'What's brought this on kit, I thought you hated the idea.'
'I've changed my mind that's all.'
'Well if you're certain of course you can go.'
'I'm very certain Daddy.'

'I hope all this is for the right reasons,' Jimmy said, 'I can't help thinking something has happened to bring on this change of heart.'

He looked down at Debbie and saw that tears were welling up in her eyes. Putting his arm around her shoulders Jimmy said softly, 'What is it, you can tell me you know?'

'I can't, it's too painful,' Debbie sobbed.

Jimmy hugged her close, 'Is it something to do with a boy.'

'How did you know?'

'I'm only old not dead you know,' said Jimmy making Debbie giggle in spite of her tears.

'It's a boy I know called Andrew, he walks me home from school.'

'And now he's stopped walking home with you?'

'Yes he's going out with someone else.'

'Well all I can say is that he can't be all there if he doesn't want to be your boyfriend.'

'Thanks Daddy, but he doesn't and I can't bear it.'

'Do you really think that going away will help though?'

'Not really, but that's not the only reason I want to go. Laura always says in her letters how great the school is.'

'It's certainly a lovely place. 'Tell you what we'll do. I'll telephone the principal and tell her we'd like to visit for a few days. If you still want to go after that we'll enrol you, how's that?'

'That sounds cool,' said Debbie brightening at the prospect of the promised trip.

By the time they reached home she was more like her old self causing Jennifer to remark, 'Someone's perked up, the walk must have done you good.'

'It was Daddy not the walk,' Debbie shouted as she took the stairs two at a time in her rush to send a letter off to Laura.

'What was all that about?' Jennifer asked.

'Our little girl has had her heart broken by some no good boy.'

Jennifer laughed, 'Really? I had a feeling that might be it.'

'Mother's intuition?'

'Woman's intuition.'

'Well whatever, she's really cut up. If I catch sight of this Andrew he'd better run fast, I'll wring his scrawny little neck.'

Jennifer laughed again, 'Oh Jimmy stop it, you can't protect her from everything you know.'

'Don't you believe it.'

'It's just part of growing up, every girl is let down at sometime or other.'

Jimmy looked alarmed, 'You don't think anything has been going on do you?'

'Don't be silly, they only saw each other coming home.'

'I hope you're right. If I suspected he'd laid a finger on her I really would wring his neck.'

'Calm down. Take my word for it, it will all have blown over in a few days.'

'By the way Debbie wants to join Laura at the Swiss school.'

'Not because of this I hope?'

'Not entirely. To be honest I think she's been wanting to join Laura for a while.'

When Jimmy told her of his plan Jennifer nodded.

'Seems sensible to me.'

The following day Jimmy contacted the school and after arranging a visit he booked a flight from Manchester for that afternoon. Next he called the River Club and instructed Mick to take over in his absence.

Explaining that he would be in Switzerland for a few days Jimmy was happy to leave Mick at the helm with temporary use of Jimmy's office.

'I'll only leave my post to collect the girls, they're in at Gatwick tomorrow.'

'Let's hope it goes OK, will you be driving or taking a train?'

'I think I'll drive, there's enough time. They're not in until four o'clock.'

'Well all the best then, see you.'

'Thanks, you have a good trip boss.'

The second call that Peter Turner took from London was to inform him that Walsh was to meet the couriers at Gatwick at 4 o'clock the following day. He called the entire operational team and told them his latest information.

'Now in view of this latest intelligence we can cancel the surveillance on Walsh, I don't want any unnecessary risks taken and him spotting us,' Peter said.

'What about tomorrow, we're going to follow him to Gatwick aren't we?' Jim asked.

'Again I think we'll dispense with that risk too. It isn't as though we don't know where he's going.'

'All the same, it seems to me we're placing a lot of faith in your informant.'

'Don't panic, the information is sound and we've checked on flights into Gatwick from Rome at that time and there's one due at ten past four.'

'So what's the plan then?'

'We meet at Gatwick tomorrow. I want everyone at the police unit at two p.m.'

'What do you want the team to do in the meantime, stay with Challoner?'

'Didn't I say? My informant tells me he's visiting Switzerland for a couple of days with his wife and daughter.'

'He seems to be bloody well informed your informant,' muttered Jim.

'He does doesn't he,' Peter grinned.

At two p.m. the next day Peter addressed his team in the borrowed conference room of the Sussex Police Airport division at Gatwick Airport. He explained to them that the team would be divided into two sections, half to watch for the arrival of Walsh and the other to cover the incoming flights in the international hall. A folder containing photographs of all eight of the women couriers was handed to each pair of officers since it wasn't known which two women were being used on this occasion.

'As soon as any member of the team identifies the two couriers they will pass the message over the radio to the rest of the team. It will be the responsibility of those same officers to keep the women under observation and to arrest them once they have handed over the drugs to Walsh. Naturally they will have first ensured that Walsh is well clear. Now is that understood?' Peter asked and he acknowledged the nodding of heads from those officers who had been assigned to wait for the women.

'Those of you watching for Walsh will keep him under close surveillance at all times, particularly when the women have passed the drugs to him. I want a mobile positioned and ready to go as soon as it's known which direction he's taking. The vehicle will maintain eyeball until the rest of the team have joined the surveillance. Any questions?' Peter asked.

'The plan still the same once he's back in Liverpool?' asked one of the sergeants.

'Yes no change there,' said Peter. 'Now in the unlikely event that we lose Walsh around the airport I want two cars to head down the M4 and two in each direction of the M25 until one of you pick him up.'

'What about the A roads?' Jim asked.

'Unlikely, Walsh is a stranger down here, I reckon he'll stick to the motorway.'

'OK, I'll sort out which cars will take the motorways.'

'Do that and then everyone get out there. I imagine Walsh will probably be early.'

By four o'clock none of the team had sighted Walsh in the airport concourse. 'Where the bloody hell is he?' a worried Jim Atkinson said to Peter.

'Held up, in traffic I expect,' said Peter trying to sound more confident than he felt. He knew Walsh would have allowed time for that eventuality. It was starting to look very much like a change of plan, possibly the women had missed their flights or had arrived earlier than expected.

'Look,' Jim said, 'the Rome flight has landed.' He was pointing to the flight information board. Peter spoke into his radio set, 'The flight has just landed. Walsh still not sighted. Imperative that we don't lose the women. Be ready for any eventuality.'

At four thirteen a radio message was sent by one of the watching officers, 'Spotted the women. They're four and six in the photo album.'

'Where are they?' Peter asked.

'At the luggage carousel,' came the reply.

'Come on Jim, let's get a bit closer,' said Peter.

They had all been issued with special airport passes to enable them to pass freely through the airport precincts without being challenged. Peter, followed closely by his Inspector, entered the luggage collection area and joined the waiting crowd around the carousel dealing with the luggage coming in from the Rome flight.

'There's one of them over there.'

'Got her, where's the other one?'

'There she is standing at the top.'

Peter spotted her.

'Looks as though they're cracking on they don't know each other,' Jim whispered.'

'You can bet it will be part of the brief from Challoner that they travel through customs separately. That way if one gets pulled in a routine check the other can still get through.'

'Does he always think of everything?'

'He certainly does. Look here comes the luggage.'

Peter suspected that the women could be using false bottomed cases which would have been supplied by Challoner. He was taken completely by surprise when one of the women pulled a small overnight case from the range of luggage which was far too small to contain a couple of kilos of drugs. Peter waited for her to claim another bag but instead she headed for the 'Nothing to Declare, Customs Green Channel' with her one small item of luggage. Peter saw that she was being followed by one of his team and decided to wait and see what the second woman collected.

Peter wondered whether she had the whole consignment in her case and thought if she had it wasn't very characteristic of Challoner. To Peter's surprise the second women also collected one small piece of luggage, again too small to contain any quantity of drugs.

'I don't get it Jim. Those cases can't contain any drugs,' Peter said, as he and Jim left the baggage claim area. He heard another radio message informing the team that the two women had now met up with each other in the main hall.

'Don't let them out of your sight,' Peter instructed. He then asked if anyone had spotted Walsh yet and was told that no one had. The next radio message confused him still further.

'Both women heading towards the rail terminus.'

'Four of you stay with the women. The rest get mobile and drive like hell into London.'

Sitting in the speeding Granada being driven by Jim down the M4 towards London, Peter started to make some notes. He knew that all the trains from Gatwick went in to Victoria Station and he was trying to anticipate what the women would do once they arrived at Victoria. There were two things they could do, presuming they intended to travel back to the Midlands. They could either catch a coach from Victoria Bus Station or else travel by underground from Victoria to Euston and travel to Birmingham by train. He decided to back both options and gave instructions for the remaining team to divide itself, half to head for Victoria and the remainder to head for Euston. He told Jim to make for Euston.

Peter now had to wait anxiously for radio communication from the officers following the women. He knew that as soon as they had a direction of travel from Victoria they would inform him. As for Walsh, Peter decided he must be waiting for them either at Euston or Victoria and the more he thought about it the more it made sense.

Challoner covering all eventualities would have reasoned that if the couriers were being watched then the greater the distance they travelled, the greater their chance of spotting the surveillance. Just then he received a radio message telling him that the women had bought tickets on the underground and were making for Euston. Peter gave his team hurried instructions to hold back once they reached Euston and to let the women enter the concourse alone. He cancelled his instructions to the officers destined for Victoria and told them to head for Euston.

'Step on it Jim, we've got to get to Euston before this pair do.'

'We'll do it, we're not far.'

They arrived at the front of Euston Station as two other squad cars drove up.

'Stay with the cars but get them out of sight. I'll tell you when Walsh starts to move,' Peter said. Turning to the other officers who had joined him on foot Peter ordered them to spread out and look for Walsh. He himself proceeded with caution as he knew that Walsh would be alerted to the police presence if he had any clue that Peter was present. He was relying on Walsh not knowing the two officers watching him.

'Walsh spotted standing near to the top of the escalator leading to the Underground,' he heard the radio tell him.

'Keep him in sight,' Peter said. He moved his own position to the timetable boards where he could see Walsh but not be seen by him. It was obvious from Walsh's position that he was watching to see if the women were being followed and he had with him a large holdall bag. It was lying on the floor at his feet, ready to abandon if necessary.

'Those women must be carrying the drugs on themselves,' Peter said to himself.

That would mean that the exchange would have to take place in private and Peter couldn't imagine anywhere less private than a busy main line rail terminus.

'It's got to be the toilets,' Peter thought. Things started to fall into place again. If the women were using body belts they would have to transfer the drugs to the holdall that Walsh would hand them and the obvious place was in the privacy of a lavatory cubicle.

'It's ingenious,' said Peter.

'Stay alert. The women spotted riding up the elevator towards Walsh,' one of his watching officers broadcasted. 'They've now walked past him with no indication of recognition. Walsh has stayed put.'

Peter could see the two women quite clearly. He hoped more than ever that the officers who had been watching the women held back long enough to convince Walsh that they were not being followed.

He watched as the two women stopped at the top of the concourse not too far from the toilets. His eyes were now on Walsh and the seconds seemed to drag like hours. Peter's heart missed a beat as he recognised one of his team emerging from the moving elevator to enter the main hall. He breathed a sigh of relief when he saw that Walsh appeared to take no undue interest. After a couple of minutes Walsh finally made his way towards the women glancing around as he handed them the holdall. Following a brief conversation the women left Walsh and walked briskly towards the ladies lavatory.

During the time the women were away Peter took the opportunity to brief his team by radio on the surveillance that was to follow. All but four of the team were to take part in the observations on Walsh. The remaining four were to arrest the two women and take them to the police station at Euston. They were to remain there while the officers recovered their vehicles from Gatwick Airport where they had left them and would then be escorted back to Liverpool. Peter also queried why Constable Berry had not obeyed his instructions and stayed back in the underground as ordered. He accepted the explanation that because of the underground the team watching the women had lost radio contact and didn't know whether the main surveillance team had actually arrived at Euston or not. It had been decided that as a precaution, Constable Berry, who it was agreed looked less like a policeman than the rest of them would, after a brief interval, enter the main concourse to keep the women in sight.

Although the radio was telling him that the women had just left the toilets Peter didn't need to hear the message as from his vantage point he could see them himself. One of the women was now carrying the holdall that had been given to her by Walsh and it was clear from her posture that it was proving quite a weight. They walked to where Walsh was standing and as he took the bag from them he took two envelopes from his pocket and handed them one each.

'The pay off,' he heard through the ear piece of his radio set.

Without further ado Walsh left the women and headed for the main entrance to the station. Peter satisfied himself that the two officers who were to begin the surveillance and the four officers who were to arrest the women were in position before he asked for Jim Atkinson's location.

'We're in the side road directly opposite the main entrance. Stay where you are. I can see Walsh heading this way.'

Minutes later he heard Jim say, 'OK come and join me. I can see Walsh going down the road, he must be parked further down.'

By the time Peter rejoined Jim in the car the two officers who had followed Walsh out of the station had confirmed that he was in his car. Chance decreed that Peter was in the vehicle most conveniently placed to follow Walsh and so he would take the lead. They watched as Walsh pulled out of the car park and Jim started to follow him.

'Eyeball commenced,' said Peter over the car to car radio. He then maintained a running commentary on Walsh's position, keeping the cars in the surveillance, informed of the route they were taking. Each of the other cars reported to him as they took their places in the surveillance.

The observation of Walsh from London to Liverpool went smoothly. He left via the A41, joined the M1 at Hendon and then stayed on the motorway taking the M62 into Liverpool.

Leaving the M62 at the 'Rocket' interchange on the outskirts of Liverpool, Walsh headed for the city centre. Peter gave instructions that the eyeball must be maintained at all costs. The surveillance team knew this order to mean contravening any of the traffic regulations if it became necessary. Following a suspect vehicle in an urban area was always difficult due to traffic, but in Liverpool it was a nightmare. The problem the officers had to contend with was not getting too close to the suspect so that he might become alerted to their presence. Equally they risked losing him if they stayed too far back. Fortunately the traffic whilst heavy was flowing well and the team had no real headaches. Walsh was followed to Allerton, a residential district of Liverpool, and he was seen parking his car outside a private block of flats. In accordance with surveillance training only one of the pursuing vehicles entered the road. Peter's vehicle was parked at the top of the road and in such a position to be able to take over eyeball should Walsh happen to drive that way. He was told over the radio that Walsh having left his car had now entered the front of the flats.

'Was he carrying the holdall?' Peter asked.

'Affirmative,' came the reply.
'How many flats in the block?'
'Looks like a three storey block and four flats on each floor.'
'Bugger,' he said, typical of our luck for him to go into a block of flats.'
'What now?' asked Jim.
'We haven't come this far to be defeated now. We'll just have to put someone on each floor. We've got to know which flat it is that they're using.'
'Just as well we've got three lads who are good in this situation.'

Peter told Jim to speak to the three officers and get them into position as soon as possible.

Twenty minutes later Walsh was seen to emerge from the block of flats and Peter was informed by radio that he wasn't carrying the holdall.

'The arrest team move in and take Walsh. The remainder stay in position until I return with the warrant. Peter had arranged with the Magistrates' Clerk if it was necessary to obtain a search warrant outside normal court hours then he would visit the home of the Magistrate and swear out the warrant before him. It was nine fifteen p.m. so Peter did exactly that. Fortunately the Magistrate had been informed by the Magistrates' Clerk and was prepared for Peter's visit. After hearing Peter swear on oath that the information contained in the warrant was the truth, the Magistrate signed the document making it legal for Peter and his officers to search the premises.

At nine forty five Peter knocked on the door of Flat twelve. It was opened by a middle aged man who Peter didn't recognise as a member of Challoner's organisation. Peter identified himself to the shocked man and showed him the search warrant authorising the search of the premises. He pushed past the protesting man and entered the flat followed by his support team. Peter made his way down the small hallway at the end of which was a room with a light burning behind the partially open door. On entering the room Peter immediately saw the holdall that Walsh had been carrying. It was on top of the dining table and beside it lay a polythene wrapped packet of white powder. Peter picked up the bag and tipped out about twenty similarly wrapped packages onto the table.

One of Peter's officers entered the room holding the man who had let them into the flat.

'Who are you?' asked Peter.
'Victor Robinson.'

'And you know what this is don't you?'
'Heroin, it's heroin.'
Peter cautioned Robinson in accordance with the Criminal Evidence Act.
'What else have you got here?'
'Manitol powder which I mix with the heroin.'
'Where is it?'
'In the kitchen through there,' Robinson pointed towards the door leading off from the dining room. In the kitchen Peter found a food mixer on the table alongside a large polyurethane bag of white powder. Peter took it into the dining room and showed it to Robinson.
'Is this the baby powder?'
'Yes.'
'And the mixer in the kitchen, is that what you use to do the blending?'
'Yes I was all set up to start mixing tonight.'
'Take him to the Bridewell,' Peter told the officer who had arrested Robinson. 'We'll we give this flat a good going over. Oh by the way Robinson, who owns this flat?'
'It was Mick Walsh who arranged for me to take the flat, but I understand Jimmy Challoner owns it.'
'That's what I wanted to hear,' said Peter smiling. 'Right take him down town.'
After the flat had been thoroughly searched and the incriminating evidence had been seized and parcelled as exhibits, Peter told the team to make their way to the Main Bridewell. On arriving at the Bridewell himself he was told that the two women couriers had arrived and had been placed in separate cells.
'Have they been thoroughly searched?' Peter asked the Bridewell Keeper.
'Yes the matron has just finished. I think it's these you'll be interested in,' he replied as he handed Peter two pairs of corsets each with a series of pockets stitched into the garment.
'Matron, were the women wearing these garments when you searched them?'
'Yes Superintendent, they were wearing one each.'
'I shall need the usual statement from you Matron and when you've labelled the garments could you hand them to Inspector Atkinson please.'
'You don't want me to enter them into the police property book then?' she asked.

'No we'll be taking all the property and exhibits with us,' Peter said ignoring the fleeting exchange of glances that flashed between the Matron and the Bridewall Keeper.

'He doesn't trust us,' the Bridewell Keeper said.

'Got it in one,' Peter said.

Peter checked the apprehension sheets to make sure that Walsh and Robinson had different cells. He didn't want Walsh to know what Robinson had told him, not immediately anyway. Peter took Jim to one side and said 'We won't interview them tonight, we'll start refreshed in the morning. I want you to charge them all with being in possession of heroin, that will do as a holding charge.'

'What about court? Do you want them in early or later in the day?' Jim asked.

'Don't let's rush things, we've got twenty four hours before we need to bring them to court. Fix it for tomorrow afternoon. Oh and Jim, Peter added, 'mark the apprehension sheets that they are not allowed visitors.'

'I'd already done that. I'll go and get them charged and then I'm off home, how about you?'

'Yes I'm on my way. The rest of the team have gone I hope.'

'Yes, nothing changes, we're last as usual,' Jim grinned.

31

The trip to Switzerland proved to be a success on every front and Jimmy felt a self satisfied contentment. Debbie was keener than ever to join Laura at the school, Jennifer was thrilled that Debbie was being given such an opportunity. Even the principal thought he was wonderful when he produced the first year's fees in advance. In cash.

On their final night in Switzerland Jimmy lay late into the night reflecting on the last twenty years as a sleeping Jennifer breathed softly against his shoulder. 'Yes,' thought Jimmy, 'the plan worked, the plan bloody worked,' and he eventually drifted off to sleep, a smile playing round his lips.

The interviews of the four prisoners had gone precisely as Peter had anticipated. The two couriers admitted they had been retained by Walsh to visit Rome as sight seers and bring back the drugs which they had concealed in the corsets he had given them. They refused to admit that they had made similar trips previously and denied knowing any of the other couriers. Robinson repeated his confession of the previous day and also admitted that he had mixed a regular weekly supply of five kilos of heroin with two kilos of Manitol Powder for the past several months. Both the women and Robinson made written statements in which they confessed their guilt. Walsh, as expected, said nothing at all.

In a brief telephone call to his Regional Co-ordinator, Peter passed on details of the arrests so far.

'Excellent, the Co-ordinator said, 'When are you nicking Challoner?'

'As soon as he returns home,' Peter said.

'Which is when?'

'I don't know for certain, a day or so I should think.'

'And they've been supplying seven kilos of the stuff each week?' the Co-ordinator asked, still unable to believe it.

'Regular as clockwork.'

'Wait until I tell the Home Office that we've stopped this little lot hitting the streets.'

'I'll leave you to tell them then.'

'Keep me posted on Challoner.'

Peter then spoke with the Prosecuting Solicitors department and arranged for the four prisoners to be remanded into police custody for the next three days. He didn't want any of them released until he had arrested Challoner.

His next call was to Mario Deponeo to tell him of the events that had taken place since their last telephone call. He was delighted to hear from Mario that as a result of watching the two women couriers in Rome the police had followed two Italian men from the Le Grand Hotel back to a small farm on the outskirts of Rome. When the police had conducted a search no less than fifteen kilos of heroin had been found. Mario was optimistic that their enquiries would eventually lead back directly to Silvana himself.

Peter put the telephone receiver back and smiled to himself. Just then Jim came into the office.

'You look pleased with yourself. Won the pools or what?' he asked.

'Almost,' Peter said and then brought Jim up to date on events in Italy.

'That's great,' he said 'particularly if they can nail Silvana.'

'Too right, and once we've got Challoner the whole organisation should collapse.'

'Talking of Challoner,' said Jim, 'do you want surveillance on his home so we'll be the first to know when the wanderer returns?'

'Good idea, arrange it will you Jim?'

On arrival in Manchester Jimmy's chauffeur met the family at the airport. Jimmy walked alongside Bill while Jennifer and Debbie dawdled behind chattering non stop about their holiday.

'How's everything been while I've been away?' Jimmy asked.

'Alright as far as I know,' replied Bill, 'there was a call from a Superintendent Harris, he wants you to ring him ASAP.'

'Now I wonder what that's about, any trouble anywhere Bill?'

'To be honest I haven't seen anyone for a couple of days, but I've had no messages for you.'

'It's probably something and nothing, maybe he wants a donation to the Police Ball.'

He was concerned enough to ring Harris immediately when he arrived home. Harris wasn't one to panic and Jimmy realised he wouldn't have rung unless there was a problem. He telephoned police headquarters and asked to speak to Superintendent Harris.

'Jimmy, at last, where the hell are you?'

'I'm at home, just got in from Switzerland. What's wrong?'

'Mick has been arrested by Peter Turner from the Regional. They've also raided a flat and arrested someone called Robinson.'

'When was this?' asked Jimmy having been taken completely by surprise.

'Couple of days ago, it seems Turner has had a secret squad watch you for some time.'

'Is Turner going to arrest me?'

'Just waiting for you to get back. That's why I wanted to warn you.'

'Thanks,' said Jimmy, 'anyone else been arrested?'

'Just the two brummies.'

Jimmy replaced the receiver and then immediately picked it up again to telephone Wakefield. He explained as quickly as he could his conversation with Harris.

'I'm on my way,' said Wakefield, 'if Turner gets there first don't say a word. Remember last time?'

'Only too well. Don't worry, he won't trick me again.'

Wakefield arrived in a flurry of scattered gravel just fifteen minutes later, five minutes before Peter Turner accompanied by another officer. In the time it had taken Wakefield to drive to his house, Jimmy had given a hurried explanation of events to a startled Jennifer. He told her about Mick's arrest by Turner and that he fully expected Turner to now come to arrest him. What he didn't say was why Mick had been arrested.

Jimmy opened the door to Peter himself.

'Hello Peter, long time no see. Is this a social call?'

'No, it's not social, I'm here to arrest you.'

'Not again, what is it this time?' said Jimmy hoping that Jennifer at least was fooled by his little display of mock impatience.

'For being involved with others in the importing of heroin.'

'What others? You're talking in riddles again Peter.'

'Don't worry, all will become clear when we get to the station.'

Wakefield stepped forward and stood beside Jimmy on the doorstep.

'I've heard the wild accusation you've just made to Mr Challoner. I'll expect you to have some very real evidence to substantiate such a serious charge,' he said.

It was obvious that Peter was surprised to see Wakefield from the look on his face.

'How fortunate that you happen to be here with Mr Challoner. If I didn't know better I might think you'd been tipped off.' Wakefield ignored Peter's sarcasm and said, 'I shall insist on accompanying Mr Challoner. I don't intend to allow you the opportunity to pull a fast one as you did the last time you wrongfully arrested him.'

'Suit yourself, we're off to police headquarters.' With that Turner took hold of Jimmy's arm saying, 'Come on, time to go.'

Jimmy turned to say goodbye to Jennifer who was standing in the hall behind him, totally bemused by this latest dramatic turn of events.

'Now don't you go worrying. It'll all be sorted out and I'll be home in no time at all,' Jimmy said as he kissed her gently on the cheek.

'I sincerely hope so,' Jennifer replied. As Jimmy was led away Jennifer ran up to Peter 'As for you, if my husband suffers any undue stress that triggers another heart attack ....'

'I have no idea what you are aware or not aware of Mrs Challoner, but I do assure you that it is not vindictiveness that brings me to your home today. It's from a professional dedication to protecting our society from people who traffic in heroin.'

Jimmy watched as Jennifer's expression changed from one of indignation to one of horror as she realised what Peter was saying.

'You didn't have to tell her that.'

Peter who was in the front seat half turned so that he could face Challoner.

'You didn't expect to keep it all secret from her for ever did you?'

Jimmy didn't reply but turned to Wakefield saying, 'As soon as you can telephone Jennifer and try to reassure her that this lot will soon be sorted.'

The rest of the journey passed in silence and Jimmy took the chance to gather his thoughts together. He remembered Harris telling him that Turner had been watching him for some time. So what? He hadn't been personally involved in the heroin transactions, he had simply managed the operation so he was happy that there was nothing for Turner to have witnessed that would connect him with the importations. Jimmy was confident that the others wouldn't involve him either. The women couriers couldn't because they didn't know anything about him. The flat had all been arranged by Mick and therefore Robinson didn't know him either. That just left Mick and Jimmy told himself that he was a professional and professional criminals didn't inform whatever the circumstances. By the time they drew up at the Police Station Jimmy had worked out his plan of action. He would state his innocence and imply that Mick was the man behind this operation. He would stick to the story, that he had no knowledge of the entire operation.

Peter Turner had been surprised to see Wakefield appear at Challoner's side when he arrived to make his arrest. It meant that Challoner had been warned and Peter was satisfied that such a warning could only have come from within the police service. It didn't matter unduly on this occasion, but it did serve as a timely reminder to Peter that he must stay alert. He must make sure that all the evidence relating to this case was kept safe in a place where it couldn't be tampered with.

Arriving at police headquarters Peter took Challoner straight to one of the interview rooms. He had already decided to allow Challoner to have his solicitor present at the interview and made no objection when Wakefield followed them into the room. Peter introduced Jim Atkinson to Challoner and Wakefield and told them that Jim would be taking written notes of the interview. Although Peter didn't expect Challoner to say anything that would incriminate himself, he intended to question him very thoroughly nevertheless. Often denials or silences to questions asked at the interview stage proved to be useful evidence in securing a conviction.

Peter began by saying that although Jimmy was not obliged to say anything unless he wished to do so, whatever he did say would be taken down in writing and may be produced in evidence at his trial. Peter then went on, 'For the past fifteen months I have led an enquiry team who have been following your trafficking of heroin.'

'If you've been watching me that long you should know I've had nothing to do with heroin or any other drug for that matter.'

'During our observations we watched you meet a man called McCann in Birmingham.'

'So? I've met hundreds of people in that time. Are you going to question me about them all?'

'McCann used to employ a number of women who he used to commit shoplifting offences.'

'The little tinker.'

'We now know that you used these same women as couriers to carry the heroin into the country.'

'No you don't. I've never used these women for anything and I repeat I am not involved in drugs in any way.'

'Do you deny you met McCann?'

'No.'

'Then you do admit it?'

'Of course I do. I took Mick to meet up with him, they're old army buddies.'

'Are you claiming it was a social visit?'

'Yes, I knew Mick wanted to go to Birmingham and it suited me because I wanted to give the new Rolls a spin.'

'But you were on your way to Birmingham when you had your heart attack.'

'Was I? That's news to me. I was actually on my way to London.'

'To meet Mr Silvana?'

'Mr Silvana?'

'That's right. You don't deny meeting him in London do you?'

'No, I've met Mr Silvana. Why shouldn't I? He's a friend of mine.'

'Then it's quite a coincidence that your pal Silvana is also suspected of trafficking in heroin.'

'Antonio, trafficking in heroin? I don't think so, he's a highly respected businessman.'

'Like you are I suppose.'

Jimmy chose to ignore Peter's remark.

'We have evidence that two women couriers travelled to Rome and brought back five kilos of heroin. We believe that you organised their trip and Silvana supplied them with the heroin.'

'Have you been spending too long in the sun? It's fried your brain.'

'I also think it was your friend Mick who collected the drugs from the women.'

'Mick Walsh? Are you sure? I wouldn't have thought Mick would get involved in that sort of caper.'

'You know Walsh has been arrested?'

'No I didn't know that,' said Jimmy 'you never said you had arrested Mick.'

'Didn't think I had to. Surely whoever told you I was on my way told you about Walsh's arrest?'

'What's Mick supposed to have done then?'

'He's been charged, with others, for being in possession of heroin.'

'No I think you're mistaken, can't believe that at all.'

'Come off it Jimmy. You know full well Walsh is involved because you employ him to be.'

'I employ Mick yes, but not to traffic in drugs.'
'What do you know about Manitol Powder?' Peter asked.
'Manitol Powder, what the hell is that?'
'It's the powder you use to mix with the heroin to make it go further.'
Jimmy turned to Wakefield who was also making his own notes of the conversation and said, 'I told you he was mad didn't I?'
'I don't suppose you know a Victor Robinson either?'
'No, can't say that I do, why?'
'He's a tenant in one of your flats.'
'Do you really expect me to know individually every person I lease property to?'
'I do when it's from that flat that we recovered five kilos of heroin and a quantity of Manitol Powder.'
'Are you suggesting I'm accountable for the actions of my tenants?'
'He's more that just a tenant. Robinson was an employee.'
'Really,' Jimmy raised his eyebrows, 'doing what?'
'He was employed to mix heroin with Manitol.'
'It appears to be a fascinating business, but it has bugger all to do with me Peter.'
'It was Walsh who took the heroin to the flat and it was Walsh who supplied the Manitol Powder. You employ Walsh and it was you who set this venture up and controlled it.'
'If you have so much evidence against Mick Walsh shouldn't you be talking to him not me?'
'Do you deny all knowledge of the activities leading to the arrest of Walsh and the others?'
'I most certainly do. If it's true that Walsh is mixed up in this I must admit I'm surprised, but it has nothing to do with me. I am not as they say my brother's or indeed Mick Walsh's keeper.'
'Bastard,' said Peter under his breath. He made the decision to end the interview at this point. It was clear that Challoner wasn't going to incriminate himself. From his answers it was obvious he was shifting the entire blame onto Walsh. Peter turned to Jimmy, 'That's all the questions I need to ask for now.'
'Superintendent, I've heard nothing in the way of evidence that would warrant you keeping my client any further,' said John Wakefield.
'Your client isn't going anywhere. I will soon be charging him with conspiracy to import heroin.'

'On what evidence do you base that charge?'

'On the evidence of association at this stage.'

'That's the flimsiest of reasons to charge anyone with a criminal offence.'

'Nevertheless that's what I'm going to do.'

'Then I shall be making the strongest of protests to the Magistrates at the Remand hearing. By the way, when do you intend to bring Mr Challoner before the court?'

'It will be tomorrow morning.'

'In that case I must ask that my client be granted bail.'

'No chance.'

Challoner was taken by Peter to the Main Bridewell where he was placed in a cell. Peter went to see Mick Walsh while he was there with the idea of telling him that Challoner had been arrested and was putting all the blame on him for the heroin charge. Walsh didn't say anything, but the news quite clearly shook him. Finally he said 'Can I see Jimmy?'

The cell door clanged behind him as Jimmy looked around the tiny cell. He walked over to the cell bed, the only piece of furniture if you didn't count the lavatory. Picking up the mattress he threw it to the floor. Past experiences had taught him that these mattresses stank of ancient urine as passed by a succession of drunken prisoners over the years. Although it was uncomfortable he preferred to sit on the wooden bench. Suddenly the cell door was thrown open and the Bridewell Keeper stood in the open doorway.

'Don't tell me I'm being released already?'

'You've got a visitor, not that you deserve one, not in my book anyway,' Jimmy didn't miss the note of hostility in the Keeper's voice.

Before Jimmy had time to ask him what his problem was Mick Walsh was ushered into the cell.

'You've got five minutes, no more,' said the Keeper as he slammed the heavy metal door shut.

'Mick what's been going on. How the hell did you let them get onto you?'

'I've no idea, it was as if they knew everything about us.'

'Well they've been watching us for months.'

'They couldn't have known what they did just from watching. If I didn't know better I'd say someone's been talking.'

'No way, they just got lucky, must have.'

'Well I find that hard to swallow.'
'Bugger that now, what have you said?'
'Nothing, I've been waiting to talk to you.'
'Good lad, then it isn't too late to sort this.'
'Sort what out? What do you mean?'
'Now pay attention. You've run this operation and from the sounds of it they've got you bang to rights. They only think I'm involved so it makes sense for you to admit it was you who ran and organised the whole thing.'
'Take the blame myself you mean?'
'Yeah, don't worry I'll see you right. You're going to get seven years whatever you say, so you may as well get something out of it for yourself.'
'If I say it was my operation I'm more likely to get ten years not seven.'
'Seven, ten, whatever. With parole you'll be out in no time and have a nice little pension fund waiting too.'
'You already owe me for the Manitol.'
'Forget that Mick. That's peanuts to what I'm talking now.'
'Just how much are you talking?'
'Now that sounds more like you. Shall we say a million.'
'Sounds good, but how do I know I can trust you?'
Jimmy adopted a wounded expression. 'Mick, how long have we been mates? Would I double cross you? Mind you if it'll make you feel happier I'll get old Wakefield to draw up a legal contract. How's that?'
'It sounds OK, but I'd have to see it in writing first.'
'Naturally. Now Mick you quite sure what you have to do?'
'Keep you out of it isn't that it?'
'Right. If Jennifer ever found out I was in drugs she'd leave me. I know the evidence against me isn't much but I can't risk it.'
'Looks like I've got to take the rap then. I want to see a contract though Jimmy, old mates or not.'
Peter Turner was waiting in the office while Walsh was talking to Challoner. He knew that he was taking a gamble letting them get together but he felt instinctively that the outcome might be to his advantage. Returning to his cell Walsh made a request to see Superintendent Turner.
'You wanted to see me?' Peter said as he entered Walsh's cell.
'I've had a talk with Jimmy and you're right, he wants me to admit to running the heroin racket.'

'And?'

'And he's not on.'

'Where does that leave us,' Peter said trying to keep the excitement out of his voice.

'It means I'll tell you all I know about Jimmy's involvement.'

'His total involvement?'

'Hang on. I'm only going to tell you about the heroin. Nothing else.'

'OK but you realise that you'll have to put it down in writing.'

'I know, I know, when do you want to begin?'

'No time like the present,' Peter replied knowing that he needed to act quickly before Walsh had second thoughts about the enormity of what he was about to do. He rang the bell inside the cell which summoned the Bridewell Keeper and as he arrived and unlocked the door Peter said, 'I'm taking Walsh to the interview room. Will you enter that on the apprehension sheet.'

The Bridewell Keeper nodded to indicate that he would. This was a routine procedure for all prisoners so that their every movement could be accurately recorded for the whole time they were held in police custody.

When they were seated either side of the wooden table in the interview room Peter began, 'I'd like you to start at the beginning and tell me everything that you can.'

'OK,' said Walsh and proceeded to recount all he knew about the heroin business from the first time that Challoner had expressed an interest. After he had finished talking and Peter had finished writing he said to Walsh, 'Did you ever meet Silvana yourself?'

'Only once, Jimmy brought him to the River Club for dinner.'

'So you don't know for sure whether it was from Silvana that Jimmy was getting the heroin?'

'No, not for sure, but it couldn't have been anyone else.'

'We could do with knowing that.'

'Then why don't I ask him? If I'm supposed to be taking the rap Jimmy will realise I'll need to know all of the facts.'

'Let me think about that. In the meantime don't let Challoner know you've been talking to me.'

'Are you mad?'

Peter was aware that from now until the trial began he would have to give Walsh full protection now that he had turned Queen's evidence.

He arranged for Walsh to be returned to a cell and then telephoned the

Prosecuting Solicitor and arranged to see him immediately. Peter explained what Walsh had done and showed him the written statement. After reading it through the solicitor said, 'It's fine as far as it goes, but as you know the evidence of an accomplice will need to be corroborated before it can be admitted as evidence.'

'I realise that and that's what I want to talk to you about. Getting anything on Challoner is well nigh impossible and I don't think I can corroborate Walsh's statement unless it comes from Challoner's own lips. Now if I was able to persuade Walsh to wear a hidden microphone linked to a tape recorder would any conversation he had with Challoner be admitted as evidence?'

'I'm aware that evidence of that kind has on occasion been admitted, it depends very much on how the trial Judge feels about it.'

'Then I reckon it's worth a try.'

'As I see it you have nothing to lose and everything to gain.'

'That's all I wanted to know.'

'Just one more thing, it would be prudent if you arranged for an independent person to equip Walsh with the device and to take charge of the tape afterwards. It will help the prosecution in the application to have the evidence admitted, show that the officers involved in the case didn't have access to the tape recorded interview.'

'Thanks for the advice. I'll keep you posted.'

Returning to his office Peter was mindful of the Prosecuting Solicitor's words and he rang the Technical Service Unit. The TSA as it was known, were offices and workshops that had been established in various parts of the country. The unit that Peter contacted was in Manchester where the head of the unit was a Detective Inspector Fisher. Peter told the inspector what was required and in view of the delicacy surrounding the intended use of the equipment, Inspector Fisher agreed that he himself would take charge of its fitting.

Peter then returned to the Police Bridewell and went to see Walsh. He explained what he planned to do and how it was imperative that he should try to repeat the conversation he had had earlier with Challoner.

'It won't be easy,' said Walsh, 'Jimmy has a knack of sniffing things out you know.'

'But you will try?'

'In for a penny, yeah I'll do my best.'

At eight o'clock that night Walsh was once again shown into

Challoner's cell. This time he was carrying a radio microphone which was attached to a small tape recorder. The equipment had been cleverly concealed on Walsh's body and unless Jimmy became very suspicious and actually frisked Walsh then he wouldn't be able to detect its presence.

Earlier that day and following his conversation with Mick, Jimmy requested a visit from his solicitor. As he expected Wakefield arrived within the hour and Jimmy was taken from his cell into one of the interview rooms where Wakefield was waiting for him.

'You look happier,' Wakefield said.

Jimmy waited until the police escort had closed the door behind him and leaving the two of them alone.

'I certainly am. I've spoken to Mick and he's agreed to take the rap, say I had nothing to do with it.'

'And you believe him?'

'Why shouldn't I?' said Jimmy, 'besides he's not doing it for love, I've agreed to pay him a million.'

'That's a lot of money.'

'I only said I've agreed to pay him, I didn't say that I would.'

'I see,' said Wakefield, 'I wouldn't be surprised if Walsh wants rather more than your word Jimmy.'

'Correct. That's why I wanted to see you. I want you to draw something up so that I can sign it.'

'That will be a legally binding contract though.'

'So? When he gets out he can sue me.'

'Very well. I'll draw up a contract for you to sign and you can give it to Walsh tomorrow.'

'Good. Now then, what about bail tomorrow morning?'

'Shouldn't be a problem, especially if we can tell the court that Walsh is going to say you weren't involved in the drugs trafficking.'

'About Jennifer, have you managed to see her?'

'Yes. I've explained that you won't be home until tomorrow but that everything is under control.'

'Did she seem happy with that?'

'As happy as she could be under the circumstances.'

'Well it'll all be over by this time tomorrow. Once I'm home I can smooth everything over.'

'I hope you're right.'

'Listen I want you to represent Walsh and the others. You can do that can't you?'

'I see no reason why not. In fact I'll make sure I have a brief word with them all just before court tomorrow.'

Wakefield summoned the Keeper and indicated that his interview with his client was over. As he watched Challoner being escorted down the corridor back to his cell Wakefield thought about what Jimmy had just told him. He was amazed that Walsh was prepared to accept full responsibility for the drug trafficking and even more amazed that Walsh actually believed that he was to receive a million pounds for his trouble.

Jimmy was pleasantly surprised when later that evening Mick was again shown into his cell. He was aware that it wasn't normal police practice but believed that it must have been arranged for him by one of the senior police officers receiving bribes from him.

'This is what you pay for,' laughed Jimmy as Mick was ushered in.

'Bit of a chat certainly helps pass the time in this shithole.'

'What it is to have friends in high places eh,' Mick grinned.

'By the way I've seen Wakefield and he's drawing up the contract even as we speak.'

'For the million pounds you're paying me to say you had nothing to do with the drugs racket, right?'

'Yeah that's about it.'

'And all I have to say is that I organised the lot?'

'Come on Mick, you know perfectly well what we agreed.'

'Just wanted to be crystal clear what I'd agreed to.'

'It's easy enough. Just tell them you ran the heroin business without my knowledge. I knew nothing, OK?'

'Yeah got it. One thing, what if they ask where I got it from?'

'Tell them to mind their own bloody business.'

'Well I'm not going to be very convincing if I don't know who I bought the bloody stuff from.'

'You could be right there. Just say you bought the drugs from some Italian who had them delivered to Rome for you.'

'Was that the Italian guy you brought to the club, Silvana?'

'Yeah, but don't mention his name again, make one up.'

'OK, but how did I get in touch with Silvana?' said Walsh deliberately mentioning Silvana by name.

'By telephone to his office.'

'Well I reckon that's all I need to know.'

'It was the only thing you didn't know. You did run that operation yourself.'

'Yeah I know.'

'Good now be a good lad and go and tell Turner. The sooner you do, the sooner I get out of here.'

'I'll tell him now if you like.'

'That's just what I'd like. I'll ring for the Keeper to collect you.'

A few minutes later Walsh was escorted from Jimmy's cell and back to his own.

Peter Turner and Ted Fisher were waiting anxiously for Walsh's return. Both knew that if the equipment had failed they were unlikely to have another opportunity. Peter also knew that the following morning at the remand hearing the prosecution would, in order to remand Challoner in custody, be obliged to tell the court about Walsh's statement in which he implicated Challoner in the heroin importation. From that moment on Walsh and Challoner would need to be kept apart at all costs.

Peter had arranged with the Bridewell Keeper that once Walsh had indicated that he wished to return to his own cell he was to be escorted to the interview room where Peter and Fisher were waiting. Once Walsh had arrived and after the keeper had left Peter said, 'How did it go?'

'Like clockwork,' said Walsh as he removed his jacket and shirt to allow Fisher to reclaim his recording equipment.

'Challoner didn't suspect?'

'He thought I was a bit slow on the uptake that's all but I got all your questions in.'

'Great, let's hope the recorder hasn't let us down.'

Fisher rewound the tape and pressed the play button. There was an audible sigh of relief from the three men when the conversation between Challoner and Walsh was heard loud and clear.

'That's excellent,' said Peter, 'you've done a good job there Walsh.'

'What now?' Walsh asked addressing Inspector Fisher.

'Well first of all we formalise this recording so that when it's produced in court, its authenticity can't be challenged.'

'By doing what?' Peter asked the Inspector.

'First Walsh will need to sign this declaration I've prepared. It states that he conducted the conversation of his own free will and without promise or favour from the police.' Fisher passed a prepared script over to Walsh who signed it.

'Secondly,' Fisher added, 'we all three sign this label as witnesses to say that this tape is the only copy that was made.' All three signed the label that Fisher produced from his briefcase.

'Now, if you will bring in the shorthand writer she can listen to the tape, take the conversation down in shorthand and type it up,' Fisher said to Peter.

When the shorthand writer returned with the typed transcript of the recorded conversation Fisher said, 'Finally the tape goes into this envelope which I'll seal and our three signatures will be signed across the seal as proof to the court that the tape has not been interfered with.'

'Right,' said Fisher, 'until instructed by the trial court this tape will remain sealed.'

'In the meantime the typed transcript will be accepted by the lower courts as a record of the conversation,' Fisher explained.

After Fisher left Peter said to Walsh, 'What made you decide to tell us about Challoner's part in all this?'

'Let's just say I had my reasons.'

'You know it won't necessarily help at your trial don't you?'

'Yeah I know. I know I won't get any favours from the court but I didn't do it for that reason.'

'Mind you,' said Peter, 'I will make it known to the trial Judge that you were of great assistance to the police.'

'What happens to me now? Once Jimmy knows the score I'm a dead man if he gets to me.'

'Yes I realise that. Don't worry unduly you're no good to me dead.'

Sitting alone in his office Peter tried to think of a way in which he could keep Walsh out of Challoner's clutches. He knew that whichever remand centre Walsh was sent to Challoner would be able to arrange his murder or maiming so that he couldn't testify against him. In desperation Peter decided that he ought to make a few enquiries at the Home Office who surely must have come across similar dilemmas.

John Wakefield asked to see his client before he was taken into court for his remand hearing. What he had to say would go down like a lead balloon and Wakefield was still trying to find the right words when Jimmy was shown into the interview room.

'I didn't expect to see you until upstairs in court, nothing wrong is there?'

'Yes there is, very wrong Jimmy,' Wakefield coughed and straightened his tie. 'The fact is Mick Walsh has made a statement to the police implicating your involvement in the heroin trafficking.'

'You don't believe that do you? It's Turner up to his old tricks.'

'Not this time it isn't.'

'How can you be so sure?'

'Because Jimmy I've seen the statement.'

'That still doesn't mean that Walsh has grassed. Turner could have written that statement himself.'

'No the statement was made by Walsh. Turner might try and pull a trick or two, but he wouldn't be able to involve the Prosecuting Solicitor, plus he showed me Walsh's statement.'

'I can't believe Mick would grass. What's he hoping for?' Jimmy asked, now in shock as the realisation of what Mick's betrayal would mean.

'A lenient sentence for starters,' said Wakefield.

'No, Mick would know he wouldn't live long enough to serve any sentence. He's a dead man and he'll know it.'

'I think the police will know all that and give him maximum protection.'

'Believe me, there is nothing, absolutely nothing they can do to keep that bastard alive.'

'I'm afraid this alters your position regarding bail this morning.'

'What?' I'm not getting bail?'

'I'll do my best naturally, but I wouldn't bet on the outcome.'

'That traitorous bastard Walsh. If I see him in court I'll kill him myself.'

Jimmy was still angry and frustrated when he was taken up the steps from the Bridewell into the dock of the Stipendiary Court. He was even more annoyed seeing the dock empty as he had a burning desire to confront Walsh.

The remand hearing only took a few minutes but in spite of Wakefield's plea on Jimmy's behalf for bail the Stipendiary Magistrate remanded him in police custody for three days.

Later Jimmy asked Wakefield what had happened to the elusive Walsh.

'He's been further remanded in police custody.'

'Until when.'

'Well that's the odd thing, until a special hearing tomorrow.'

'What do you suppose that means?'

'I'm not sure Jimmy, but if I had to guess I'd say it's to give the police time to consider where to put him.'

'Doesn't matter where they put the bastard, he'll never be safe. Now look John, I want you to get a message to Terry Pritchard. You'll get his number from the River Club, it's in Manchester somewhere. Just tell him I want to put a contract out on Walsh. Explain to him why and he'll do the rest.'

'Right, I'll see to it this morning. Now what do you want me to tell Jennifer?'

'Tell her Turner has concocted the evidence again. She'll know what you're getting at. Ask her to come and see me so that I can explain it all myself.'

'Consider it done. Well I'll get off and get started then,' said Wakefield eager to leave.

'Just one more thing before you go,' said Jimmy, 'am I right in thinking that without Walsh the police have got nothing on me?'

'Nothing that would convict you.'

Jimmy smiled, 'As I thought John, as I thought.'

32

After leaving the office of the Prosecuting Solicitor, Peter contacted Mr Steen at the Home Office hoping to hear a solution to the problem of how to protect Walsh in the coming weeks. The simple answer would have been to repeatedly remand Walsh into police custody, but the law doesn't allow a prisoner to be remanded for more than three days under normal circumstances and only seven under extreme circumstances. Giving Walsh bail was another solution which nose dived. Challoner would have him silenced within hours.

Steen was sympathetic but couldn't offer any answers. He did tell Peter he would get onto the prison department for their advice, promising to telephone Peter back within the hour. True to his word Steen rang Peter back almost immediately.

'Not really very positive news Peter. Apparently until a person is actually convicted they cannot be classed as a 'Supergrass.' The Prison Department haven't had the resources to make special provision in remand centres for vulnerable cases on remand such as Walsh. It seems only the convicted are entitled to protection.'

'Did they know of any other similar cases and more importantly of any other cases which had found a way round the problem?' asked Peter.

'They have and they asked me to pass on what they consider to be the only solution you can go for.'

'Which is?'

'Bail Walsh and with his agreement remand him into your protective custody.'

'I'm not keen. It would mean putting him up in a 'safe' house, risky to say the least.'

'May I make a suggestion on a place of custody,' Steen said, 'what about a police establishment?'

'Now that is a possible solution, but the snag is I can't see a force anywhere rushing to have Walsh as a lodger.'

'That's where I can use the Home Office's not inconsiderable influence

Peter. If you approve the idea and Walsh agrees to the conditions, tell me where you would like him to go and I'll speak personally to the Chief Constable concerned.'

Peter thanked Steen for his help, replaced the receiver and then spent the next half hour considering the proposed plan for Walsh's protection. He knew the courts would have no power to make it a condition of Walsh's bail that he stay in a police establishment. It would have to be Walsh voluntarily agreeing to abide by whatever rules Peter saw fit to impose. To all intents and purposes Walsh would be a prisoner, housed in a police cell. The significant difference was that he wouldn't be subject to the legal requirements of court appearances.

Peter was in no doubt that this was the ideal solution. One in which he would have complete control. Unfortunately what Peter thought was irrelevant if Mick Walsh rejected the plan.

Mick Walsh saw immediately that Peter's proposal was realistically his only choice and he agreed to surrender himself into protective police custody.

After discussing possible locations with Jim Atkinson, it was decided that a rural police station in Cumbria would be appropriate. Such a venue would meet with the standard of security required and the likelihood of corruption amongst the officers was considerably less.

Peter told the Regional Co-ordinator where he had decided and it was agreed that in the interests of security the only people who would know of Walsh's future whereabouts would be the two of them and Jim Atkinson. Peter spoke again with Steen and suggested the force area where it was hoped to house Walsh. Steen promised to discuss the matter with the Chief Constable of Cumbria and accept his recommendation on the actual location of the police station where Walsh would be housed. As an added precaution it was also agreed that Walsh be given a new name.

Jimmy's delight at seeing Jennifer for the first time since his imprisonment was tempered by the fact that he was only too aware of what was at stake if she saw through his charade.

'Oh Jennifer, I'm so sorry you have to see me in this terrible place,' Jimmy said as he held Jennifer tightly against his chest.

'What's happening Jimmy? I expected you home today.'

'I should have been but Mick Walsh is trying to shift the blame to me and with Turner's help they've convinced the Magistrates that I'm somehow involved.'

'You're not though, are you?'

'Of course I'm not,' Jimmy stroked her hair and looked indignant. 'This is all just a stupid waste of everyone's time, all cooked up by that idiot Turner and now Mick as well.'

'Have you asked Mick why he's doing this?'

'No, I haven't seen him since he told Turner I was involved.'

'According to John Wakefield there are others involved. Surely they must have told the police you're not connected with them.'

'I'm sure they have but Turner wouldn't let a little thing like the truth stop him when he's got the bit between his teeth.'

'I don't understand how he's able to do this.'

'Let's just forget it for now, believe me the truth will out. Now then, how's my Debbie?'

'Debbie is fine. I haven't told her where you are of course. She thinks you're away on business.'

'Good, I don't want her to know anything about this.'

The half hour visit passed all too quickly. As Jennifer stood up to leave Jimmy said, 'Will you do something for me, will you telephone Antonio for me. Just tell him that my friends are in hospital and won't be able to go over for a while. Tell him I'll ring him myself as soon as I can.'

'What friends do you mean?'

'Some friends from the River Club, nothing important,' said Jimmy as he bent to kiss Jennifer, ignoring the waiting police officer who was to escort her out.

The next morning Jimmy had a visit from a puzzled John Wakefield.

'What's up?' Jimmy asked.

'I only wish I knew. Walsh has just been granted bail at his special remand hearing.'

'That's great news,' said Jimmy, 'he'll be dead tonight. You did get in touch with Pritchard didn't you?'

'Yes and I agreed the usual fee.'

'Excellent. It'll be goodbye Mr Walsh before we know it.'

Wakefield still had a worried look. 'It's a mystery why they've agreed to bail Walsh, I mean even the prosecution must have given some thought to the fact that he could be intimidated.'

'Maybe that was one of Walsh's conditions in making the statement.'

'Perhaps.'

'Don't worry about it. Just make sure that Pritchard is told he's out on bail. It'll make his job that bit easier even though he's the master at making anything look like suicide.'

Peter and Jim drove Walsh to Cumbria themselves. As they pulled away from Liverpool they were careful to ensure that no one was attempting to follow them. Walsh was to be lodged at Ullswater police station and the Inspector in charge was waiting to meet them after their two hour journey. During the drive Walsh advised Peter that if he ever wanted to convict Challoner it would have to be outside Liverpool.

'I've thought about that,' said Peter, 'I know better than most just how far his influence can extend.'

On his return there was a message for Peter to call and see the Prosecuting Solicitor which he did immediately.

'It's about the transcript of the tape recorded conversation between Walsh and Challoner. I think I ought to serve a copy on the defence. Do you have any objections to that?' the Prosecuting Solicitor asked Peter.

'No, I'm fine with that, they've got to know sooner or later.'

'Good. I don't want to give the defence any reason to challenge our actions and manage to get that piece of evidence excluded because of a technicality,' the solicitor said.

'Couldn't agree more,' Peter replied.

'You do realise that this case will need to be referred to the Director of Public Prosecutions?'

'Yes of course. There is one other thing I'd like to ask, can this case be tried outside the Liverpool area?'

'Why do you ask that?'

'I'm concerned that if I don't, with his local network of contacts Challoner might just see his way to perverting the course of justice.'

'There is nothing in law to stop the case being heard outside Liverpool, particularly since in the charge we specified the United Kingdom. Just to be absolutely sure I'll have a word with the DPP's office and let you know.'

Peter thanked him and went back to his office. So far so good, Challoner was safely locked away. Walsh was out of harms way and Peter had high hopes that given time he would provide further evidence that would help to convict Challoner. Peter intended to make regular visits to Walsh especially as the trial date approached. He knew that Walsh needed all the moral support he could muster.

The next day he heard from the Prosecuting Solicitor that the case could be heard in somewhere other than Liverpool. It was proposed that at the Committal Proceedings the case would be referred to London for the trial. Peter was delighted with the news because he doubted that even Challoner's influence extended to the capital.

'Don't look so bloody miserable, I'm the one banged up,' Jimmy greeted Wakefield at their next meeting.

'Sorry, there's more bad news I'm afraid.'

'Go on, let me have it.'

Wakefield went to his briefcase and gave Jimmy the transcript of the conversation he'd had with Walsh. He watched as Jimmy read it without comment.

'The bastard is worse than I suspected.'

'He's got it in for you alright.'

'Good job he won't be around to give evidence then.'

'That's the other bad news. Even without Walsh that tape can still be used in evidence against you.'

'Then I'll have to make sure the tape goes the way of Walsh.'

'How can you do that?'

'You don't need to know. Just leave it to me.'

'Well if we get that tape the court won't accept the transcript,' Wakefield started to look happier.

'Has Pritchard been in touch?'

'Only to say Walsh isn't at any of his usual haunts and he wondered if you had any clues as to his whereabouts.'

'The bugger could be anywhere. He'll have taken off for a few days, but he won't leave Liverpool for long. Tell Pritchard to be patient.'

'Will do. Is Jennifer coming to see you today?'

'Yes, she'll be here later. Now what about tomorrow. Will I get bail?'

'Shouldn't think so especially now the prosecution will produce that transcript at tomorrow's hearing.'

'Can't you fix it for my case to come up in one of the courts where I've friends on the bench?'

'Afraid not, the prosecution are insisting on the stipendiary himself hearing your remands.'

'That miserable old sod. He always turned down invitations to the River Club.'

'Given that you won't get bail you should prepare yourself for Risley. After tomorrow they can't remand you in police custody any longer.'

'Yeah I realise that.'

After Wakefield had gone Jimmy asked the Bridewell Keeper if Superintendent Flanagan could be requested to visit him. Flanagan appeared within the hour, none too pleased.

'What on earth have you asked to see me for? Don't you realise this visit goes on the apprehension sheet? The entire force will be putting two and two together,' Flanagan said crossly.

'Tough,' said Jimmy, 'you didn't mention any of this crap when you took your money. Thing is, it's time to earn it.'

'Forget it, Turner will know exactly who it is if anything goes wrong.'

'Then you'll have to make sure nothing does won't you?'

'What is it you want done anyway?'

'Not much. Just get me the tape recording of the conversation I had with Walsh, I want it destroyed.'

'Not much? Are you on another planet? That's Turner's main piece of evidence.'

'Exactly,' said Jimmy, 'that's precisely why it must be destroyed.'

'When you call in what's due you really go for your pound of flesh.'

'It's called insurance,' Jimmy smiled, but his cold stare made Flanagan wince.

'Some cover, it's my career on the line here.'

'Only if you cock this up.'

'OK, I'll try but don't blame me if I don't find it. Since that statement business a few years ago Turner has been very cagey about where he leaves his tea cup never mind vital evidence.'

'I'm sure you'll do what has to be done,' Jimmy said as Flanagan left his cell. It amused Jimmy to see how these corrupt men of power reacted when it was pay back time. None of them were very happy taking orders instead of a brown envelope. For this reason Jimmy tended to spread the workload and it had been a long time since Flanagan had earned his keep.

Peter unlocked his office door and stopped in his tracks. The room resembled a war zone. Completely ransacked with files of paper strewn over the floor and furniture lying upturned. The filing cabinet had been forced open as had the drawers of his desk. Peter's telephone started to ring and he eventually traced it to beneath a bundle of papers on the floor.

'Turner,' he said.

'The Prosecuting Solicitor here, just to say my office has been ransacked in the night and my court files broken into.'

'Anything missing,' Peter asked.

'Not as far as I know.'

'I've just found my office in the same state,' said Peter.

'What do you suppose they're after? Something to do with the Challoner case?'

'The tape's my guess.'

'Really. Then it would have to be someone from inside the force wouldn't it?'

'Without a doubt.'

Peter ended his conversation with the Prosecuting Solicitor and telephoned Inspector Fisher at the Technical Resource Unit. 'Turner here,' he began.

'You must be psychic. I've just tried to ring you, but it was engaged,' Fisher said.

'You wanted to tell me your office has been turned over, right?'

'Not only my office, the whole unit.'

'Did they get what they wanted?'

'Not if you mean the tape. That was in the safe and whoever broke in stopped just short of blowing it.'

'Only because they weren't equipped with explosives.'

'In that case I'd better get the tape moved to another secure location.'

'I agree,' Peter said. He then telephoned his Regional Co-ordinator and reported the three incidents of burglary to him. He was advised by the co-ordinator not to pursue the matter himself, but to leave it to the force who would carry out the necessary investigation once the Chief Constable had been informed.

After the remand hearing at which Challoner was remanded to the Risley Remand Centre for seven days, Peter went to the Bridewell where Challoner was being prepared for his journey.

'Too bad it didn't work a second time,' he said to Challoner.

'What are you on about.'

'You know perfectly well what. Well once bitten twice shy.' Challoner's face fell. He watched as Jimmy, handcuffed in a line of prisoners was led from the Bridewell to the waiting prison coach.

'How have the mighty fallen?' Peter muttered to himself.

That afternoon Peter drove to Ullswater to spend a couple of hours with Walsh. The Cumbria Police had allowed Walsh as many privileges and as much license as they could for which Peter thanked them. During the visit

Peter asked Walsh if he could tell him anything more about Jimmy's involvement in the heroin trafficking.

'I've told you all I know,' Mick said.

'Just wondered if you knew what he'd done with all the cash he 's got together.'

'Most of it's invested. He's got a good accountant to sort that out for him.'

Even so, there's only so much you can invest legitimately.'

'Well there's always the bank accounts.'

'What bank accounts?'

'I don't know all the banks he uses, but I know he always uses the same six names to open the accounts.'

'Can you remember them Mick?'

'Yeah, it's always the same Christian name, Joseph Alan. Then he used Brown, Black, Green, Grey, White but I can't remember the last one.'

'All colours, was the last one a colour do you think?'

'Not exactly, yeah I remember, Cherry it was Cherry.'

'Excellent, it always helps if you can tell the courts where some of the money that's been made has been deposited.'

'He's got a Swiss bank account too.'

'I suspected he would have, Jimmy always did hedge his bets.'

'He must be worth millions.'

'Yes that would be about right I should think,' said Peter before he took his leave of Mick and drove back to Liverpool.

The next day Peter's squad members visited every bank in the Merseyside area and made enquiries about a customer going by the name of Joseph Alan Black or any of the alternative names that Challoner was now known to have used. Later that day sixteen bank accounts had been traced and in each case the bank had been given identical instructions which were that no correspondence must be sent to the address of the account holder, which proved on investigation to be fictitious. Each was a deposit account and each contained twenty thousand pounds.

'Not bad,' Peter said to Jim Atkinson, 'three hundred and twenty thousand safely tucked away.'

'It's a bloody fortune.'

'To us it might be but to Challoner it's just pocket money.'

'And they say crime doesn't pay.'

Peter said nothing, but his thoughts were not too far removed from

Jim's last remark. Whoever would have thought that Jimmy Challoner would have made so much money?' Not Peter. He'd always believed that Jimmy would succeed at something, but a multi millionaire, never.

'Right, back to business,' Peter said 'first thing tomorrow Jim I want court orders so that those bank accounts we've unearthed can be frozen.'

'Sure,' Jim nodded. Peter was glad that his squad now thought as one. No longer did they question his motives in not taking anything for granted where Challoner was concerned. Jim obviously agreed that if the accounts were not legally frozen then Challoner would somehow find a way for the cash to be withdrawn.

'By the way,' said Jim 'did you hear that Superintendent Flanagan has resigned?'

'No I hadn't heard,' Peter replied, but then he wasn't surprised either by the news.

33

Jimmy Challoner was sitting in one of the small interview rooms at Risley Remand Centre waiting for a visit from John Wakefield. Jimmy looked idly around and saw that this section of the Remand Centre had been purpose built for inmates to be interviewed by either solicitors or police officers. There were six small interview rooms on each side of a wide corridor, at either end of which was a security door with a prison warder in attendance. Each of the interview rooms had large glazed sections facing the corridor presumably so that the two warders could see into the rooms for the purpose of supervision. The exterior windows Jimmy noted were barred to prevent any attempts at escape. The interview rooms each had their own door so that there was at least a degree of privacy when the door was shut.

'Pity this section couldn't be used for social visits as well,' said Jimmy to himself. Looking up as he heard the security door being opened Jimmy saw the warder escorting Wakefield to the room allocated to them.

'You look well,' Wakefield said to Jimmy as he sat down at the small wooden table opposite his client.

'I am well. I've got things pretty well organised in here.'

'I'd heard that one or two of the prison staff were bending the rules a bit.'

'Well you have to make the most of these set backs.'

'Well I'm glad you feel like that because there's been another.'

Jimmy's grin faded and he looked anxiously across at his friend and legal adviser knowing from the look on his face that bad news was imminent.

'Go on, let me have it,' Jimmy said slumping in his chair.

'The prosecution are going to ask for your trial to be held in London.'

'What. Can they do that?'

'I'm afraid they can and will.'

'But why would they want to do that.'

'At a guess because they feel that there is less chance of interference in the case if you get my drift.'

'Oh I get it alright,' interrupted Jimmy, 'and they'd be right. I don't like the way this is going John. That bastard Turner is behind all this.'

'There's something else too.'

'Go on.'

'The prosecution are going to commit Walsh and the women separately and get their trial heard quickly so that Walsh can give evidence against you at your trial.'

'What would be the advantage of that?'

'It's going to look better if Walsh has been convicted and sentenced. It means that the defence can't suggest he's only giving evidence in the hope of a lighter sentence.'

'Turner again.'

'Undoubtedly. Now what I do want to go over is our own strategy.'

'Let's hear it then, you're the legal eagle.'

'At your committal hearing I think we should accept all of the evidence the prosecution submit with the exception of Walsh's evidence. It's my opinion that he should be called to give evidence orally so that we can assess the content and style he presents it in.'

'Can we insist on that?'

'Yes we can. We have the right to hear any of the prosecution witnesses give evidence if we want to.'

'Let's go for it then, always assuming that Pritchard doesn't get to Walsh first.'

'We must plan for the worst scenario Jimmy. That's why I'm going to suggest that from the outset we employ a barrister from the London circuit to defend you.'

'Suits me, who do you reckon?'

'David Arrowsmith QC is just about the best criminal defence lawyer in the country.'

'Get him. I want the best.'

'He doesn't come cheap.'

'What price liberty?'

'Fine, I'll get onto him straight away.'

'Do that and find out where and when Walsh's committal is going to be held. As soon as you know make sure that Pritchard does too.'

'Got it,' said Wakefield as he rose to leave.

One more thing.'

'Yes?'

'I want you to get in touch with Michael on the yacht. Tell him to bring it to Britain and berth it at Poole.'

'You're not thinking of doing a runner are you?'

'Not yet I'm not,' Jimmy's face looked murderous and Wakefield breathed a sigh of relief as he made his way down the corridor to be escorted out of the grim surroundings which comprised Risley.

Peter Turner was preparing the file of evidence for the committal proceedings of Michael Walsh. It was unfortunate that Walsh had to appear in person as Peter would have preferred to have kept him out of the public eye. However the law decreed that the accused must be present at the committal hearing even though none of the evidence was to be challenged. Peter had heard along the grapevine that someone from Manchester had been looking for Walsh and he knew that the committal hearing would provide a golden opportunity for anyone determined enough who wanted to kill Walsh.

It was with this in mind that Peter was discussing with Jim Atkinson his own ideas on keeping Walsh in one piece.

'As I see it we have three problems to consider. First how and when we collect him. Secondly his protection in court and thirdly his removal from court and his return to Cumbria.'

'The court house must be the most vulnerable place,' suggested Jim.

'True, but it's also very public and whoever the hitman is he'll know he would have much less chance of escape.'

'So logically the best time to get Walsh is after the court hearing, either by hijacking or by trying to follow him back to where he is being kept.'

'That's what they would like us to believe, but I reckon they'll plan it a little differently.'

'How do you mean?'

'It's my guess that they'll plan on us taking action to prevent the obvious,' answered Peter.

'Which would be a hijack.'

'Right. Now put yourself in their shoes. How would we in the Crime Squad go about finding where someone is being kept?'

'We would follow whoever would lead us to the hide-out.'

'Exactly.'

'Give us some credit, we wouldn't be stupid enough to allow ourselves to be followed.'

'We wouldn't if we were aware we were being followed but what if they were using a tracking device?'

'Is that likely. Tracking equipment is relatively new, we've only got it recently ourselves.'

'If it's available to us it's available to anyone. It's only a radio transmitter and a scanner after all.'

'I see what you're getting at but even if they have got the equipment the transmitter has got to be attached to the target vehicle. How are they going to know which one we'll be in?'

'If we were to collect Walsh under normal circumstances we would use an armoured prison van and as we've only got the one the choice is simple.'

'You know I think you could well be right. It's so simple and it almost fooled us,' Peter knew exactly what Jim meant. If a tracking device was to be used then the vehicle carrying the scanner could remain well back out of sight since the range of the transmitter was about a mile. The surveillance squad would only be alert to those vehicles trying to keep the target vehicle within their sights. They would be unaware of a vehicle carrying a scanner which would be informing its operator from a safe distance of the route being taken.

'Modern technology can be a double edged sword,' said Peter.

'What do we do then? Remove the thing before we set off?'

'No, we still need to arrest the hitman otherwise he'll just have another go. What we'll do is let the prison van carry on as though it was being used to go and collect Walsh. Instead of going to Cumbria we'll pack it off to North Wales and if we use a bit of nous selecting the route then once we get it out in the open the lads should spot the vehicle with the scanner and arrest the hitman.'

'And what about Walsh?'

'You and I will go for him during the night. That way we'll know by vehicle headlights whether we're being followed or not.'

'Just as a precaution,' Jim added, 'I'll check our car out for a radio transmitter.'

Walsh's committal hearing had been fixed for a Tuesday morning and Peter had arranged for the prison van to make its decoy run on the Monday. During the Sunday night he made sure that the van kept to its normal routine and that it was left in its usual garaging space while being watched by members of his team. When Peter arrived at his office on the Monday morning he was told that a radio transmitter had been placed on the underside of the prison van.

Peter breathed a sigh of relief on hearing this news as it meant that his hypothesis was becoming a reality. Later that morning he punched the air in a rare triumphal display when he learned from Jim that the surveillance team had made an arrest in North Wales. Three men had been captured in a vehicle equipped with a scanning device tuned into the radio transmitter which had been recovered from the police van. One of the arrested men was Terry Pritchard from Manchester. CID at Manchester were able to say that they had long suspected Pritchard of being a hired killer but had never had the evidence to substantiate this belief. Peter was satisfied that he now had sufficient evidence and instructed that Pritchard be charged with conspiracy to commit murder.

The committal of Walsh and the two women continued without further incident and since all of them were pleading guilty to the charges an early hearing at Liverpool Crown Court was requested by the prosecution.

The Director of Public Prosecutions had appointed a member of his own staff to prepare and prosecute the committal case not only against Challoner but against Walsh and the couriers as well. Peter had met Mr Bridley several times in order to discuss the case with him. It had been at Bridley's suggestion that Walsh and the women should be tried separately and before Challoner. That way Walsh would be a convicted and sentenced prisoner by the time he gave evidence at Challoner's trial. Peter had been impressed by the logic of this idea. He knew that Walsh's evidence would carry more credibility in court when it was pointed out that his motive was to see justice done rather than any preferential treatment he might expect to receive from the courts for doing so.

Due to the cancellation in the Crown Court calendar at Liverpool, Walsh's trial was listed for hearing two weeks after he had been committed. Peter was relieved to hear the news and knew that Walsh would also be pleased. The sooner he was convicted the sooner he would start serving his expected lengthy term of imprisonment. Once Walsh was convicted Peter wouldn't be able to provide his personal protection. From the moment he received his sentence from the Judge, Walsh would come under the control of the prison authority.

To ensure his safety Walsh must be granted the status of 'super grass,' and Peter knew that he must begin his campaign with the Prison Department immediately. It had long been recognised by the Prison Department that prisoners who had agreed to testify against acknowledged major criminals required extra security and certain prisons reserved a wing especially for these super grass prisoners. Prisoners with super grass status were completely segregated from other prisoners and the prison staff were carefully vetted. However because of the limited accommodation available for such prisoners the granting of super grass status was far from routine.

Having made enquiries into the required criteria needed to qualify for super grass status Peter then had to obtain a written agreement from the Director of Public Prosecutions confirming that Walsh's circumstances fitted the criteria as laid down by the Home Office. Without this written authority Peter knew he wouldn't make any progress. He contacted Mr Bridley and arranged to meet him at the Director of Public Prosecutions office at Queen Anne's Gate in London.

Obtaining the letter of authority from Bridley, who was authorised to sign on behalf of the DPP, was as Peter had expected it to be, merely a formality. Bridley was by now very familiar with Walsh's circumstances and shared Peter's view that Walsh merited maximum protection in order to ensure his appearance at Challoner's trial.

Peter next arranged a visit to the Home Office to meet with the Police Liaison Officer who was attached to the Home Office Prison Department. Here Peter was required to make out a detailed report listing his reasons why Walsh should be afforded super grass status. The Police Liaison Officer explained to Peter that in spite of the strong recommendation from the DPP's office which was to accompany Peter's report, there was still only an even chance of the Prison Board approving it. Travelling back to Merseyside Peter felt a sense of anti climax. He had wanted to go back to Walsh with the news that he was to be given protection. Otherwise how could he expect the man to give evidence that without the protection of the law was tantamount to signing his own death warrant.

34

With only a week to go before Mick Walsh's trial was due to begin Peter was worried that he hadn't heard from the Prison Department. He still was none the wiser whether Walsh would be categorised as a super grass or not. Although he had discussed with Walsh what he was attempting to set up for him he hadn't broached the subject of what he would do if the application was refused. Peter was on the point of telling Walsh that it looked probable that he would have to serve his sentence as a routine prisoner when to his relief word came through. Once Walsh received his sentence he would be taken directly to one of the locations reserved for inmates termed super grass. The actual location was to remain confidential, known only to the Prison Department and to Peter. Walsh would remain at one establishment for the duration of his sentence after which he would be given every assistance to integrate himself back into society. This would take the form of a new identity and such financial help as was necessary for him to take up his life again. Peter set off straight away to pass on the good news to Walsh at the secret destination, taking all the necessary precautions before setting off.

On the day of Walsh's trial Peter and Jim collected him as they had on the day of his committal hearing. The journey passed without incident and Walsh was handed over to the prison officer in charge of all the prisoners at Liverpool Crown Court.

It was known that Walsh and the others intended to plead guilty and as a result the hearing was listed for a half day only. When a prisoner pleads guilty the need for a jury or witnesses for the prosecution, other than character witnesses, is eliminated which speeds matters up. Peter Turner was a character witness for Walsh explaining his assistance and anticipated assistance at the trial of Challoner, had been invaluable in bringing the case to court. When sentencing Walsh, Mr Justice Fraser told him the Government and the courts, were anxious to bring to trial the people who were controlling the importation of illegal drugs into the

United Kingdom. Anyone who gave the police assistance in bringing these felons to justice could expect a degree of leniency from the courts. He went on to inform Walsh that the normal sentence he could have expected for his part in the drugs conspiracy was ten years. In view of his assistance to the police this would be reduced to five years. Peter was delighted with what could only be described as a light sentence. He was convinced that Walsh would honour his pledge to give evidence against Challoner and would be the major influence in securing a conviction.

After the case Peter went to speak to Walsh explaining that Challoner's defence wanted him at Challoner's committal hearing.

'I was hoping to spare you that but they insist.'

'No problem.'

'It'll be a rough ride and then you'll have it all again at the trial.'

'I'll look on this as a practice run.'

'Don't take the committal too lightly. This case could be dismissed at any time you know.'

'Believe me as far as Jimmy is concerned I don't take anything lightly.'

'No, I don't suppose you do.'

The two men said their goodbyes and Walsh was taken into the protective custody of the Prison Department. Peter found himself hoping that Walsh would survive to take up his second chance.

Jimmy Challoner sat at the back of number eight Court. One of the nine courtrooms which made up the Liverpool Magistrates' Courts. He looked around and saw the usual faces associated with the judiciary system. Sitting directly below him was his defence counsel, David Arrowsmith, and alongside him was John Wakefield. To the fore of them and to their right sat the Prosecuting Solicitor. The Magistrates' Clerk was sitting facing him just below the bench which awaited the arrival of the Magistrate who would hear the committal. Jimmy's first plan had been to arrange for one of the Magistrates he had carefully cultivated over the years to preside over the hearing. Since his defence had decided not to fight the case at this stage it was irrelevant who sat on the bench and plan A had been shelved. Added to which Wakefield had advised him that Turner would have anticipated such a move on Jimmy's part and would have taken steps to ensure that a neutral Magistrate presided.

The arrival of the Magistrate signalled that the case was about to begin. It was at this stage that Jimmy became aware of the extra uniformed police officers in the court room and guessed they were there to safeguard

Walsh. Jimmy looked down to where Peter was sitting on one of the side benches in the well of the court and as their eyes met Jimmy grinned broadly. He couldn't have been more delighted that he had caused Peter such trouble.

It had taken all Jimmy's powers of persuasion to stop Jennifer coming to the hearing. He suspected that if Jennifer heard the unchallenged prosecution case she would doubt his innocence. He had finally convinced her the hearing was merely a formality which would be very brief and there wouldn't be any opportunity for them to meet.

The case began with the Prosecuting Solicitor standing in front of the Magistrate and reading out all the statements of prosecution witnesses who were not present in court. After an hour Jimmy's attention was wandering but he sat up with a start on hearing the prosecutor say 'Call Mr Walsh.' This section of the trial was to have his undivided attention and he turned to watch as Walsh made his entrance through the doors at the back of the courtroom. Walsh was handcuffed to two prison warders and although he tried to avoid Jimmy's gaze, just for a moment he found himself looking into Jimmy's hate filled eyes. An involuntary shudder went through him as he turned away and took his place in court. Looking at Walsh Jimmy was consumed with rage, some of which was directed at himself. Walsh should have paid the ultimate penalty at the time of his first betrayal and Jimmy vowed that never again would he allow sentiment to cloud his judgement. Walsh and Turner had it coming Jimmy thought to himself and he couldn't wait to deliver.

Walsh entered the witness box and was released from his handcuffs, although the warders stayed close by. The clerk handed him the testament and a card on which the oath was written and which Walsh read out in a firm voice.

It had been previously agreed between David Arrowsmith and the Prosecuting Solicitor that Walsh's statement would be read out to the court rather than for the prosecutor taking Walsh through it verbally. When the prosecutor had finished he sat down and David Arrowsmith rose to his feet. There was an intimidating air about Arrowsmith and when he started to speak in his loud, resonant tones everyone in the courtroom, including Jimmy, was transfixed and listened with rapt attention.

'Tell me Mr Walsh, do you believe in the oath you have just taken?'
'Yes I do.'

'Good. Then this shouldn't take too long.'

Jimmy watched as Walsh visibly relaxed on hearing this.

'The statement that's just been read out to the court, did you make it Mr Walsh?'

'Yes.'

'Why did you make it Mr Walsh?'

'I don't understand.'

'It's a simple enough question. Why did you make the statement?'

'To tell the police exactly what had been going on.'

'Is what you said in your statement the truth?'

'Yes.'

'It isn't the truth though is it Mr Walsh?' said Arrowsmith raising his eyebrows and staring at Walsh.

'It is the truth,' stammered Walsh growing uncomfortable under Arrowsmith's gaze.

'Then maybe Mr Walsh you will explain to the court what it was you meant in your statement when you said that Mr Challoner had recruited the women from Birmingham?'

'I meant that Jimmy had organised their recruitment.'

'Mr Walsh, we all need to hear your answer. Now will you repeat that.'

Walsh repeated his answer.

'But Mr Walsh, it was you who recruited the women was it not?' Arrowsmith's voice boomed out across the courtroom.

'Yes.'

'Is it not true that Mr Challoner never even saw the women let alone met them?'

'Yes.'

'So you were in fact not telling the truth when you made that statement were you Mr Walsh?'

'It was the truth. You've twisted my words.'

'Was it the truth or was it not.'

'No,' said Walsh, 'but ….'

'Thank you Mr Walsh,' said Arrowsmith not allowing Walsh to finish speaking. 'Now how much more of that statement is lies I wonder?'

'The rest is the truth.'

'We shall see,' Arrowsmith replied. 'Now Mr Walsh, let us leave the statement for the time being and concentrate on the typed transcript of the tape recorded talk you had with Mr Challoner. You do remember the talk you had?'

'Yes I was wearing the tape recorder strapped to me.'

'Really?' Arrowsmith said, 'and was this apparatus visible to Mr Challoner?'

'No, it was hidden on me.'

'So it would be true to say that Mr Challoner would not be aware that the conversation was being taped?'

'Yes, that is he didn't know.'

'Thank you Mr Walsh. Now why was the conversation you had with Mr Challoner recorded?'

'Mr Turner wanted Jimmy to admit his involvement in the drugs business.'

'Then it was Mr Turner's idea?'

'Yes.'

'And did Superintendent Turner suggest to you which points he wished you to raise in this conversation with Mr Challoner?'

'Yes.'

'And did you ask those particular questions?'

'Yes I did.'

Mick Walsh appeared to have regained his composure and was looking a little more confident than he had a few minutes ago.

'Thank you Mr Walsh. Now let us turn our attention to something else. In what capacity were you employed by Mr Challoner?'

'I was his number one.'

'Doing what?'

'Well mostly I helped run the clubs.'

'And would you describe the club business as a legitimate enterprise?'

'Yes, it's all above board.'

'How much did you get paid for this?'

'I was paid thirty thousand a year.'

'Really,' said Arrowsmith adopting a look of surprise, 'thirty thousand is a handsome salary is it not Mr Walsh?'

'Yes, but I earned it.'

'I'm sure you did Mr Walsh. Would it be true to say that Mr Challoner paid all of his employees a fair wage?'

'He did but he wanted his pound of flesh in return.'

'Doesn't every employer?'

'I suppose so.'

'Tell me Mr Walsh, did Mr Challoner know what all of his employees did in return for their wages?'

'More or less.'

'If those employees were asked to do something extra in addition to their usual duties would they receive extra payment?'

'It would depend on what they did.'

'Let me give you an example of what I mean' Arrowsmith said as he shuffled the case papers on the bench before him. 'Take your case for example. You have said that you are employed by Mr Challoner to run his club business,' Arrowsmith looked across at Walsh and saw that he was nodding in agreement, 'now let us suppose Mr Challoner had asked you to do something entirely different from those duties. Would you have expected to be paid extra money for doing whatever it was that he wanted you to do?'

'You'll have to explain a bit more, I already do other things from time to time without any extra pay.'

'Let's assume that you were asked to run another section of Mr Challoner's business?'

'In that case I'd expect to be paid considerably more.'

'If you didn't receive that extra payment what would you do?'

'I would refuse to carry out those extra duties, but I don't think that would happen. If he wanted you to take on extra responsibilities Jimmy always paid for them.'

'Then tell me Mr Walsh do you consider that the heroin business which you stated Mr Challoner organised but you ran would constitute the extra responsibility that Mr Challoner would pay for?'

'Normally yes I would.'

'Normally, what do you mean by that?'

'I mean it should have been something I got extra money for but I didn't.'

'And in spite of not being paid for this extra responsibility you didn't refuse to carry out these duties?'

'No.'

'Thank you Mr Walsh, that's all,' and with that Arrowsmith sat down.

Jimmy continued to stare at Walsh who appeared relieved as he was handcuffed to the prison warders and led from the court. Jimmy was surprised at Arrowsmith, it seemed to him that he had Walsh by the throat and then just let him go. Jimmy just hoped he knew what he was doing.

When called Jimmy stood and faced the Magistrate who told him that on the evidence that had been submitted before him there was a prima facie case for him to answer and that he would be remanded in custody to stand trial at the Old Bailey in London.

Immediately after Challoner's committal hearing Peter Turner was talking to Mr Bridley from the Director of Public Prosecutions office.

'What did you make of that lot?' the solicitor asked Peter.

'Quite a lot,' Peter said. 'For a start Arrowsmith is every bit as good as they say he is.'

'Yes he's certainly got a reputation for winning, but don't panic we'll employ someone who is his equal to present our case,' said Bridley.

'I'm relieved to hear that. From what I gathered today Arrowsmith is going to challenge the statement that Walsh made on the grounds that it's not the truth. It also looks as though he's questioning the way in which the tape recorded conversation was instigated and if that's not enough he's going to suggest that Challoner didn't know that Walsh was running the heroin trade.'

'I think that's an accurate summary of the defence tactics,' said Bridley as he gave a wry smile.

'The thing I don't understand is why the defence have given us so clear an insight into the way they intend to fight the case.'

'Legally it was very shrewd of Arrowsmith.'

'Firstly he knows how Walsh stands up as a witness and how best to undermine him. Secondly he has put on record and introduced onto the court transcripts several important issues that will tie the hands of the eventual prosecutor in this case.'

'We can always introduce further evidence if we want to.'

'We can but we can't materially alter the case we've now presented.'

'Don't look so fed up Superintendent,' Bridley said. 'The defence have got some formidable hurdles in this race.'

'They're off to a good start though,' said Peter as he made his way back to his office.

Looking through Walsh's statement again Peter was reasonably happy, in spite of Arrowsmith's inferences that the contents were inaccurate it would still stand up as evidence.

The remarks Arrowsmith made regarding the introduction of the tape recorded conversation were a different matter. They couldn't be denied because they were true, he had instigated the tape's use. The issue was whether his actions had been those of an 'agent provocateur.' If the court rules that Walsh had been used as such then by law the tape of the conversation could not be used in evidence. In Peter's view Walsh hadn't been used as an agent provocateur. To do so would have been for him to have incited Challoner to commit an illegal act. In essence he hadn't made any proposition to Challoner, he simply had a conversation with him.

It was clear to Peter that Arrowsmith would claim that Challoner had no knowledge of the heroin business. He had cleverly elicited the information that he wasn't paid for running the drugs business from Walsh, but if the tape was passed as evidence then Challoner was sunk anyway. If the tape was excluded as evidence then Peter feared the outcome.

35

Jimmy Challoner was furious. He was pacing up and down his cell in Risley like a caged animal. Informed that he was to be transferred to Wormwood Scrubs in London he was not a happy man. He held no particular affection for Risley, but at least it was home territory, the prison staff knew him by reputation and were on occasion suitably biddable.

On hearing of his transfer Jimmy sent immediately for Wakefield. Having heard the news of Jimmy's transfer, he was already on his way having correctly anticipated that his client would want to see him and quickly.

'What the hell's going on John?'

'Calm down Jimmy.'

'I bloody can't. What are they going to do next?'

'Just sit down and let's talk about it.'

Jimmy stopped pacing the floor and sat down opposite Wakefield.

'That's more like it, you were making me nervous.'

'Tell me now John, can they do this? Send me to London?'

'I'm afraid they can.'

'Isn't there anything you can do? Appeal or something?'

'I can ask for the date to be delayed, but that would only be for a week or two at most.'

'Well that's something.'

'There is one thing, how about letting Jennifer visit. The poor woman badly wants to see you.'

'No, never. She's not setting foot in this rathole John.'

'Well remember your trial date could be months away, are you prepared to go without seeing her for such a long time?'

'Months? Why the hell is it going to take so bloody long?'

'The Old Bailey's case load is that far behind that's why.'

'I don't believe this is happening to me. It's all down to that bastard Turner, but believe me he'll pay for this.'

'Forget Turner and think of Jennifer. Let her come and see you.'

'OK. Arrange it.'

'Excellent, I'll arrange it for tomorrow. Now do you want me to go for a deferment or not?'

'Let me think about that one. I'll talk to Jennifer about it first.'

Incidentally, Walsh was followed as you asked and he was taken to Bedford Prison.'

'Was he now,' said Jimmy brightening, 'so now at least I know where to arrange Mr Walsh's long overdue comeuppance.'

'Do you want me to do anything?'

'About Walsh? No, I'll fix it myself from in here.'

The following day Jimmy was sitting with the other remand prisoners waiting for Jennifer to arrive. The visiting hall was an extension of the canteen which was open for cups of tea and snacks. Jimmy was sitting as far away as possible from the other prisoners and nobody was foolhardy enough to invade the space he had created for himself. At three o'clock the door at the far end of the room swung open and there was a babble of noise as the wives and girlfriends surged into the room. He watched as Jennifer came in. She looked anxiously around the room and he watched her face light up with recognition as she spotted him. Jimmy stood up holding out his arms and she fell into them, her head burrowing into his shoulder.

'Christ, I hate seeing you here.'

'Jimmy I couldn't care less where I see you as long as I see you,' Jennifer said taking both his hands in hers across the table that now divided them.

'Did John tell you about my move to London?'

'Yes.'

'We won't see each other at all.'

'Yes we will, I'm going down to the cottage. I'll be close enough to visit as often as I'm allowed then.'

'What about all your committees and things.'

'I've told you Jimmy, nothing matters but you. Committees and things will still be there when all this is over.'

'What about Debbie? We can't pretend for ever.'

'I'm going to tell her the truth. She's old enough to understand, she'll cope.'

Jimmy looked at this, decisive, feisty woman opposite him and realised that she was made of sterner stuff than he had ever imagined.

When the visit came to an end Jennifer kissed Jimmy saying 'Just hang on for a few more weeks darling. Remember Debbie and I love you and that's all that matters.'

'And I love you too,' murmured Jimmy, 'believe me heads will roll Jennifer when the truth comes out.'

At the prospect of frequent visits and reassured of Jennifer's belief in his innocence, Jimmy's spirits soared and he whistled jauntily as he swaggered back to his cell.

Operating throughout all the prisons and remand institutions in the country is a prisoner's intelligence network. This is used by inmates to communicate either outside of or within the prison service. It didn't take Jimmy long to establish who was Risley's contact man and he arranged a meeting in the communal exercise yard. Jimmy explained that he wanted to take out a contract on a prisoner in Bedford Prison, a permanent contract.

'That will be expensive,' the contact man looked at Jimmy. 'That's not a problem for you though is it?'

'How much?'

'Five thousand.'

'Who to and where.'

'When the contract's agreed you'll be given the number of an account. Pay the five thousand in and the contract will be honoured.'

'Suits me. You know I'm on the move to the Scrubs in a day or so?'

'No worries. You'll be contacted there when the contract has been agreed. Now better give me the details.'

Peter was pleased that his request to have Challoner removed to London had been agreed by the prison department. At Risley Challoner's cronies were far too close for Peter's liking and he suspected that Challoner would have the means to orchestrate his own break out should he choose to. He dreaded seeing Jimmy evade prosecution and escaping to Spain or Brazil where he could remain free as Britain had no reciprocal agreement with either to extradite fugitives. For the last four weeks there had been no indication from Challoner that he was planning an escape and Peter felt that for the first time in a long time he could safely forget about Challoner, if only for a while.

A telephone call from the prison department shattered his complacency in the space of a minute when they told him it had picked up on the grapevine that Challoner had arranged for a contract to be taken out on Walsh. Sending for Jim Atkinson, Peter cursed his own stupidity in allowing his guard to come down with a devious opponent such as Challoner in the other corner.

'Doesn't this guy ever give up,' said Jim.

'No and we must never forget it again.'

'What are we supposed to do, Walsh isn't our responsibility now?'

'That's right and we can forget about Walsh. He's in the supergrass wing and he's safe. The thing is Challoner won't know that yet and when he does he'll need an entirely different plan.'

'In other words we've got to be half a dozen jumps ahead of him.'

'Exactly. Once he knows that he can't silence Walsh he'll have to plan his defence differently so I want you to go away and think hard about what he might do next.'

'I'll do the same. Let's put ourselves in Challoner's shoes and see what we come up with.'

'Oh another of your brainstorming sessions is it,' Jim laughed.

'Certainly is and I'll thank you not to knock them.'

Peter smiled to himself as Jim left the office. He was aware that the squad could be cynical about his attempts to reach a conclusion by bouncing ideas off them. In his experience he had found the ploy yielded too many positive results to ignore.

'Right Jim,' said Peter when he caught up with him later in the day, 'hit me with it, what have you got?'

'Not a lot.'

'OK, what would you do next if you were our lad?'

'Plan my escape.'

'How?'

'Bribery probably.'

Peter was writing down the key words, escape, bribery.

'Means of escape?'

'Commercial airports and seaports are out so it would have to be by private plane or boat.'

'Destination?'

'Spain I suppose.'

'Now,' said Peter, 'let's assume that escape is out of the question, what then?'

'Well with Walsh still alive, I'd have to consider nobbling the jury.'

'What if the said jury are given police protection?'

'Christ I don't know. I'd have to arrange my own bloody jury.'

'Thanks Jim,' said Peter 'that's been most helpful,' as he scutinized the list of key words he had written down.

'I don't see it myself,' replied Jim totally unconvinced.

'Well for starters it's brought home to me that we've overlooked the obvious. We know Challoner has his own yacht, and we haven't checked with all the port authorities to see if it's over here or not.'

'Yes that had been overlooked,' Jim admitted, 'I'll get on to it right away.'

'Good,' said Peter as he scanned the list again. 'The rest of the words are not so obvious in giving answers but given time I'm confident they will. They just need a bit more thought.'

'To be honest I don't see what else there is to think about. Once we give the jury full police protection what can he do? Not even Challoner can select his own jury panel.'

'Maybe, maybe not.'

Life improved as far as Jimmy was concerned with the move to Wormwood Scrubs. Grisley Risley had earned its nickname in his opinion and the atmosphere at the Scrubs suited him. Added to this Jimmy received regular visits from Jennifer and long optimistic letters from Debbie in Switzerland. He wished that the fantasy Jennifer and Debbie believed so implicitly were true. Unfortunately things were not looking too rosy from his side of the fence. Arrowsmith had warned him that in spite of any evidence the court might be persuaded to reject he could still be convicted if Walsh's testimony was accepted by the jury. Knowing Arrowsmith's reputation that statement made Jimmy nervous. The fact that Walsh was being too closely guarded for the contract on him to be carried out didn't inspire him with confidence. He had come to the conclusion that if taking out Walsh before the trial proved impossible he would find a way to silence him before the retrial which Jimmy was already planning for himself.

Jimmy was kept informed of his business affairs in his weekly meetings with John Wakeley. Any decisions to be made were made by Jimmy. In that way he remained in control while various managers had been delegated to manage the day to day running of the organisation. He was well aware that if he was imprisoned for any length of time one or two of these now trusted servants were likely to get ideas above their stations.

For the present he was grateful they were holding the business together. Business matters over Jimmy asked Wakefield.

'Does the majority rule still apply in the case of juries John?'

'It certainly does. The Judge will always try for a unanimous verdict. If that is not forthcoming he will accept a majority verdict of ten to two against.'

'So if the jury members were three against and nine were for, what would happen?'

'The Judge would have no option but to order a retrial. Why do you ask?'

'I'm just considering one or two options.'

'If you're thinking what I think you're thinking how the hell are you going to pull that one off?'

'There is a way,' Jimmy replied, 'better that you know nothing. All I want you to do is contact a solicitor called Ray Rowlands. He has an office in Camden Town, just get a member of his firm to pay me a visit, he'll do the rest.'

'That all?'

'That's it.'

Wakefield was wise enough not to pursue the subject further.

'Ah yes, I had a call from the yacht. Michael said the vessel is in great shape and he's waiting for instructions.'

'I suspect I'm not going to need it after all, tell him to sail the thing back to Greece.'

'Right anything else before I go?'

'No, everything seems OK. What about the house? Is it being looked after?'

'Being well looked after, no problem there,' Wakefield said closing his briefcase and standing up. He shook hands with Jimmy, 'Until next week then.'

'Yeah see you then.'

Four days later Jimmy was on his way to attend the meeting set up by Wakefield. He had known about but never used the 'Jury Firm' as they were referred to. They were a London based organisation who offered a service to those criminals who could afford them and whose trials were scheduled to take place at the Old Bailey.

As Jimmy entered the interview room to meet Ray Rowland's representative he was somewhat taken aback to see a woman waiting for him.

'Mr Challoner, good to meet you. I'm Sandra Tushingham.'

'Nice to meet you,' said Jimmy taking her hand. Sandra Tushingham was in her early thirties, tall and slim with an authoritative manner.

'I'm surprised to see you're a woman. I was expecting a man.'

'Everyone is,' she smiled. 'We've found that the prison authorities don't ask too many questions when a female arrives claiming to be a member of the legal profession.'

'And are you?'

'Ray Rowlands is a solicitor and he's retained by the firm as our legal adviser. Since we do most of our interviews in prisons we use his name as the simplest way of gaining admission and being granted privacy. So Mr Challoner to answer your question, no I'm not a solicitor. I work for the firm and am using the office of solicitor to facilitate my talk with you.'

'I'm impressed.'

'That's good, because we pride ourselves on our professionalism and guarantee a professional service.'

'So what do I need to do?'

'Not a lot. We've already done our homework on you, if you know what I mean.'

'And do I pass?'

'I wouldn't be here if you didn't.'

'How much is this service just as a matter of interest.'

'I presume that you want a jury to disagree on a verdict?'

'Correct.'

'Then the price is one hundred thousand pounds.'

'That's a lot of money.'

'Not when it's measured against a lengthy spell in prison.'

'I've still got a retrial to think about.'

We both know that the likelihood of anyone being convicted at a retrial is remote. Anyway from what I've heard Mr Challoner conviction in your case is unlikely,' Sandra said as she met Jimmy's gaze. He assumed that she meant the contract on Walsh.

'Right,' said Jimmy, 'consider yourself hired.'

'That's fine. Now all you have to do is authorise Mr Wakefield to deposit the money into an account he will be given details about.'

'Consider it done.'

'Leave everything else to us. Just one thing, don't allow your legal representative to make any objections to any members of your jury. He might just exclude one of our own people.'

'I'll bear that in mind.'

'Good, anything else you want to ask?'

'Well I must admit I'm curious as to how the whole system works.'

'It's simple really. We have someone working within the jury selection administration at the Old Bailey. When the lists are compiled for trials, our man substitutes the names of three members of our organisation for three of the genuine members.'

'Simple yet ingenious, clever.'

'I assure you Mr Challoner it's foolproof. We never give the prosecution any reason to suspect what we are doing.'

'Well this is going to make the wait easier, knowing I'm off the hook.'

'I'm glad. Before I go I've been told to pass on some advice Mr Challoner.'

'Advice, what advice?'

'As soon as Walsh has given his evidence you must have him silenced.'

'I don't understand.'

'Well once it becomes known that your case is to be retried the authorities will reintroduce extra security measures for Walsh.'

'Ah, got it.'

'We have considerable experience in these matters and we're only too happy if we can assist our clientele,' said Sandra as she rose to leave.

'You were right about Challoner's yacht. It's anchored off Poole Harbour,' Jim said.

'Right under our bloody noses and we nearly missed it.'.

'Do you seriously think he'll make a run for it?'

'He will if he thinks all else has failed.'

'What do you want to do about this yacht then?'

'I've no idea. I'd better ring the DPP's office and see if we can legally impound it.'

'I'd like to see the look on the property clerk's face when I tell him to make room for a yacht,' Jim said. Peter laughed at the thought but just the same he thought it would be advisable to check on procedures to safeguard the yacht.

The solicitor conducting the prosecution thought that the yacht could reasonably be assumed to have been bought with money made from drug trafficking and therefore it would be prudent to impound it. He left Peter to deal with the physical problems this would involve.

Peter could only think of one body who might be able to solve his problem. He contacted HM Customs & Excise and explained it to them. They agreed to impound the yacht and issued an order to the Harbour Master at Poole instructing him not to allow the vessel to sail. In the meantime they would arrange for it to be taken by the crew of a coastguard cutter to their own mooring where it would be kept under close supervision. Peter authorised the Customs to release any crew members that may be aboard the yacht.

Having identified and dealt with one of the issues that had emerged from his brainstorming session with Jim, Peter concentrated on the other worrying issue now looming. He believed that Challoner would realise that his jury would be given round the clock protection to ensure that no attempt was made to corrupt them. Logically then his only recourse would be to find out before the trial who his jury members would be and to the best of Peter's knowledge that was impossible.

A jury panel was selected randomly on the first day of a trial from a number of jury members who had been summoned. There didn't seem to be any way that anyone could know in advance which jury members were likely to be selected for a certain trial, particularly when several courts were sitting at the same time which they did at Liverpool and would most certainly do at the Old Bailey. He would need to check however just to make sure he wasn't harbouring any misconceptions.

Telephoning Liverpool Crown Court Department he asked them if it was ever possible to know who the members of a particular jury might be.

'Not until the actual day of the trial,' came the reply, 'we could only tell you that say sixty members of the public had been warned for jury service and that forty eight would actually be required. We wouldn't know which individual member would sit on each of the respective four juries until the actual day.'

'Well that's clear enough,' Peter thought. Even so he arranged to see the senior administration officer in charge of selecting the juries for the Old Bailey Courts. He wanted to make absolutely certain that their system matched that of Liverpool.

'Let me explain our system,' the court official said. 'Firstly we send out letters to members of the public warning them for jury service and telling them to report to the Old Bailey on a certain date. From this list of names a jury for a particular trial is randomly selected on the morning of the trial beginning.'

'In your experience do you think Challoner would be able to somehow obtain advance information on who the jury members might be?' Peter asked.

The court official leaned back in his chair and thought about the question Peter had just asked. After a moment or two he said, 'I don't honestly believe that it's possible for someone to gain that kind of information. You see it's the court ushers and not my department who are responsible for the final selection from the comprehensive lists that we provide them with.'

'Wouldn't it be possible for one of the ushers to arrange for three people to have their names called even though they were not on the list?'

'Yes it could be done, but it would be discovered as soon as a clerk of the court checked the names of the jury members against an identical list we provide him with.'

'Then how does the clerk know which people the usher has chosen from the list?'

'When the usher calls the name of a potential jury member, as long as that person is present he will tick against the name. He shows his list to the clerk who in turn ticks his own sheet. If the names didn't appear on the court list the clerk would immediately query it.'

Peter frowned, he knew that however foolproof a system appeared, if it was administered by human beings then it was open to abuse. He tried to analyse the present system and decided that if certain members in that system colluded then it should be possible to arrange for selected people to sit as jurors. Peter put it to the senior administration officer, 'Wouldn't it be possible for the clerk who compiled the list and one of the court ushers to get together and fix a jury of their own choosing?'

'Not in practice. The ushers aren't told until the morning of a trial which court they are to be responsible for.'

'I see,' said Peter, 'so for that theory to work the usher would have to know with certainty that he was to be responsible for the trial in a particular court.'

'Exactly,' said the administrator, 'and with twenty courts in use you can see for yourself what the odds against that would be.'

'So in your opinion it's simply not possible for anyone to have advance information on jury members?'

'It is possible to obtain advance information on potential jury members, but as I understand it your question is, would it then be possible to arrange for nominated people to sit as jury members at a specific trial. The answer to that is no.'

'Unless,' said Peter, ' several people were involved in the conspiracy.'

'Obviously if that were the case then yes, in theory it would be possible. The fact is for collusion to take place on that scale it would have to include myself and I assure you superintendent I am too near retirement and my pension to be that silly.'

Peter laughed, 'No I'm sure you're not.'

36

The prison coach was making slow progress through the traffic clogging the London streets. The continuous stopping and starting was irritating Jimmy who was one of fifteen people in the coach making its way to the Old Bailey Courts. In Jimmy's case it would be the first of many similar journeys he would make over the next five weeks which was the estimated length of time that his trial would take.

In an effort to take his mind off the journey Jimmy was concentrating on the throng of pedestrians all scurrying along the crowded pavements like so many white rabbits. They couldn't all be late for very important appointments thought Jimmy to himself.

Turning his attention back to the coach Jimmy studied his fellow passengers. Some were on their way to a first day in court while others were on the second and third week of their trials. It amused Jimmy to compare the eclectic code of dress chosen by his fellow inmates ranging from bovver boys in jeans and T-shirts to the smartly turned out ex city man who was on trial for fraudulent trading. Jimmy was relieved that he could attend the trial dressed in his own clothes. It would have been the last straw if prison uniform had been insisted on. Jimmy had selected his own outfit with care. He was dressed in a dark pin striped suit, hand made by his tailor in Liverpool and hoped that his immaculate appearance would give the intended impression which was that of a law abiding, successful businessman.

At ten twenty five precisely Jimmy was taken up the steps that led from the cell complex beneath the courts and into the dock of number two court. Jennifer was sitting just behind the dock on the front row of the back benches reserved for witnesses and family of the accused. Jimmy returned Jennifer's beam of recognition and mouthed, 'I love you,' before he was escorted to his seat.

Looking around the courtroom where he would spend most of his waking hours during the next five weeks he was surprised at the similarity between this court and the main Crown Courts in Liverpool. Having only appeared before the Liverpool Courts it had never occurred to Jimmy that courts in different areas would be virtually identical.

He acknowledged the nod of greeting from his solicitor, John Wakefield, who was sitting on the front benches of the court immediately behind his counsel David Arrowsmith. The Clerk of the Court called for silence and when the court fell silent His Honour Mr Justice Randles entered from behind the high bench where he would sit in order to preside over the court. Jimmy turned to grin at Jennifer and gave her a thumbs up sign.

The first business of the day was to swear in the twelve people who would in time decide on Jimmy's innocence or guilt. Arrowsmith had been annoyed at Jimmy's insistence that he was not to make any objections to any members of the jury.

'That's nonsense. The law allows us to make up to a total of three objections and it can be important to do that.'

'No,' Jimmy said, ' no challenges.'

Although Arrowsmith failed to understand his reasons he had reluctantly agreed to accept the first twelve people who were called.

Having been sworn in by the Clerk of the Court the eight men and four women sat down and looked around self consciously as the charges against Jimmy were read out.

His voice rang out firm and confident in reply. 'Not guilty my Lord.'

At this stage Jimmy was requested to sit and the prosecuting barrister stood and turned to the jury.

'Members of the jury, I am to prosecute this case on behalf of the Crown and my learned friend, Mr David Arrowsmith QC is to act for the defence. During the course of this trial it will be the prosecution's contention that you will hear evidence that will leave you in no doubt whatsoever of the guilt of the prisoner, Challoner, to all of the charges you have just heard put to him. You will hear how he set up a system of women couriers who were paid to carry the evil drug heroin into this country. Challoner sold this heroin to innocent young people in return for vast sums of money which all went towards amassing him a personal fortune worth millions of pounds. Challoner, who is a ruthless man, was the head of a syndicate which traded on the human weaknesses of those who do not have the will to resist the evils of the drugs he was trafficking in. Fortunately for the prosecution a former member of Challoner's syndicate is to appear and will be giving evidence against him. You will be told by his Lordship of the legal points you must take into account when listening to the evidence of Mr Walsh. Whilst you are listening I would ask you to remember the courage Mr Walsh has displayed in giving this evidence against his former employer. The courage, ladies and gentlemen of the jury and the will to eliminate from society the evil that men like Challoner inflict upon the often unsuspecting and more vulnerable members of the public.'

Jimmy was completely unmoved by this opening speech. He was far too experienced in the ways of advocacy to take offence at what was being said about him. He knew that whatever was said in this opening address would be quickly forgotten as the case unfurled. The time to worry about what was said was in the barrister's speeches at the end of the case. A good speech by either side at that stage of the proceedings usually made an impact and had a lasting impression on the jury members.

Having come to the end of his opening address the prosecuting barrister called for Michael Walsh.

At this Arrowsmith rose to his feet saying, 'My Lord, before the jury is allowed to hear the evidence of Mr Walsh, I wish to make an application on a point of law about how some of that evidence was obtained.'

'I had anticipated such an application Mr Arrowsmith,' the Judge said. Turning to the jury he continued, 'Members of the jury, learned counsel and myself must debate a point of law and whilst we do so you will be temporarily excused. I must now ask you to retire from the court and go to the jury room for a short while.'

Jimmy took the opportunity of this enforced break to turn around and smile at Jennifer. Her smile in return was perfunctory with none of her usual warmth. Jimmy hoped she hadn't been listening too closely to the opening address but he didn't worry too much. He had warned her to expect a tissue of lies throughout this trial.

Hearing his barrister begin to speak he turned his attention back to the court.

'My Lord, as you will no doubt have gathered my application concerned the manner in which the evidence regarding the taped conversation between the witness Walsh and my client was obtained. It was, My Lord, at the instigation of the police and with prepared questions that Mr Walsh, wearing a concealed tape recorder, was placed in a cell with my client. My client was completely unaware that his conversation with Walsh was being recorded and gave no thought to his answers to those questions so cunningly asked. Now I might reasonably suggest that this action amounted to 'agent provocateur' but I don't think at this stage I need to go to such lengths to satisfy your Lordship that this piece of evidence should not be admitted. My submission therefore is this My Lord. Since Mr Walsh was so obviously being used as an agent of the police, he would in my view have needed to conform to the rule of evidence in the same way that the police themselves would have been required to. If that is the case My Lord, my client should have been cautioned as to the outcome of his answers. He was not so cautioned and it is therefore my contention that the tape recorded evidence was obtained by subterfuge and as such should not be admitted as testimony in this case.'

David Arrowsmith sat down leaving Jimmy in awe of his eloquence and confident he had the right man for the job. He was only half listening to the prosecution barrister who then stood before the Judge arguing that the taped evidence had been obtained fairly and should therefore be admitted as evidence. His concentration lapsed completely when the barrister began quoting lengthy sections from a huge tome on the law.

Jimmy grew increasingly bored but he sat up with a start when he suddenly realised that the prosecuting barrister had finished speaking and was sitting down. Jimmy listened in rapt attention as the Judge began to speak.

'I have listened with interest to the submissions that have been made before me but without the benefit of previous specific case law to give me clear guidance, I have had to form my own opinion. I have therefore decided that in the interests of justice, this particular piece of evidence should not be given.'

David Arrowsmith rose to his feet and said, 'I am obliged My Lord.'

'Me too,' Jimmy whispered.

'First round to Jimmy,' Peter muttered.

He knew there was absolutely nothing he could do though, it was pointless to brood. His faith was at least partially restored by the able way in which Mr Seymour-Jones had presented his arguments on behalf of the prosecution. He had been David Arrowsmith's equal on every count and would, Peter believed, prove equally convincing to the jury. Peter had been non-committal when his Detective Inspector had expressed surprise that the defence had not exercised their legal right to replace up to three of the jury members. In similar trials the defence usually objected to anyone who appeared to be middle aged and middle class in the belief that they would be more likely to be prejudiced against drug offenders than a younger person. It didn't always work in their favour, but was a calculated risk that the defence often preferred to take. The fact that the first twelve jurors had been allowed to sit unchallenged was unusual.

At the request of the prosecution Mr Justice Randles had previously heard their application in his chambers for the members of the jury to be given police protection for the duration of the trial. He had granted the application and would later advise the members of the jury accordingly.

'Let's hope that the protection will be sufficient to stop Challoner from attempting to get at them,' Jim said to Peter as they watched the jury file back into court.

'Call Michael Walsh,' Peter heard the court clerk call out.

'Here goes, let's hope his nerve holds out,' Jim said.

Peter had seen Mick before court began and his morale appeared to be high. In fact Peter suspected Mick was looking forward to the task ahead and felt honour bound to caution Mick to take nothing for granted especially now that the tape was excluded from the evidence.

'Mr Walsh, are you a convicted person,' Mr Seymour-Jones addressed Mick Walsh after he had taken the oath.

'Yes.'

'Are you presently serving a five year term of imprisonment?'

'Yes.'

'And was that prison sentence given as a result of your participation in drugs trafficking?'

'Yes.'

'Could you, Mr Walsh, tell the court how you came to be involved in that offence?'

'You mean from when I first met Jimmy Challoner?'

'Yes, that would be a good starting place.'

Mick Walsh then spent the following hour and a half giving a convincing account of his association with Challoner and his part in the heroin trafficking. At its conclusion Mr Justice Randles adjourned the hearing for lunch.

As he left court Peter went over and spoke to Seymour-Jones.

'I was a bit disappointed by the Judge's decision not to allow the taped evidence,' he said.

'Yes, I had rather hoped the decision would have gone our way.'

'How does it affect our case?'

'A minor setback that's all, we may have lost a battle, but we're still out to win the war.'

At two o'clock the trial recommenced with Mick Walsh again standing in the witness box. Seymour-Jones rose to his feet saying, 'Mr Walsh, before you are cross examined by Mr Arrowsmith there are a couple of points I'd like to clarify.'

'Were you at any time offered any inducement by the police to give evidence against James Arthur Challoner?'

'No.'

'Isn't it true to say that when sentencing you to your term of five years imprisonment the court took into consideration the fact that you were to give evidence against Challoner?'

'Yes they did, I expected to get at least ten years.'

'Then was that the reason that prompted you to give evidence against Mr Challoner?'

'No, when I told the police about Jimmy I didn't know it would make a difference to my sentence. I just felt it was time the truth came out about Jimmy.'

'Thank you Mr Walsh. Please stay where you are,' Mr Seymour-Jones said as he took his seat.

Jimmy looked across from the dock to the witness box where Mick was standing and tried to fathom what had turned Mick against him. Hadn't he always treated him well, given him status within the organisation, paid him over the odds? Jimmy was mystified.

It irked Jimmy that his present predicament was largely of his own making. Twice in his life he had shown uncharacteristic benevolence, once in sparing Walsh's life and again in not killing Peter Turner. It certainly wouldn't happen again Jimmy vowed. Wheels were already in motion regarding Walsh and once he was released he would remove the thorn from his side which was Peter Turner. Permanently.

Having listened to Walsh giving evidence Jimmy had to grudgingly acknowledge that he had sounded both convincing and sincere. However, that was the easy part thought Jimmy, 'Let's see how you come out of this,' he said to himself as Arrowsmith took the floor.

'Mr Walsh, you have just told the court that your motives for giving evidence against Mr Challoner were entirely without thought for any benefit to yourself?'

'I just wanted to see justice done.'

'That suggests to me Mr Walsh that you believe an injustice had been done. Is this true?'

'It would have been if Challoner was allowed to get away with his part in all this.'

'I'm interested in what you think to be an injustice. Do you mean that an injustice has been committed against yourself?'

'It would have been if I had taken the blame by myself.'

'But as I understand it Mr Walsh, you were to blame.'

'Well yes, I was.'

'Exactly. You were to blame and to minimise the sentence that you so clearly deserved you agreed to give evidence against Mr Challoner.'

'No, that's untrue.'

'If is isn't true Mr Walsh, what are you doing here in this court.'

'It's true that I agreed to give evidence against Jimmy but not for the reason you just said.'

'Really, is that so. Then tell me Mr Walsh was it your own idea to give evidence against Mr Challoner?'

'Not exactly.'

'No? Then who was it who suggested that you should try to involve Mr Challoner?'

'It was Superintendent Turner.'

'Superintendent Turner asked you to involve Mr Challoner?' Arrowsmith gasped, turning to face the jury to maximise the effect of the shocked expression on his face.

'He didn't actually ask me to involve Jimmy.'

'Then just what did he ask you to do?'

'He told me that Jimmy was putting all the blame on me and I should think about making a statement saying what his involvement was.'

'How long had you been in custody before you were asked to make this statement?'

'A few days.'

'And had you considered making a statement prior to this conversation with Superintendent Turner?'

'No, I'm not usually a grass.'

'That's very interesting Mr Walsh. So it was at the suggestion of the police that you made the statement in which you involved Mr Challoner?'

'Yes.'

'Let us leave the statement for a moment. I want to first clarify why you decided to give evidence against Mr Challoner. Am I right in thinking that it was because the police suggested that you should?'

'In a way.'

'Then let me put it to you another way. If the police hadn't suggested that you involve Mr Challoner would you have done so?'

Mick looked uncomfortable as he answered, 'I don't suppose so.'

'Then Mr Walsh, you only said that Mr Challoner was involved because the police suggested that you should.'

'Yes, but he......'

'That's all on that point thank you Mr Walsh,' Arrowsmith said, cutting Mick off mid-sentence. 'Now, let us turn back to the statement that you made to the police, why did you make this statement?'

'Superintendent Turner said I would need to put what I had said in writing.'

'So it was the police again who told you what to do.'

'Told me what to do but not what to say.'

'Are the contents of the statement correct?'

'Yes.'

'Mr Walsh, you will recall that at Mr Challoner's committal hearing I asked you if what you had said in your statement about Mr Challoner recruiting women couriers was true or not?'

'Yes.'

'And what was your reply?'

'I said it wasn't exactly true.'

'Perhaps you will now explain to the members of the jury just what it was that you meant to say?'

'I put in my statement that Jimmy had recruited the women but really it was me.'

'So you were trying hard to involve Mr Challoner in something that he was innocent of?'

'I meant to say that Jimmy had organised for the women to be recruited, not that he actually did it.'

'If Mr Challoner had organised the recruitment of the women, how did he do it Mr Walsh?'

'Through someone I knew.'

'Through someone you knew, not somebody that Mr Challoner knew then?'
'That's right.'
'Would you describe the recruitment of the women couriers to be important to the importation of the heroin?'
'Vital, without them the drugs would have had to be smuggled in a different way.'
'So I suppose it would be vital to whoever was in charge of the importation of heroin to know that the women were suitable?'
'Yes.'
'Mr Walsh, did Mr Challoner meet any of the women couriers?'
'No.'
'Did you meet them Mr Walsh?'
'Yes I did.'
'Thank you Mr Walsh.'
'Mr Arrowsmith'
'Yes My Lord,' replied Arrowsmith.
'If that is a convenient place in your cross examination to stop I would like to adjourn the case for today.'
'It is most convenient My Lord.'
'I'm obliged,' said Mr Justice Randles.
'Now members of the jury, before I adjourn the court I must tell you that in this case I have granted an application by the prosecution for each one of you to receive personal police protection for the duration of the trial. This will mean some slight inconvenience to you. It is the fear of the prosecution that you could be approached in order to attempt to corrupt you into giving a decision that would not be compatible with the evidence. To guard against this a police officer will be assigned to you twenty four hours a day. It is perhaps not as bad as maybe it sounds. They do not expect to be taken into your homes, unless of course you wish it. It is usual for them to keep a vigil outside your home. They will be obliged to accompany you wherever you go so it would be helpful if social activities could be kept to a minimum for the duration of the trial.

Telephone calls will be intercepted and checks made before a call is passed through to you. I realise that this might seem to be a restriction on your civil liberties, but I do assure you that it is very necessary. Finally I would like to thank you in advance for the public spirited way in which I feel sure you will all respond.'

Jimmy paid little attention to the Judge's address to the jury. He knew that it was both a waste of time and rate payers money, but there was nothing he could do about that. He analysed Mick's cross examination and was pleased that it had gone so well. Arrowsmith had been superb in the way he had steered Walsh into saying exactly what he wanted him to say before cutting him off. The jury must now be wondering exactly what his real motives were for giving this evidence. On the whole Jimmy was satisfied with this first day of his trial. He looked across to Jennifer's seat and was shocked to discover it empty. In spite of the heat in the room Jimmy shivered.

37

Peter Turner arrived at the Old Bailey early the following morning. He was staying with his squad in a Metropolitan Police Hostel, a somewhat spartan establishment. To escape his surroundings he had risen early and walked the three miles to the court. He had considered a morale boosting visit to Mick Walsh but common sense prevailed and he thought better of it. Prosecution witnesses were not supposed to communicate with each other until after each had given their evidence and it would undoubtedly have been misinterpreted had the visit been observed. The last thing Peter wanted to do was to give the defence any ammunition to use against the prosecution. 'Indeed Arrowsmith didn't seem to need any. He was managing very nicely on his own,' Peter thought to himself. As a professional himself Peter had to admire the way in which David Arrowsmith was conducting the cross examination. He was skilfully drawing out from Walsh the tit bits most useful to the defence, just drawing the line between fact and fiction in such a way that an impartial observer would think that he and Walsh had plotted against Challoner. It was unfortunate that recently there had been extensive coverage in the media on cases where a small percentage of police officers had been found guilty of fabricating evidence. 'I only hope the jury in this case are bright enough to see what's really going on,' Peter thought as he walked up to the court.

As he entered the Old Bailey he was informed by the police officer on duty that Mrs Challoner had asked to see him.

'Where is she?'

'She's sitting in the hall outside number two court sir,' the constable replied. Peter made his way upstairs and because of the hour, which meant the building was almost deserted, he saw Jennifer immediately.

'Mrs Challoner?, you asked to see me?'

'If I can Superintendent.'

'Of course, how about a coffee?'

'That would be lovely, thank you.'

Peter led the way to the cafeteria and brought two coffees to the table where Jennifer was seated.

'How can I help?' Peter said gently, sensing that this was a woman in shock.

'I believe you have known Jimmy since you were boys.'

'That's right. Closer than brothers at one time.'

'What went wrong?'

'Who knows? Different interests, different outlook?' Peter shrugged his shoulders and smiled.

'Superintendent, may I be frank with you?'

' Feel free so long as I can be frank too.'

'Thank you. I adore Jimmy and I can't believe he's even remotely connected with the charges brought against him.'

'But,' Peter said as she faltered.

'I have some questions I would dearly like answers to.'

'I'll answer any I can but I'm not allowed to discuss the case itself I'm afraid.'

'No, I realise that. My question is, why have you persecuted Jimmy over all these years?'

Peter returned her gaze and said quietly, 'Is that what Jimmy told you?' Jennifer nodded in reply.

'Then you must decide for yourself the truth of that. All I will say to you is that I have never fabricated evidence against anyone in my life.'

'Jimmy says that you and Mick Walsh have joined forces against him,'

'How well do you know Walsh?' Peter asked.

'Reasonably well.'

'Now do you honestly believe that he would join forces with the likes of me to get at Jimmy?'

'I don't know. I just don't know.'

'Then allow me to offer some advice. Listen to the evidence, all of it and then decide for yourself.'

'If you and Walsh are plotting against Jimmy the evidence will be a pack of lies anyway.'

'True,' said Peter, 'but I have enough confidence in the evidence to believe that once you have heard it you'll be left in no doubt where the truth lies.'

Jennifer nodded again struggling to retain her composure as tears threatened to fall.

Peter took her outstretched hand saying, 'Look I'm really sorry I can't tell you what you want to hear. Can I escort you back to the court Mrs Challoner?'

'Thank you anyway but no. Thank you for sparing the time to talk to me Superintendent, I appreciate it.'

'Then I'll say goodbye,' Peter said gently hoping that the coming day in court wouldn't be too hard on Jennifer Challoner whose only mistake was to fall for such a con man.

'Goodbye and thank you again.'

Jimmy was already at his place in the dock when he saw Jennifer enter the court and take her seat just behind him. He waved and smiled in her direction expecting her to do likewise. The jerky little wave of acknowledgment and the quick mechanical smile that flitted across her face made him wonder if the travelling every day was becoming too much for her. Jimmy decided he would ask John Wakefield to have a word with her in one of the intervals.

Just then the Judge entered the room and as the assembled throng rose Jimmy looked towards the jury and catching the eye of one or two of its members he bowed his head slightly in a gesture of confidence. He hoped that these small gestures, together with his undoubted sartorial elegance would help to create the impression that he was quite simply a businessman and nothing more.

As Jimmy had expected, Mick Walsh didn't look as confident as yesterday going into the witness box.

'Mr Walsh,' began Arrowsmith, 'how long have you been in the service of Mr Challoner?'

'Over twenty years.'

'Can you describe to the court the position you held in Mr Challoner's organisation?'

'I suppose you could say I was the general manager.'

'General manager of what?'

'The club business.'

'Would you describe your position as one with some degree of responsibility?'

'Yes I look upon myself as Jimmy's number one.'

'So I take it from your reply that Mr Challoner trusted you to run that section of his business which he had delegated to you.'

'Well just the day to day running of it.'

'Does that imply Mr Walsh,' the QC said, 'that Mr Challoner was involved in the decision making process?'

'Oh very much so, Jimmy kept his finger on the pulse of all his operations.'

'That's very interesting,' Arrowsmith said pausing to look at the jury, 'does that mean then that Mr Challoner knew at all times what was going on within his business?'

'He certainly did. Nothing happened that Jimmy didn't have personal knowledge of.'

'Really Mr Walsh. How fascinating. May I presume then that if something was occurring within Mr Challoner's business that he had no knowledge of then it had nothing to do with him or his business.'

'That's perfectly true.'

'Tell me Mr Walsh, did Mr Challoner have any part in the purchase of Manitol Powder which you told the court about earlier?'

'No, but ….'

'Thank you Mr Walsh,' Arrowsmith interrupted him, 'a simple no will suffice. Was Mr Challoner involved in the mixing of the heroin with this Manitol Powder?'

'No, he had nothing to do with that.'

'Was Mr Challoner concerned in the sale or distribution of the heroin?'

'No he wasn't, but ….'

'Thank you Mr Walsh, you have answered the question.'

'Now, I think I should recap for the benefit of the jury. You have told the court that Mr Challoner had nothing to do with the recruitment and the control of the women couriers. You have said that Mr Challoner wasn't involved in the purchase of the Manitol Powder or with its inclusion with the heroin. You have stated that Mr Challoner was not involved with the sale or distribution of the heroin. Is that a correct summary of what you have told this court?'

'Yes, but ….'

'Yes will suffice Mr Walsh,' Arrowsmith interrupted skilfully. 'Now Mr Walsh, it does seem to me, as indeed I feel sure it will to the jury, the Mr Challoner you describe as the successful businessman and the man with his finger on the pulse has been singularly lacking in his knowledge and control of this heroin venture.'

'That's because he wanted to keep his name out of it.'

'Thereby allowing you to take full responsibility for the heroin business?'

'Yes, that's the way Jimmy wanted it.'

'Mr Walsh, will you tell the court what your average earnings were when you were in the employ of Mr Challoner.'

'About thirty thousand a year.'

'You seem to have been very well paid Mr Walsh.'

'Yes Jimmy paid well.'

'How long have you been earning that kind of money?'

'I've always earned that sort of money,' Mick said.

'How long has the heroin business been running?'

'Two to three years.'

'And in that time Mr Walsh, have you received a substantial wage increase?'

'No, just the usual annual increments.'

'But didn't you just say that Mr Challoner always rewards his employees when they took on more responsibility?'

'I was supposed to have been paid extra for the heroin business but it never materialised.'

'Precisely Mr Walsh. It never materialised because Mr Challoner didn't employ you to traffic in heroin.'

'He never paid me specifically.'

'He never paid you at all Mr Walsh because he didn't know anything about the heroin business.'

'He did, he knew alright.'

'Mr Challoner is innocent and you know it.'

'No, he's guilty as hell.'

'I put it to you Mr Walsh that you deliberately and maliciously set out to involve Mr Challoner in order to try and lessen the part you played in this evil trade.'

'No, that's not true, Jimmy was the mastermind not me.'

'One final question Mr Walsh. Do you yourself take drugs?'

There was a long pause before Mick Walsh answered and only after he was prompted by Mr Justice Randles.

'Yes,' Walsh's voice was no more than a whisper.

With that Arrowsmith went to his seat leaving Walsh standing bewildered in the witness box.

Peter was sitting outside number two court along with the other prosecution witnesses still waiting to give their evidence.

It was a rule of the English legal system that witnesses who were to give evidence at a trial were not allowed to be present in court before they had actually given that evidence. This was to provide a fair a case as possible for the accused. As a result Peter didn't know what David Arrowsmith was putting Mick through, although he wouldn't have to wait too long. He had placed one of his officers, who wasn't giving evidence, in the public gallery and he kept Peter up to date with events as they unfolded in the courtroom.

Peter was jolted out of his boredom induced reverie as the court doors opened to reveal Mick Walsh being escorted out. Peter saw how bewildered Mick looked and although he knew he shouldn't, he went over to Mick.

'Is that it Mick? Over?.'

'It's been adjourned until after lunch, I've got to be re-examined or something.'

'Oh that's nothing. Just our own barrister who will ask you questions to clear up some of the points that were raised during cross examination.'

'Well there were plenty of those, Jimmy's barrister was bloody quick.'

'That's what Jimmy's paying for,' Peter said, 'plenty of less able barristers would have set out to attack your character, but Arrowsmith knew that it wouldn't help his case.'

'He just led me into trap after trap getting me to say what he wanted to hear. The trouble was he would shut me up before I could explain what I really meant.'

'Don't worry about it. The case has got a long way to go yet.'

'The way it's going I wouldn't be surprised if the bugger beat the rap like he did with all the others.'

'Mick, thanks for giving evidence, it will really help.'

'Look, it had nothing to do with you, this is personal.'

'All the same …thanks.'

'We're quits OK? I appreciate the fact that I've been kept alive.'

Peter nodded, 'Quits sounds OK to me.'

The remainder of the afternoon was taken up by Seymour-Jones. During his re-examination he allowed Mick to develop his answers so skilfully curtailed by the defence barrister. Towards the end of the afternoon he asked had Mick ever been to Italy to which Mick replied 'No.'

'It does seem strange that someone who allegedly masterminded this heroin importation has never once visited the country the drug was collected from. Tell me Mr Walsh, to you knowledge has Mr Challoner ever been to Italy?'

'Yes'

'Mr Walsh, do you know anyone who comes from Italy?'

'Not really. I've met some Italians but I wouldn't say I know them.'

'Who are they?'

'A Mr and Mrs Silvana, friends of Jimmy.'

'Where did you meet these people?'

'The River Club. They were staying with Jimmy and he brought them down one night.'

'I see. And it was Mr Silvana who provided Mr Challoner with the heroin ....'

At this David Arrowsmith leapt to his feet scattering his case papers, 'Objection My Lord,' he cried totally ignoring his papers covering the floor of the court. As his clerk attempted to retrieve them he went on, 'My learned friend knows only too well that he cannot introduce new evidence during re-examination. No mention hitherto has been made of Mr Silvana.'

Before his lordship could pronounce his own ruling, Mr Seymour-Jones stood up. 'My apologies My Lord. I completely withdraw my last remark.'

Mr Justice Randles then instructed the jury that they must completely ignore the reference to Mr Silvana. Everyone present in the courtroom knew that it was an impossibility.

Peter said a brief goodbye to Mick, he had completed his evidence and was returning to Bedford Prison where he would serve out his sentence.

As he was on the point of leaving Peter saw John Wakefield coming out of the court room with Jennifer Challoner. He heard Wakefield say to her, 'Jennifer, please don't pre-judge the issue, it's early days yet. Jimmy is completely innocent, please believe that.'

'Is he John?' Peter heard her say. 'I'm not convinced any more. Give Jimmy my message will you please?'

'Won't you reconsider, this will be such a blow to Jimmy.'

'Just give him my message.' Jennifer said quietly before walking away.

'Mrs Challoner,' Peter said as she hurried past him but with head bowed she ignored him and continued walking.

Peter looked back at John Wakefield who simply shrugged his shoulders.

Jimmy Challoner sat in one of the cells beneath the courts, furious at the prosecution's remark about Antonio Silvana. Until that point he believed the day had gone favourably for him. Thinking that he wouldn't see anyone until the prison bus left at six o'clock Jimmy was surprised when at four thirty the police officer on duty told him he had a visitor. For a split second Jimmy thought it might be Jennifer and his face fell when John Wakefield was ushered in.

'It's your solicitor,' the officer announced, 'you'll have to see him in your cell, we haven't the staff to take you to an interview room.'

'That's alright by me.'

'I'll have to lock the door you understand.'

'Just ring the bell when you're ready to leave,' the officer said as he banged the heavy metal door shut.

'You're not going to like this,' Wakefield began.

'It's Jennifer isn't it. I knew by her face something was wrong. She isn't ill is she?'

'No, she isn't ill.'

'Then what's wrong John?'

'She's not coming to court anymore.'

'Well I can understand that,' said Jimmy sounding relieved.

'There's more to it than that, she doesn't want to see you for a while.'

'Doesn't want to see me? What the bloody hell are you on about?'

'She says she needs time to think.'

'I can't believe it. How the hell does she think I feel eh? The last thing I need right now is a bloody domestic.'

'Is there anything you want me to do?'

'No, just leave it for now. She'll come round especially when I'm found not guilty. It's Walsh's evidence that's to blame, she's let it cloud her judgement.'

'You could be right but Jennifer is no fool Jimmy.'

'No John, it's Walsh alright, good job I've fixed for him to be taken care of.'

'Well if there's nothing you want me to do I'll go. I have to meet David Arrowsmith.'

'No there's nothing you can do about Jennifer. What did Arrowsmith make of the reference to Silvana?'

'That's what I'm seeing him about. Now it's been raised by the prosecution we'll need to dispel it from the jury's minds that it was

Silvana who was supplying you with the heroin.'

'Why don't we just say that Silvana and I were business colleagues?'

'Arrowsmith will know what to do, let's leave it with him.'

'Suits me, he's doing OK so far.'

'Excellent,' said Wakefield as he pressed the bell to summon the police officer to let him out of the cell.

38

The trial had now entered its fourth week and had so far been taken up with the witnesses for the prosecution which included the police evidence of the surveillance and arrest of Challoner. Peter, the last of the prosecution's witnesses delivered his evidence in a professional and practised manner. The case had been temporarily adjourned for lunch when Peter received a message to contact the Governor at Bedford Prison. He had to wait until the court adjourned for the day and as he was waiting to be recalled for cross examination he wondered what it was that the Governor could want to talk to him about.

David Arrowsmith rose briskly to his feet as soon as Peter took his place in the witness box.

'Superintendent, how long have you known Mr Challoner?'
'All my life, we lived in the same street as boys.'
'And were you friends?'
'The best of friends.'
'Are you still friends?'
'Hardly.'
'Then when did the friendship break down?'
'I suppose it was in our late teens.'
'Was there a reason for that break down in your relationship with Mr Challoner?'
'We just went our different ways.'
'Was it not because you became jealous of Mr Challoner's success?'
'Not at all. I have never been jealous of Challoner.'
'Then why Superintendent have you used your position as a police officer to repeatedly harass Mr Challoner?'
'That is untrue.'
'Really, you surprise me Superintendent. Maybe you could tell me whether you have ever brought a prosecution against Mr Challoner?'
'Seymour-Jones sprang to his feet saying, 'I must object My Lord to

this line of questioning, it has no relevance to the case in question.'

'On the contrary My Lord,' said Arrowsmith, 'it has every relevance as I intend to prove.'

'Very well Mr Arrowsmith, continue,' said Mr Justice Randles.

'Thank you My Lord. Now Superintendent perhaps you will answer my question?'

'The answer is yes.'

'Was my client ever convicted?'

'No.'

'On what grounds was Mr Challoner acquitted?'

'Through lack of evidence.'

'How many such cases have you brought against my client?'

'Three.'

'And in each case was the result the same?' Arrowsmith raised his eyebrows theatrically.

'It was.'

'And were each of these prosecutions instigated by yourself?'

'Yes, they were.'

'And you still maintain Superintendent that you haven't harassed Mr Challoner?'

'Yes I do. I have simply done my job and attempted to uphold the law.'

'I wonder whether the members of the jury will see it like that. I put it to you Superintendent that you are motivated by jealousy and have waged a personal vendetta against my client using your office as a weapon.'

'That is untrue. I have only ever done my duty.'

'Your duty to yourself.'

'No, my duty to the community at large.'

'If that were so don't you find it odd that in every case you brought against my client each was dismissed through lack of evidence. You are not that bad a police officer are you?'

The court was hushed as everyone waited for Peter's reply. He knew that whichever way he answered Arrowsmith use it to his own advantage. Since he was on oath Peter answered truthfully, 'No.' He realised that in answering in this way it was like admitting he had brought the prosecutions of Challoner purely from malice.

'Yes,' said Arrowsmith, 'that is precisely what I expected you to say and as I see it the members of the jury can draw only one conclusion from your answer.'

Peter was relieved when the Judge chose that moment to adjourn the case for the day. Remembering that he had to telephone the Governor at Bedford Prison, Peter went to the police room where there were private telephones.

Having made the call Peter replaced the handset and sat staring into space for several minutes. Pulling himself together he went in search of his Detective Inspector.

'I don't believe it,' Jim Atkinson said after hearing Peter's news. He had known from Peter's face as he approached that something was wrong, but he wasn't prepared for what Peter had to say.

'I'm afraid it's true.'

'It can't be. Why on earth would Mick Walsh hang himself.'

'Come on Jim, he didn't. Mick was murdered.'

'How can you say that? What would be the motive now he's given his evidence.'

'The motive hasn't changed and if I'd been thinking straight Walsh would still be alive.'

'I don't get it, you'll have to explain.'

'It's all part of Challoner's long term strategy. He's still blocking up the exits. If he doesn't get off he'll be aiming for the next best thing.'

'A split jury?'

'Exactly.'

'But that would mean he'd rigged the jury and we know he hasn't approached them, we've kept an eye on them throughout.'

'Even so I'm convinced Challoner will be expecting a retrial at the very worst and with Walsh dead he knows it wouldn't even get to first base.'

'That makes sense if he'd rigged the jury, but not otherwise.'

'You'd better believe it, not that it makes me feel any better to say it, because I should have foreseen this and prevented it.'

'No you couldn't, besides the prison authorities wouldn't have accepted that Walsh might be required for a retrial. They wouldn't and couldn't have kept up the special protection, they just don't have the resources.

'I'll never forgive myself for not trying. Now all I can do is make sure Walsh's death isn't recorded as just another cell death statistic. This was murder and the prison had better investigate it as such.'

The following morning Peter knew he had to put his frustration at Walsh's death aside and concentrate on the job in hand, namely his cross examination.

'Superintendent, we have heard that during the police surveillance of Mr Challoner he was observed making a trip to Italy. Is that correct?'

'It is.'

'My learned friend seemed to be suggesting to the court that this visit was of a sinister nature. Was it?'

'Well we know he went to meet Mr Silvana.'

'Was there anything sinister in that?'

'Not that we can prove.'

'And we know do we not that if you had any evidence that the meeting was anything other than two friends meeting socially, then it would have been produced before this court?'

'Yes.'

'We can also expect Superintendent, from the very detailed and professional manner in which your squad carried out their enquiries into this case, that you made similar enquiries into the background of Mr Silvana?'

'Yes, we did.'

'Perhaps then you will share with the court exactly what your enquiries concerning Mr Silvana revealed.'

'Mr Silvana appears to be a successful businessman. His main business interests seem to be licensed clubs and gambling casinos.'

'It would appear then that Mr Silvana and Mr Challoner have much in common as a result of their business interests.'

'Yes,' said Peter wishing he could have added, 'plus the common interest in heroin dealing,' but his evidence had to be strictly factual.

'Then it seems perfectly natural to me that Mr Challoner and Mr Silvana would meet in order to pursue their common business interests as businessmen do all over the world. Would you not agree Superintendent?'

'Yes.'

'And what could be more pleasant than in Italy. Now please tell me Superintendent, from your enquiries into Mr Silvana's background, did you find him to be a man of unblemished character?'

'He doesn't have a criminal record if that's what you mean.'

'That is exactly what I mean,' Arrowsmith said. 'Would you now please tell the court if you have any evidence to prove that Mr Challoner and Mr Silvana were dealing in drugs?'

'No I have no evidence that Mr Challoner and Mr Silvana were trafficking in drugs.'

'Hardly surprising one must conclude. Thank you Superintendent, that is all.'

Peter paused for a moment to see if Mr Seymour-Jones wished to re-examine him but he didn't. He had to admire the masterly way in which Arrowsmith had evaded the inference that Silvana was the man responsible for supplying Challoner with heroin. His final question had been carefully and expertly phrased. By asking Peter directly if he had proof that Silvana and Challoner were engaged in drug trafficking he knew that Peter had to answer directly and so miss the opportunity to suggest that they were. He also knew that had he had the benefit of the tape as evidence it would have proved that Silvana was the supplier.

Peter left the witness box and took his seat on a side bench. Glancing over at Challoner, Peter was galled to see Jimmy smugly grinning at him, his gloating countenance leaving Peter in no doubt as to which way he thought the questioning had gone.

39

Jimmy knew that with the end of Turner's evidence came the conclusion of the prosecution case. This meant that it was now the turn of the defence to begin. During Peter's cross examination Jimmy's concentration had been patchy due to his mind not unnaturally being given over to Jennifer's desertion. He convinced himself that being acquitted was the only way in which Jennifer would accept his innocence and he approached the witness box in a determined frame of mind. This was war.

'Please be sworn in Mr Challoner,' Arrowsmith said. Jimmy took the testament that was handed to him by the clerk of the court and held it aloft in his right hand as he read the oath in a loud firm voice.

'Please state your full name,' Arrowsmith said.

'James Arthur Challoner.'

'Mr Challoner, why do you suppose you are in this court room today?'

'To clear my good name.'

'We are now aware that this is not the first time you have been required to undergo such an ordeal in order to clear that good name.'

'No, Superintendent Turner has brought other false allegations against me in the past.'

'Which were all proved to be completely without foundation.'

'Yes.'

Do you know of any reason why Superintendent Turner should believe you to be a criminal?'

'None whatsoever. We were both brought up to respect the law and I have always been faithful to my upbringing.'

'In that case why else do you think Superintendent Turner would wish to try and discredit you?'

'I really have no idea. I'm at a complete loss trying to understand his motives.'

'I would suggest his motives are prompted by jealousy.'

'I find it hard to believe that Peter, sorry Superintendent Turner would persecute me purely out of jealousy.'

'Whether you like to believe it or not, I think you must now accept that it seems to be the only logical answer.'

'Yes, I'm afraid you may be right.'

'Have you ever considered reporting the Superintendent's conduct to his superiors?'

'Oh no, I wouldn't do a thing like that. He could have been in trouble if I had.'

'And for that reason you have never been able to make a complaint about him?'

'No, I still remember how close we were.'

'And what about your relationship with Mr Walsh. Were you surprised when you learned that he was to give evidence against you?'

'I was devastated,' Jimmy said, 'especially since Mick was for some reason telling a pack of lies.'

'Do you know of any reason why he should do that?'

'Only that he must have been put up to it, there can't be any other reason. Mick was like a brother to me.'

'You still maintain that Mr Walsh gave untruthful evidence to the court?'

'It was anything but the truth. I have never been involved in any way in drug dealing.'

'Do you bear Mr Walsh any animosity for what he tried to do to you?'

'Lord no, I could never hold a grudge against Mick.'

'Are you aware Mr Walsh has been found hanged in his cell?'

Although Jimmy knew this full well after being informed by prison grapevine he feigned surprise at the news.

'No, not Mick. He was like a brother to me.'

He started to sway in the witness box and for effect he grasped the sides of the structure as though to steady himself.

'Mr Challoner, are you alright?' Mr Justice Randles asked.

'It's the shock your honour, I can't take it in. Mick of all people.'

'Would you care to sit for a moment?'

'No, no I'll be fine, but perhaps a drink of water?'

'Certainly,' the Judge replied. As a glass of water was ceremoniously delivered to the witness box Jimmy dramatically took out his handkerchief and with studied deliberation wiped his eyes and noisily blew his nose.

'Do you feel able to continue?' Mr Justice Randles asked.

'Yes I think so.'

'I'm sorry to have to be the bearer of such distressing news to you,' said Arrowsmith. 'Have you any idea why Mr Walsh would do such a tragic thing?'

'I can only guess. Knowing Mick as I do, I imagine he couldn't live with the shame of knowing what he had attempted to do to me.'

Jimmy dabbed at his eyes as the jury looked on with a mixture of shock and dismay on their faces. Arrowsmith had been right when he had said that the news of Walsh's suicide in such a dramatic way would gain the jury's sympathy. Spurred on by the success of his initial efforts Jimmy turned to face Peter and shouting in a voice choked with emotion, pointed and said,' 'By making Mick tell such lies against me you've as good as murdered him. I hope you're satisfied now.'

The deathly hush in the court room was broken by Arrowsmith asking Jimmy if he felt able to continue.

'I would like to ask you about your meeting with Mr Silvana?' said Arrowsmith.

'I'll carry on,' Jimmy gave a brave smile.

'We first met the Silvanas by chance on a holiday. Now our family friendship has become very close, our daughters even go to school together in Switzerland.'

'Have you had any business dealings with Mr Silvana?'

'Yes that's why I went to Italy. Antonio, that's Mr Silvana and I were considering going into partnership to develop property in Greece.'

'And do you still intend to go into partnership with Mr Silvana?'

'Indeed I do.'

'So your reason for going to Italy was to discuss the prospect of property development in Greece?'

'Yes, I'd never visited Italy before so it seemed to be the ideal opportunity to combine business with pleasure.'

'Tell me Mr Challoner, what is the nature of your business?'

'I own several licensed clubs and restaurants, plus I have a large property development company.'

'Can you tell me the approximate annual turnover of all your business interests?'

'Approximately twenty million pounds.'

'And are you the sole owner of these businesses?'

'Yes.'

'It is evident Mr Challoner that you are a very wealthy man.'
'I suppose I am.'
'Mr Challoner, why do you suppose people traffic in drugs?'
'I presume for the money.'
'Exactly, yet from what you have told the court money is not an incentive for you these days.'
'No, not for a long time in fact.'
'Thank you Mr Challoner, that is all.'

At this point Mr Justice Randles turned to the jury and said, 'This appears to be a suitable juncture in the proceedings to adjourn for the day. We will recommence in the morning.'

'Can you believe that,' Peter said. Having Mick murdered and then using his death to gain the jury's sympathy. I'd like to bloody ring his neck.'

'Steady on,' said Jim. 'Don't let it get to you.'

'I can't help it Jim, I knew Jimmy would try anything to avoid prison, but that charade in court takes the biscuit.'

'The problem is that charade worked on the jury. I was watching them and if you ask me they swallowed it hook, line and sinker.'

'Me too and I reckon you're right. We've bloody lost this case now.'

'It does look that way, but we've still got Seymour-Jones to pull something out of the hat when he cross examines.'

'No chance. Challoner's a born actor, if he carries on like he did today we're sunk.'

'All our hard graft for nothing.'

'Be honest, we need a miracle to save us now.'

'That's alright then, I've always believed in miracles.'

'Well get on your knees right now and pray like hell Jim.'

Jimmy's mood of jubilation disappeared fast when he was handed a letter on his return to prison. He recognised Jennifer's handwriting and as soon as he was alone he ripped the envelope open. Immediately his heart sank as he read the contents.

'Jimmy, I realise that you don't want to hear this, but I feel honour bound to be honest with you. I don't want to believe that you have been involved in drug trafficking, but there are too many question marks over your past actions. I can't continue to have blind faith in you however much I love you. I believe the only thing we can do is go our separate ways and I will be seeing Debbie and telling her the same thing in the next few days. I cannot shield her from the truth much as it will hurt her. I wish you well, Jennifer.'

Jimmy read and reread the letter several times hoping against hope he had misinterpreted the message. Finally he had to admit his marriage was over. For the first time in his life Jimmy tasted the bitter flavour of regret. For the first time wealth and power seem a shallow goal and through the long sleepless night, Jimmy wept.

The next day in court Jimmy had to draw on all his reserves of willpower to stand up to Seymour-Jones' cross examination. However his innate antagonism when faced with the law kicked in and he managed to answer convincingly when questioned. By the mid-day recess he was confident that things were still going his way.

At precisely two o'clock Mr Seymour-Jones resumed his cross examination.

'Mr Challoner, you have given the court the impression that all of your businesses are conducted within the letter of the law. Is that correct?'

'Most definitely.'

'In that case Mr Challoner, why did you find it necessary to make bank deposits in so many fictitious names?'

'Objection My Lord,' Arrowsmith interrupted, 'this questioning is not proper.'

'On the contrary My Lord,' Seymour-Jones said, 'it is most proper in order for me to challenge the defence's claim that Mr Challoner was a legitimate businessman.'

'Objection overruled,' Mr Justice Randles called out.

'Now Mr Challoner, why did you feel it necessary to open so many bank accounts in so many names?'

'It's not illegal.'

'Maybe not but neither is it normal business practice.'

'I opened those accounts because I didn't wish my wife to know what my financial position was.'

'Did you declare the contents of these accounts to the Inland Revenue?'

'No.'

'Not I would suggest the actions of an honest man. However let us turn now to the drug smuggling.'

'I deny any involvement.'

'Very well Mr Challoner, now maybe you will tell me in what capacity was Mr Walsh employed in your organisation?'

'Like I said, he was my general manager.'

'He was not your business partner then?'

'No.'

'From your own very considerable experience as a businessman, would you say that to run any type of business venture is time consuming?'

'It can be.'

'More so if that business is engaged in trading with a foreign country wouldn't you agree?'

'Yes I would.'

'Do you keep control over your employees, that is, do you know where they are and what they are doing, when they are working for you?'

'I certainly do, it's essential in business.'

'Did Mr Walsh take much time off work?'

'No, that was one of Mick's strong points, he worked most days of the week.'

'Then how do you explain to the court how it was possible for Mr Walsh to run a drugs business without your knowledge?'

'He must have done it in his spare time.'

'But Mr Challoner, you told us that he didn't have any spare time.'

'He had some.'

'Enough to organise and run an international drugs operation?'

'He must have because I didn't know a thing about it.'

'Where did you think that Mr Walsh was when he went over to Amsterdam to purchase the baby powder?'

'I can't remember, probably visiting a friend or something.'

'I suggest to you Mr Challoner that you knew exactly where he was and what Mr Walsh was doing when he was organising the drugs operation because he was working for you.'

'He was working for me but not in peddling drugs. I didn't know anything about that.

'I also suggest that the money deposited in the bank accounts under fictitious names was the proceeds from the sale of drugs.'

'I've told you why the money was in those accounts.'

Seymour-Jones paused to read a piece of paper that had been handed to him by Superintendent Turner.

'Now Mr Challoner, let us turn to your association with Mr Silvana. You did tell the court that you were both in the same line of business didn't you?'

'I did.'

'And did you tell the court that your meeting in Italy was to further one of those common business interests did you not?'

'I did.'

'And do you still stand by that statement?'

'Yes of course.'

'Good. So I am correct in my assumption that whatever it is that Mr Silvana does, you Mr Challoner are similarly engaged.'

'We have similar business ventures, yes.'

'As I suspected. Now tell me Mr Challoner, is Mr Silvana engaged in drug trafficking?'

'Antonio? Don't be so ridiculous. He's about as much involved in drug trafficking as I am.'

'What does that mean?'

'It means this. If Silvana is engaged in drug trafficking then so am I.'

'That is most interesting Mr Challoner. I have here a copy of a telex message from Interpol.' He held the message up, 'sent to Superintendent Turner.' He produced his spectacles with a flourish and began to read, 'Antonio Silvana arrested this date in possession of forty kilograms of heroin.'

'Didn't I tell you that miracles do happen' said Jim to Peter as they left the court room together. Mr Justice Randles had adjourned the case for the day upon the application of Mr David Arrowsmith who had requested time to consider the impact of the news concerning the arrest of Antonio Silvana and the effect it would have on the defence case.

Peter grinned at Jim, 'I loved the way old Seymour led Jimmy up the garden path before dropping the bombshell.'

'Touch of Perry Mason there.'

'I'll never forget the look on Jimmy's face when it sank in what he'd said.'

'Serves the bugger right after all that acting in court over Mick's death.'

'I don't think he enjoyed our dramatics quite as much.'

'I'd say Silvana's arrest just about cooks Challoner's goose, what do you reckon?'

'I wouldn't presume anything, but it will certainly do our case no harm at all.'

'Well you look younger already,' Jim smiled.

'Shows that much eh?'

'Just a bit.'

'Why don't we go back to the section house, get changed and then I'll buy you a pint. I think we deserve something.'

'I won't argue with that,' Jim said with feeling.

40

Jimmy Challoner sat with David Arrowsmith & John Wakefield in one of the small interview rooms beneath the main courts. Arrowsmith had been analysing the damage that the news of Sylvana's arrest would have on their own case.

'If I hadn't been so bloody stupid and said what I did, we might have found a way round it.'

'What's done is done. What we have to do now is try and minimise the effect that the news has on the jury.'

'And how for Christ's sake do we do that?'

'When I re-examine you tomorrow we'll attempt to give the impression that the news of Silvana's arrest for drug trafficking was as great a shock to you as it was to them.'

'Well it was.'

The following morning in spite of two restless nights Jimmy arrived in the dock of the court looking surprisingly fit and alert. He knew he must give the performance of a lifetime answering Arrowsmith's questions.

'Mr Challoner,' Arrowsmith began, 'when the case was adjourned yesterday evening the court had just been informed of Mr Silvana's arrest. Were you surprised by the news Mr Challoner?'

'Stunned. It was the very last thing I expected to hear.'

'Why was that?'

'The Mr Silvana I knew was never anything but a strictly above board businessman.'

'So you had no idea that he was involved in drugs in any way?'

'I did not. Had I suspected at all I would have stopped dealing with him immediately.'

'In your answer to Mr Seymour-Jones you said that Silvana was no more involved in drugs than you were. What did you mean by that?'

Jimmy paused, looked over to the jury for effect and said, 'I know that I am not nor have ever been involved in drug trafficking. I thought I knew Mr Silvana sufficiently well to make the comparison with myself. It was a figure of speech that's all.'

'Thank you Mr Challoner, that is all.'

'No further questions of this witness,' Seymour-Jones said addressing Mr Justice Randles.

'Return Mr Challoner to the dock,' the Judge instructed the prison officer who sat alongside the witness box where Jimmy was standing.

'That concludes the case for the defence My Lord,' Arrowsmith said.

'Thank you Mr Arrowsmith.'

'Are you ready to commence your final speech?' the Judge asked Mr Seymour-Jones.

'Thank you My Lord, I'm quite ready.'

The remainder of the day was taken up by the closing speech from Mr Seymour-Jones for the prosecution and David Arrowsmith for the defence. Jimmy was aware that Arrowsmith had done his utmost in pursuit of a not guilty verdict, but at this stage he was not optimistic. He prepared himself for the worst which in this case was a retrial.

The following morning Mr Justice Randles summed up the case, going through the evidence and reminding the jury of the testimony given by various witnesses.

Although he was attempting to be impartial and not give the jury any indication on which verdict he thought they should deliver, Jimmy detected a slight bias against himself. At the conclusion of his summing-up the Judge turned from where he had been facing the jury and stared directly at Jimmy sitting in the dock. Jimmy stared defiantly back at the Judge before his honour turned back to the jury and said, 'And now ladies and gentlemen of the jury, will you kindly retire in order to consider your verdict.'

As the jury members filed out he looked at Jimmy again. To Jimmy the look clearly said 'I hope they find you guilty.'

Jimmy smiled wryly at the Judge and said to himself, 'I'm about to trump your ace your honour.'

'The jury are coming back in,' Jim whispered to Peter who was sitting outside the court room talking to the solicitor from the DPP's office. He checked his watch, two and a quarter hours since the time that the jury went out to decide their verdict. Experience had taught him that when the jury returned to court as quickly as this then the verdict was usually in favour of the accused.

'Don't look so sick, it could mean we've won,' said Jim.

'Or it could mean the jury require further guidance from the Judge,' the DPP's solicitor added.

'Well we'll all know shortly,' Peter said as he followed the other two into the court room.

Peter sat in his usual place on one of the side benches in the well of the court. He looked up at the dock and saw that Jimmy was already waiting. Peter momentarily met his gaze but neither man was giving anything away. Peter knew that Jimmy would be aware that if the jury had reached their decision so quickly the chances were that it favoured the defence.

There was an undercurrent of excitement in the hushed court room as Mr Justice Randles took his seat on the high bench.

'Ladies and Gentlemen of the jury, have you reached a verdict?' the words of the court clerk rang out. The jury member who had been elected foreman replied nervously, 'We have.'

'And is it the verdict of you all?'

'Yes.'

Peter looked across at Jimmy who was sporting a broad grin of triumph.

'On count one on the indictment how do you find the accused, James Arthur Challoner, guilty or not guilty?'

'Guilty.'

Peter heard Jimmy cry out, 'No that can't be right,' before the judge banged his gavel and called for silence. The triumphant smile was replaced by a look of horror as Jimmy realised what this verdict would mean.

Peter sat quietly as the remaining guilty charges were given to the other charges on the indictment. He experienced a tremendous wave of relief but not the euphoric high he had imagined that he would. Instead there was a feeling of emptiness which for the present he found inexplicable. His attention was swiftly diverted by the judge who was about to pass sentence on Jimmy.

'James Arthur Challoner, you have quite properly been convicted of a series of crimes which can only be described as the most despicable charges that can be laid against a person. For profit and greed you traded in death and the public has a right to be protected from the evils of people like yourself. This country, through the legal system, will clamp down very hard where it is able in order to deter others from spreading the evil and danger that drugs can bring upon a society. It is the sentence of this court that you will go to prison for fourteen years on each of the charges, the sentences to run concurrently. I also intend to exercise my right under a recent Criminal Justice Bill to forfeit any assets that I deem to have been derived from the profits of your illicit drug dealing. I therefore proclaim that the cash held in all of your bank accounts opened in fictitious names, to be direct proceeds from your drug trading and they will be confiscated. I also deem that the yacht, 'Jennifer,' which has been impounded by the authorities, to have been purchased from the profits of your drug dealing and I order it to be sold and the money realised from its sale, together with those from the aforementioned bank accounts, are all to be paid into police funds. These will help to finance new resources in an effort to help combat the growing menace that drug trafficking brings. Take the prisoner down.'

In the solitude of his cell Jimmy tried to analyse what had gone wrong. He dismissed the thought that the jury firm had ripped him off. They were after all in business and that business depended on total trust. A trust that would have been instantly destroyed had they taken such a course. No, he reasoned, he had been thwarted by the only person who could outsmart him and that person was Peter Turner. Jimmy's vanity was such that he had to know just how he had been out foxed and ringing his call bell he made a request to see Superintendent Turner.

It was nearly an hour later before his cell door opened and Peter Turner walked in.

'Peter, I thought you weren't coming.'

'I very nearly didn't.'

'Cheer up. You've won, got what you always wanted, me behind bars.'

'Oddly enough I really don't get any pleasure from your conviction.'

'Well I would in your shoes.'

'That's where we're different then. Now what is it that you wanted to see me about?'

'I want to know how you did it?'

'Did what?'

'Found out about the jury firm?'

'I learned from my previous mistakes with you. I knew you'd think up something to ensure your acquittal.'

'And.'

'And knowing how your mind worked. I knew that you would be looking to cover every eventuality and that somehow you had to find a way to get at the jury.'

'But how did you actually do it?'

'Stroke of luck really.'

'Not for me it wasn't.'

'Well I knew that in order to nobble the jury you would have needed to know in advance who would be sitting on your panel. At first it seemed the procedures were tight enough to ensure that this information couldn't be got at in advance. Fortunately by raising the question I put a doubt in the mind of the senior administrator responsible for selecting juries. He examined the jury lists going back over several months and found that occasionally an extra three names had been added to the official list.'

'How did he notice that?'

'He didn't at first, that's why it went undetected. It was only because he was looking hard that he noticed a slight variation in the type and he was able to spot a pattern.'

'I see what you mean by luck.'

'Yours had to run out sooner or later.'

'How did you find out who was working for the jury firm?'

'Once we had spotted how the names appeared on the lists, we monitored every new list until an extra three names had been added. Now in order to make sure that it was those three names that were to sit on a chosen jury panel we knew something had to happen at the stage the ushers were randomly selecting names from the list.'

'So you kept watch?'

'Exactly and it wasn't long before I saw one of the administrative clerks go up to one of the court ushers and give him a message. The clerk took over the list while the usher left and when he returned the clerk had selected the named people he had added to the list.'

'Pretty ingenious.'

'Indeed it was.'

'And when it came to my trial you obviously stopped the clerk sending the usher on a wild goose chase.'

'No, I didn't want to alert you or anybody else that the jury panel were not as you had planned so we let the system run in the usual way.'

'Then how in hell …?

'Simple, we just replaced the three names that had been added by the clerk with three names from the public list.'

'I've got to hand it to you Peter, that was pretty cool thinking.'

'Well now you know, does it help?'

'I like to know where I went wrong so that I never repeat a mistake.'
'I hope there won't be a next time.'
'Maybe, maybe not.'
'This is it then Jimmy, I doubt we'll see each other again.'
'Why's that? I'll be out in ten years. I'll see you then.'
'When I retire in a couple of years Jean and I are moving away from Liverpool so it's unlikely.'

'No hard feelings then,' said Jimmy holding out his hand. Peter looked at the outstretched hand and then slowly raised his gaze to Jimmy's eyes.

'Just one,' he said, 'Mick Walsh,' and with the words ringing in Jimmy's ears Peter walked out of Jimmy's cell without a backward glance.

Epilogue

Jimmy Challoner had served two of his fourteen years sentence. Including the time he had spent in custody while on remand, with time off for good behaviour, he had less than seven years to serve. As a category A prisoner he had to be held in one of the top security prisons and he found himself in Parkhurst on the Isle of Wight. He had created a comparatively comfortable life for himself by the payment of bribes to officials and prisoners alike and all things considered his lifestyle was acceptable.

His one disappointment was that Jennifer never once replied to his letters. He drew comfort from the fact that she had never started divorce proceedings and through John Wakefield he learned that she wasn't seeing anyone else.

His surprise knew no bounds therefore when he received a letter from Jennifer asking for a visitor's card to enable her to visit him. Jimmy counted the hours until her visit weaving endless fantasies in his head, all of which ended with Jennifer melting into his waiting arms.

'Hello Jimmy,' Jennifer's voice was icy.

'Jennifer.'

Whatever he had expected from this visit it wasn't this, Jennifer looking at him with such ill concealed contempt, unable to hide her revulsion.

'Jennifer, I had hoped this meant you had forgiven me.'

'It means nothing of the sort. I wanted to tell you something and I wanted you to hear it from me.'

'What is it?'

'Just this, Debbie the daughter you professed to love so much, is dead.'

'Dead?' Jimmy stared at Jennifer, 'Dead, what do you mean?'

'I mean dead as in my beautiful daughter has gone Jimmy, dead as in not alive Jimmy, dead from a heroin overdose sold to her by a lousy murderer just like you Jimmy.'

'No,' Jimmy cried as Jennifer turned on her heel and strode out of the room.

Jimmy attempted to chase after her but as he stepped forward he suddenly stopped and clutched at his chest. Jennifer ignored the commotion behind her, any remnant of feeling she had ever had for Jimmy had died alongside Debbie.

Later as he lay in his hospital bed Jimmy wondered who had lost the most all those years ago, the milkman delivering in Chesham Street … or himself.